CRONE

Jeannie Wycherley

DEDICATION

In memoriam
Herbie Longfellow Alderdice

9th September 2006 - 29th July 2016

PROLOGUE

The cracking and snapping of dry bones reverberated through the stillness of the night. In the freezing air, at the very heart of the wood, in the slumped ruins of a long-forgotten dwelling, something dark began to manifest itself.

Little more than a mummified corpse, she unfolded her outer layer in a shower of dust and dry mould. Her skin, what remained of it, creaked like ancient leather and her flesh stretched taut over foul stringy innards. Then reaching, stretching, groaning, retching, she hauled herself upright. Once risen, she floated inches above the ground, while the mist—salty from the nearby sea—enveloped her like a pall and covered her foul nakedness.

She slipped out of the shack. The wildlife in the undergrowth shrank from her black charisma, keeping their distance from her rancid stench, the stink of putrefaction.

In the treetops, caught out by her rapid return to sentience, an owl blinked uneasily. Fearful, he observed her as she moved beneath him, then hopeful of evading her gaze he casually pivoted his head, pretended she was unseen and he was unseeing. But Aefre, even in her newly woken state, was both observant and deadly.

She was fast: lashed out at the owl, a missile of energy directed from her mind and he died instantly. Shedding a cloud of downy feathers, he slipped from his perch into her ready grasp. Her deformed claw-like fingers caught the remains and stuffed him into her mouth, whole. She chewed once, twice. Swallowed. A single line of blood dribbled from her chin, and the thinnest layer of fresh skin started to form a mouldering translucent veneer.

There was a halo of light to the east. Civilisation. For Aefre, the time was ripe. She was awake. It was time to bask in the thrill of the hunt. This time she would locate her sisters and join them in a merry dance of carnage.

First things first, however. She needed sustenance. She headed for town. She would find everything she needed there.

*

The boys tumbled out of the multiplex, blinking in the garish sodium lights of the car park, high on an adrenaline kick after enjoying the latest Hollywood blockbuster. Max was grateful that James now had a driving licence and a car to go with it and they weren't dependent on the non-existent bus service. It was hell being stuck in Abbotts Cromleigh with nothing to do.

Max was completing his A levels this year, and come September he would be off to University in a city where you didn't need a car. Everything he needed would be on his doorstep. Live music venues, sporting facilities: Sheffield promised to be everything his small Devon home town couldn't be.

He'd miss *The Storykeeper* though. Sheffield had bookshops, sure, but The Storykeeper was something special. It was housed in a higgledy-piggledy Elizabethan structure that had been added to time and again over the years, and thus appeared to stretch back and up endlessly. Shelves meandered like mysterious rivers throughout the building, stacked with volumes containing millions and millions of words. Max found magic in words. If he was honest, he would rather have his nose in a book than go clubbing, but he was canny enough to realise that this wasn't a cool thing to admit at almost eighteen. He didn't mind. He had all of his life to read as much as he wanted, starting with his English Literature degree.

Smiling broadly, he tussled with Euan about who should sit in the front seat. Euan, who was shorter than Max, gave up easily enough and sprawled indolently in the back of the ageing Peugeot 205, trading insults with Max who folded himself up into the front seat next to James and resumed munching on the popcorn he'd carried out of the cinema.

"You can't be hungry, Max, surely?" James asked as he slid the key into the ignition. "You ate all of your bucket and most of mine. Whose popcorn is that anyway?"

"God knows. I picked it up as I left." Max smiled

impishly.

"Gross. Well don't spill it over the insides of my car or you'll be on your hands and knees licking it up, arsehole."

Euan laughed from the back seat. "James, you're so precious about this damn car. Anyone would think it was a Ferrari or something."

"You can laugh, but one day I am going to be at the wheel of a Lamborghini and it won't be Maxie here sat beside me playing with my gear stick. Oh no, I'll have some luscious blonde with huge tits and a tiny waist to keep me happy."

Euan roared with laughter. "Dream on."

James flicked through the available radio stations, before leaning across in front of Max to pop open the glove box. "Pick us out a tune, dude," he instructed and Max rifled through some old-school cassettes to find something he fancied. The Peugeot had previously belonged to James's aunt and was so antiquated it didn't even have a CD player. James had inherited the cassette collection along with the car. Max found one simply labelled 'Hits 1994' and clumsily tried to slide it into the open mouth of the cassette player. After fiddling and getting it jammed, James intervened, flipping it easily into place. 'Girls and Boys' by Blur filled the car and simultaneously all three of the boys broke into song.

*

She'd had some luck feeding, but in spite of appearing more robust Aefre felt as wobbly as a new-born foal. Her hibernation had been relatively short this time, an interval of only fifty or so years. The world had continued without her, as it always did, and she needed to acclimatise to the changes.

The wood itself was far smaller than it had been. Every time she woke she was witness to a shrinking natural world. Once she might have walked for some time to find a settlement, but now there were humans everywhere, practically on her hearth. The more humans there were, the more difficult it became to locate her sisters. She lifted her head, her sharp beak of a nose, as yet without skin, scanning the horizon. She could make out others like her—the Guardians were close—but not her sisters. She needed to grow strong again, and quickly. Her power to discern who and what and where was too weak.

The stench of this new world overpowered her senses. Deeply unpleasant smells that she had no context for. The very air throbbing with an energy she only vaguely recognised. Electricity had been around for some time but now it pulsed and vibrated everywhere, and the great arc of artificial light from the nearby town masked the stars. They could not shine brighter than manmade illuminations.

The hunting ground that she and her kind had once freely roamed was being destroyed and it made her unhappy. She bitterly detested the passing of time. Her anger flared, hot and poisonous.

*

The ageing Peugeot ambled through the dark country lanes. James, in spite of his age and gender, was a careful driver, and valued the freedom driving allowed him. He was alone among his friends in actually owning a car of his own. His folks were well off and wanted him to join the family firm when he finished school. Yes, he was going to spend the rest of his life designing, printing, and selling paper bags and cardboard containers. He realised that to many kids his age—intent on living hard and fast and travelling and playing—such a life might sound like an almighty burden, but he had always known where he was destined to end up. He planned to one day take over the firm from his uncle.

And he would have that Lamborghini if it killed him.

*

Aefre floated stealthily down the hill towards the Sentinel tree. The foul reek of petrol and diesel fumes lingering in the lanes made Aefre gag. The vapours made her dizzy. But standing in front of the tree her excitement grew. Perhaps soon she would be strong enough to cross the portal and search for her sisters. At this time of year, when the shadows were long and bonfires burned, when the frost held the Earth in a tight grip at night, and the leaves were damp underfoot during the day, the threshold between this world and the other was more easily crossed.

Across the lane from the Sentinel, the lights of White Cottage twinkled. Aefre cursed. The cottage had been purposefully built overlooking the great oak tree, the portal she needed to use in order to cross between planes to find her sisters. The Guardians were still in residence in the cottage. Damn them and their interfering ways. When would they die out?

Her lingering thoughts naturally drew their attention. As she drew level with the cottage she felt the occupants reaching out—searching, enquiring. Their power touched at the edge of hers, and she hurriedly withdrew. She wasn't strong enough to take them on.

Not yet.

The lights of a modern carriage driving her way momentarily blinded her. Aefre's anger sparked once more.

*

The lane wound its way left and right, and James skilfully went with it, managing the curves with ease. The road was quiet this evening with little traffic about, so progress was relatively smooth. In places the mist was thick and he slowed down to accommodate it, elsewhere it was non-existent. Blur had given way to The Prodigy and then The Cranberries. Euan and James sang along to the lyrics they knew.

The sky was dark, the moon backlighting a few clouds so that they shone, otherworldly, silver and grey. On this part of the journey, heading back through the rolling, fertile countryside to Abbotts Cromleigh, much of the sky was obscured by overhanging trees anyway.

The cassette tape jammed. James lent forwards to flip it out, when from nowhere, a figure stepped out of the mist in front of the car.

James yelled as he saw the movement—but it was too late. He yanked the steering wheel sideways with his left hand to avoid colliding with the figure, but he pulled too hard. Max screamed as the car ploughed forwards, hitting the verge on the left hand side of the road before crashing into a huge oak tree.

The tree was centuries old. It was a scarred warhorse. An immovable force.

Unfortunately, the car was not. The bumper hit the tree, followed immediately by the bonnet of the car. Metal and plastic crumpled, glass fractured and exploded, the engine was crushed, one wheel spun off. James's body was flung forward, his chest impacting on the steering column. His head was flung forwards and sideways, twisting viciously and snapping his neck, before colliding with the side window. His skull fractured like a soft boiled egg. He was dead before the noise of the crash had travelled as far as the cottage across the road.

Simultaneously Euan, who was not wearing a seatbelt, was thrown forwards against James's seat. His right wrist splintered and his right leg was crushed as James's seat crumpled back towards him. His back twisted and his head flailed. He lay against James's seat, winded and unable to breathe, until gradually he became increasingly aware of his surroundings and his breath rasped into the sudden silence.

Max was luckier. The right hand side of the car had taken the brunt of the impact. His legs were trapped under the crumpled dashboard and the airbag had broken his nose, but he was alive. He slumped back into his seat, his eyes closed, his heart pounding, waiting for the adrenaline to subside and the pain to begin.

Total stillness after the violence of movement and noise. With all his heart Max wanted his Mum. He called for her and started to cry.

In the back seat, Euan was making strange noises that spoke of a world of pain and discomfort. Max tried to say they were going to be all right. Help would come. But he could only mumble.

Max sensed rather than saw movement close by. Someone opened the rear door and a shadow invaded the car. Euan screamed in pain. Max sensed someone looking over his shoulder at James, before withdrawing. Euan whimpered. Then the door opened next to Max, and someone was reaching in. Thank goodness. Help was here.

A hand reached out to him, an old woman's hand, liver spots on the yellow flesh. It was followed by a face, ancient and leathery, black eyes glittering hungrily. Lank hair brushed his cheek and she breathed in as he breathed out. A heavy fog began descending on Max. His breathing became laboured, his heartrate slowed. His chest tightened, so tight he thought his heart would burst. The woman was sucking his breath away. His vision blurred, and then he knew no more.

*

A savage encounter. She enjoyed it. Now it was over, she needed to take the time to reacquaint herself with her surroundings. The landscape was recognisable, but only barely. The tiny village of Cromleigh, population of one hundred and thirty-two within a two-mile radius, had exploded to many times its original size since her time. The town now boasted large municipal buildings, housing estates, and roads where once there had been country lanes and ramshackle farms and cottages.

One hundred years or so ago, Aefre had hunted among the factories and warehouses. Some of those were dilapidated ruins now, while others had been torn down to make way for housing. A century ago she had been entranced by the elegant parade of shops on Fore Street but now only the bookshop remained. In the hands of the same owner too. She knew him, Kephisto, The Storykeeper. Knew him well. Had considered visiting him several times so they could become reacquainted.

She skirted a group of new houses: little identical boxes sharing what had once been woodland and then a field. If she listened closely she could make out the sounds from inside: snoring, babies crying, moans of lust emanating from warm beds. The noise was overwhelming. This world was a crowded place. She yearned for the deep silence of her country of old.

Where she could gain access to the houses, she did. She stalked through homes, gazing down at innocents as they slept, leaning in and inhaling the mustiness of their breath, glowering a warning at anything that moved.

When dawn peeped above the horizon, she slipped like a shadow back into the wood. Tomorrow was another day. Humans were easy pickings.

Somewhere close by, a dog barked a warning. Nobody was listening.

ONE

HEATHER

Three Years Later

Tendrils of cold mist slipped their fingers down the neck of my fleece. I barely noticed. Pressing one hand against the bark of the tree in front of me, I traced the old scars still evident in the bark. Was Max somehow here? Probably not. But this was where I felt closest to him. Here, where his life had been extinguished. Seventeen years of age. Too young. Forever young.

I placed my flowers against a jutting root of the huge oak and kneeling, collected up some of the rubbish gathering in the hedgerow, stowing it away in a plastic bag for later disposal. I was careful not to disturb a fresh bouquet of carnations. Red for Liverpool FC. James's favourite team. These friends, once inseparable in life were now inseparable in death.

My breath caught in my throat and stuck there. My eyes filled with tears. I could never come here and not weep for my only son. Three years on and the pain, while no longer the hysterical, screaming kind, was a constant, aching reminder of my loss. I gathered some dead leaves into my hands, crushed them between my fingers, crumbled them to ash, and scattered them on the breeze, then kissed the fingers of my left hand and gently touched them to the tree, offering some vague blessing, before walking away.

The road here was narrow, no more than a lane, so I had parked farther up where it was a little wider. I strolled towards the car, in no real hurry. As I approached the bend in the road, I turned back for one last look. The oak stood tall, its trunk gnarled and twisted, branches skeletal. It dominated the road. Most of the leaves were gone; winter had a tight grip of the countryside.

This road descended from the small town of Abbots

Cromleigh at the top and travelled in a south-westerly direction, ending twelve or so miles down the hill at the larger coastal town of Elbury. The huge oak tree was nestled in a dip in the road, a slight valley, with tall hedgerows on both sides. To the left was a cottage and a field, known locally as Pitcher's Field, joining the wood that stretched out for miles, heading briefly uphill once more, before tumbling towards the cliffs that overlooked the sea.

On days like today, when the sky was an ominous slate grey and the mist was rolling off the sea, it was a grim and forlorn place. A number of crows were perched in the oak tree, and they gazed down at me now, their eyes black and bright. One of them cawed loudly and flew across the road in front of me before settling on a ramshackle wooden fence that belonged to a neat cottage with a thatched roof.

I had on occasion seen a woman pottering in the garden. A young woman, perhaps late twenties or early thirties. Once I had seen an elderly lady, dressed in black, watching me from the door of the cottage. She had given me a half smile but turned away when I had self-consciously acknowledged her. Smoke always drifted from the chimney, even during the summer. These cottages could be cold in spite of their thick walls.

Neither woman was in the garden on this freezing afternoon, but thin curls of dark smoke rose above the thatch as usual, scenting the air. Logs were piled against the front of the house, and a number of lanterns hanging from the front porch shone in the dimming light.

Dusk was falling. It was time to head home and walk Pip, Max's old lurcher. Pip was getting on himself now and didn't need to walk as far as he had in his younger days, but he liked to get out and about and have a good sniff among the leaves. I whispered my goodbyes to Max again.

I had to shake off the feeling that someone was watching me as I headed for the car. Stupid, I know.

TWO

MIKEY

Mike leant against the old wooden beam, holding a pool cue lightly in his hands. His head was buzzing. It was not an unpleasant feeling, but it reminded him that he had drunk enough beer for now, tomorrow being a work day.

Fraser racked the balls up again, but it was winner-stays-on and Mike had lost, so he guessed it was his round. He returned his cue to the wooden rack and shouldered his way through the crowd to the bar. Last one, he promised.

It was busy for a Thursday and he had to wait, but he was an easy-going kind of guy and, besides, he was standing next to Maddie Ledden. He'd known her at school—all the boys had known Maddie. She had boasted Abbotts Cromleigh's greatest cleavage even at fifteen years of age. Now they were all approaching their early-twenties and Maddie had two kids, but her breasts were still a joy to behold. Mike tried not to leer and smiled warmly down at Maddie, while she adjusted her top so that he could get a better view.

"Looking good, Maddie, really ... swell."

Maddie giggled. "You should come and see me sometime Mikey. It's been an age."

"Yeah, I should." Mike recalled the times he had buried his face in Maddie's magnificent chest and smiled. "Who are you with tonight?"

"The usual crew, you know," Maddie gestured over to a table. Mike recognised many faces from school.

He nodded. "Good stuff. Can I buy you a drink?"

"No I'm fine thanks. Let's take a rain check, huh?"

"Sure." Mike put his arm around Maddie and hugged her, his fingers accidentally brushing her right breast. She laughed, winked, and twisted from his grip, picking up her drinks and sashaying back to her table, knowing full well he was watching.

Mike collected his drinks and returned to the pool tables

at the rear of the pub but as he did so he felt his skin prickle and crawl. The feeling began on his scalp and worked steadily down his spinal column to his thighs. He shivered.

"You cold mate?" asked Fraser, taking his pint of ale and glumly watching his girlfriend Sally make mincemeat of his game.

"Nah. Just tired. Need to get going really. Due on site tomorrow by eight." Mike stroked his forearm with the hand that wasn't clutching his beer, trying to make the goose pimples disappear.

Fraser nodded. 'Love Shack' by the B52s came on the jukebox, and there was a roar of approval from the front of the pub. Fraser looked up, and someone at the door caught Fraser's eye. He nudged Mike.

Mike followed Fraser's gaze. A beautiful stranger posed in the doorway, her gaze raking across the clientele and fixing on Mike. Mike shivered again. The sensation of fingers digging around in his head made his bowels churn and his heart beat faster. For one moment he felt violated, and yet the feeling was quickly gone, replaced instead by a warm glow of desire.

The woman regarded him steadily, an open invitation. Next to Mike, Fraser cleared his throat. "I think she likes you, mate."

Mike remained where he was; his mouth open; his mind sluggish. Fraser nudged him with his elbow and hissed, "Go on! Christ! She's practically begging you to go over and say hello. Who is she anyway?"

Confused, Mike shook his head. He didn't recognise her. She was stunning. Long hair as black as a raven's wing. His ultimate fantasy. Pretty gothic looking, in a bottle green dress, velvet—not that he knew about such things—moulded to her curves. Her dark eyes glowed like the embers of a long burning fire.

"Never seen her before." Mike's throat seemed a little constricted; his voice husky.

The woman smiled. Mike cleared his throat.

"Go on!" ordered Fraser frantically, and Mike moved

obediently away. "Make sure you bring her over here and introduce me, you bastard!" Fraser shot after him.

Up close, she was perfect. Flawless. Her alabaster skin was smooth and pale, her lips plump and moist, naturally a dark pink. Her eyes, now that he was close enough to see them, were a deep emerald green with flecks of brown around the pupils, outlined by long, fluffy eyelashes. She was the ultimate airbrushed fantasy, and she quite took Mike's breath away.

He stammered out a greeting. "I'm Mike."

She nodded. "I know."

"You do? What's your name? Are you from around here?"

"My name is Aefre. And yes, I come from these parts. I've lived here all my life."

Mike wondered how old she was. Maybe thirty or so. He couldn't really tell.

"Ether? Well I'm pleased to meet you. Can I buy you a drink?"

Aefre studied the bar, the optics, and the gaily coloured drinks in bottles. She shook her head and smiled widely at Mike, displaying white, even teeth. "No. It's not a drink I'm looking for."

The smile knocked Mike's socks off.

Aefre took Mike's arm. Her grip was surprisingly firm. "Let's go."

*

In the soft light of Mike's bedroom, he found he could not quite believe his luck. Here was the most beautiful of women. She asked no questions and demanded nothing of him. Mike was dazzled by her beauty. Her skin was as soft as a new-born's, her limbs long and supple. Her touch, at first tentative as she explored his body, had become more confident and self-assured. She was a passionate woman. Her hair tickled his chest when she straddled him, and he was cocooned in a bubble of desire.

13

"Why me?" he breathed as she moved with him.

In answer, Aefre bowed her head to his face, her eyes glowing, alive with need. She bent down to him, as though for a kiss, but instead started to inhale deeply, her mouth closing around his. His eyes widened as the breath was drawn from his body.

When she had emptied the air from his lungs, she began drawing out his soul.

*

The local papers were awash with the news of Mikey's death, and he was mentioned on the local news at 6.30 pm. I perched at my kitchen table thinking about the Mikey I'd known. He'd been in the same class at primary school as Max, a sweet lad, polite when he came to birthday parties at our house. He had been good with his hands, loved to build things. The Legos would be scattered across Max's bedroom floor, and complicated and colourful structures displayed on the windowsill. The newspaper stated that Mike was employed at Buskin's, a local construction firm. The trade he had chosen was so apt.

His mum would be devastated.

I should send her a card. What was her name? I ferreted around in my brain trying to remember but drew a blank. I'd kept all of my condolence cards, along with other mementos to my son in a box under the stairs and located them easily enough. I flicked through but quickly became frustrated with the task and impatiently set the thick pile to one side. They teetered on the table before one escaped from the pile, slipping to the floor. I stooped to pick it up. The message inside simply read, *Heather, so sorry to hear about the loss of Max. He was a good and gentle boy and Michael has memories of fun times at your house. In our hearts always, Sarah, Russ, Michael, Lewis, and Siobhan.*

*

Mike's funeral was delayed for a few weeks while the coroner and the police tried to establish the facts of his death, although the papers lost interest once there appeared to be no scandal or wrongdoing and moved on to the local MP's expenses row instead.

The day of the funeral was dismal. Drizzle dropped relentlessly from a heavy, grey sky. I approved. No-one should be buried on a beautiful day when skies are blue and the sun warm. It's only fitting that the weather reflects the miserable situation of loss.

The church was full to bursting with family and friends. Taking a pew at the back, out of the way of those who had a greater claim to Mikey, I found myself struggling to hold it together. Watching the coffin being brought into church, carried solemnly by six young pall bearers, including Mikey's younger brother Lewis, loss etched on his pale face, was more than I could handle. And so as the coffin was arranged at the front of the church and the pall bearers took their seats, I slipped away to wait for the service to finish.

I meandered around the small churchyard, until my reverie was interrupted by a tall young man in a dark grey suit, with brand new shoes, the leather stiff and shiny, and no doubt uncomfortable. Visibly distressed, he lent the palms of his hands against the wall a little way from me. I watched him as his face worked and his Adam's apple gulped. Eventually I could bear it no longer.

I moved towards him and placed my hand on his back. The tears streamed silently down his face.

"It's ok," I said. "You're allowed."

He erupted. Great heart-rending sobs. He cried and cried. It was a ferocious outpouring of grief, and I wept quietly with him, empathising with the pain of the gangly man in front of me. When eventually he quietened I handed him a tissue from my bag. I had plenty. He blew his nose noisily and wiped his face.

"I'm sorry," he said.

"No, don't be," I replied firmly. "It's better out than in." I studied his face, vaguely familiar. He was pale skinned, slightly freckly, and blotchy from the crying. "You were a friend of Mikey's?"

"Yes. I was with him … the night … the night before …"

I nodded.

"I'm Heather Keynes."

He nodded down at me, his eyes still full of tears. "I know. You're Max's mum. I was at his funeral too. I'm Fraser Gray."

"Oh, I'm sorry," I began, "I don't remember—"

He waved my apology away. "He was a popular guy, in his own way. Quiet wasn't he? Max? Just like Mikey was. Mikey, you know, he wasn't the big 'I am' or anything. Just a fun loving guy. Liked to play pool. Liked a beer. Occasional night out in Elbury. Once in a blue moon to Exeter. He was a simple man."

Inside the church the sounds of the first hymn started up. Tears pricked at Fraser's eyes again. He rummaged in his jacket pocket and found his cigarettes and lighter. He flipped a cigarette out but his hand was shaking and he couldn't get the lighter to work. I took it off him, cupped my hand around the lighter, flicked until the flame burned and then offered him the light.

He inhaled deeply. Forced his shoulders back and down before slowly releasing the smoke from his lungs. He offered me one, but I shook my head.

He indicated the cigarette in his hand. "I'd given up, you know? But what's the point? Live or die. When your number's up …" He pulled on the cigarette again and started to relax. "It was funny …" he paused, his eyes glazed over.

"What was funny?"

His opaque eyes were tired and confused. "They never found her."

"Who?"

"The woman. Mike met a woman that night, his last night. They left the pub together."

"Was she a friend?"

16

"No. He'd never seen her before. Neither had I. She was gorgeous. Not from round here. I'd know her."

"Who was she then?" I'd never seen a mention of a woman in the papers.

"I don't know. He never introduced her. Hell, he only spoke to her for a few minutes and then they left the pub together. Didn't say goodbye or anything. Next thing I know, he's dead."

"You told the police about her though?"

"Yeah, yeah. They wanted to talk to her." He shrugged. "But they couldn't trace her."

"Did anyone else at the pub know her?"

"No. No-one remembered seeing her."

Puzzled I stared at Fraser and ran through what he had told me. "But you saw her?"

"She was beautiful," Fraser nodded sagely.

"You both saw a beautiful woman in the pub and Mikey went to say hello."

"My girlfriend was with me, but this woman was only interested in Mikey anyway. Giving him the come-on."

"So Mike goes over and he talks to her for a few minutes, and they leave together?"

"Without so much as a seeya."

That did seem odd. "This woman was the last person to see Mike alive, but no-one remembers her or knows where she is to talk to?"

Fraser sighed. "That's about the long and the short of it. I've not seen her since. No-one has."

How odd. "The police have said they don't think there are any suspicious circumstances about his death," I pointed out.

"No, that's right. But still …"

Fraser finished his cigarette. He ground it out against the wall. He nodded towards the church door to indicate he was going back in. I smiled and stepped away from him. He slipped quietly back inside.

I considered what he had said. Fraser was right. The woman was a loose end that made Mike's last evening and

17

unexplained death just a little untidier. I had to sympathise with Mikey's mum. Sarah would want to know how Mikey had died, just as I had wanted to know the details about Max.

But maybe there are no answers in life.

*

I spent an hour at the gathering after the funeral, but I needed to get home to Pip. I said my goodbyes to Sarah and donned my coat, hat, and scarf. I considered speaking to Fraser again, but he was immersed in conversation with a group of other young men and women. In the semi-darkness of the function room it was difficult to make out the people he was with. One man, well-hidden in the shadows stared at me as I observed the group. I couldn't see him properly, but as I made my way to the door I could feel his eyes burning my back. Unnerved, I was glad to get away.

*

Margaret had completed her evening routine and it was time to go to bed. She had finished her cocoa and three custard creams, washed the milk pan and her mug, and left them to drain for the morning. Finally, she let Colin, her cat, out. Now it was time to tuck herself in.

Earlier in the evening the timer on her electric blanket would have automatically switched on so that by the time she made her way upstairs, brushed her teeth, and changed into her nightdress, the bed would be nice and warm. She was thankful that her daughter and son-in-law had bought the new blanket for her. Roy said it was safer than the old ones, and Cathy claimed it was more economical. That was good to know.

Margaret wheezed into the bathroom to brush her teeth. Out of habit she never let the water run, considering it wasteful. Tap on, tap off. Rinse, spit, done.

From downstairs she distinctly heard a click. She paused for a moment, listening hard. She didn't want to negotiate the stairs again.

A yowl. That silly cat. Must have come back through the

cat flap. Margaret hoped he hadn't brought any little presents with him.

Out of the corner of her eye Margaret caught a flash as something streaked past the bedroom door. She turned, but whatever it was had disappeared.

"Colin!" she scolded. "You know you're not supposed to be in the house at night." It was half-hearted of her, telling Colin off. Margaret loved her furry companion to bits.

She rinsed her mouth and swooshed the sink clean carefully. She returned her toothbrush to its little blue pot with a pleasing clink and headed into her bedroom. The room smelled fresh, Margaret liked to sprinkle lavender on her sheets. She undressed, folded her clothes neatly onto a chair, and pulled a plain white cotton nightdress over her head.

She moved Mr Barnaby, her childhood bear, from his place in the centre of her bed, gave him a hug and a kiss as she had for virtually every day of her eighty-six years and lay him down on Alf's pillow. If she awoke in the night, there would be something to reach out to and touch. She settled back against the pillows and closed her eyes, feeling cosy and started to doze, until she became aware of a rustling noise in the room with her, and a dank smell.

"Colin," she murmured. He shouldn't be in the bedroom.

Her body felt leaden, as though something was draining her already depleted reserves of energy. Margaret opened her eyes and for a moment she thought she saw her late husband Alf standing in front of her. She blinked. Lifted her head to have a better look. It *was* Alf. She tried to reach out to him but found she couldn't move.

Alf came closer. He leaned over her, and for a moment she thought he would kiss her. Instead, he sniffed her. Margaret shrank away, confused. "Alf?"

He lashed out; his long nails raked her face and knocked Mr Barnaby off the bed.

Margaret panicked. This was not Alf. He was never anything except gentle and kind. He would never hurt her or disrespect her things, including Mr Barnaby, whom he had always tolerated with total sweetness and understanding.

Margaret tried to scream, but her throat was dry. Her mouth opened and closed in terror as Alf climbed onto the bed. He pulled the bedclothes roughly down from her chest and stared down at her bony figure in its prim nightdress.

Margaret shrank back in fear, any humiliation quickly replaced by terror. Her insides turned to ice, her heart began to beat hard in her chest, and her breathing hastened.

Alf climbed over her, straddled her, and stared down into her eyes. His weight alone was enough to suffocate the frail Margaret, and she feebly tried to push him off. His lips parted, and he bent his head to her. Instead of a kiss, he breathed in.

Margaret was rigid underneath Alf, her arms taut, but as the kiss went on, her body relaxed, her heart rate started to slow, and her mouth opened slackly. As he breathed in, she breathed out until there was no air left to exhale. She lay weakly on the bed looking up at someone who couldn't possibly be her husband. There was no pain, but suddenly she longed for more time. A chance to see her daughter and tell her how special she was and how much she was loved.

It was a futile last wish. As Alf's shape shifted and Margaret stared up into the face of a hideous woman, a crone far older than she, her heart stopped, and her body—already deprived of oxygen—began to shut down. Death followed swiftly.

Colin observed the scene from the corner of the room. His eyes glowed with alarm in the darkness, until he turned tail and raced down the stairs. The crone turned her head to watch him, smiling with grim satisfaction when she heard him tear through the cat flap.

*

The strength that Aefre had drawn from Mike could only last so long. Playing sexual games with him had been fun but it depleted her energy, and the shapeshifting always caused rapid drain. Given that she had duped a whole crowd of people in the pub into believing that Mike had left alone, she had a right to feel tired.

She had become adept at finding easy victims over the centuries. That was the reason she had sought out Margaret. Elderly people were always a good bet. They were on borrowed time anyway, so people expected them to die suddenly. Four or five like Margaret allowed Aefre the time she needed to build her strength so that she could take on the Guardians and gain access to the portal. She wanted to track down her sisters. There was strength in numbers. If they could join forces, there was nothing they couldn't do. No end to the fun and games. They could wipe out whole communities. Lay waste to towns. She wanted her sisters to join her. She intended to find a way.

*

I paused in the midst of my supermarket shopping to have a quick flick through the newspapers. Today the local newspaper the *Cromleigh Chronicle* had caught my eye, and I turned a few pages, wondering if there was anything new about Mikey. Instead, I noticed another article of interest, smaller and tucked away on the bottom of page five.

"GP's Concern for Elderly Cromleigh Residents" ran the headline. A local GP was raising an alarm about the unexplained deaths of seven local pensioners over the past three weeks. Apparently these patients had been fit and healthy, and while it was not unnatural for the elderly to pass away suddenly, the GP pointed out that it was standard procedure to request post-mortems be carried out where the deceased had died alone and without warning. The hospital in Exeter had found itself a little inundated. I recognised one of the names. Margaret Hannaford, had been my neighbour while I was growing up, and I felt a regretful pang at her passing.

Poor Margaret. She had been a sweet lady, who doted on her daughter and her grandchildren.

As I tucked the paper into the trolley and moved on, the hairs on the back of my neck prickled. The feeling emanated somewhere between my shoulders and travelled to the top of my skull. Somebody was watching me. I spun around. No-one was looking my way.

Maybe I was imagining it, but the feeling came again several minutes later and while I scolded myself for being paranoid, I couldn't shake the feeling off, I remained uneasy for the rest of the afternoon.

THREE

CLAIRE

It was a word that Claire was fond of. Extraordinary. She liked the fact that it had all those syllables. Ex tra ord in air ee. She kept saying the word in her head over and over as the others talked. She perched on a stool by the Aga in her kitchen listening to the half a dozen other women and several men who were grouped around the large wooden table. Claire periodically rose to quietly fill cups and glasses with her hot and spicy ginger and lemon cordial. Perfect in this cold weather. Candles sputtered at various points throughout the room, shadows flickering against the walls.

Outside the wind was ferocious and the rain was beating down on the thatched cottage so hard that torrents of water poured from the roof and pooled on the path outside. If this kept up, the run-off from Pitcher's Field would flood the road, causing misery for travellers on the road to Elbury.

Although why anyone would want to travel to Elbury in the early hours of a miserable day in February, Claire had no idea.

The people grouped around the table had come from far and wide but they were a hardy lot who wouldn't let poor weather stand in their way. They varied in age, with Claire as the youngest, to a very wizened centenarian, Mercy Greengrass, who had travelled from Somerset, only thirty or so miles away.

Mercy listened calmly as Claire's mother, Dorothea, explained the recent disturbances in Abbotts Cromleigh. She spoke of the deaths of Mike, Margaret Hannaford, and eight other elderly or infirm residents from within the local community.

Solange Pendennis pursed her lips. "We can't know for sure that Aefre walks. She was awake so recently... when was it? Just three years ago?"

"She is walking," Dorothea argued firmly. "And feeding. We have sensed her movement. And what's more she's already building her strength. Remember, three years ago she was extremely aggressive but fairly weak. We moved swiftly then to banish her from her hunting grounds. We nipped it in the bud, and we need to do that again. Quickly."

"We must find a permanent solution. It simply isn't wise to keep chasing her back to her hide in the forest. This has all been going on for too long." Mercy was grave, and Solange nodded in agreement.

Dorothea sighed. "But these days we cannot even call together a full meeting of the Guardians. We are becoming weaker. There seems so little we can do to counteract Aefre."

"Our numbers are diminishing, there's no denying that. You made a wise decision to call an extraordinary meeting, but not everyone could attend at short notice." Mercy settled back in her seat and smoothed out her long dark skirts.

There was that word again, thought Claire. Extraordinary.

Like her mother, Claire recognised the danger. She had sensed the power of Aefre's evil as it hovered near the cottage. Even working together Claire and Dorothea struggled alone against Aefre's force; the emaciated fingers of which invaded warmth and happiness where they found it, while she sucked the love and light out of everything.

Three years ago the combined wisdom of the Guardians had managed to put a quick stop to Aefre's murdering spree and she had returned to her miserable dwelling to sleep. They had hoped she would hide for longer, but she had already returned—and she was hungry. This was a testament to her growing strength and their weakening powers. The Guardian's enchantments were no longer binding Aefre to the earth for long enough.

"What if ..." Claire started but stopped. Was it her place as the most junior member of the Guardians to speak? Mercy's dark eyes glittered, and she cocked her head at Claire. Her benign look appeared encouraging.

"What if Aefre becomes powerful enough to take us on?"

Claire asked.

Mercy nodded. "It's a likely proposition."

"We have to ensure that doesn't happen," said Dorothea firmly. Claire realised that Dorothea was as fearful as Claire was, after all, her family was the most vulnerable of all, here in the cottage, so close to the Sentinel.

"It is going to happen, however, and sooner than we would like." Mercy was direct.

"It feels different this time," said Claire, and Dorothea agreed.

"She is different. Stronger. Perhaps because we are weaker, perhaps because she has a great purpose." Mercy looked thoughtful. "We have to consider what we can do without instigating a battle with Aefre or putting ourselves in jeopardy." To Dorothea she said, "You need to monitor her closely—but without antagonising her—and keep us informed of her movements."

"And the town? And the Sentinel? How do Claire and I protect those?"

"You're not alone, Dorothea, never alone. Someone will come." Mercy stared through the window into the darkness beyond as though she could see someone out there. "Someone … a stranger … will come. One who is known to you but not known by you … she will come and she will help us." Rose nodded and smiled. Mercy gathered her dark cloak around herself and gestured at the assembled Guardians, her bony hand graceful, the skin as smooth as it had ever been. "We are all here for you."

Dorothea nodded. "Very well. Blessed be." Claire set about blowing the candles out as the group dispersed through the darkness.

*

Aefre retreated further into the hedgerow, in the pouring rain some distance from the cottage, far enough away so that no-one would spot her. Even so she had seen Mercy Greengrass pointedly glare in her direction. That enfeebled bitch had bat-like senses. Mercy reached out for her, and Aefre mentally slapped her away; impatient, annoyed. The Sentinel was protected, wrapped up tightly in a mystical charm of the Guardians' making and she couldn't break it yet but one day she would unlock it, and when she did her wrath would fall like fire from the sky.

FOUR

THE EYE

Late Spring

I drove out of Abbots Cromleigh and turned on to Elbury Road with trepidation. Just three weeks previously, a group of five young people had lost their lives at exactly the same spot on the road as Max and James. I wanted to pay my respects, but also to ease my own fresh pain. Old wounds had been reopened by the media coverage of the accident: the harrowing images of the tangled metal being shipped away on the back of a truck; the tearful parents, siblings, and partners of the young people at the crash scene; and coverage of the funerals.

A carpet of once colourful flowers, now in varying states of decay, stretched out from the tree like a bride's train. Bouquets and soft toys were tied to branches with ribbons, and cards were tacked or stapled all over the trunk. I carefully removed two cards so that Max's plaque was visible once more, then I took a handkerchief from my pocket to wipe its surface clean.

I tried hard not to process what I could see—fresh, clean scars in the bark—but of course I knew what they meant and I shuddered. All around me the ground was churned up. The car had been travelling at some speed down into the dip and had hit the tree without braking. The two women in the back had been thrown through the windscreen, suffering horrific non-survivable head injuries. The driver and front seat passenger had both died on impact, and another lad who had been sitting between the girls had succumbed to his injuries later in hospital.

I slumped in sadness. The tree, heavy with new foliage, also drooped in sorrow. Cards attached to bunches of flowers flapped idly in the breeze, the messages, lovingly written, were already beginning to fade in the sunlight. There was a deep stillness all around, and for a moment I was lost in melancholic reverie.

The flapping of a bird overhead startled me. Looking up I could see a number of crows perched on branches glaring at me with beady, black eyes. I frowned up at them.

One of them had a tight grip of something in its beak. I wondered what it could be. The bird kept flapping around on a branch, causing a kerfuffle among the others. Suddenly all the birds started squawking and cawing at each other. The noise was loud in the stillness of the warm and sunny afternoon, and I grew alarmed. The bird with the item opened its beak and dropped it. I watched whatever it was tumble towards me, seemingly in slow motion, the sun reflected from it, causing it to sparkle as it fell. It landed on the ground beneath my feet. I peered down, searching the carpet of flowers around me.

Kneeling among them, I explored gently with my hands for whatever had dropped. It couldn't have gone far and hadn't sounded like it had bounced away. I tenderly parted stalks and petals, careful not to damage the tributes, searching for the item with my fingertips. My left hand found something. I curled my fingers around it and drew it out from between some slightly browning chrysanthemum blooms.

I was unable to comprehend what it was at first. I stared at it for a second or two before I realised, and then with a shriek, I threw it away, hard, towards the hedgerow. It was an eyeball. I scuttled backwards, away from it, scattering flowers as I went, before losing my balance and sprawling sideways. The eyeball hit the leaves and dropped to the ground, rolling back towards me before coming to rest, looking up at the tree. It was blue. The sun shone on it, the cornea sparkled, and for a second it appeared to slightly swivel to look my way. I cried out and rolled to my feet, feeling a sharp pain in my hand as I put my weight down to push myself up.

I moved away, into the centre of the road, staring at the eye in disbelief. Where the hell had that come from? Surely it wasn't from the accident? It was too fresh. I imagined a possible scenario, the devastating injuries, particularly of the girls who had punched through the glass with their faces. Then I thought of Max …

My knees gave way. I squatted in the road and raised shaking hands to my face. A crimson river ran down my left hand and wrist. Blood dripped onto my jeans and the ground below. The palm of my hand had been gashed quite deeply on a sharp object hidden among the flowers. The wound gaped. It would need stitches; there was no doubt about that.

I breathed deeply and stood, feeling disoriented, but needing to get back to my car.

Somewhere, a woman laughed long and shrill. Mocking me. It was an ugly sound.

Startled, dizzy, nauseous, I turned about. Who was it?

"Who's there?"

Silence. The blood dripped between my fingers. I needed to wrap the wound and get to a hospital, assuming I could drive, but I had dropped my handkerchief at the base of the tree. I didn't want to go back and retrieve it. I didn't want to see that eye again.

The blood flowed, spattering on the road in front of me. I lifted my left hand up, supporting it with my right. There was no way I would be able to drive like this. I needed help. The only answer was the cottage across the road, and with relief I saw the young woman who lived there standing at the gate watching me. Her head was tilted upward and she appeared to be scenting, the way Pip did when I took him out walking and there were rabbits in the vicinity.

"Excuse me," I said, my voice shaking. I raised my bleeding hand.

The woman grimaced and nodded, then held the gate open. I walked through, down a few steps towards the patio area. The cottage's lamps swung in the warm breeze and the smell of herbs greeted me. There were pots and tubs of all shapes and sizes, full of plants I didn't know the names of.

"Come through," she said briskly.

"I'm so sorry to be a nuisance," I began, but the woman shook her head. I followed her into the cottage.

"Please don't worry," she said and led through me to the kitchen and an old-fashioned porcelain sink. She ran the tap. I tentatively put my hand into the stream of water. It was cool but not too cold. I watched bright blossoms of blood turn the sink red before the water rinsed them away, becoming rosy pink as it did so. My hand steadily dripped, the flow unceasing. "Stay there," the woman said, "I'll only be a moment."

She went into a room at the back of the kitchen, a pantry maybe. Bottles clinked before she returned to check on the wound. "It's going to need stitches," I said. "If we could just clean it up and then perhaps bind it, even with kitchen roll, I can get back to my car and drive to the hospital."

The woman shook her head. "You won't need stitches, my pet. Don't worry." She smiled before disappearing into her pantry again. I pondered on her calling me her 'pet'. It was a strangely old fashioned expression, and she was younger than me. The gentle thudding and scraping noise of a pestle and mortar drifted my way. Such a familiar sound. Once I had made curries and blended my own spices. Max had loved my curries. I didn't make them anymore.

After a few minutes, the woman reappeared clutching a small clay bowl containing a thick green paste. She took my hand and carefully dried it on a muslin cloth. It wept and bled, and she dabbed it carefully until the edges of the wound were as dry as she could possibly make them. She smeared the paste neatly over the wound, until it began to act like a plug. The bleeding was contained.

"Sit." She motioned to a wooden chair at the table, and I sat gratefully. The woman set a large iron kettle to boil on her Aga and pulled a bright yellow teapot down from a shelf.

"You look pale," she said softly.

"I'm ok. I feel a bit shaken, that's all," I replied. My knees were still wobbly. I badly wanted to lie down.

"You'll be fine. You're strong."

I studied her properly then. She was somewhere in her early thirties, but her curly brown hair was greying at the temples and she had made no effort to dye it. She had a few crow's feet around her eyes, but otherwise her face was unblemished and unlined. She wasn't beautiful, but she wasn't plain either. Her eyes were as grey as a November sky over Elbury. I took in her clothes. She wore a simple dress, with a three quarter length skirt and a pair of clogs. It was at once effortless, draped casually over a slender form, and somehow timeless.

She smiled, perhaps at my obvious curiosity, before turning her attention to the teapot. She served up a cup of hot sweet liquid that was the precise same yellow as the teapot; it may have been tea, it may not. It warmed me through and calmed me too. After a few minutes the shaking stopped, and I began to relax a little.

"Now," the woman said. "I've seen you before."

"Yes." That was likely, after all I recognised her.

"Your son was killed in an accident out there?"

I nodded curtly, not wanting to talk about Max.

"Not this time," the woman said referring to the recent car crash practically outside her front door, "but the time before." It was a statement not a question. "I've seen you here, often."

I nodded again. My eyes filled with tears, and I impatiently willed them away. No-one had time for my grief and self-indulgence anymore. I kept myself to myself, cocooned in my bubble of loneliness and sorrow.

"You miss him." The woman sounded sad. Absurd. Of course I did. I sniffed back my tears. With a huge effort of will, I changed the subject.

"I'm Heather."

The woman hesitated. "Claire," she said eventually, seemingly reluctant to offer more.

"Thank you for helping me out today."

"I knew you were coming."

I regarded her in surprise. "What do you mean?"

Claire only shrugged and poured more tea. She urged me to drink again. "What did you see out there?"

"Pardon?"

"You saw something. It scared you." She studied me intently, searching my face.

I swallowed, the memory returning, "I saw …" The bile rose in my stomach.

"You saw?"

"I saw an eyeball."

"Yes." Claire was solemn, but neither surprised nor horrified. She wasn't aghast in the same way I was. Assuming it was a human eye, why had the emergency services not cleared the scene properly?

"Did you see me with it?" I asked her. She shook her head and shrugged again. Her gaze was steady, if anything she appeared curious about me and my reactions.

A sudden realisation crossed my mind and I shook my head fiercely. "Look, I'm not crazy."

I wasn't, was I? A wave of anxiety flooded through me. What was happening to me? Was I becoming unhinged? Or had I really seen an eyeball? Panic made me babble, suddenly the tears were falling.

Claire's hand was on my shoulder. "Easy," she soothed. "It's the shock. Drink the tea."

I drank the tea, my head full of memories. I wept. The floodgates opened. I sobbed for Max. For James. And for Euan who had survived but with life-changing injuries. And for the latest car full of reckless kids. I cried for myself. Time passed. Claire was kind. She spoke soothing words, plied me with the yellow tea, and handed me tissues.

*

A few hours later I was standing in my own hall and Pip was rising stiffly from his basket in the kitchen. My left hand was bound up and throbbing nicely, my car was parked on the road directly outside, and my keys lay on the little telephone table where they always lived when I was at home. The thing was, I couldn't remember driving home. I had no memory of negotiating the winding lanes or busy streets of Abbots Cromleigh. I didn't recall parking, or dropping my keys in their habitual place.

I felt drained. My head pounded. I let Pip into the back garden before feeding him, then climbed the stairs to drop on my bed like a stone and sleep like the dead.

I slept more soundly than I had in months, years maybe. A full eleven hours. Pip usually stirred for a morning wee at around 6.30 but today at 8 he was still curled in his basket, snoring contentedly. I woke slowly, warm and comfortable under the covers. When I rolled over to check the time I found myself tangled in the bandage that Claire had wrapped around my hand. I sat up and pulled at the rest of the dressing gingerly, afraid of what I would find underneath. I fully expected a congealed, icky mess of blood, but the bandage fell away easily from the dried green paste that covered the wound. There was no mess.

I swung out of bed and padded through to the bathroom where the sun was streaming through the frosted glass. Holding my hand up to the light, I examined the dry paste and picked at the edges with my thumbnail. It crumbled away like chalk. I gently picked a little more and then rubbed harder with my fingers. Dust coated the sink in lurid powder. There was no evidence of the laceration from yesterday under the dry paste. I washed my hands with soap and water until they glowed pink and then towelled them dry. I could see the faintest pink line across the palm of my hand.

Nothing more.

*

Over the next few weeks, in idle moments, I found myself looking at the palm of my hand in wonder. I decided to visit Claire again and ask her about the wound.

This time I approached her cottage clutching a bottle of wine and feeling strangely nervous. I didn't know what she would say to me, but I sensed we had unfinished business.

A number of crows, pulling at the innards of some unfortunate roadkill victim, fluttered reluctantly away from me as I walked down the lane towards them. Others sat on branches and stared at me insolently.

The cottage door opened as I bent to unlatch the gate. Claire waited for me, not exactly smiling but seemingly not too displeased. Once in the kitchen, it became apparent she had been expecting company. This time a green teapot and two pretty mugs waited for the kettle to finish boiling. I handed my wine over awkwardly. "Sorry, I don't know whether you drink wine, but I just," I stumbled over the words, "I just wanted to say thank you. For last time."

Claire took the wine. She studied the label for a second, her head bent over the bottle, her hair tied back in a loose bun with little curls falling over the nape of her neck. Her hair had an amazing sheen. She smiled graciously. "Thank you. I'll enjoy this." She placed the bottle on a shelf on the dresser at the rear of the kitchen. "But you really didn't have to, you know."

"I know." I hesitated. "I guess…"

"You wanted to come back."

"Yes."

She nodded and indicated a chair.

"If you're expecting somebody I'll leave you to it." Claire shot me a puzzled glance, so I indicated the mugs and the teapot standing ready.

"Ah. No. I expected you."

I frowned. She'd said that last time.

I watched her bustle around, filling the pot and rattling the mugs. She offered me honey to stir into my tea. "You should," she said when it appeared I would decline. "It really brings out the taste and the honey is from our own hive." I took the honeypot from her and stirred some in. She was right. It tasted glorious.

We made a little small talk before lapsing into silence. I felt I should ask her about the wound on my hand she had treated but didn't know how to start.

Claire may have sensed my discomfort but she ignored it. Instead she rose and removed a candle from a drawer. She lit the candle with a taper from the stove and stood in front of a mirror. I hadn't noticed the mirror before, it was covered in a thin green silk scarf that blended in with all the plants—the drying herbs, flowers, and vegetables hanging from the ceiling. In fact, I hadn't noticed the décor at all during my previous visit. I had obviously been too busy bleeding and crying.

I looked around now. The room was basic, with rough-hewn walls and a neatly laid stone floor, with furniture that was original and rustic. People would pay a fortune for such furniture these days and yet the solid table and chairs, the dresser and free-standing cupboards appeared to have been in situ for a very long time. Everything was spotlessly clean. A homemade lissom broom rested idly in the corner waiting to be pressed into service.

Claire carefully removed the silk scarf from the mirror and folded it. The wooden frame was ornately carved to resemble a huge knot in a tree with the mirror at its centre. At its north, south, east, and west points there were clusters of leaves and acorns, berries and blossoms.

Claire held the candle in front of the mirror. The flame flickered and burned brightly for several seconds, leaping towards her reflection before she blew it out. The sooty black smoke twirled in the air, clouding the mirror. Claire stared intently through the swirls, looking deep into the glass. When the final wisps cleared, Claire turned back to me.

"I knew you were coming because I have the sight."

"The sight?"

"I can see things that … most others can't."

"What sort of things?" I tried to suspend the disbelief from my voice.

"All sorts of things. Things that have happened. Things that will happen. I know that you and I are going to become good friends. I know we're going to work together towards a common aim."

I sat back in my chair and pursed my lips. Did she think I was a fool? I stared around the room suspiciously, studied the mirror again and the strangely dated items that cluttered the shelves and hung from the ceiling. Coloured bottles and labelled jars were everywhere. "You know this how?"

"I know, because I'm a witch," said Claire simply.

"Oh yes?" I answered politely. *Hello*, said my 42-year-old brain, *No such thing, no such thing!* I was not a great believer in the occult or anything remotely similar. Hell, I hadn't even read any Harry Potter books, although I'd watched a few of the films.

"Yes." Her cool grey eyes fixed me to my chair. There was no challenge in them. She merely wanted me to know and to understand. "There is such a thing." She offered me a slightly amused smile. Perhaps she had read my mind.

Maybe.

No.

It was obvious what I was thinking and she had guessed correctly.

"My mother is a witch, as is my grandmother, and the knowledge and the wisdom they've accumulated has been handed down through generations. I'm an only daughter."

"Claire isn't a very witchy name, is it?" I was abrupt, slightly rude. "Shouldn't you be called Agnes or Griselda or Gertrude or something?"

She laughed warmly. "No it isn't very witchy, that's true. But Claire is just one of my given names. Perhaps Griselda is another." She twinkled at me.

I frowned. She seemed serious. I took a moment. "So, the healing of my hand? That was what? Magic? And my getting home? I couldn't figure that out."

"A kind of magick, if you like, yes." Claire didn't add anything else. She twisted her mug in her hands and stared into the depths of her tea.

My own green mug was dangling loosely in my hand. I knew nothing about magic or spells or the sight. In fact, my only brush with the occult came about when a friend showed me a love spell when I was thirteen. I wrote the name of my true love on a piece of paper in my untidy scrawl and slept with it under my pillow for a week until my mum changed my bed and it was washed with the bedlinen. It hadn't made poor Ian Todd fall in love with me though.

This was hocus-pocus nonsense. Why would Claire tell me? Surely if witches were real they kept schtum. "Why do I need to know? You could have just bound up my hand and sent me on my way. You didn't have to put that gooey green stuff on it. I don't have to know what … who … you are."

"It's not my choice. You do need to know who I am, apparently, because you are going to need my help. And we are going to need yours."

"I'm going to need your help? What do I need your help for?"

"Maybe not right now, but you will," Claire answered calmly.

"To do what?" I challenged.

"I can't tell you that yet. You will come to me of your own free will when the time is right."

I gawped at Claire. She really believed what she was saying.

There was a creaking from upstairs that startled me. We weren't alone. Claire glanced up at the ceiling and smiled. "I'm sorry. You'll have to go now. That's my grandmother." For some reason the thought of Claire's matriarchal witchy grandmother hovering above my head, able to hear every word we were saying, perturbed me more than a little. I had assumed we were alone.

I rose and walked to the front door of the cottage. I noticed the entrance to the living room here, beyond which a fire burned brightly in spite of the warmth of the day. Several rocking chairs were angled close to the fire, one covered by a patchwork blanket. A cat, black of course, sat dangerously close to the grate. As I took in the room and its contents, a crow landed on the sill of the open window. I started in alarm.

"*Volare procul*," ordered Claire, and the crow squawked almost angrily at her before flying away.

At the front door I hesitated, turning back to Claire.

I was incapable of thinking of anything to say that seemed to fit the odd conversation we'd shared. "Thanks again," I said. It was all I could manage.

"Thank *you* for the wine. I'll see you soon." She smiled and closed the door.

FIVE

ETHAN

Ethan Carnegie consulted his map once more. This appeared to be the correct route. If he cut through the field he would come out on a tiny B road called ... where was it ... oh yes, Elbury Road. That was perfect. From there it was a seven-mile hike into Elbury and he would pass by The Traveller's Rest, an inn which had received four stars on TripAdvisor and which Ethan felt warranted a visit. He intended to have a spot of lunch before hiking on to the coast.

This was his third weekend in succession in Devon, and he was enjoying walking along the Jurassic coast. He was recently divorced and fighting fit. Everything felt good in his world.

He tramped down Pitcher's Field spying a sweet little cottage off to his right. Even in the warmth of the summer sun, the chimney was emitting smoke. He admired the cottage, then climbed the stile that led to the road. He hadn't gone much further when he spotted a woman up ahead of him. In spite of the sun, he shivered, goose bumps appearing on his skin. He rubbed his hands together to get rid of the prickling sensation and dismissed his feeling of unease.

The woman was leaning against a huge tree at the side of the road, wearing khaki shorts and a cheerful yellow t-shirt. She was slim and sporty looking with boyish hips. Her ash blonde hair, straight as a rule, was pulled back in a tidy ponytail. She balanced on one foot, a walking boot lying in the road next to her rucksack, while she pulled at a yellow sock.

"Hi there," he said breezily as he came alongside her. "Everything ok?"

Her pale green eyes flashed in the sun. Ethan was struck by the woman's skin, so clear and glowing with health. He smiled appreciatively.

"Good afternoon," she said. "Yes, everything's fine. I had

a stone in my boot and seem to have cut my foot, but I'll live."

Ethan indicated her sock. "Would you like me to take a look? I have a first aid kit in my rucksack."

"Oh I really don't want to be any bother," the woman murmured casting her eyes down.

"It's no bother, I promise." Ethan set down his own rucksack and flipped open one of the side flaps but got no further.

"No, I suppose not," the woman said.

Ethan glanced up. The woman's eyes were dead. She smiled and lashed out at him.

*

From the familiarity of the kitchen table I examined accident photos in the local newspaper. Abbotts Cromleigh buzzed with the news of the death of the walker on Elbury Road, and while the police initially appealed for witnesses and information, it soon became clear that nobody knew anything. Nothing helpful anyway.

The *Cromleigh Chronicle* identified the man as Ethan Carnegie, divorced and from Reading, Berkshire. He had been a keen walker. Although police didn't give away many details they had announced that they were treating the death as suspicious and were considering whether the walker had been in collision with a vehicle of some description.

Results of the post mortem were of limited assistance. The man had suffered catastrophic head injuries, a broken wrist, and a broken rib. A collision with a vehicle seemed the only rational explanation. Officially.

The problem remained: there were no skid or brake marks on the road, suggesting that if there had been a vehicle it had made no effort to stop. The absence of debris indicated that any vehicle had suffered no cataclysmic damage itself. It was a complete mystery. Police enquiries in the vicinity of Elbury and Abbotts Cromleigh regarding vehicles with dents or broken windows or headlights had drawn a blank.

I supped my tea and studied the image in front of me.

The photographer had taken the photo pointing up the hill towards Abbotts Cromleigh. In the near distance, slightly out of focus, not one hundred metres from the scene of the walker's accident I could see the oak tree, Max's tree, surrounded by withered floral tributes.

I sat forwards over the paper, elbows on the table, and rubbed my face. This was such an unlucky stretch of road. All of these accidents and all of these deaths. Surely they could be prevented in some way? Perhaps it would help to have more signposts about the bend, or to slow the traffic right down in the area opposite Claire's cottage.

I played back the road in my head. Elbury Road was a typical Devon lane, curving this way and that way, climbing and dropping, tall hedges on both sides. The odd thing to me, was that visibility was actually pretty good on this stretch and the road was relatively straight. Obviously driving too quickly and meeting something in the road would cause problems, but otherwise there was no particular reason for this to be an accident black spot. The oak tree itself did not obscure the road ahead.

I knew all this thanks in large part to the police report into Max's death and his inquest. The experts had concluded that speed had not been a factor in the accident, but that James had lost control of the vehicle due to a lapse of concentration caused by circumstances unknown. It was unclear why James had failed to apply his brakes.

Very little had made sense about Max's accident, and nothing made sense about this walker's death. For me it was all too emotive, and somewhere a family must be grieving just as I had. Just as I was. All these wasted lives. So many families wanting answers. We were all waiting for something indefinable.

*

Later that afternoon I sat in a café in Abbotts Cromleigh stirring a cup of tea. Feeling unsettled, I'd decided to speak to my old family liaison officer, DC Ivy Lawrence, about the accidents on Elbury Road. I'd phoned her on the off chance she had some free time and could chat. When she walked into the café, I did a double take. Ivy was dressed in civvies and was very pregnant. I had no idea.

"Wow!" I said in greeting, my eyes getting wide.

She smiled, and I stood up to give her a hug. It was difficult to reach around her.

"I didn't know you were on leave," I apologised.

She laughed and then scolded me. "I haven't seen you for ages! How are you doing?" Her eyes were wise, and I sensed the warmth of her concern and the compassion that made her so good at her job. Ivy had spent a great deal of time with me after Max's accident even though, in the end, Max had not been a victim of crime and nobody had been found to be at fault. I waited while Ivy ordered a milk shake. She had a craving for strawberries.

"I'm ok," I said, my standard response. We both laughed. "No, I am, really. Well I think I am. You know. Some things rock the boat."

Ivy nodded. "The recent accident down Elbury Road? I thought of you."

"Yes." The image of the eyeball came back to me in a flash, and I shuddered. I hesitated and frowned. "Yes. That's what I wanted to ask you about."

Ivy smiled and shook her head. "I haven't been working with those families, and I don't really know all of the details." I felt this was only a half truth. Just because Ivy wasn't involved didn't mean she didn't have her ear to the ground.

"Do they have a cause for the accident yet?"

Ivy took a beat and narrowed her eyes. "Driver error." Of course. "Were you expecting something else?"

"No. I don't know. Not really." I paused. "Ivy, this may sound crazy. In the light of the walker's accident as well, I just figured there might be something happening along that stretch of road."

If Ivy considered me stupid, she was too professional to show it. "I don't think there's a link between the two accidents, and certainly not between those and the walker's death," she said, not unreasonably. "After all, this latest was a hit and run."

"Officially?"

"Officially."

"And unofficially?"

Ivy remained guarded. "Unofficially I can't comment, you know that."

I nodded. "Ok. But …" I tapped my fingers on the table as I considered my next question. "What about that stretch of road? What makes it so dangerous? I mean, six deaths in a matter of weeks?"

Ivy stretched and rubbed her lower back. I was sorry to harangue her. I hoped she didn't consider me an angry mum with too little in my life to distract me, obsessing about the death of my only son.

"When Max was killed, they said the accident was caused by driver error. James's fault."

"Yes. That's what the coroner ruled," Ivy said carefully.

"But there was nothing to indicate that James was intoxicated. No alcohol or drugs in his blood."

"No."

"And on the night in question, the roads were quiet. The weather was okay. Cold, some patches of mist. No rain."

"That's right."

"And he wasn't driving excessively fast for the conditions."

"No, a little over thirty miles per hour, within the forty speed limit, but it would be very difficult to build up much speed on that stretch of the Elbury Road."

"So it was down to James."

"We know from the directional marks that he swerved slightly. He must have been trying to avoid something. A badger or another animal in the road possibly. There was no evidence he hit anything besides the tree. No other vehicle involved."

I knew all of this. I wasn't about to argue that James wasn't a careless driver, that he wouldn't have been driving too fast or taken any risks, because what did I know? James had been eighteen years old. He had held a driving licence for less than three months. All of the statistics show that young teenage males are the most at risk of dying in road accidents.

"And what about the latest accident?"

"Pretty similar," Ivy concurred. "The car was travelling much faster but it didn't brake at all. The weather conditions were good."

"It didn't brake at all?" My insides quaked at the thought. I thought of the two occupants who had been flung through the windscreen.

Ivy reached across and squeezed my hand. "Have you been to the site?" She knew I was a frequent visitor to lay flowers for Max. I nodded grimly. "It amazes me that that old tree is still standing. It's a solid beast that one."

That damn tree. I pictured it there, standing like some kind of sentinel on Elbury Road. Dwarfing the other trees around it. The scars on its trunk, the decaying flowers scattered around its roots. It would outlive me and everyone I knew.

Ivy slurped her milkshake. "Driver error. In both cases. With speed as a factor in the latest incident. It was just a coincidence that this latest accident occurred in the same place."

"And the hiker?"

"Coincidence," she repeated. We studied each other in silence. Ivy really believed there was nothing more than that to these occurrences. The case was closed. I admitted defeat and smiled ruefully.

"When are you starting maternity leave?" I asked instead and Ivy grinned. For the next thirty minutes or so we chatted about her baby and all of her preparations and I tried not to feel anything but pleasure in her obvious joy for her firstborn. But my firstborn had been reduced to bone and dust by now and my happiness for Ivy was entirely bittersweet.

*

Once home I tried to attend to various household chores

to distract myself from the frustration building inside me. Pip followed me around, stuck to my legs like a limpet. Sometimes he needed lots of fuss and attention, and today because I'd been out and about I suppose he just wanted to feel loved and grounded.

I decided to tackle the kitchen worktops. I had a terrible tendency to pile everything up and leave it lying there. When I subsequently sorted through the piles I would invariably find birthday cards that I had bought and written and never posted, unopened bank statements, newspapers that had been half read, along with appointment slips for the GP, the dentists, and hairdressers. Of course I could never find anything when I actually tried to. My organisational skills were a nightmare.

I hadn't always been that way. But nowadays I placed one foot in front of the other and carried on. I wouldn't call it living so much as surviving with disinterest.

I sifted the first pile. There were newspapers folded to articles about the car accident on Elbury Road, plus obituary notices for Mikey. My thoughts turned to Fraser and the mystery woman in the pub. Had the police found her, I wondered, or had Fraser been drunk or hallucinating? I hadn't heard any more about Mikey. I ought to touch base with his Mum Sarah to see how she was faring.

I scanned the reports in the paper, but quickly stopped myself. I would only end up feeling maudlin. That was no good. It took a supreme effort of will, but I threw the papers into the bin and started sorting through another pile.

Once I could see my worktops I felt a great sense of accomplishment. I was considering having a cup of tea before tackling the contents of the fridge when the phone rang. I checked the time. It was 5.50 pm. I had been away with the fairies.

I picked up the phone and was surprised to hear Ivy. We exchanged pleasantries before she cut to the reason she had called.

"I've been thinking about our conversation. I know you're still hurting and … I'm worried you're beginning to look for conspiracy theories." I tried to interrupt but she cut me off. "You asked me about that road and what has made it so dangerous. Well, that's the thing."

"What? That it's suddenly dangerous?"

"No. Quite the reverse. It hasn't become more dangerous recently. It's always been a black stretch of road."

"How so?"

"What I mean is that there have been accidents and unexplained deaths on that road since … well … forever."

"Have there? I didn't know that."

"No. Time passes and people forget. The thing is, when I joined the service, twelve years ago, I served with a guy named Brendan Chadwick and he had twenty plus years on the force at that time. He's retired now. He told me about an accident that happened when he was a young constable—and this would be in the days before seatbelts I guess—when some kid flew out of his car and ended up suspended in the oak tree. That's the same oak tree."

"Jeez," I said.

"In the '90s, I understand the council considered widening the road, or putting measures in place to slow the traffic but they didn't have the money and to be fair, none of the accidents have been proven to be speed related."

"I see." Silence. I didn't know what to say.

"I'm sorry, honey," Ivy said softly. "I don't have the answer as to why Max died."

"No."

When we hung up, I lay my head against the smooth, cool surface of my kitchen table. I stayed that way for some time, pondering, until without really understanding why, I returned to the bin and retrieved the newspapers I'd thrown away earlier. I shook them off and smoothed them out and started looking for the Elbury Road stories.

SIX

THE PROFESSOR

The lecture theatre was warm and stuffy, and I feared I'd fall asleep. Against my better judgement, I'd agreed to attend an open lecture at the University of Exeter with my friend, Mel. Mel fancied herself a little bit alternative, a bit new age, a tad fae. She believed in an ancient goddess and wore her spirituality like a patchouli-scented, rainbow-coloured cloak. I figured most of her beliefs were total and utter poppycock, but Mel was a good friend and a kind person, so I let her be who she wanted to be, and she ignored the fact that I was a miserable curmudgeon.

Mel had wooed me to the lecture with a promise of coffee and cake at her favourite vegan café afterwards. She had also claimed that the professor leading the lecture was, in her words, a 'real hottie'. This opposed my image of a 'professor' as an absent-minded, greying, bearded male, wearing brown cord trousers and a smoking jacket of some description who would routinely drop papers everywhere.

It was therefore a pleasant surprise to clap eyes on Professor Trenton Redburn for the first time. He was average height with clean, dark hair that flopped over his forehead. He had a sporty build and obviously worked out, his shirt was snug against his chest and his shoulders were broad. Best of all he was late thirties and free of any distracting facial hair. He was wearing suit trousers, a pink shirt with rolled up sleeves and a brightly coloured tie, casual but smart. On this occasion I found myself agreeing wholeheartedly with Mel's judgement and sat up straighter when he walked onto the podium. Professor Redburn was obviously of the Brian Cox school of lust worthy academia.

The title of the lecture was 'The Wisdom of the Ancients and the Natural World'. I observed Professor Redburn for a while, he was an animated speaker and his slides came quickly, but really I wasn't following what the man said at all. His slides contained images of demons and flowers and fruit and all manner of oddities, but after a while, the warmth of the lecture hall, the brightness of the sun, and his soothing voice made me a little dozy. The lack of engagement with the audience reminded me of my own short-lived University days.

I hadn't lasted long at University; I'd found myself pregnant before the beginning of the second year and had remained at home to have Max without telling the father. He didn't know about Max's death either, because he had never known his son existed. How strange that Max, who had been a part of that man, had never existed in his world.

I distracted myself from my sad thoughts by observing the audience. In front of me floated an ocean of frizzy hair in varying shades. I tried to guess how old people were on the basis of the backs of their heads. It was inappropriate behaviour, but it kept me amused for a while.

Yawning widely, aware of a pressing need to pee, I turned my attention to the lecture once more. Professor Redburn flipped the slide, and I stared at a huge photograph of a giant oak tree. For a moment I saw Max's tree and my breath caught in my throat. It wasn't his of course. It was some tree in America. I tuned back into the content of the lecture. The professor was addressing the notion that in myth and folklore, many communities of ancient people had believed that trees were inhabited by spirits. Some saw trees as centres of healing energy, full of love and light. That was right up Mel's street. Other trees were just the opposite, full of dark unpleasantness.

Time froze as I processed what the professor was saying. He made a joke about tree-huggers and the audience laughed. I forgot my need to visit the bathroom, my mind working overtime. I was considering Max's tree. Surely if ever a tree was ill fated, this one was. All those accidents that Ivy had told me about. It was a magnet for death and disaster.

And what of Claire and her mother and grandmother? Were they really witches? Why did they live in such close proximity to the tree? Were they linked to it in some way?

"Jesus. It's the tree," I exclaimed. The woman sitting directly in front of me turned around and shushed me. Mel regarded me oddly. I sank back into my seat, waiting impatiently for the lecture to finish.

As soon as the lecture was over I scrambled down the stairs, pushing past Mel hurriedly, and barging against other people in my rush to get to the lectern. The professor was gathering up his papers, and this part of my stereotypical preconception was correct. The man had armfuls of paper and files to carry, along with what appeared to be an old school satchel, bursting at the seams. He flung the satchel over his shoulder and hefted several supermarket bags full of student marking in one hand.

"Excuse me?" I lay my hand on his arm urgently, and he turned towards me and smiled. He had a gentle, handsome face. I flushed, instantly tongue tied, fearful of coming across like a complete fool.

He observed me kindly, perhaps sensing my distress and unease. "Did you have a question?" he asked. "Only I have a taxi coming."

I was flustered. I needed to talk to this man and it was vital that he didn't think I was a total nutcase. I wanted to ask him about the oak tree, maybe he could explain Max's death to me, but I wasn't at all sure how to phrase what was on my mind.

I didn't have much time. "Tell me more about the trees!" I blurted the words out. He looked slightly taken aback. "I mean ... How can I know? How can I know that a tree has a spirit? Or that it's a bad tree?"

Bonkers, I thought. He'll think I'm totally bonkers.

"Ah!" he breathed, looking oddly pleased. "Walk with me?" he led me out of the lecture theatre and into the corridor beyond.

"As I said in the lecture, certain cultures have a belief that some trees house spirits." I nodded. "These cultures have provided anecdotal evidence that tree spirits keep themselves to themselves nowadays, fearing extinction." He glanced at me and my face must clearly have been asking, *Do you believe that bullshit?* because he laughed out loud at my expression. "They say, you can only tell if a tree has a 'bad spirit' as you put it, if it deigns to show you." I blinked at him nervously. He increased his pace, and I practically had to run to keep up with him. He was smiling, mocking me perhaps. But suddenly he pulled up short. I almost ran into him. He studied me curiously. "Why do you ask?"

I frowned, confused by my own thoughts. Was I so desperate for answers to Max's death that I was going to listen to the claptrap this guy was preaching? Dear God. I was turning into a fruit loop.

"Ah well," I stuttered. "I don't rightly know."

"I see." He seemed disappointed and slightly bemused. "Perhaps we can keep in touch and if you do come across something interesting, it would be great for my research. In fact, give me your email address so I can send you some more reading."

I nodded. "Ok." I scrabbled in my bag for a biro and then scrawled my email address on the top file in his arms. He nodded at me and headed for the waiting taxi. I followed him a little way behind. "Professor," I said as he moved to shut the door. "Do you believe in witches?"

He regarded me oddly. "Yes. Some of my best friends are witches."

I thought of Claire and how she was adamant that our paths would cross again. "Oh," I replied.

*

Two days later I hadn't heard from Professor Redburn, and I had decided he wasn't the complete ticket. How could a tree have a spirit? And did he really believe in witches too? He and Mel were made for each other. How could people be hoodwinked by his daft lectures? His line of study was ridiculous.

I checked my email for about the nine hundredth time that day, just as a missive flew in from T J Redburn from a

University address.

He had kindly sent through a variety of links, scanned documents, and photographs for me to look at. I spent well over an hour printing everything out and collating it, neatly stapling sections together. Flicking through them I found that for the most part, the documents were far too academic for me but I took them up to bed anyway and tried to decipher the content. Needless to say, I slept well.

Fortunately, in amongst the academia, there were a few newspaper and magazine articles that were more accessible for the lay reader. One contained a story regarding a huge cypress tree in Mexico that had a reputation for attracting bad fortune. The news report suggested that, in the previous thirty years alone, the tree had claimed over eighty lives, from car crashes and pedestrian accidents and even a number of suicides. The latest was the hanging of a young itinerant.

In another article, a tree in Norway was chopped down after seven traffic collisions in two years. In both Mexico and Norway, the locals were convinced that the trees were evil, living entities attracting death and misfortune. In the case of the Mexican tree, legend had it that the tree was inhabited by the spirit of a bandit who had been strung up on one of the higher branches by a vigilante in the 1930s. The locals were now too scared to chop it down so they brought offerings of bowls of food and sacrificed chickens at the roots of the tree in an attempt to ward off evil and keep their families safe.

I sifted through all the material, not sure of what exactly I was looking for, or what I expected to find. What was I trying to prove? In among the articles and documents were photo print outs of trees shaped like people or parts of people. There were trees with carved heads and bodies and some beautiful artwork. None of this meant anything. My tree looked like a tree.

I riffled through the images. Dozens of them. Finally, my eye fell on an early black and white newspaper photo of a huge oak tree, standing tall and haughty, skeletal of frame and denuded of all its leaves. The quality was poor and there was no story with it. I placed it on the slush pile but before turning to the next image I returned to it. In front of the tree was a man with an axe. To the left of the tree across the road was the top half of a cottage. Several women, dressed in black clothing and shawls, posed with folded arms outside the cottage looking at the man with the axe. The photo wasn't clear enough to make out the facial features of the people depicted, but the stance of the women suggested that they were disapproving of whatever they were observing.

I scanned the cottage and then the tree. The cottage appeared familiar. I compared them again. Cottage and tree. Again. Tree and cottage. There was no doubt: this was Max's tree and Claire's cottage.

My hands were shaking as I reached down and retrieved the picture from the pile. Judging by the clothes I guessed that this had been taken in the early part of the twentieth century, or late nineteenth. Why had the man with the axe wanted to chop the tree down? He obviously hadn't succeeded, so what or whom, had prevented him? These women? Where was the story that went with the photo? Frustrated, I shuffled the papers once more, but couldn't see a lone piece that matched the image.

I was stumped, but knew instinctively this was something worth pursuing. Perhaps Professor Redburn would know more. I checked the email he had sent. His department address and phone number were highlighted under the body of the text so I quickly dialled him up. No answer. The call went straight to voicemail. Damn. I suppose with it being the summer holidays he was taking time off.

There was nothing for it but to email him and hope he picked it up quickly. I was brief, and asked whether he had any further information about the photo and attached it to the email. I added my own contact details and as an extra flourish marked it as urgent. It wasn't, but I wanted to get his attention. Within seconds I had a response, but my hopes were dashed when I realised it was an automated out-of-office reply.

I slunk around the house for a while, unsure of what to

do next. The house was stuffy and I was antsy so I decided to expend some energy by taking Pip out. I needed the fresh air and it was a glorious afternoon, such a shame to waste it indoors. The park wasn't far away and it was pleasant to walk around, watching children feed the ducks and teenagers canoodle on the grass. I recalled knocking back cider with my friends one afternoon when we should have been at school, and being chased out of the park by a warden after he caught us. Happy days.

Pip enjoyed a good run and barked at various objects— both animate and inanimate. I focused on the green of the well-kept grass and the bright hues of the flowers; they gave me a chance to rest my eyes, tired and scratchy from all the reading. Tired and scratchy was a good description of how I felt generally.

I arrived home to see the answering machine blinking at me. I hurriedly pressed the button, knocking the handset out of the cradle in my hurry. I listened as Professor Redburn's cheery voice informed me he had some good and bad news.

He had the original newspaper clipping but no story with it. However, he would send over a scan of the reverse side of the newspaper so that I could use that for clues to the date and origin. If I needed any help he would be happy to oblige.

I raced over to my laptop and logged back into my email. There it was.

I waited impatiently for my printer to warm up so that I could print the scan. Squinting, I scrutinized the tiny type on the article that had appeared on the reverse of the image carefully. There was a reference to a tug-of-war competition between Elbury and Abbotts Cromleigh on 28 August. The Elbury team had won the trophy, after Abbotts Cromleigh had taken it in 1907. This photo had to be contemporary to 1908 then.

Excitedly I grabbed my car keys and headed into town. The library had the local newspapers on microfilm and fifty minutes later I was sitting at a microfilm reader next to an attentive librarian. She had narrowed down newspaper options to one of three printed in the region, including the *Cromleigh Chronicle*, but judging by the typesetting she had decided it was the long defunct *Elbury Evening Telegraph*.

I started with the 28 August 1908 and moved forward. I didn't have far to go. On 1 September I came across the photo and the story. I read excitedly. According to the *Telegraph*, on 14 August 1908, Thomas 'Smiley' Earnshaw and his fourteen-year-old son John had been killed in an accident on Elbury Road. Their horse had apparently been startled by crows and had run amok. The cart had overturned and hit the tree. The horse had subsequently been destroyed. The Earnshaws had died of their injuries.

The newspaper mentioned a number of other accidents in the area and stated that some residents from nearby Abbotts Cromleigh were claiming that the tree was cursed and were demanding its removal. The photographer had captured local farmer Elias Caldecott as he set about preparing the way for the tree's imminent destruction.

So what had happened then? The tree was still standing.

Puzzled, I scrolled through the microfilm until I came to the next day and there was the headline, 'Tragedy! Local Farmer Killed by Falling Branch'. High winds had apparently caused some of the branches to break. Caldecott had taken his axe to the tree but was felled by a branch from above, before he could strike the first blow. The tree had been saved.

I asked the librarian for copies of the stories and accompanying photographs, and on second thought opted for blow ups. I paid what I owed and was about to leave the library when my attention was drawn to the local history section.

A striking woman, sitting at a table there, stared at me in quiet fascination. Her eyes were as green as white wine bottles, clear but piercing. I glanced at her somewhat uneasily, wondering why she was watching me so avidly. I guessed she was in her late fifties or early sixties. She wore no makeup and her long white hair fell about her shoulders. "There's some interesting reading here," she said. I opened my mouth to reply, and she nodded in dismissal and politely squeezed past me.

I gaped after her as she left the library without further ado. She didn't look back. The smell of sharp, fresh lavender lingered long after she walked away.

On the table in front of me were a number of books. Had she been reading these? There were three volumes. Each was leather-bound with gold lettering on the spine. I reached out and drew the first one to me, flipping the cover, and turning it so I could see what was written there. What I read made me sit down in a hurry. The volume, written in the 1830s, was entitled *The Myths and Tales of Elbury and Her Surrounding Villages and Hamlets.* The book fell naturally open at a page describing the history of the tree on Elbury Road. Startled, I had a quick look at the other two volumes. They were both of a similar age and ilk. I flicked through the pages of each, and again, naturally and quickly located information pertaining to the oak tree.

Local folklore had it that the tree was a dangerous landmark. The communities of Elbury and Abbotts Cromleigh, along with the neighbouring hamlet of Talerton, and village of Awlcombe, knew that the area should be avoided wherever and whenever possible. It was claimed that during the eleventh to the fourteenth centuries, the tree had been used as a place where vagrants, beggars, and thieves were hung, and many people had shied away from using that route on the off-chance they would be waylaid by the souls of the damned. But then as now, the route had been the quickest way to get to Elbury from Abbotts Cromleigh. Over the centuries the tree's bad reputation had continued to fester and was writ largely in the lives of locals as an arbiter of death and disaster.

The third book, *Witchcraft in the Western Counties of Old England* mentioned—almost in passing—that a tree near the port of Elbury was rumoured to have held a special fascination during the fifteenth and sixteenth centuries, when witches for miles around would visit the tree at Samhain. They believed that the tree was a gateway to a world beyond this one. Which world was not clear and the detail was sparse.

I sat back on my chair and exhaled noisily, trying to release tension.

This was all so ridiculously fantastical, and I was totally caught up in it. I didn't want to believe all this ridiculous superstition, but what if there was something to it?

SEVEN

TRENT

It was with some trepidation that I invited Professor Redburn to my house the following weekend. Trent, for he insisted that I call him that, was excited—in a way that I guess only academics can ever be—about my odd snippets of information. He was absolutely thrilled that I might have something that he could use in his research. I was equally certain that the whole thing was crazy. The tree was starting to inhabit every thought I had. But hey ho. In for a penny, in for a pound, as my mother liked to say.

After I had photocopied a couple of dozen pages at the library from the books left behind by the mysterious woman, I had come home and started sticking things together in one of Max's old folders. Feeling a little like the history undergraduate I had once been, albeit temporarily, I carefully started to cut things out, stick them to blank cards, and annotate them in my neatest handwriting. I then slipped them into plastic wallets and inserted them into the file. My thinking was that this would allow me to move things around and make connections more easily than I would have been able to had they been fixed by glue in a scrapbook.

Taken altogether, in what must surely have been the most cursory piece of research ever undertaken, the contents of my collection already appeared impressive to me. The question I was posing to myself: Was it believable that the tree was an ill-fated harbinger of death and destruction? Was there anything to these stories at all? My gut instinct was that it was all hogwash, but I was willing to look into anything that might help me understand what had happened to Max.

Trent turned up promptly, driving a car that was even more battered than mine. I was struck again by how young he was for a professor, no older than thirty-six or thirty-seven I would have guessed. I was nervous as I held the door open for him, but he was warm and friendly, and apart from being really quite geeky at times in manner and speech, and obviously extremely well educated, he came across as a likable man.

He greeted Pip with great gusto, and Pip returned the welcome, getting himself over excited and resulting in a coughing fit. I calmed them both down and took Trent through to my newly cleaned and tidied kitchen, which was still doubling as a study for my tree research. Trent looked around at my shabby belongings, and I grimaced. It had been a while since I had felt the urge to be house proud.

"Please," I said and indicated the chairs around the kitchen table. "Would you like something to drink?" He opted for herbal tea. This was fortunate as I was completely out of coffee but had a cupboard full of various flavoured herbal teas. I always fancied them when I spotted them on the supermarket shelves but never usually got around to drinking them.

When we were both sitting at the table with our drinks and had finished chatting about Pip and the weather—unfathomably warm and sunny for July in England—he turned his attention eagerly to the folder in front of us.

I pursed my lips. "I don't know how to start."

Trent smiled. "When my students get stuck or tongue-tied, I tell them to jump in anywhere and then we can retrieve any lost nuggets of information later."

"Ok," I said. I folded my hands in my lap to prevent fidgeting, examining them before taking a deep breath. "My son was killed just after Christmas three years ago. He was seventeen. The car he was travelling in hit a tree on Elbury Road. My son, huh," a familiar hitch in my speech. I breathed. Tried again. "My son, Max, was a passenger. He and the driver were killed. There was one survivor." Trent looked stunned and didn't immediately respond.

"A few weeks ago there was another bad accident at exactly the same spot. This time five teenagers died. The week before last a hiker was killed on the same road." I took one more deep breath, articulated the thought that caused me the most consternation. "And I think it's the tree."

I stopped. I didn't know how to continue. None of it made any sense. Surely what I was saying would sound ridiculous to anyone who wasn't party to what was going on in my overly-anxious head with its busy internal meanderings.

Trent surprised me then. He leaned forward and took one of my hands in his. His voice was soft. "I'm so sorry. About your son."

My eyes clouded with tears, and I smiled a smile that was more of a grimace than a grin. I nodded and fought the wave of emotion that engulfed me, as it always did. "Thank you."

We sat in silence for a moment. I felt emotionally exhausted. Eventually Trent gestured towards the file on the table. "May I?" he asked.

"Oh, of course. Sorry. Yes."

He pulled the file towards himself and began to flick through the pages. I had placed everything in what I thought was chronological order and recorded the source of information where it was readily available. He read everything and studied the photos. When he came to the photo he had originally sent me he whistled as he read the notes.

"You actually know this cottage?"

"Yes. It's the cottage across the road," I replied.

"So this photo was from your local newspaper?"

"Yes, the *Elbury Evening Telegraph*," I pointed to where I had made a note of that on the photocopy from the library. "It's closed now."

"We may actually be able to get our hands on the original copy of the photograph even so."

"Really?"

"Yes. The paper will have had a pictorial archive that may well have been moved somewhere else. It's worth checking out where that could be. You never know what other details a clearer image might throw up. Anything can be helpful."

"What are we actually looking at here?" I asked, bemused. "I mean, if we find out the tree has some sort of bad karma, or I don't know, a reverse magnetic force field or something scientific," I was clutching at straws, "what are we going to do?

59

Excommunicate it or something?"

Trent smiled, amused by my gruffness. I wasn't trying to belittle him and was frightened of what we could possibly find out. I guess I still did not believe in any of this hocus pocus, spiritual claptrap. And yet... and yet ...

"Let me just look through the rest of the file, ok?"

I nodded. I left him and changed the water in Pip's bowl, standing at the window in front of the sink for a while, gazing out into my back garden. I knew what was coming up in the file. Trent was going to find the various pieces of information I had collaborated about Max's death along with photos taken of the crash scene and Max's death certificate.

I had also included cuttings taken from the local newspapers and printouts from the BBC news website about the accident involving the five teenagers, and the death of Ethan Carnegie. That was pretty much everything I had. I doubted any other stretch of road in the UK was as unlucky as Elbury Road.

When Trent had finished looking at the file, I heard his chair scrape back. He came and stood next to me, clutching his mug. "Would you like a refill?" I asked.

"Sod that," he replied, his eyes sad. "Can we go and get a drink somewhere? I could really do with one."

*

Hefting the file, I led Trent the half mile or so into Abbotts Cromleigh town centre. There was a lovely pub there called The Admiral Nelson, a long-time favourite of mine. There was no music, no pool table, no game machine. No mod cons at all in fact, just hard wooden benches and huge kegs of beer. Years ago it would have been a spit and sawdust pub, now there was a notable absence of sawdust but pretty much everything else remained the same.

Trent was enamoured straight away. It transpired that he loved real ale.

It was a beautiful afternoon so we opted for the neat beer garden out the back. It was lovely to sip a beer, to have the sun on my back and shoulders and feel that warmth. It was a rare moment of contentment for me. I knew the old Heather would have thought it was cool to be in the company of this handsome and intelligent man, but the new version of me was obsessing about the tree and the role it had played in Max's death.

"What do you think?" I asked.

Trent fiddled with the file. "I think that it's worth looking into. But, and this is a big but," he took a swig of his pint, "even if we can prove some sort of link between the tree and the various deaths that you've found," he grimaced, "I'm not sure what our plan of action could be."

"Maybe we could have the tree cut down?"

Trent shook his head. "Maybe. But I think it's more likely that people will think we're a bit … well they won't want to know. They'll dismiss you as a grieving mother, a bit …"

"Unhinged?" I finished for him bitterly. "Hey, people already think that, believe me. And maybe they're not far wrong." I thought of the citalopram and the diazepam lined up neatly on my bedside table.

Trent tapped the file. "There's something here. This is just a few instances you've found where the tree seems to be the focus of odd activity. There may be more. We can't get access to many historical records because they don't exist anymore—or they were never written down. But as your research has already shown, there are rumours abounding locally suggesting this specific oak tree has garnered itself a bit of a reputation for being deadly.

"What interests me as a cultural anthropologist, is that it doesn't appear to be a part of public awareness, and nothing has been done about it at all, apart from one attempt by an unfortunate farmer to chop it down. I don't know how far he would have got with that measly axe he was carrying though."

I sighed. "So there's probably nothing we can do."

Trent shook his head, looking solemn. His eyes soft with sympathy. "So what happens elsewhere when these trees are uncovered?"

"You remember the tree in Mexico? Yes?"

I recalled Trent's lecture. "They gave offerings."

"That's right. They leave gifts to appease the spirits or they offer sacrifices, generally animals—chickens, pigs, or goats—in the hope that the spirits will be satisfied with some bloodletting and decide to leave the community alone."

"I do remember." I recalled the slides he had shown of the trees swathed in ribbons and surrounded by bowls of fruit, and in one memorable case, a goat's head. "But what if that doesn't work? What do they do then?"

"In some cultures it's not unheard of to have some sort of Guardian by the tree. I've seen that in Asia." Trent fiddled with his now empty glass. I wondered if he fancied another pint. It was my round.

"How so?" I asked rooting around in my shoulder bag for my purse. I could never find anything in my bag. My house keys had split the cotton lining and my personal effects managed to hide themselves mercilessly from me in some secret compartment I had no knowledge of.

"They sometimes build a little house near the tree and the occupant will keep an eye on it. They pop out, sometimes several times a day, to perform rituals that cleanse the tree's spirit, or satiate its needs, whatever they might be." Trent appeared hopeful as I found my purse.

I was about to stand up and head for the bar when what he had said permeated my slow-witted brain. "Wait. You said they build a little house near the tree and keep an eye on it?"

"That's right." Trent handed me his glass, but I sat down again, much to his dismay. "What?" he asked.

"After the lecture I asked you whether you believed in witches."

"Ah," he looked bashful. "You did, yes."

"And you said, some of your best friends are witches."

"Well."

"Well?"

"I figured you were a nutter, and I wanted to humour you."

I was stunned into silence for a moment. It was what I had been afraid of, and yet, it seemed ironic that a man who believed in tree spirits thought that I was the weirdo.

"I hoped at first you had some genuine information that I was going to be able to use, but when you asked me that question, I must admit I decided you were strange." Trent had the grace to look embarrassed but then burst out laughing. I joined in. It was the first time I had genuinely laughed in what felt like a long time. I was odd, yes, but so was he.

"Trent," I said. "Get your things together. We're going back to my place to collect my car and then we're going to take a drive. There's someone I want you to meet."

*

I parked in my usual spot and led Trent down the lane towards the cottage. A faint smell of wood smoke perfumed the air in spite of the heat of the day, and I wondered whether Claire had a bonfire on the go.

I was aiming straight for the cottage but unsurprisingly Trent wanted to take a look at the tree so I allowed myself to be side-tracked. The flower tributes were still there, lying in an ever decreasing state of decay: the stems wilted, the blooms brown and sorry looking. However, there were some fresh flowers laid there too. Another grieving mother looking for solace in the shade of this gargantuan tree.

Trent turned back to me as I hung back, feeling unusually reluctant to approach. The sun shone down on us as he asked me if I was ok, and then he took my hand and pulled me forward to stand next to him. His touch sent a frisson of pleasure through me, something I was unaccustomed to. I didn't let go of his hand, and he didn't let go of mine, so we examined the debris of flowers on the ground together, a memorial to the lost, and for the first time in three and a half years I was able to stand at the point of my son's demise without wanting to scream out in agony, loss, and frustration.

I closed my eyes and breathed deeply for a moment. An image of Max smiling at me filled my mind and quickly disappeared. When I opened my eyes, Trent squeezed my hand.

"Not much sign of a malevolent entity around here, is there?" I smiled.

Trent prodded the tree. "No, not really. It all seems pretty regular."

Very regular, apart from the fact that there was a mountain of flower tributes here, and a smaller pile of fresher flowers slightly farther down the lane where Ethan had been found. Apart from that, yes, everything was normal.

Trent dropped my hand. He scrutinized the tree from all angles and gazed up. The tree was thick with leaves at this time of year. I saw his face register surprise and followed his gaze. A number of crows roosting above our heads stared down at him, silently appraising us with their beady black eyes.

"They're awfully quiet, aren't they?"

"They weren't the last time I was here. One of them dropped an eye on me." The memory made me shudder.

"An eye?"

"An actual eyeball. A human eyeball."

Trent grimaced. "Are you sure? Where did they get that from?"

I gestured at the churned up ground around us. "You tell me."

Trent followed the faint yellow marks on the road that the police had left after investigating the scene. He noted the deep ridges carved into the verge where the car had left the road. He examined the recent scarring on the trunk, the splintered creamy wood starkly contrasting with the bark and moss. The devastation of the area demonstrated how hard the car had hit the tree. "Not nice."

A movement in our periphery caught my eye. It was Claire. She had come out to her gate and watched us. When she caught my eye, she gave me a knowing look and gestured for us to come over. I nodded.

"Trent, the woman I wanted you to meet is over here."

He followed me across the road, and I introduced them.

"I've put the kettle on," Claire said and when we entered her kitchen, three china mugs awaited is. "Is raspberry tea acceptable for everyone?"

"That's my favourite," said Trent earnestly.

I smiled slyly. What a coincidence.

The sumptuous scent of fresh baking made my mouth water. "What have you been baking? There's a lovely smell in here."

I waited for Claire to claim she had been making frog leg quiche or rabbit innards cupcakes but she simply said, "Raspberry sponge. We have a glut of them in the garden and my grandmother loves sponge."

"Sounds delicious," said Trent, possibly hoping she would offer a slice. I had to agree. I watched him take in his surroundings and clock all the herbs and spices. He looked twice at the veiled mirror.

"So what can I do for you?" asked Claire who in turn was surreptitiously appraising Trent whenever his attention was elsewhere.

"Well." Where to start? I was tongue tied for a moment. This whole situation was frankly ridiculous. Claire claimed to be a witch, from a line of witches. Trent believed in the existence of tree spirits. I believed in neither. Trent thought the idea of modern day witches was absurd. I had no idea what Claire thought of tree spirits. It was time to find out. "Trent is a professor of anthropology at the University of Exeter."

"My specialism is historical cultural anthropology, particularly in relation to folk myths and lore." Trent nodded, as though that meant anything to anybody except himself.

"I brought him here, because we've been looking at the number of accidents on this road, right outside this cottage in fact, and ah, we were wondering whether there is some sort of connection between the tree and the deaths." We had left the file of research I'd undertaken in the car, but from the way Claire suddenly twitched I figured she knew exactly what I was talking about and wouldn't need to see my 'evidence'.

She shrugged. "All these accidents, they are a coincidence

surely."

"But they aren't, are they?" For the first time I was certain I was right. Claire's odd resignation to what I was saying proved there was something strange going on. My heart began to beat faster in fear and panic. Did I want Max's death to be a pointless accident, not down to someone or something else? No. If Max had died from something other than a freak accident I wanted to know. "Claire?" I heard a note of hysteria in my voice.

The world suddenly went grey, the strength sapping out of me. For a moment I thought I would faint. Claire moved quickly, to grab the mug from my hand before I dropped it, then placed her hand on my head, pushing it down so that my head was between my knees. My head vibrated and in the back of my mind something slim and slick coiled and uncoiled. I closed my eyes and allowed the vision to pass. When I came back to the present, Claire was telling me to breathe slowly and deeply and pressing a cool, freshly scented citrus compress to the back of my neck.

I kept breathing in and out, letting the strength return to my limbs. Trent reached across and took my hand. "Are you ok?"

I sat back up, smiling ruefully. "Yes, I'm fine. I'm sorry. The reality of Max … sometimes … if I'd ever thought someone was to blame … I couldn't rest if I thought someone had caused his death. If someone caused the accident, then I would want to find them."

"What if it's not someone but something?" asked Trent solemnly.

"If it's the tree, what then you mean?" I asked.

Claire's face was as cool as the compress I held in my hand. "How could a tree be to blame for your son's death?" She shook her head. "I can't help you."

"Tell me about the tree." I said.

"I can't. Don't ask me to."

"But you must. I need to know."

Claire's gaze was steady, her eyes clear and forthright.

"What you want to know," she said slowly, "it is not something that is in my gift to offer you. I am not able to share what I know with you."

I waved her off. "Trent was telling me that sometimes a tree has a Guardian who lives close by. Who gives the tree offerings and ensures that it is pacified? Is that what you do?" I hated how irrational and crazed I sounded. "Is that why you live here, in this cottage?"

Again Claire shook her head. It wasn't a denial of what I was saying, it was a refusal to speak of it.

"Can I destroy the tree?" I asked.

"That's unlikely," Claire said. "There is magick, deep magick, that is far stronger than an axe or a chainsaw."

"Magick?" Trent asked, leaning forward in his chair, interested. "You know about magick?"

Claire smiled, a small movement at the corners of her mouth. "You could say that, yes."

"Claire claims she is a witch," I put in. "She healed my hand when I thought it would need stitches and she … she says she has the sight." Saying it quickly in this way made it all seem plausible.

The pair of them each had their own strange beliefs. I had lost my son and was vulnerable to any kind of shit anyone offered. I shouldn't be mixing with them, or listening to their preposterous claims. Max was dead. It had been a simple accident and nothing to do with witchcraft, magick, or a possessed tree.

Trent was taken aback but then beamed at Claire. "That's just amazing. Then … there is something in it? The tree? It has a malevolent spirit of some kind?"

Claire sighed. "This is beyond me. I can't tell you anything. I need to speak to my grandmother. She's resting just now. I'll talk to her. You'll have to come back another time."

*

Outside it was twilight. Trent and I walked in silence to my car. The lane was shadowy and the hedges were high.

There was nothing to see, nothing that could be seen, but Trent stared out of the window all the way back to the Abbotts Cromleigh crossroads. We passed a pub at the crossroads and I almost suggested we pull in, but I was scared that if I stopped to have a drink, I might have another and another.

I drove back to my house instead; Trent's car was there after all. I pulled into my drive and saw Trent staring at the tattered exterior of my house. He was quiet. What did this man really think of me? Did it actually matter? Would I ever see him again?

I broke the silence, scared of being left alone once more. "Would you like to come in?" I asked. So British, so polite. "Maybe another herbal tea?"

He turned to me and laughed. His face was so animated. "If you have anything stronger that would be excellent, and erm, if I could use your facilities so much the better. All that fruit tea has gone straight through me."

*

My patio had seen better days; it was badly in need of weeding and the flags were broken. I had let things go since Max's death but barely noticed. It takes one person, one outsider, to throw your life into stark relief. For the first time, in a very long while, I caught myself caring what a stranger thought of me.

It was dark however, the only light coming from the kitchen behind us, and Trent appeared oblivious to the state of my garden. Instead he was processing everything that had happened since he had turned up at my house a mere six hours earlier. I left him to his thoughts and returned to the kitchen.

We hadn't eaten. I thought of Claire's homemade raspberry sponge with regret and gathered together some cheese, crackers, and a jar of Branston Pickle, before opening a bottle of red wine. Fortunately, while I was often out of anything edible, I was never short of wine. I loaded up a tray and carried it outside where we nibbled and drank. The stars popped out, slowly at first, before spreading across the night sky like measles. This was one of the blessings of living rurally—there was much less light pollution and on some nights, like tonight, the map of the heavens was fantastic.

Trent chatted amiably about his research and teaching. He obviously loved what he was doing although he told me he had never wanted to be an academic. "I thought about the law," he said, because his father was a barrister, "but I just wasn't cut and thrust enough, so I settled for history. It's much gentler."

I smiled at that. "Isn't history all about wars and dictators?"

"No, no. Well it can be. I just ignore those bits. Did you go to University?"

"Temporarily. It's a long story."

"Why did you leave?"

"Well ..."

"Are you going to tell me it's a long story again?" asked Trent, amused. His eyes were soft in the moonlight, sympathetic. He placed his wine glass on the table in front of us and then put his warm hand on my cooler one. "I have the time to listen if you want to tell."

And so I told him everything. More than I'd ever told anyone. More even than I'd told the bereavement counsellor allotted to me in the weeks after Max's accident. I told him about meeting Max's father at University. He'd been a postgraduate and my seminar tutor. Maybe it wasn't particularly ethical on his part, but I had a crush on him and we were consenting adults and we somehow ended up in an entanglement. I was far too young to handle a proper relationship, while he was happy to have undergraduates throwing themselves at him.

"I saw him one night when I was out clubbing with some of my friends. We'd both had too much to drink. We flirted. It went too far. But I was so into him." It was a short lived fling. I discovered he was seeing someone else. It wasn't until I returned home for the long summer break that I found out I was pregnant. There was never any question of going back to University. I lived with my mother until Max was born and then I found somewhere else for us both to live.

"I brought him up by myself. In spite of everything people say about being a single mum, it wasn't really that difficult. My own mum was hugely supportive, and he was such a good baby. Slept well. No problems at all. I found a job in admin and then I trained up to work in the IT department at the local college, and Mum helped me look after Max." When my mum died I inherited enough to buy this slightly tatty house and now I worked at home as a web designer.

"Max was everything to me. He was the easiest child to love. He was a sweet intelligent boy with a ready smile and a great sense of fun. Parents always say that, don't they? When their children pass on? But he really was a lovely kid. He wasn't particularly adventurous, but he liked spending time with his friends and he wouldn't shy away from trying things out. He was a bookaholic. He read anything and everything. He lived in the bookshop downtown at weekends. The Storykeeper? Do you know it? He wasn't an A star student in anything except literature, but he was on course to get good A levels and he was heading to University. He wanted to go north, to Sheffield. Used to joke he wanted to get away from me. Maybe he really did want that. We were all the other had. Perhaps he was suffocated by me." I'd often considered that. It would have been hard to see him go to Sheffield, but he was so excited and thrilled with the prospect, how could I have stood in his way? It was infinitely harder to know now that I would never see his face again.

"All he ever wanted to study was literature. Books were the magic in his life."

"Then he died." I skipped over the details. What devastation that had been. I'd completely lost the plot for a while and had been on some serious medication. It had been hard clawing my way back to some semblance of sanity. "But you have to go on, because what is the alternative?"

We were quiet for a moment as I reflected on Max and the boy he had been. I didn't need to say that there was a huge void in my life; it must have been obvious.

I changed the subject a little, and we talked about the more recent accident. Trent had heard about this one on the regional news. He didn't know about my visit to the crash site afterwards however. "That was when I cut myself and first met Claire."

"You said she …"

"Healed my hand. Yes. Magically." I snorted. "I was pretty sure it would need stitches." I held my hand out to Trent. He took it and twisted it into the available light from the kitchen window. There wasn't much.

"I can't see anything."

"There's not much to see. It's just a thin pink line. But it was a deep gash. At the very least it would have taken a while to heal. Claire put a paste over it, and the next day, the cut was healed. There was nothing there."

Trent frowned. He didn't understand either.

"Tell me about they eyeball," he said. "You're certain it was human? Not a sheep? Cow?"

"Definitely human."

"Are you sure?"

I blew my cheeks out, shook my head, and grinned wryly. "No. How can I be sure? I'm not an anatomist. But it was a blue eye. I thought it was human." I shuddered.

"Jesus."

"Yeah. Weird. And there's one more thing you need to know." Trent nodded and picked his wine glass up. "A man named Ethan Carnegie was killed a few weeks ago. The police say he was hit by a car, but they've never found any trace of a car and no driver reported an accident. His body was found maybe twenty or thirty feet away from the oak. There is something amiss with that damn thing, Trent, I know there is. It can't just be a coincidence." I sat back and shivered a little. I was emotionally drained and that made me feel cold and vulnerable.

But I liked Trent. He didn't offer faux sympathy or empty platitudes. Even now he simply nodded and sat with me in silence for a while, cogitating, until eventually he said, "Max sounds like the type of student I would have loved in my class. You know … one who actually reads. You'd be surprised how many students think that they can get through their degrees without reading anything more demanding that their Facebook page."

I laughed. It was a tonic. A release.

"We need to think about what to do next," said Trent slowly.

We. He'd said we. He didn't think I was a crackpot after all. I nodded. "I suppose we should wait until Claire gets back in touch with us. If she wants to talk to us."

"That works out well for me. I have to be in Leeds for a conference on student retention this week, but maybe you could look into finding a copy of the photo from the newspaper."

"The farmer by the tree you mean?"

He nodded.

"Ok, I'll see what I can find out. Anything else?"

He hesitated. "If you do have any spare time, you could look back through the local newspaper archive and see if there are any similar stories we can add to the folder. Then I suppose we'll just have to wait for Claire."

"It's ridiculous, isn't it? All this."

He smiled. "Possessed trees you mean? Maybe. But strange things happen. And people around the world believe in tree spirits, or possession, so we can't discount anything. I suppose I'm inclined to agree with you. I've never seen any actual evidence of a tree spirit, but I have heard some amazing tales."

"Do you think Claire's straight up about being a witch?"

"Don't you?"

"I don't know what to think." I pondered for a moment. "She has been able to do some strange things. But what does being a witch mean in this day and age?"

"She makes a mean cup of raspberry tea," said Trent.

*

72

The house felt empty once he had left, or maybe it was just that I felt more alone. He had cheerfully bid me goodbye after squeezing my shoulder once. There was no awkwardness. I missed him now he was gone.

Darn. I was attracted to him. But I was at least four years older than him and he was a good looking man. I suppose I wasn't bad looking, for a woman in her forties, but nothing sensational. I wasn't into pimping and preening. I went long months between haircuts and didn't bother with makeup and manicures. Surely men of his age in his position would look for women years younger than me, glamorous women, or women they could start families with.

On the other hand, he could be married already, or in a relationship, or gay or something for all I knew. There was no ring on his finger, but what did that mean? Some men don't bother with them, do they? Maybe I should have asked him, but looking back on our conversation there had been no point where I could have investigated his personal circumstances without appearing obviously interested in him.

And that would never do.

Nonetheless I could have kicked myself. I was far too out of practice to get involved with anyone anyway. I bet my heart would creak if anyone tried to unhinge it.

I busied myself with clearing up, attempting to ignore the fluttering feeling inside my stomach. I was in the first throes of a crush, like some silly schoolgirl. It had been a ludicrously long time since I had felt this yearning anxiety for another.

There was nothing to do except enjoy it while I had the chance.

EIGHT

BRIAN

The next morning, I did a Google search for information about the *Elbury Evening Telegraph*. It transpired that the *Telegraph* had long ceased to be an independently run local newspaper, having been taken over by its parent company known as the Western Media Syndicate or WMS. The WMS headquarters was located in Plymouth. The WMS website had a contact phone number so I rang them, and that was how my day started.

WMS claimed not to hold the archives for any newspapers prior to when they had taken over the *Telegraph*. Previously, a smaller company had also owned *The Cromleigh Chronicle*, the *Telegraph* and another local newspaper, the *Herald*. They had been defunct since the '90s and unfortunately the helpful lady at the WMS didn't have a clue who would hold the archives.

I was stumped. Perhaps the archives had long since been destroyed. I had a vague recollection of a series of newspapers that tended to come out in the summer up until a few years ago that had been popular with tourists and locals alike, named something like *Bygones*. Who would have published something like that, I wondered? They had contained a fabulous array of fantastic vintage photographs. Max had bought them in The Storykeeper bookshop, and pored over them, enthralled by the retro photos of Abbotts Cromleigh, comparing old landmarks to their present day settings.

I jumped when my mobile phone clanged. It was a text. Texts were a rare occurrence in my life. I picked up the phone and clumsily found the screen that contained my messages. The number was an unknown one, or at least not saved into my contacts anyhow. I pressed open the text to see, *On my way to Leeds. Thanks for yesterday. Odd, interesting, enjoyable. How are you getting on?*

My heart skipped a little. I read and reread the message for any hidden connotations and decided there were none. One positive, I decided, was that Trent didn't use text speak. I hurriedly typed back, spuriously imagining time was of the essence if he was to receive my return message, *Drawn blank. No archives. Change of company. What now?*

A moment later another clang. That was fast. Perhaps he'd been awaiting my reply. I smiled hopefully at the phone. This time he suggested, *Try public archives in Elbury and if not, Exeter.*

Ah, I thought. It made sense to ask a researcher where he would locate the archives. I found the number of the local history section of library services in Elbury, rang them to discover, unsurprisingly, all of the Elbury archives had been sent to the public records office in Exeter.

Back on Google I was able to find the Public Records Office and print out a map of its location. I hated driving to Exeter, could never figure out the road system, but nonetheless I jumped into my car and set off.

Finally, by lunchtime, I was sitting in the car park gathering together things to take inside the building with me. The website had warned that bags were not allowed. Once inside I had to register, show proof of identification, and stow all my personal items into a locker. The staff were extremely security conscious and rightly so I figured, if they had documents that were irreplaceable.

I was greeted by the muffled sound of people talking very quietly and the noise of machines whirring. The atmosphere within the main reading rooms was quiet, studious, and professional. Occasionally there was a rustle of paper or the scratch of a pencil. I was intrigued to think this was how Trent spent a great deal of his time.

I approached the main desk, as instructed by the receptionist, clutching my brand new visitor's pass. I quietly explained that I was looking for a copy of a photograph that had appeared in the *Elbury Evening Telegraph* in September 1908. The woman listened carefully and jotted down some notes.

Then she asked whether I had a photographic reference number, which of course I didn't. She showed me to a computer and demonstrated how to use the software to search for images. I could narrow down by year and month, and also subject matter, although the categories were pretty generic.

And that was as simple as it was. Within ten minutes of arriving at the records office I was staring at a scanned version of the photograph of Farmer Caldecott in front of the oak tree, bearing his axe. The photograph was much clearer on the screen than it had been in the blurry newspaper image that Trent had provided me with. Underneath the photograph was the reference number that I would need to use if I required a copy. I politely asked the elderly gentleman to the side of me whether I could borrow his pencil to write down the number and he happily obliged. As I wrote he leaned over to take a look at the photograph.

"Well, fancy, that's Black Cottage in the background there, I'll wager?" His voice was low but excited.

Puzzled, I whispered back, "Black Cottage?"

He pointed at my screen at the cottage. "Black Cottage. It's actually called White Cottage but all us locals used to call it Black Cottage when I was growing up."

"You grew up in …"

"I grew up in Awlcombe, next village along." The gentleman nodded.

"That's right," I murmured. "Some beautiful cottages there. Very *des res*."

"They weren't desirable back in the '30s and '40s I can tell you. Simple labourer's cottages then. Falling down ruins." His accent was broad.

I smiled. "You don't want to know what they sell for these days, then."

"Oh I know already. Second homes. Holiday cottages. Damn Londoners. Not really progress, is it?"

An assistant shushed us and the old gentleman winked at me gleefully. He probably hadn't been told off in years. "I can tell you some stories about the old days," he nodded his head at the exit. "I'm going to have a cup of tea. Why don't you join me in the tea room?"

I whispered that I would. First of all, however, I made my way back to the help desk again and asked for a copy of the photograph. They were able to provide a scan on photographic paper for an astronomical fee. I agreed, because I knew that I needed to have something to show Trent. They printed it out for me and I carefully took it with me as I went through the exit and found the tearoom opposite the locker room.

Inside the tearoom were a number of vending machines serving a variety of hot and cold beverages and sweets and crisps. Nothing particularly healthy. I bought a bottle of water and a plastic cup of tea that tasted like chicken soup and sat at a round table in the window, next to my brand new friend.

The gentleman smiled and held out his hand. "Brian Miller. Retired school teacher, local amateur historian and genealogist."

I shook his hand. "Heather Keynes. Web designer and erm … extremely amateur researcher. Research for a friend really." I decided I didn't really want to get into what I was doing.

"What's your interest in Black Cottage?" asked Brian.

I wondered how much I should tell him. I didn't want to chat about Max or possessed oak trees, so I played it cool.

"I found this photo in a newspaper cutting and I wanted to know the story behind it," I answered, truthfully.

"May I see?" asked Brian. I handed the picture to him. He took a magnifying glass from his jacket pocket and inspecting the image.

"Do you know who the farmer is?" he asked.

"Yes, I believe his name was Elias Caldecott."

"Ah, that would make sense yes. I was at school with his grandson. And I knew him for a while afterwards too. We should have been in National Service together. A tragic family."

"Really? How so?" I asked, my interest piqued.

"You undoubtedly know that Farmer Caldecott here was

killed by a falling branch, or so I heard, but his son also died quite tragically. He was killed when some German bombers dropped their bombs on East Devon as they flew out to sea and home to Germany. 1943 it was, '44 maybe. I think the Germans were aiming for Exeter and overshot. Anyway the farmhouse was hit and he and his wife were killed. They were young. Very sad."

"But you knew the grandson too?"

"Yes, we were at school together. Graham he was called. Was a bit of a rebel. Brought up by his Aunt and Uncle in Cromleigh, but just ran wild really. Got himself a reputation. A bit of a lady's man. Had a few flings with married women. All a bit hush hush of course. Not the done thing at all. Used to hang out with a Polish lad who was just as bad, and he came to a sticky end too."

Brian sipped at his tea. He'd brought a thermos with him. He obviously knew how bad the vending machine's tea was here.

"What happened to the Polish lad?" I prompted.

"Nobody knows really. Luka or something, Lucas. He'd been in The Plough and Harrow. He was most nights. He liked to chat up the ladies, pick one up if he could, maybe escort them home. Most times it came to nothing. Decent girls wouldn't have had much truck with him. He'd be lucky to get a bit of a kiss and a cuddle really. On this last night Lucas and Graham were with a mutual friend of ours called Bill 'Tucker' Tuckman."

I twiddled with my plastic cup. Brian obviously liked to tell a tale. I nodded, hoping he would get to the point.

"The way Bill told it afterwards, was that some stranger came into the bar. Beautiful young woman. Bill saw her, all the guys saw her, but Lucas fell madly in love with her instantly. Like a fairy tale." His tone was mocking but I started. This sounded familiar. Too familiar.

"Really? Why? What was so special about her?"

"Bill said she was the most beautiful woman any of them had ever seen. And she had, you know, if you'll excuse me saying so, real sex appeal." He whispered the last few words in case I was shocked.

"Go on," I said.

"The way Bill described it, the moment she came through the door all eyes in the place were on her but she only had eyes for Lucas. Lucas being Lucas ... well it didn't take him long to make her acquaintance. Graham was most put out. Lucas and this lady, they sat at the bar, friendly as you like. Then they left—nobody saw them leave though. Lucas was found dead in bed in his lodgings the next day. No-one knew why he died. Just that he did. And no-one apart from Graham and Bill remembered the woman afterwards."

The plastic cup crumpled in my hand, the gruesome tea spilt unnoticed on the table. I sat straighter, my mouth open in shock.

"Are you sure?"

"Yes, oh yes. There's not many people left to verify the story any more, I suppose. Bill told me all about it because he found it very odd. Not long after that I had to go and do my National Service."

"So what happened to Graham?"

"He disappeared. It was all a bit of a mystery really. He had lodgings with Mrs Adams on Curzon Street too, do you know it? Big Georgian house. She was an interesting character. Lost her husband in the war so kept the house on by letting rooms to young men after that. Rumours abounded about her. She would have been in her fifties by the time he moved into her boarding house."

"And Bill?"

"I haven't seen him for many a year, but I think he lives in sheltered housing in Elbury nowadays. I bump into his sister Maeve from time to time."

My mind was reeling. What had happened to Lucas? Hadn't Fraser told me virtually the same story just a few months ago about Mikey? This was like some urban legend that gets repeated every few years or so. Was Brian having me on?

Brian's chatter brought me back to the present. "So you see, it was a tragedy from start to finish with that poor Caldecott family."

"And the tree was never destroyed."

"No. It does seem to attract its fair share of mishaps, doesn't it? A coincidence?" Brian appraised me, becoming curious about my enquiries. I quickly changed my line of questioning.

"Brian," I turned the photo back to him, "tell me about the cottage and its inhabitants."

"As I said, it was known in my day as Black Cottage because, and I know this sounds foolish ... the rumour was that a number of witches lived there."

"Witches?" I feigned surprise.

"Yes. That's what folks said. My mother certainly thought that was the case. Different times. We don't believe in such things now, do we?"

"No." I decided discretion was the better form of valour. "And people what ... hounded them out?"

"Oh no. My mother, like most of the villagers thought these women were wonderful. If you needed a lotion or cough mixture or if your children had a fever, the ladies in Black Cottage were always happy to prepare something for you. Yes. Their family had always been there and people just accepted them. No-one was frightened of them. Totally innocuous. My mother didn't talk about such things, but I heard that in the days before the NHS, when people actually had to pay the doctor for their services rather than simply pay their national insurance contributions, these ladies were very much in demand in our part of the world. I heard that Dorothea particularly was renowned for her ability to aid fertility for example."

"She helped women to have babies?"

"That too, but my understanding was more that she knew how to stop babies coming, and as such she was very popular with the young women in the village and roundabouts, and also with some married women too." Brian winked at me.

"And is this Dorothea in the photo?" I asked.

Brian took his magnifying glass out again and examined it closely. The photograph was much clearer than the newspaper article had been.

"Well you know that's very odd," said Brian.

"Why?"

"Because this photo was taken in 1908 and yet I knew Dorothea in the 1940s, that's forty years after this photo was taken and yet, yes I'm almost certain that's her. She never aged a day." I moved around to Brian's side of the table to look through his magnifying glass with him. "And that's her daughter." He tapped the image of the other, younger woman, also swaddled in a long black cloak. "Oh what was her name? It's on the tip of my tongue."

I recognised her now that I could see her clearly. "Claire!" I said in disbelief.

"That's it!" said Brian. "How did you know?"

*

I exchanged contact details with Brian and promised I would let him know if anything ever came of my research into the photograph. Fortunately, I managed to keep his questions at bay about what I was looking for exactly, but I decided he was an excellent source of local information.

I drove home lost in thought. For once the ridiculous traffic queues in the city didn't bother me, but it was still a relief to get back out into the country on the familiar roads back to Abbotts Cromleigh. The weather was sultry, so I wound the windows down and relished the breeze as it flowed through the car.

Once home I wrote up as much of the conversation with Brian as I could remember. I made a mental note to buy myself a notebook and some pencils. I was turning into an amateur sleuth. I decided the next step was to attempt to discover whether Bill was still alive and if so, where he lived.

Feeling unusually energised, I headed into the back garden to tidy up, something I hadn't wanted to do in a long time. I worked exhaustively, pulling up dead plants and flowers and digging up weeds, emptying my old pots and containers and trimming back the bushes that were running wild. Pip meandered around the garden, getting in the way and generally being a nuisance but extremely good company at the same time. When the light started to fail a few hours later I was able to sit back with Pip on my knee, stroking him with hands that were bloody and scratched, and nails ingrained with dirt. I felt good.

My late dinner was a simple affair, cheese on toast shared with Pip, and then I slumped under the shower and washed away the scent of dusty archives and fresh sweat. I fell into bed, totally exhausted.

And then I couldn't sleep.

Insomnia had been my constant friend since Max's death. For the first eight months I had needed sedatives just to get through the day. It had been rare for me to sleep for more than four hours a night and I had felt continually fatigued. Recently things had improved, but even so I rarely went the whole night without waking, and the dawn often found me in the kitchen nursing a mug of tea.

Tonight I was hot and overly tired. I tossed and turned, thinking about Trent. I was just drifting off and on the edge of a very strange dream when I heard the clang of my mobile. The text was from Trent of course. My heart gave a little skip of delight.

Just thinking of you. How did you get on? Would phone but late I know. Been at conference dinner. Dull.

He was thinking of me, as I lay thinking of him. In the dark, I blushed a little and pondered on how to reply. In the end I opted for, *Sorry to hear conference dull. Exciting day here. Need to catch up.* I scanned the words a dozen times before pressing send.

The reply came back swiftly. *Sounds intriguing! Back Thurs. Beers?*

It felt good to know that I would see him so soon. *Yes. Catch up over beers.* I was pleased with how laid back I sounded.

Great. Sleep well X came the response. I stared at that kiss for a long time until it was imprinted on my brain. When I finally slept, the X was carved on my heart.

NINE

SARAH

The next day was spent catching up on all the jobs I had to complete for clients. It was a long day, and I was hot indoors. The house was airless, and I was frustrated because I badly wanted to be doing something else—anything else, but I was behind on deadlines and needed to get back on track. I finished the day's work by issuing invoices to my clients, before taking Pip out for a walk.

We went to the park and had a slow wander and a sniff. After a while I sat on a park bench and watched the teenagers in their hoodies and low slung trousers messing around with their phones. The park was a mecca for this age group. I'd hung out here with my friends twenty-five years ago, and Max had done the same.

Thinking of Max and his friends reminded me of Mikey. At Mikey's funeral, Fraser had mentioned that both he and Mikey had attended Max's funeral. I couldn't remember whether Max had known Fraser particularly well, but because I hadn't recognised him I assumed they hadn't been great mates.

Fraser's story about Mikey's final night matched Brian's about Lucas. What did that mean? Was there some sort of link between the two deaths? The deaths were fifty years apart but there was a mystery woman in each case. A beautiful woman. One that nobody remembered afterwards.

I was beginning to see conspiracies everywhere.

I pondered on this and decided to call Mikey's mum. Perhaps she had news, or maybe I could find out more about the woman he had met. In any case she would have Fraser's details. I dug through my bag until I found my mobile. There was hardly any battery left. I scrolled through my list of contacts. I'd taken Sarah's details after the funeral and spent some time with her since, talking about Mikey and Max, and dealing with bereavement. I located her home number and selected it. It rang and rang.

For a moment it seemed no-one would answer but finally Sarah picked up.

"Hello?" That one word encapsulated her weariness. She was beaten. I recognised this so well. Bereavement is tough. Initially people take an interest and support you but after a while all of the support disappears and you are left to cope as best you can on your own. In many ways I had felt worse six months after the death of my son than in the immediate aftermath. If that was possible. Maybe it wasn't. But the ensuing loneliness made everything more difficult.

"Hey Sarah," I said quietly, "it's Heather. How are you doing?"

"Heather." She sounded relieved. "It's good to hear from you. I'm ok, you know. Surviving."

"Yeah. Are you getting out and about?"

"I try. I do try. I don't sleep well. I'm so tired."

"I know, honey."

There was a difficult silence as she fought to bring her emotions under control, and then she asked the question I dreaded. "Does it get better, Heather?"

I blew out a breath. I owed her the truth. "I won't lie. It does and it doesn't. No-one will bring him back." I heard her breathing change as she started to weep. "That pain will always be relentless and sharp, but not as fresh as it is now. Eventually you start to live with it."

"Everyone says it takes time."

"We all have a lot of time, Sarah. Sometimes too much. And sometimes, time is all we have. We have to be strong."

"I don't know if I can be."

"Yes you do know you can be. You've come this far. You can get through this, or if not through, you can bear it. Maybe that's the most we can hope for."

My battery gave a warning buzz. The phone was going to die any minute. "Sarah, the reason I rang was that I'm trying to track down a friend of Max's. His name is Fraser and I saw him at Mike's funeral. Would you be able to put me in touch with him?"

"Fraser? Yes. He and Mike were great friends. I don't have his number but I can find out and give you a ring if you like?"

"Yes please, or we can meet up for coffee?"

"That would be nice. I'll be in touch."

*

I met Sarah in a sweet little cafe in Abbotts Cromleigh. They made a mean cream tea. I ordered the works for us to share, but Sarah only wanted a pot of tea. I struggled with the scones and cream by myself.

She appeared pale and drawn and had lost a great deal of weight. This curvy, bubbly woman was being reduced to a shadow of her former self, thanks to the unexplained death of her beloved middle child.

I smiled warmly at her and took her hand, freezing in spite of the beautiful August weather we were having. "Tell me how you are," I said.

Sarah waved away my concerns, but I persisted. Slowly and painfully she dragged out her feelings and shared the terrible difficulties she was having. She couldn't concentrate, didn't want to spend time with anyone, and was unnaturally irritable. Particularly with those who didn't warrant it— supermarket checkout operators, bank clerks, the people answering the phone for her gas company. She told me about her cold, hard anger when she saw young couples in the street living their lives as though nothing had changed in the world.

"And I know that only my world has altered. But it feels so wrong to me. And then I feel stupid and guilty because I am jealous that other young kids get to live their lives while my Mikey can't."

"I know," I said, and I did. "I look at people in their early twenties now and I wonder what Max would be doing. He would have completed University. Where would he be working? Would he have a nice girlfriend?" Everything Sarah was going through, it was all so familiar, and I realised I had come a long way, further than I might have thought possible when Max died. But there is no real coming back after the loss of your child. Sarah had a hard road to traverse ahead of her.

"But on top of everything, I have these dreams …"

"What sort of dreams?" I asked curiously.

"Strange, horrid dreams. I see Mikey quite often in them … and he's calling out for me, and there's this woman in them …" Her voice trailed off.

"Who is the woman?"

"I don't know. She always has her back to me. She's hunched up, and she has long flowing hair but it's dry and matted … and I can see her fingers … they're horrible. Claw like. Great talons on the end of them, sharp. Filthy. And the knuckles are twisted. And it's like she's realised I'm there and she starts to turn around and I can hear Mikey shouting … I'm walking towards her and I can't reach her. I know I want to kill her. I want to do something to save Mikey, but I can't reach him." Sarah slumped back in her chair.

"And?"

"And that's it. Usually I wake up but the dream seems to go on and on before it even reaches that stage. I'm always fighting to get close to her and she seems out of reach. She's always on the verge of turning around and I'm frightened, so frightened."

I commiserated with her. It sounded awful. "Have you spoken to your GP?"

"No. He gives me enough pills without adding more." She fiddled with the dainty cup and saucer in front of her. "Did you dream? After?"

I nodded and lifted the teapot to top her up. "Yes a little. I would dream that Max was still alive." I would waken to realise he was dead. The pain was a stone that would incapacitate me for the whole day. "But nothing like you're describing."

Sarah buried her face in her hands for a moment and then pulled herself together. She changed the subject abruptly. "I have a contact number for Fraser." She located the slip of paper in her purse and handed it to me. It was a mobile number. "He's a good lad. Was so cut up about Mike. He's been around to see me a few times."

"Thanks, that's great. I shall look forward to having a quick catch up with him."

I paid the bill, and we walked out of the tea shop together. I hugged Sarah, feeling her fragility in my embrace. She was a little bird—just bones beneath my touch. For a second I felt dread, some sort of premonition maybe, and I held her tighter, but the moment passed and we said our goodbyes.

TEN

MR KEPHISTO

I needed to buy some bin bags on the way home. I headed towards Taylors, the hardware store down the road from the cafe, looking lazily into all the windows as I went. It was the time of year for fetes and fayres, and many of the shop windows were decorated with summer bunting and pastel coloured balloons. Abbotts Cromleigh was a lively community, small enough that most of the shops were independently owned, reflecting the people of the town and their interests rather than the interests of anonymous multi-nationals with their corporate branding and laissez-faire attitude.

Taylors had changed little over the years. As a girl I had occasionally been sent on errands to the shop, for items such as fuses and lightbulbs. I remembered one occasion where I had tripped and dropped the paper bag containing a lightbulb in its flimsy paper box as I raced home. The filament hadn't survived and I had sensed my father's quiet disapproval as he handed over more change and instructed me to take more care on my repeat journey. My right knee shredded and swollen— the blood left to congeal—remained unsoothed until much later in the day when my mother noticed it. That's how it had been in my house. My studious father, older than my mother, stern and joyless. My mother, a caged bird, so vibrant and loving; a free spirit, trapped in my father's house. I had never understood their relationship. Too late now; they were both gone.

I bought my bags and began to retrace my steps back to the café and my car parked beyond. Coming up on my right, across the road, was The Storykeeper bookshop. The fabulous building was in a small block that contained the oldest architecture in town. Elizabethan originally, The Storykeeper had been extended outwards and upwards a few times. Now, cartoon like, it careened at crazy angles, lurching over the narrow road as though drunk. It was one of a handful of listed buildings in the town, and all native Cromleigians, as we called ourselves, were ridiculously proud of it.

I crossed over, drawn as always to the display of tomes in the window. Max had inherited his love of literature from me. I had been obliged to bring him here at least once a fortnight from the time he had been old enough to understand that the books I read to him every night had originated, in large part, from here. Once he was older and had a little more independence, he would cycle down here on his own. He spent so much time in The Storykeeper and at the library that I had worried he would stand out from his peers, but it was a measure of my son, that he balanced his life and interests beautifully and surrounded himself with other lovely boys who appreciated him for himself. He was never bullied, never found himself in a fight. Maybe he would have one day.

I balanced on the narrow pavement and pressed my forehead against one of the squares of glass, looking in at the display. Photography and art seemed to be the theme. On the right were a number of abstract art books, full of dynamic rainbow swirls. On the left were black and white photography books. In between, someone had cleverly laid out books in a spectrum of colour. It was enticing.

A figure came out of the shop to my left, and aware of the narrowness of the pavement, I started to turn so that we could negotiate passing without either party stepping in front of the traffic behind us.

"Good afternoon!" said a cheery voice. For a moment I was flummoxed, then I recognised the man—Brian Miller from the public records office.

"Brian! What a coincidence."

"It's a small world indeed, Heather. I was just thinking about you." He brandished the packet in his hand. "In fact, I have something you'll be very interested in." He jerked his head back the way he had come. "Let's go back inside and I can show you in there."

I followed Brian as he negotiated the three worn stone

steps leading up to the front door of the shop. The bell jangled as we entered, and somewhere I heard a bird cawing. Mr Kephisto, the eccentric owner of The Storykeeper, kept a crow. He'd always had one. As a child it had scared the living daylights out of me, but Max had often insisted we go upstairs to visit him. It had a name, didn't it? Caius or something. If it was the same crow. How could I have forgotten the bird? It was free to come and go as it chose, but most of the time it appeared happy to be settled on its perch on the mezzanine level, watching everybody mooching around among the books on the ground floor below.

Brian navigated past the lines of shelving, until we reached the staircase. We climbed the stairs, me with my heart in my mouth. The stairs teetered and wobbled, sponge like under my weight. They were flimsy and old, held up only by their placings in the wall.

The mezzanine floor held a small area approximately six metres square. A balustrade marked one edge, with a wall and a door into the rooms opposite it. On either side books were displayed on shelving, and in the middle of the space, two old over-stuffed high backed armchairs were poised at slight angles to each other. In the centre of the floor was a huge vintage globe atop an old Persian rug, the colours of both dulled by long use. Caius, unfazed, remained on his perch as we appeared, but he watched us as we moved around, his jet black eyes unblinking.

"Look here," said Brian excitedly. He dipped his hand into his brown bag and drew out a couple of books. Casting one aside he held the other out to me. He had clearly been looking through the local history section on this floor, the book in my hand was entitled, *Abbotts Cromleigh through the Lens of Time*.

I flicked through, wondering what I was looking for. It was a slim volume, with plenty of photographs, and wouldn't take long to read. Brian took it back. "Here," he said, quickly finding what he wanted and returning it to me.

It was a short section about the village of Awlcombe.

There were several photographs of the village. One with a line of old houses that I recognised, including The Traveller's Rest public house, and a lovely one of the old thatched post office, once the centre of the community but now sadly sold off.

Turning the page, I saw what Brian wanted me to see. There were several photographs of White Cottage. I had seen the black and white one in the records office, the other was a more recent colour photograph, possibly taken in the 1940s at a guess, because of the odd tint. The photo was zoomed out wide, meaning I could see the whole of the front of the whitewashed cottage, with Elbury Road disappearing up the hill beside it. What was interesting to me was that part of the oak tree was in shot, and standing next to the oak tree was a woman, dressed head to foot in black. A long black skirt under a long fitted black jacket. She was in side profile so I couldn't see her face. It wasn't Claire though. How could it have been? This was decades ago.

"Interesting, isn't it? Hasn't changed a jot, that place." Brian looked satisfied with how intently I was studying the photo. "Keep it," he said as I closed the book to hand it back to him. I started to protest, and he gestured at the wall. "There's loads more copies here. I'll buy another one."

"You don't have to," I said, but he waved me away. I stared at the photos in the book again. That couldn't be Claire.

"Do you believe in witches?" I asked Brian, remembering what he had told me about the inhabitants of White Cottage.

Brian pursed his lips and frowned. "No."

I stared back down at the book. "Neither do I."

"Strange things have happened in Abbotts Cromleigh from time to time. With what happened to Graham, for example."

And Mike, I thought. Coincidence. Surely, that's all it was.

"You know you really ought to go and have a chat with Bill Tuckman, the old guy I was telling you about. He's not quite the full shilling I've heard, but he was there. He lived in Mrs Adams's letting house too. He could tell you more about what happened. Fascinating I'm sure. I saw Maeve this morning as it happens. She tells me that he's in The Elbury Valley Residential Home, over on Cromleigh Pass." I knew the one. Built in the '80s, but as grim looking as a Victorian workhouse. I shuddered. It was where people with no money, no family, and no hope ended their days. Soulless.

Brian noted my expression. "He could do with a visitor."

That would be the case, living in that place.

"Ok."

"Take him a newspaper and some mints. He'll like that."

I smiled. Out of the corner of my eye, I saw movement. Mr Kephisto had appeared on the mezzanine level. He was a small, thin man, always impeccably dressed in a three-piece suit with a handkerchief poking out of one pocket. Today the suit was a sapphire blue, and the handkerchief was bright red.

He smiled at me. "Nice to see you after so long, Heather." He hadn't changed in forty years. Not at all. He'd appeared old to me when I was a young girl, but now, over thirty years later, he didn't look any older than seventy or so. A puzzle.

"I was so sorry about Max," Mr Kephisto, went on quietly. "He had a wonderful imagination. He is much missed here." It didn't seem possible that I hadn't visited the shop since Max died, but evidently this was the case. "Well, I have business to attend to, but I'll see you soon, I know." With that he passed through the door, quietly closing it behind him.

I smiled nervously at Brian, who was looking slightly embarrassed. Perhaps he hadn't known about Max, perhaps he had chosen to say nothing. That was the reaction I usually had—an embarrassed or uncomfortable silence. I was used to it, but I didn't like it very much.

I squeezed Brian's arm, hoping to make him feel better. "I'll look Bill up," I promised.

"Bill Tuckman." Brian seemed relieved.

"Thanks for the book," I said. "I have to dash, see you soon." I turned on my heel and made my exit down the stairs as fast as I dared, moving swiftly through the shelving and out to the front of the shop. I sensed Brain looking over the edge of the balustrade watching me go, so I threw a vague wave. The crow cawed as I pulled open the door, the bell jangled once more, and I slipped down the stairs into the fresh air outside.

I crossed the road and stared back at the beautiful crooked façade of the book shop. The bulging front made it look for all the world like an Elizabethan ship. I tilted my head back so I could see to the second and third floor. From a small window far above me, I spotted a face looking down at me. It disappeared as I watched.

ELEVEN

NABB'S HILL

Pip was crossing his legs in desperation by the time I arrived home. I decided to make up for ignoring him all day by taking him for a walk on top of Nabb's Hill, part of the forest that lay to the east of the town. Walk far enough across the ridge of the hill and you could turn down a path and meet Elbury Road if you so wished.

I grabbed my car keys and Pip's lead and with a tired sigh locked the house back up again, but my fatigue soon melted away as we parked up in the little fenced off dirt area and began to stroll purposefully under the forest canopy.

I adored the forest, and I loved this walk. The air was fresher here, my head clearer, my thoughts reinvigorated. I breathed deeply, inhaling the scent of the spruce and the organic wholesomeness of the leaf mulch. The sun was still relatively high in the sky, but the light was softly dappled, filtering prettily through the trees. The green moss glowed neon, growing freely, on trees that were living, as well as those that had been felled. The forest floor rolled this way and that; the soft colouring and gentle lighting was restful to my eyes. I relaxed, dropped my shoulders, and walked on.

I could wish for no better companion than Pip. He scurried this way and that, picking up smells with his super-sensitive nose and following them for a time before abruptly losing interest. He would belatedly remember he was accompanying me and career back in my direction, swinging away just as a collision appeared imminent. He was a good dog. I gazed after him fondly. He was getting on, the white in his muzzle gave his age away. I shut down those thoughts. Kept walking. Intent on living in the moment.

Soon enough though I began to think of the people of that day. Mr Kephisto in The Storykeeper. What had he said? *I'll see you soon, I know.* The phrasing was odd; it wasn't your usual pleasantry. Had he been the one watching me as I left the shop? That pale face at the window?

And Sarah. The dreams she was experiencing sounded awful. The pain that skittered sharply in my own chest, barely dulled by time, was reawakened by the rawness of her grief. Thinking of her and what she was going though brought it back to me, and I was momentarily overwhelmed by sadness. My eyes filled with tears. I rested for a moment, leaning my weight against the trunk of a large beech tree, its branches spread wide all around me, sheltering me from direct sunlight. I sniffed hard and swiped at my eyes and dug around in the pocket of my dog walking fleece for a tissue.

Something underneath my back shifted. Something large, not an insect.

I leapt away from the tree and turned, expecting to see a mouse or a vole—or something fairly sizeable at any rate—scuttling away, as alarmed as I. There was nothing on the tree, nothing moving in my eye line.

In panic I contorted my arms and brushed at the back of my jacket, rather ineptly, before deciding that the best—and only safe—course of action was to pull it off and check it over. I practically ripped the fleece from my body and threw it to the floor. I turned it over, flipped it this way and that. There was nothing to see. No creatures making a nest where they weren't welcome.

"You cretin." I laughed softly, more a moment of relieved hysteria than amusement. "There's nothing there. Nothing there." I blew out my lips, giggled nervously again, and glanced around. I couldn't see anyone. My humiliation had been private.

A branch cracked behind me and I jolted, startled. My head shot in the direction of the sound, my breath caught in my throat. It was Pip. "Only Pip," I whispered. I wanted to hear relief in the words but my heart was beating hard and my breathing was jagged. I was suddenly out of breath.

"Come here, dafty," I urged him loudly and held my hand out. He walked towards me and then stopped stock still, six feet away from me. He gazed at me and then the beech tree behind me, his back rigid, his tail straight up. "What is it?" I asked in a low voice. In answer Pip started to growl, his eyes glowing with anger.

I turned slowly, followed the direction he was looking in, puzzled. I could see nothing, just the beech tree and the trees beyond. Maybe there was something in among the ferns that littered the forest floor, but I couldn't see anything. "There's nothing there, Pip, it's ok," I soothed and walked towards him, holding my hand out to placate him. Something in my mind shifted: a giant centipede, a segmented worm, or a snake ... coiling and uncoiling.

The hackles on Pip's neck stood up and he snarled and spat, his lips curled back from his teeth. Alarmed, I backed up. "Pip!" I said urgently, but he ignored me, it wasn't me that was worrying him.

Pip snapped and growled, frantic in his anger, lowering himself closer to the ground and inching towards the tree. I started to walk backwards, trying to put some distance between me and the tree. "Come away, Pip. Good boy. Let's go home." He wasn't having it, but at least the snarling dropped to a low throaty growl.

In front of us I heard something rustle. A branch snapped, about twelve feet from where I was standing. Pip exploded with anger but made no attempt to leap at anything coming towards us, he merely danced in place, barking and snapping at whatever was heading our way.

I scrutinized the forest in front of me but I could still see nothing at all. Nothing at head height, nothing lower down. Maybe it was a badger or a fox, hidden by the undergrowth, perhaps it was injured and would hurt me if I went too close. That had to be what Pip was picking up on. He was protecting me.

Pip advanced. If an injured animal lay among the ferns and brambles it could be dangerous. I had to stop him going in there. I dashed forward to intercept him before he went much farther. As I did so, something tall and dark moved past my vision just feet away. I had the sense it was a woman because her clothing was loose and flowing. I reared back in sudden shock, staring in the direction the woman had taken, but she had melted into the trees. I took a step forward to get a clearer view, and it was then that I was pushed sharply and firmly, not by a person, but by a wall of strong, warm wind. I quite clearly heard the word "Away" as I flew backwards. I landed on my backside and rolled on to my side. Pip came to rest next to me, smacking the ground hard. He lay still.

I shrieked.

"No, no, no, no, no." In horror, I twisted and crawled towards Pip. His eyes were open and vacant, and he lay stiffly in the dirt. For one miserable moment I feared the worst, but as I reached him, he snuffled and wheezed and rolled on to his stomach. On my knees, I stroked his soft head. He was alive, just winded. Thank god. Thank god.

Looking up at the beech tree, I was momentarily giddy. The markings on the tree, the cracks in the trunk, and the whorls and knobs slipped and ran into each other, sliding this way and that as though they were melting. The earth beneath my knees vibrated, and beside me Pip began to whine. I gripped his collar tightly with my right hand and stood. It was time to beat a retreat.

Before I had taken more than two steps, a shrill keening rent the air around me. Terrified, I dragged Pip away. I hurtled back to the shelter of my car, running hard, my knees pumping, my breath wheezing in and out as I fought for oxygen, stumbling occasionally on loose branches, kicking up leaves and dust. Pip raced beside me, the whites of his eyes showing his own fear, but he stayed with me, refusing to leave my side. As we ran, the eerie screaming followed us, filling my head with a red hot haze of panic.

I pounded down the final part of the hill to the deserted car park, fumbling breathlessly in my pocket for my car keys. They were there. We were ok; we were going to get away. I unlocked the door and Pip jumped in with no urging from me. As I threw myself into the driver's seat and swung the door closed, I heard a giggle. My blood turned to ice. Something had followed me.

Sobbing with fear now, I slammed my hand down on the driver's door lock and punched the key into the ignition. Only when the car had started did I dare to peek behind me. A solitary woman, in a long dark cloak, standing sideways at the edge of the forest, started to turn to look after us. Simultaneously she lifted an ancient wizened hand to her hood. I slammed into first gear, floored the accelerator, and released the clutch, letting rip with a squeal, swinging the car out onto the road oblivious to oncoming traffic, and without looking right or left.

I had no intention of hanging around, and no desire to see what that woman looked like.

*

Sitting at my kitchen table, Pip by my feet, I clutched a small glass of cherry tightly in my pale hand. The house was deathly quiet. Too quiet. I shifted uncomfortably, looking out into the hall at the front door beyond. The stained glass panels were backlit by the fading sunshine. I feared that a shadow would fall over them. I feared that whatever had been in the woods was going to find me at home. I feared I was going crazy.

Ridiculous. I refused to countenance the existence of spirits or demons or the supernatural. Whatever had happened this afternoon would be explained rationally, either that or perhaps I was in the middle of a psychotic break, or simply unstable. My hand shook as I raised the brandy to my lips.

Unsteadily, I placed the glass on the table and bent down to brush more dirt and debris from Pip's coat. He was subdued but calm. I counted my blessings. I couldn't bear to lose him. Not yet.

Please.

I felt so alone. I needed someone to talk to but I didn't want to impose or be a burden to others. Who could possibly understand what had happened to me recently? The odd woman, the eyeball at the oak tree. I shuddered. Where was this all coming from? There had to be somebody who could help me.

I moved into the hall and picked up the house phone. I should make an appointment with my GP. Investigate my mental state. I was about to dial the number when from the kitchen came the clang of my mobile phone, muffled by all the necessities I kept in my shoulder bag. I examined the phone in my hand. Sighing I replaced the receiver and went in search of my mobile.

Was just thinking about you. Everything ok? it read. Trent.

The message brought fresh tears. Maybe somebody did care after all. I liked this man, but given my grief, neuroticism, and general screwed-up-ness, I figured he should take a long walk in the opposite direction. What man in his right mind would find me attractive? But then again, I was a woman of forty-two for heaven's sake. And Trent was an adult. I needed to give him credit where it was due. And I badly wanted to stop hiding from everyone.

I fumbled with the mobile. Started to reply and deleted it. Debated with myself. Eventually I settled for, *You must be psychic. Strange afternoon.*

I returned to my seat at the kitchen table and picked up the brandy. Trent would be busy. He had sent a polite message. I wouldn't hear from him again.

My phone rang. I jumped and scanned the screen. It was him.

I thumbed the receive button and lifted the phone to my ear. I tried to say hello, but I was suddenly overcome with emotion and couldn't trust myself to speak.

"Heather?" Silence. "Heather? Is everything all right?" There was a long pause. I swallowed, and my throat clicked audibly.

I took a deep breath. "Sorry," I said.

"Are you ok?"

"I, ah, I'm a bit shaken."

"Are you at home?"

"Yes."

"A strange afternoon, you said?"

"Yes." My voice was husky, dropped to a whisper. "But, I …" I couldn't say anymore. Couldn't tell him about it. I was frightened, of what I had experienced certainly, but also petrified that I was going crazy.

"It's fine. It's fine." His voice was soft but strong. "You don't have to talk. I'm sorry I'm not there. I've had an odd sensation that something was wrong all afternoon. But you're safe?"

The front and back doors were safely locked. The light was growing dimmer. Soon night would fall and I wouldn't be able to tell whether there was anybody outside or not. I would shut and lock the windows, draw the curtains and pull the blinds. Maybe I would bar the door to my bedroom too.

"Yes," I said, and my voice was stronger.

"Good." There was a pause and our electrical signals pulsed and danced during the silence. "I'm coming back tomorrow, so I'll come and see you. But Heather?"

"Yes?"

"If you need me in the meantime, just text or call, ok? There's nothing I can't get out of here. Promise me?"

I promised him.

*

Trent arrived back into Exeter late the following evening and rang as soon as he was home. He wanted to come straight over and see me, but I had made an effort to have a chilled out day and was feeling calmer. I couldn't entirely dismiss the afternoon in the forest as something that hadn't happened, but I was attempting to let it fade from my memory.

I lay on my bed and told him all about my meetings with Sarah and Brian. "Everything feels odd, doesn't it?" I said. "Like there's something I can't put my hand on. It's as though a number of peculiar things are happening here. That oak tree opposite White Cottage …"

"There's a definite centre of attention there."

"Do you think I should get in touch with Fraser and speak to him again?"

"It couldn't hurt," Trent replied. "You might find out something new. In fact, if you can set up a meeting over the next few days I could come with you. Two heads are better than one when you're sleuthing."

"Ok." I hesitated for a moment but decided to tell him the rest. "There's more. This may sound pretty absurd." I mentioned Mr Kephisto in the bookshop, and then with a deep breath I told him about my walk in the forest with Pip and what had happened. "There has to be a rational explanation," I finished.

"Perhaps an eccentric bystander."

"I feel like a fool."

Trent laughed. "Maybe I'll come with you the next time you decide to walk in the woods."

"Pip would like that," I said shyly.

"It would be excellent research for me," Trent answered, and I felt momentarily stung. He must have sensed this because as an afterthought he added, "And I'd love to spend more time with Pip too."

I smiled, appeased. "Ok then."

"Ok then," repeated Trent, and I heard my smile returned in his voice.

TWELVE

FRASER

I agreed to meet Fraser at lunchtime on Friday. Rather than swing by mine, I suggested Trent met us at The Plough and Harrow on Putts Lane. He drove over from his home in Exeter, and I walked from mine. He smiled broadly when he saw me arriving and hugged me affectionately. It felt good to be in his company.

If nothing else, we hoped that the location would serve to remind Fraser of the last evening he had spent with Mike. We were early, so found ourselves a table opposite the bar, overlooking most of the pub. Trent ordered a couple of ales at the bar. We waited, scanning every face that walked through the door.

Just as I was beginning to worry that Fraser wasn't going to show up, he sauntered in. He was easy to spot given his height. I'd forgotten how skinny he was too. He seemed the wrong size and shape to be working on building sites as he had no bulk to speak of, but I expect his wiriness belayed his strength. I waved him over.

"Hi Heather," he said and studied Trent curiously.

"Good to see you again Fraser. This is Trent. He's a friend of mine. He's interested in finding out what happened to Mike too."

Fraser appraised Trent for a moment. "All right," he said.

"Let me get you a drink. What are you having?" Trent stood.

"A pint of the Otter. I'll just have the one. I'm back on site this afternoon."

While Trent was at the bar I asked Fraser what his job was. "Are you a builder, like Mike was?"

"No. I'm an electrician. But Mike and I worked for the same company. We were practically in each other's pockets. We were mates at school together too, you know? But we started to hang out a lot more when we were apprenticed together."

I nodded. "And how are you doing now?"

He knew what I was asking. "I'm ok. I miss him. Can't believe he's gone."

"I understand," I said. "He's still … almost within touching distance."

"He was there a few weeks ago, yes. And now he isn't."

Trent returned with a pint for Fraser, and he knocked half of it back in one swallow. "Tell us about that night, Fraser. Mike's last night in here," I said.

"Well, I don't know what else I can tell you really. It was as I said."

"Tell me everything you can remember. No matter how trivial."

Fraser took a deep breath and stared towards the back of the pub, turning his mind back to that night. "We met up about eight. It was busy in here. There were loads of people in fancy dress. In fact, yeah, Maddie Ledden was here. Mike had a thing for her once, when we were all at school. But then I think everyone did."

"Maddie Ledden?" I asked. The name rang a bell.

"Yeah. She was at school with us all. She left school early. She was having a baby. I think she's got two kiddies now."

I vaguely recollected Maddie. Cheerful young blonde girl with a pleasant face and a pleasant personality, but not particularly well-gifted with brains. She had been in Max's reception class, and now here she was with two children herself. How time flies.

"Mike talked to her at the bar. I was with Sally my girlfriend. We were all playing pool, out the back." He gestured towards the rear of the pub.

Trent and I turned and had a look at where the pool tables were located. Depending on where you were standing you would have a good view of the right hand entrance of the pub.

"And you saw this woman come in?" Trent asked.

"Yes," Fraser said. I could see him casting back through his memory. After a pause he said, "You couldn't miss her. She filled up the whole room."

"How so?"

"She was gorgeous. Stunning. But that wasn't it either. It was just this vibe that she gave off. She was somehow larger than life. I really don't know how to explain it. There was something … I don't know, shiny is not the right word. But she shone, she kind of … zinged."

"Zinged?" Trent sounded a little puzzled.

"Yes. I can't think of the words to describe her. But she just went pow." Fraser made an exploding gesture with his hands. "It seemed like every guy in here was looking at her standing there in the doorway and desiring her. You know? She looked around, took everything in. Sized us all up." He stared at the door, remembering. "That's right. There was something kind of calculating about the way she appraised us all. But in the end she only had eyes for Mike. She clocked him and that was it."

"Did Mike usually chat to strange women in the pub? I mean, it takes some bottle to chat up a complete stranger, doesn't it?"

Fraser shook his head. "No. He wasn't a shrinking violet like, but even so, most of the women he chatted up, he'd known for years. I seriously thought he was going to ask Maddie out again. They'd have made a really nice couple. And then this woman arrives, and for a minute there, I was thinking he wasn't going to go up to her, but it was obvious she wanted him to speak to her and I kind of encouraged him. It didn't take much." Fraser laughed. "I had an ulterior motive you know? I was hoping he would introduce me to her, but they had one drink and then they left and he never came over to say goodbye or anything."

"So they had a drink together, where?" Trent wanted to know who else had spoken to the woman.

"They went up to the bar. Roy the landlord served them and he couldn't take his eyes off her—he was practically dribbling. She, meanwhile, seemed entranced by the optics and all the coloured bottles."

"She didn't speak to the landlord then?"

"No, but she was standing right there with Mike at the bar. Then she turned all of her attention to Mike. And after that drink, Mike didn't say goodbye, he just left. I was dead jealous."

For a moment Fraser appeared incredibly sad. My heart went out to him. I often thought back to the evening that Max had left with his friends. I had been upstairs. He had shouted up to tell me he was off, and I didn't get a chance to hug him or say goodbye. I had been changing my bed or something and had glanced out of the window and seen James waiting in the car. Max had jumped in the car without looking up at my window. Maybe I had smiled. Maybe I hadn't. That was it. The last glimpse of my son alive.

Fraser was still talking. "I was playing a shot. I looked up as he went out the door with her. I remember wondering whether they would go to the car park for a quickie, but that didn't seem to fit the scenario. She had some sort of purpose. She moved with such," he struggled to find the right word, "assurance? I remember thinking he had hit the jackpot." Fraser's chin dropped to his chest. He was still grieving. His shoulders hitched and then he took a deep breath and offered a wry smile. "At the time I wanted it to be me, I was jealous, but now I'm just so glad that it wasn't. But," he breathed deeply, "I wish it hadn't been him."

I nodded. We all considered that for a quiet moment.

"The police couldn't find any trace of her, And the people here," Fraser indicated the pub in annoyance, "were just so vague about it all. Almost as though they had forgotten she had ever been here. One or two remembered a woman coming into the pub but most people the police spoke to, they couldn't remember her at all. It's bullshit!" Fraser banged his hand down on the table, and I jumped in alarm. The landlord glanced over at us. "Sally, my girlfriend, she can't remember a thing about that night. I mean, that's not right is it? If she can't remember, and no-one else can remember, then that's like some sort of mass amnesia. How is that possible?"

At that moment the landlord chose to come over to clear the table of our empty glasses, perhaps in the hope we would buy more, perhaps to check we weren't getting too rowdy. The pub was quiet this lunchtime. Trade was slow.

Fraser nodded at him and then gestured towards me. "Hey Roy. I was just telling my friends here about the night that Mikey went missing."

The landlord nodded. "Mike was a good bloke. He's missed by a lot of people."

"And I was mentioning that gorgeous woman who came into the pub and struck us all temporarily dumb."

"Oh right," answered Roy. "What woman was that then?"

"You don't remember a woman coming in that night?" asked Fraser.

"No son. I just remember you two louts lounging across the pool tables most of the night." Roy sniffed and went on his way.

Fraser turned to us and his face was pink. "You see what I mean? It's like some damn conspiracy of silence. It's like I made it up. She talked to him. He should have remembered her. I don't understand it."

I didn't either, and from the look on Trent's face, neither did he.

*

Subdued somewhat, Trent and I walked back to his car. "Maybe Mikey didn't meet a woman in the pub at all," Trent mused.

"And Fraser made it all up?" I could see what Trent was getting at. How could we be sure that Fraser's version of events was true? It did seem far-fetched. But what motivation did he have to lie? Uneasily, I remembered my run-in with the tree in the forest, and how something that had appeared so out of the ordinary just a few days ago, was explained away easily when you applied rational thought to it. "Perhaps he was drunk. Or high. Or something."

Trent started the car. I was reminded of the woman with the cloak in the forest, the way her skinny, twisted hand had resembled a claw. I peered behind me. Nothing there. I shuddered. Stupid.

"Are you cold?" Trent reached forwards to turn the heating on, but it was a warm and muggy day, so I stopped him. My fingers brushed his hand, and I felt a small jolt of electricity. He looked at me quickly. I smiled and blushed and blew my hair out of my eyes to cover my embarrassment. I was behaving like a schoolgirl. What must he think of me?

"While we're looking into this stuff, shall we take a trip out to the residential home?" he asked.

"To see Bill Tuckman?" I pondered on this. "Do you think there's any point?"

"Who knows? Maybe I'm just in the mood for chatting to crazy people." He smiled at me, and my stomach did a happy jig. He was so handsome. My face was burning I was sure.

"Why not?" I tried to sound casual, but inwardly I was celebrating the chance to spend another few hours in Trent's company.

Trent had his eyes back on the road and nodded. "You'll have to direct me."

"Ok." I wound my window down to allow the air to blow against my hot face.

"You're warm now, then?" Trent asked.

I laughed and fanned myself.

THIRTEEN

MRS ADAMS

Elbury Valley Residential Home was a sad little place. It had been built, as many buildings in the early 1980s were, extraordinarily quickly. I remembered at the time marvelling at how rapidly it had been thrown up, with little care, and less grace. Brand new it had appeared fairly smart, but now the small rectangular windows and sandblasted concrete finish were dated and unattractive. I hoped against hope I would never end up here myself.

Brian had promised to phone ahead to let Bill know he would be receiving visitors, and the member of staff we met at reception greeted us happily. Bill didn't receive many guests, she explained, and led the way to the visitors' lounge.

The lounge was actually a pleasant conservatory at the rear of the building that opened out into a sizeable garden and the forest beyond. Bill was seated at a large table in front of an open window, painting with water colours. He smiled absently as we drew closer but became more animated once Trent had introduced us and explained who we were.

"Oh you're the folks Brian said would be visiting." He had a broad Devonian accent, and reminded me of my grandmother. "I don't know what I can tell you, I'm sure, but I'm happy to help."

We pulled up chairs as Bill began to clear his things away. "We don't want to inconvenience you, Mr Tuckman," I started to say, but he waved an arthritic hand at me.

"No inconvenience. I could do with a rest anyway. And a nice cup of tea." I twisted in my seat and spotted a tea trolley.

"I'll get them," Trent said, but a care assistant noticed us looking that way and pre-empted us, wheeling the trolley over so we could choose. Once we were all settled with a mug of slightly stewed tea, and a couple of cheap digestives, I considered Bill with interest. He was in his late seventies, early eighties. His hair had receded quite a way, but what was left of it was snow white, soft and fine like baby hair. His watery eyes were a pale blue and he had a weathered face, leathery and slightly yellow in his old age.

We locked eyes, and he laughed cheerfully. "I was a bit of a ladies' man in my day," he said, as though I had suggested he couldn't possibly have been, "just like your young man." I blushed at the insinuation that Trent and I were an item, but Bill didn't notice.

"I'm sure you were," I appeased him. "How old are you, Mr Tuckman?"

"Ha! Call me Bill. No point standing on ceremony, is there? I'm eighty-four," he said proudly. "And I intend to live another ten years at least."

"No reason why you shouldn't," said Trent.

"What did you do before you retired, Bill?" I asked.

"I was a fisherman. On the trawlers. Out of Exmouth. Finished that in the mid-1980s. Worked here, there, and everywhere after that and lived in Elbury and all around this area. Did whatever job I could to earn money. Came here a few years ago. Just spend my days painting now."

I studied the watercolour he was working on. It was a fantastical ocean scene. Mermaids and seahorses in beautiful blues and greens. The watercolours were oddly vibrant. He was talented.

"It's beautiful," I said, and I meant it.

"Thank you. I loved art at school. Didn't get much down time when I was at sea, but as I got older I picked it up again. It's all I do these days. That and listen to the radio. I don't like the telly. It's all a load of old rubbish, isn't it?"

"It is," agreed Trent.

"Bill," I felt we needed to get to the point, "we wanted to talk to you about a few things. Lucas…"

"Luka? He died. There's nothing to tell."

"And Graham Caldecott? What happened to him?"

"At the boarding house?" Bill's eyes hardened.

"Yes." I felt strangely uneasy. "But if you'd rather not tell us?"

There was a long silence. I felt uncomfortable and glanced at Trent. I was about to apologise and change the subject when he sighed deeply. When he spoke again, the tone was quieter, less jovial than it had been. He spoke in a low voice so Trent and I had to lean in to hear him.

"The thing is, I never talk about it. I never have. Because I've always thought no-one would believe me. They didn't at the time, no-one seemed overly bothered when Luka died, and so I've always kept quiet about Graham as well. If I was to say anything now, they would dismiss me as an eccentric geriatric with some sort of degenerative brain disease." He laughed wheezily, but I sensed an underlying fear in his words and recognised the truth in what he said too. I was feeling defensive myself.

Trent nodded. "We promise not to judge you. Or to repeat what you say to us to anyone else." Bill waved that away as though it wasn't important.

"The thing is, Bill, we lost a friend, a young man …"

"Mikey Short? Yes, I know about him. I knew his grandfather, Sarah's dad, way back when. He was a good man. Hardworking. Mikey was just like him. Hadn't seen either of them for a while though." He looked at me, his watery eyes unblinking. "What I'm going to tell you can't possibly be related to what happened to him though. What happened to Graham was years ago. Years and years. I was a young man."

"Tell us," I urged.

He sighed. "Well let me see. I was twenty-three or twenty-four—something like that. I had been working on the trawlers, but my mother wanted me to learn a trade. She didn't want me to be a fisherman like my father. He lived and breathed fishing, lived for the sea, and then the war came and he rushed off to join the navy. He was killed on the *Hermes* when it was sunk by aircraft off Ceylon in 1942." Bill smoothed the table in front of him.

"So I did what she asked, and I found myself a carpentry apprenticeship. I'd been doing that for a few years when my

111

mother passed away, and because I'd been living with her I had to find myself somewhere else to live. This was 1954, and in those days, you couldn't simply rent a flat like nowadays. You just had a room. So I ended up in a boarding house. Mrs Adams's boarding house."

"Where was this?" asked Trent.

"It was on the high street, top end. It's still there. The Georgian houses there. Number six." Bill shuddered.

I knew exactly where he meant. The whole of the upper end of the high street had been lined with Georgian houses, homes to wealthier merchants in the town once upon a time, now there were only ten or so left. The rest had been bulldozed in the late '60s to allow for the extension of the row of shops in the high street. That was when there was a demand for retail space. Those shops were still there—ugly as they were—but many were boarded up or home to cut price discount stores and charity shops.

"It was incredibly run down at that time. As a result of the war, and rationing and stuff, you know? Nobody had much money in Abbotts Cromleigh in those days. Those houses were a bit rough round the edges. Some still had outside lavatories. All a bit different now, eh?"

He wasn't wrong. While the houses might have gone for a song back in the '70s and '80s, these Georgian houses, along with The Storykeeper and the little Elizabethan block the bookshop occupied, were easily some of the most expensive properties in the town nowadays, much valued and celebrated for the historical heritage they brought to Abbotts Cromleigh. The Victorian and Georgian houses had proven to be particularly attractive to property developers over the past twenty-five years, having been bought cheaply, renovated and sold on, often several times, they increased in value with each sale.

"I can still remember seeing the place for the first time. This terrible green paint everywhere downstairs. Must have been a job-lot. Ancient rugs on the floors, covering this old stained linoleum. Then upstairs it was all chipped paint and badly fitting doors. Mattresses that were stuffed with horse hair."

Bill stroked the table again, his eyes far away. "It was clean though; I'll give it that. I had a room up in the attic, tiny, but it did for me. I didn't have much in the way of possessions, never have. So a single bed and my dad's old trunk, that was it.

"Mrs Adams, she ruled that house with a rod of iron, she did. She was a respectable widow, and she ran a respectable house, that's what she always used to say to me. She only took in gentleman lodgers, and never allowed women into the property, apart from the girl who came in to help do the cleaning. What was she called now? Oh, it escapes me."

Bill was quiet for a time, thinking. "I can't remember. Lovely she was. I only met her on a Saturday, because other than that I was always at work and she didn't come on Sundays. Maybe it will come to me. Sometimes, these memories, it's like everything just happened a few days ago, you know, and it's as clear as a bell in my mind. But other times, things are foggy.

"Mrs Adams was a tall austere woman. Always beautifully made up, with finely drawn eyebrows and a beauty mark on her cheek. I was young so she seemed very grown up and mature to me. She wore her hair the same way she would have done during the 1940s, had the same eyebrows and pale face, and she always wore bright red lipstick. I think she had a cruel look to her, but maybe that's with the benefit of hindsight. She was a cold woman."

"Was there a Mr Adams?" I asked.

"I never saw evidence of a husband. I assumed she was widowed during the war like many other women her age. Very sad it was, for those ladies."

"Perhaps there never was a Mr Adams," suggested Trent. "It was common in those days to claim you were married, or had been married, especially if you wanted to hide a dubious past or have a measure of respectability with the bank or other places and people in authority. It would be easier for a woman to claim to be married or widowed if she wanted to run a business."

"I never saw any photos of Mr Adams, so you may well be right, young man."

Bill lapsed into silence once more. We waited.

Eventually Bill came back to us. "But you want to talk about what happened to Graham, don't you?"

I nodded.

"He was about the same age as me, short and well built. A farmer's lad he was, but he had the urge to find respectable office work. After he finished his stint in the army, he came back to Abbotts Cromleigh to find a career. He was good with numbers, worked in banking or at an accountancy firm or something. Always very well turned out. Nice suits. Polite young man.

"I began to sense that Mrs Adams had a thing for him. I couldn't understand it because she was at least a foot taller than him, and over twice his age, but there you go."

"What made you think that?"

"Just the way she was with him. It all started when … well, we all had breakfast in the breakfast room every morning. Usually it was porridge and toast and that was it. She started to offer Graham eggs, and jam, and real butter. Not that awful margarine we had back then."

I smiled, unconvinced that this demonstrated Mrs Adams 'had a thing' for Graham. "She didn't offer anything like that to the rest of us, is my point. It wasn't just the breakfast though. When one of the lodgers moved out she offered Graham a new room. It was a big room at the front of the house on the first floor. Big double bed. Nice and close to the bathroom. So there was that, but it was in the small things she did too. The way she talked to him. It was all 'Mr Caldecott' this and 'Mr Caldecott' that. She would touch him. On the arm or the shoulder. She never touched anyone else. It wasn't done."

"Do you think Graham was interested in her?" asked Trent.

"I think he was probably flattered. We all would be,

wouldn't we? If an older woman took a shine to us? But I don't know that he was interested in her."

"Did he have a girlfriend?"

"I don't think there was anyone special."

Trent nodded. "Tell us about the night Graham disappeared."

Bill sighed and lapsed back into silence. I watched his eyes moving. He was thinking.

"I was sick. Eaten something that hadn't agreed with me I think. Unusually I'd been at home all day. In bed, apart from trips to the lavvy every ten minutes, with the worst case of the trots I'd ever had. Forgive me dear," he said to me. I shook my head.

"It was beginning to calm down. I had taken some ancient kaolin and morphine I'd found in the bathroom cabinet and of course I hadn't eaten all day. But I was making my way down the attic stairs for one of my visits to the floor below me, when I heard someone coming up the main stairs from the ground floor. I was a bit embarrassed about being caught in my pyjamas or being overheard on the lavvy—I think I said that the doors weren't particularly well fitted—so I paused on the attic stairs and let whoever it was coming up, go to wherever they needed to, before I went in."

"Who was it?"

"It was Mrs Adams. Even if I hadn't seen her I would have known it was her. She always wore the same perfume—lily of the valley or some such. But I did see her. She crossed the landing and tapped on Graham's door. I don't know if she had a response from him but she went in.

"I crept past the door and nipped through to the lav. I sat and made my will for a bit and then I heard some muffled cries. I couldn't understand what it was. I finished what I was doing and came out into the hall. The commotion was coming from Graham's room."

Bill cleared his throat and frowned. "I didn't know what to do. I just stood there for a while, in my pyjamas, listening. I thought maybe they were, you know …"

115

"Doing what comes naturally?" suggested Trent.

"Exactly. I wasn't a man of the world, by any measure of the term. But the more I listened, the less it sounded like people enjoying themselves and the more it sounded as though someone was in distress." Bill shifted uncomfortably, remembering this, but I nodded to reassure him. "I didn't do anything immediately; I didn't think I should interfere. I tip toed back to the stairs and was going to take myself back to bed, but something stopped me. I couldn't just walk away. I wasn't sure what was going on." Bill swallowed and the sound clicked in his throat. Trent and I waited.

"I went back to the landing, treading carefully. Holding my breath. Trying not to make a sound. There was a chink of light coming through the door. It can't have been closed properly. I eavesdropped in front of the door, my ear close to it. I could hear someone moaning, not in a pleasurable way. I was confused and … and … yes I was frightened. It sounded like a man. It had to be Graham. I pushed the door open a crack and peered through."

Bill caught his breath. He was pale, and I began to worry that retelling this story was all too much for him.

"What did you see?" asked Trent quietly, calmly.

"The lighting was muted, so most of the room was in shadow, but the bedside light was on and I could see them. She was on top of him. On the bed. Her skirt had ridden up and I thought I'd made a mistake, because they were obviously engaged in … you know. His hips were jerking underneath her. But I could only see her back. It was strange, because from the back, riding him like that, she looked like a young woman. Her hair was long and loose, and lighter. It shone. I remember that shine, and her thighs were firm. She was hunched down over him."

Bill shook his head. "I should have backed off. Left them in private. I wanted to. It was wrong to eavesdrop. But it felt odd. Maybe because Graham was clothed. I pushed the door a little and stepped to the side, and I could see her. She was sucking his face. Not kissing him. This wasn't reciprocal," Bill stumbled over the word, "she was literally sucking his face up into her mouth." Bill lifted his hands to his face and dramatically pressed them together. "It was like a hoover sucking up material. That's the only way I can explain it. And Graham was helpless. His eyes were rolled back, and he was juddering underneath her, like he was having a seizure on the bed, and she just sucked the life out of him. That's how it seemed to me. That's what I saw."

Bill coughed and his eyes ran. I tried to catch the eye of one of the care assistants, worried that he was too overcome, but he shot his hand out and grabbed mine. I jolted in shock, his hands were icy cold, and his grip was fierce. "And then she turned around. It wasn't Mrs Adams, not as I knew her. Not at all."

I shivered. "What do you mean?"

"The woman on top of Graham was old. Ancient. A hag. Decayed. Her skin was the skin of something long dead, rubbery and brown. Her arms and legs were like branches from a tree, knotted and gnarled. Her hair was dry and wild. She wasn't beautiful at all." Tears began to roll down Bill's face. I grasped his other hand in mine.

"It's ok. It's ok."

I gestured to Trent to get one of the care assistants. He rose, but Bill croaked fiercely, "No!"

He took a deep breath and then another, and his grip in mine started to relax. "She was a demon, a thing possessed. She stared at me standing there and then she shrieked, and I was hit full in the face with a blast of hot air. It knocked me backwards and she screamed 'Away' at me."

I regarded him with horror. "Away?"

He started to whisper now. I had to lean forward. "And I was so scared. So very scared. I shat myself. A twenty-four-year-old man. I'd done my national service and spent time in Egypt, I'd been on the trawlers, and I'd seen some stuff, and yet I shat myself like a baby." He leaned back in his chair. "I ran back upstairs to my room and locked the door and cleaned myself up as best I could. Jesus it stank, but I daren't go back

117

down to the bathroom. Then I sat up all night. I heard steps coming up the stairs and walking around the tiny attic landing from time to time, and I watched shadows moving under the crack of the door.

"I fell asleep when it started to get light, and a few hours later," his tone was incredulous now, "I heard Mrs Adams calling everyone down to breakfast, as though everything was normal. I raced down to the first floor landing and waited for Graham to come out of his room, but he didn't. I tried his door, and it was locked. I heard Mrs Adams calling me, and I picked up my jacket and flew down the stairs and out the front door, and I got the hell out of there."

Bill swiped at his eyes. "I found a room at another boarding house. Graham was reported missing. The police came to speak to me, and I tried to tell them what I had seen, but you could tell they thought I was out of my mind. For a while I thought maybe I was."

My own hands were shaking.

"Sorry love," said Bill, "I've frightened you. I didn't mean to."

"No, it's fine," I breathed deeply, pulled myself together. "I believe you, Bill. I believe you saw all that." I surprised myself by saying the words out loud. I couldn't explain what had happened to him any more than I could explain what had happened to me, but I knew he was telling the truth.

Bill sank back in his chair, exhausted. A nurse came over to check on him, and I took my cue from her concern.

"We should go," I said, and he nodded weakly. We rose. Trent shook his hand, and I leaned down to kiss his cheek. "Thank you for sharing this with us."

"Do you think it will help you understand what happened to Mikey?" asked Bill quietly.

"I don't know," I answered honestly. "We have no idea what's going on, but I really do hope so."

*

The whole day had left me feeling confused and out of

sorts. I had the beginnings of a headache and was glad when Trent offered to drop me at home. We drove most of the way in silence, but when he pulled up outside the front of my house and turned to me, I gestured for him to turn the ignition off.

"I don't know where this takes us at all," I said into the silence. "We've heard some really strange things, but what does it all mean?"

"At the very least it means that two women may have gotten away with murder," mused Trent.

"Do you believe Bill?" It all seemed so incredulous. "Could he just have imagined he saw something out of the ordinary because he was ill?"

"That seems to be as useful an explanation as any other." Trent sounded troubled. He had believed Bill's story then, just as I had.

"Poor Bill. He's lived with those memories his whole life." I felt sad for him. It was hard to live with demons taking up residence in your head.

"Are you going to be ok tonight?"

"Yes, yes. I'll be fine." My house was dark, but Pip was in there waiting for me. I wondered whether to invite Trent inside. I wanted nothing more than to take some ibuprofen and put myself to bed.

"I have to get back. Work do to attend," Trent said as though reading my mind. I speculated again about whether he was single or not. "But listen. I'm ah, free tomorrow night? Would you like to go out for a meal somewhere? We could catch up on everything, put the world to rights, have a drink or three."

My stomach rolled with excitement. This sounded like a proper date.

"That would be lovely," I said coolly and hoisted myself out of the car.

Leaning over to my side before I shut the door, Trent said, "Say hi to Pip," before winking and letting me go. I shut the door, stood back, and watched him pull away.

FOURTEEN

THE CHARMS

By the following evening I was both excited and apprehensive. I had buried myself in a pile of work to keep myself busy and prevent myself overthinking things, but by lunchtime we had exchanged a number of texts and I was giddy.

I tried to keep my cool of course. I didn't think it was befitting of a woman my age to be skipping around like a thirteen-year-old. And I didn't quite understand why my body was behaving the way it was, but I was obviously attracted to the poor man. Maybe he didn't feel the same way. Perhaps he was only interested in me because he wanted to write a research paper about the old oak tree on Elbury Road. I didn't want to make a complete and total idiot of myself, but I was certain that was exactly what I was doing. Even so, I couldn't seem to stop myself.

The afternoon dragged, but finally it was time to think about getting ready. I had a long shower and dried my unruly hair more carefully than usual. I spent ages picking out suitable clothes, initially choosing my usual look—aging hippie—jeans, embroidered cotton blouse, and a string of beads, but eventually I opted for soft and feminine and I pulled on a pretty dress in cream with vintage blue flowers. I'd bought it for a wedding years ago, and it had rarely had an outing since. I rubbed some cream into my arms and legs to soften my skin after the shower and then applied mascara and a touch of eyeliner. I skipped blusher and foundation given that my cheeks were flushed enough, and I didn't want badly applied makeup running down my face if I began to glow during the warm evening.

Excited barking alerted me to Trent's arrival. I took a few deep breaths to compose myself. Pip, however, ruined any chance I had of appearing calm and sophisticated, by throwing himself at Trent in ecstasy the moment the door was opened.

He dashed into the street, loudly letting the neighbours know that Crazy Heather at number fourteen had—unusually for her—a gentleman caller.

I didn't have shoes on so I was largely ineffectual in catching my errant hound, hovering by the door, inanely calling Pip to heel and being roundly ignored. He showed Trent how poorly I had trained him by peeing against the wheel of Trent's car and skipping into the road straight into the path of an oncoming pizza delivery moped.

Trent was able to grab him by the collar, and laughing, we hooked him back inside. I closed the door with relief.

"That was an enthusiastic welcome!" Trent grinned at me. He held out two gift bags he was carrying. "For you," he declared.

"Oh presents," I said, trying to hide my excitement.

"There's a bottle of wine there, to replace the wine I drank here last week," explained Trent, "and then I thought I should bring you something back from Leeds, but to be honest I didn't really know what you'd like. They do have amazing shopping there though."

The second package was beautifully gift wrapped. "The assistant did it," Trent explained when I exclaimed over it.

I pulled at the ribbon covering the expensive paper. Underneath was a small leather case sheathed in a cardboard outer. I carefully prised the case open and found myself staring down at a beautiful silver necklace. The chain was plain but strong, and dangling from it were two charms—an oak tree leaf and an acorn.

"Oh my word," I was stunned. "Trent, it's gorgeous, but I can't—"

"Yes you can," he said firmly, "and in fact you must. I bought it for you. I can't take it back because I'm not going all the way to Leeds just to return a gift, and besides I don't have anyone else to give it to. And there's a story behind it. It was pretty weird how it came about."

I was getting used to weird. "How do you mean?"

"I had a free hour or so and went for a wander around

town, and I spotted this quaint little side street, with some dinky little shops, including a jeweller. There was a tray of charms in the window. Lots of different ones, but these really stood out because they reminded me of you. I hoped they might bring you good luck."

"You shouldn't have."

"No, probably not, but I felt compelled. The jeweller gave me quite a good deal. In fact, I bought two charms and she gave me one for free," he said and gestured at the bag he had handed me earlier, "but these were the two I wanted for you. To symbolise strength and hope."

"They are beautiful," I said, truly thrown. It was such a generous gift. And he had mentioned he didn't have anyone else to buy for. My heart gave a happy skip. I drew the final charm out of the bag, wrapped in tissue paper.

"I asked the sales assistant to just pick one at random, so she dug through to the bottom of the box. You don't have to like this one." I dropped the shining charm onto my upturned hand and we stared in silence at a solid silver, five-pointed pentagram.

*

We lounged in the garden of the Smuggler's Inn on the cliff top in Elbury. It was a warm evening, and the garden was decorated with fairy lights. Beyond the cliff edge all we could see was the sea, glistening softly as the sun dropped. It was pretty and romantic.

Trent was puzzling over the pentagram charm, twisting it over and over in his fingers. "I don't really shop much, but on Wednesday I'd sat through as many conference papers and lectures on retention as I really cared to. Academic conferences—you have no idea. They can be so dry. Completely lacking in any form of creativity. I was finding it hard to stay awake at some points. I needed some fresh air and just fancied a walk. There was a shuttle bus from the campus into town so I hopped on and wandered around for a bit, found myself outside this quaint old jeweller's. I saw the charms in the window—and the acorn seemed just perfect for you but I figured the oak leaf was a good symbol too."

"And you didn't see her choose the pentagram?"

"I swear."

I took the charm off him. "What does a pentagram symbolise?"

"It's an ancient pagan symbol. The five points of the star represent five elements—spirit, water, fire, earth, and air. It's supposed to ward off evil spirits, or provide protection."

I grimaced, wondering what to do with it.

"It was entirely a coincidence I promise you," said Trent, frowning. "I know given everything that has been happening it seems impossible, but it was."

I nodded. "Strange." It was.

He took the necklace from me and slipped the pentagram over the hook so that it nestled behind the leaf and the acorn. Then he handed it back to me and said softly, "Please?" How could I resist? I looped the chain around my neck and fastened it. The chain was long enough so that the charms fell into the top of my cleavage. Trent's gaze rested there, and I blushed.

"That's gorgeous," he said, and I laughed shyly at the innuendo.

We passed a pleasant few hours after that, eating and drinking. He told me more about his conference and outlined his own paper. It had gone well. He made me laugh talking about some of the other guest speakers and the dull world of academia, as he witnessed it.

"So you didn't get to have any fun?"

"Oh, I met a few people I knew, and there were some younger academics there, escaping from their partners and kids. There's always a party crowd somewhere."

"Were you one of them? Glad to be away from partner and a dozen kids?" I teased.

"Oh yes. I'm a regular Old Mother Hubbard."

I raised my eyebrows in mock surprise, and he shook his head.

"No children. No wives. No ex-wives. A couple of ex-girlfriends, including a complete lunatic from Southern Ireland. Fortunately, she's lecturing in the states now. That was a close shave."

I smiled and gave myself a mental high five. Hooray. Confirmation that the man was indeed single.

"What about you? No men on the scene?"

"No, goodness me, no," I said earnestly, surprised he considered it feasible that I would be in a relationship with anyone. "I mean, not for a long time. There was a guy for a while, but I think he found it difficult that I had Max. I didn't really want any more children, and I think he did. So we sort of … fizzled out. That was a few years before Max was killed."

"No-one since?"

"No," I replied honestly. "It put me off."

"And now?"

"And now? Honestly? I don't know. I don't know how dating works anymore. In fact, I don't know if anything works anymore." He winked at me. We had both established that the other was single.

It was easy to talk to Trent, and we continued to chat amiably about anything that caught our attention. We discussed music and films and growing up. He was originally from Lincoln but had moved to Exeter to complete his PhD and never left. I started to ask him about his family when a loud rumble of thunder interrupted me. It had grown dark while we were distracted, and the air was oppressive. We hadn't noticed that out to sea the clouds were roiling and boiling, thick, and such a dark grey they were almost black. Now they were heading inland towards us.

"I think we're going to have a storm," Trent said.

"It's quite welcome; my grass is like straw."

We finished our drinks. Trent took the empties back to the bar, and I visited the ladies. While washing my hands, I studied my face in the mirror. My cheeks were flushed; a combination of the heat and the pleasure of being in such good company I guessed. I glanced down at the chain around my neck, the charms glistening. Was I ready to be with this man? In all senses of the word? Could I do this?

I felt insecure, out of practice, lacking in confidence, but oh, I liked him.

I joined Trent in the car park as rain began to fall onto the thirsty Earth in huge warm drops. Laughing, we ran to the car and dived inside, slamming the doors just as the heavens opened. The rain was heavy, coming down in great strings. It thundered on the roof and within seconds the parched ground around us was shiny with water, and the potholes in the parking area were beginning to fill up.

We pulled out of the pub car park, Trent driving with me shaking my wet hair out. Trent switched the radio on and some smooth jazz blasted out of the speakers. I turned it down and then because we had started to steam up the car, I fiddled with the air controls to try and get some air circulating to demist the windows. Unfortunately, it was an old car and nothing worked particularly quickly. I cracked my window a tiny bit and let the air from outside in, without too much of the rain.

We drove down the hill into Elbury, and then once we had navigated the seafront and the one-way system, turned onto Elbury Road heading for home. Within a mile of the town centre there were few if any houses or cottages anymore and the roadside lighting was long gone. The road narrowed until it became a lane with pull-ins here and there for oncoming traffic. Occasionally there were left and right turns, virtually hidden, but at these places the road widened slightly.

It was widest of all as we travelled through Awlcombe. I gazed out through my side window into the blackness and the pouring rain and tried to imagine what it would have been like living here throughout the 1940s and 50s as Brian had. No wonder everyone was known to everyone else. The place was tiny with just a smattering of thatched cottages.

The road wriggled its way along, and we headed towards The Traveller's Rest, the well-known landmark halfway between Elbury and Abbotts Cromleigh. I surveyed the area ahead through the windscreen, lulled into relaxation by the beer I had consumed, the gentle motion of the car, and the swish of the windscreen wipers.

We rounded one bend and then another but the inn did not come into view. I frowned.

"Have we taken a wrong turn?" I asked puzzled.

Trent kept his face turned towards the road. "I don't think so. Why?"

"I'm expecting to see The Traveller's Rest any second that's all, but we haven't driven past it yet."

"I haven't turned off anywhere …"

"That's strange."

"Maybe the lights were off and we've missed it?" suggested Trent.

"Maybe," I answered. But it was not quite ten o'clock yet. There was no reason for The Traveller's Rest to be in darkness, unless it had suddenly gone out of business, or there had been a power cut. I thought back to Awlcombe. The lights had been on in the homes we had passed there.

I peered out of the window, face up close to the glass, trying to recognise a landmark. The road was beginning to straighten and the hedges along the verges grew taller. The trees on each side of the road spread their leafy boughs across the road, branches entwining in the centre, creating a long dark tunnel that spread dramatically ahead of us. The headlights picked out the tarmac, relatively dry here where the trees shaded the road. I was confused. The Elbury road was not this straight on any stretch of its nine miles. The road curved and bent, waxed and waned. Paradoxically, given my experience, it was what made the road safe, the inability to speed through any part of it.

"Damn," Trent muttered, and I looked at him in alarm.

"What?"

He nodded forwards. It took me a second to realise that the headlights were dim. Where they had been throwing their beam a fair distance before, now we could only see about fifteen feet in front of us. Ten feet. Trent was slowing down so he could drive within the limits of the beam. I reached for the radio and turned it off. Trent applied the brakes again. The car started to cough and hiccup.

"Shit!" said Trent. "I don't believe this. What's wrong with the car?" He changed down through the gears trying to find some power but the car cruised to a gentle halt, the engine failing. He pulled on the hand brake, slipped the car into neutral, and turned the key in the ignition. The engine clicked but did not roar into life. Red lights flashed on the dashboard and an alarm beeped quietly at us.

We sat there for a moment in silence before Trent said, "I am so sorry about this. I had the car put through the MOT a few weeks ago, and there was no hint of a problem."

"It's fine." I was about to say more when all of the electrics in the car died and we were plunged into total darkness.

"Damn, damn, damn." Trent frantically tried to start the car again. We heard the dry click of the solenoid but nothing else.

"We should get out," I said. "We don't want a car to suddenly come around the bend and run into the back of us."

Trent tried to flick the hazard lights on, but they weren't working either. No power, no electrics, and no battery. A complete electrical failure.

"I have a triangle in the boot. Let me go and set it up." He clambered out of the car, moving quickly to the rear to retrieve what he needed. I twisted around to watch him run through the rain, back the way we had driven, to set the triangle up, a little way down the road.

I sat in silence, listening to the rain thundering on the roof. This was a sudden summer squall, that's all it was, it would soon pass. So why did I have such a profound sense of unease? Trent was out of sight now and something didn't feel right to me at all. I turned to the front, stared into the gloom beyond, my breathing shallow and uneven. What was keeping Trent? I reached for my bag on the floor of the car and fumbled for my mobile. No signal. No surprise there. We were in a mobile black spot.

Something thudded into the side of the car. I jolted

sideways in shock, ready to scream, but it was just Trent scrambling around and trying to open the door and get back into his seat.

"You scared the living crap out of me!" I hissed.

"Sorry!" he said, and then he giggled. He was soaking. "I slipped in the wet and collided with the door. I think I've broken my knee." I giggled along with him for a moment.

"This has 'Wake Up Little Susie' written all over it!"

"I can assure you I'm well past the age of considering the backseat of my smelly old car for a first date."

I smiled into the darkness. Trent turned the keys in the ignition once more, with no luck. I considered our options. "We'll have to walk up the road," I suggested.

"Which way?"

I was stumped to tell you the truth. Had we passed The Traveller's Rest? And if so, had anyone been there? Under normal circumstances I would have suggested that we go that way, but because I was unsure of our exact whereabouts, and because I was certain we had covered half the distance from Elbury, I figured we should head towards Abbotts Cromleigh. Trent thought about it and then agreed. "With any luck, Claire will be in and she can give us a lift on her broomstick," I joked.

"Maybe I should go alone," said Trent.

"Are you crazy? What am I going to do?"

"Sit here with the doors locked and don't open them for anyone except me," said Trent.

"I don't want to sit here alone," I protested.

"But look at how you're dressed!"

He had a point. I was wearing my pretty dress and a pair of lightweight sandals. I didn't have so much as a cardigan let alone an umbrella or a mac.

"Oh," I said. And then I inspected what Trent was wearing. "Yes, but you're not much better." He had opted for smart casual three quarter length shorts, a flowered short sleeve shirt and sandals. Well, it had been a warm dry evening.

"This doesn't count because I'm already wet through." It's true, he was.

To be honest I couldn't bear the thought of him heading out into the darkness without me. I had been unnerved enough sitting alone in the dark waiting for him before, knowing he would only be a few minutes.

"No," I said, making up my mind, "I'm going with you." I opened the door before he could protest and jumped out into the rain. Out of the car I could smell the damp earth and the rain crushed scent of leaves and bushes. The rain was heavy and unusually warm. It really wouldn't take long to soak through my clothes.

Trent reluctantly exited his side and reached back in for the keys. He joined me at the front of the car, and we grimaced at each other before heading down the road. As he had given me the option of remaining warm and dry in the car, it would be wise not to moan about how wet I was getting at any stage. Instead I hummed 'Singing in the Rain' and Trent chuckled beside me.

We stuck close together. The darkness was complete. The trees were thick along the roadside and above our heads, a cave made entirely of trees. We found ourselves stumbling forwards, arms stretched out for safety. Trent's shirt was pale in colour, as was my dress. I could just about make him out in the thick gloom. Occasionally one or other of us would use our mobiles to light the way.

I heard Trent yelp slightly to the front and side of me and assumed he'd turned his heel or trodden on a stone so I moved towards him, colliding with him in the dark. "Ow!" he said sotto voce.

"Sorry," I whispered back.

"I just walked off the road. Look down."

I shone the light of my mobile to the ground. The tarmac of the road had given way to a dirt track. There were stones and debris strewn ahead of us. Crouching, I followed the edge of the tarmac. The road had finished. Only the dirt track remained.

"This is all wrong," I said quietly, perturbed by what I was seeing. "Elbury Road does not just tail off. Where have we come to?"

"Maybe we've wandered off the main road somehow?"

"We must have; I just don't understand how or where."

Tent placed his hand on my arm. "Do we go on? Or go back to the car and wait until someone drives by?"

I glanced back the way we had come. Total inky darkness. Nothing to see. "What if we can't find the car?" I asked, hoping my nerves wouldn't betray themselves. I moved close to Trent, breathed in the scent of his warm skin and musky aftershave. "What if no car comes this way? Maybe it's a farm track. I think we need to take a chance and go on. We didn't pass any houses on the way to this point so what else can we do?"

Trent thought for a moment. "Agreed." He shone his mobile onto the path in front of us, and we edged forward. The trail was rough, the going slow and treacherous. I slipped once or twice, my shoes completely impractical for the terrain. I stubbed my toes on rocks numerous times, and then turned my ankle. It was painful progress.

The trees began to close in on us, the path narrowing. Without the light from one or other of our phones the darkness was completely impenetrable. I felt anxious, every nerve in my body alert. The weight of our surroundings pressed down on me. I had never suffered from claustrophobia but now I felt enclosed in a dark box, with no escape. My breathing was shallow, and I was sweating. We crept forwards for what seemed like an eternity, until I stumbled. Righting myself I noticed that we were trekking uphill now. The path was becoming steeper and steeper as it became narrower.

I stopped for a moment to catch my breath, leaning against a tree with one hand, panting, but intent on catching Trent up as quickly as possible. I listened as he continued slowly up the path. Although the rain was hardly penetrating the canopy here, the atmosphere was hot and steamy. I could have closed my eyes and imagined myself in the jungle.

I trembled slightly with the exertion of walking uphill in my useless sandals. As my breathing slowed down I became aware of a distinct smell and wrinkled my nose. Something smelt bad; meaty, not quite right. Maybe an animal had left its prey here. It coated my throat and made my stomach queasy.

At the same time, I became increasingly conscious of the sounds around me. The woods were awake. Things lived here. I heard a shuffling quite close, something scuffling about on the floor, the snap of small twigs breaking and dry leaves crisping to dust. Above my head, the leaves whispered and rustled. I wondered about the animals that inhabited this wood. Badgers were likely, foxes certainly, squirrels, perhaps deer, smaller mammals. Insects. I shuddered and peered into the gloom of the trees. Nothing to see but foliage and shadow.

A moan, low and pained, sounded in the darkness some way behind me. I spun around, held my breath. My eyes darted here and there, looking for the source of the noise. I could hear someone moving through the trees, heading towards me. Someone slow and heavy, struggling with the climb, more than I had been. "Who's there?" I called.

Silence. Just the sound of the rain hitting the canopy above my head. I held my breath again. No response to my query. No more noise at all, not even the rustling of the leaves, or the movement of small creatures. "Hello?" My voice was barely perceptible, and there was no hiding the quiver of fear. What the hell was I thinking? I should have stayed in the car. But then what? Trent would have been out here alone.

For a fraction of time, the moon came out from behind the clouds, and the trees above my head must have thinned out slightly, because for a second I could see back the way we had come, much farther than the light of my failing mobile phone would allow. Yet, all I could see, as far as my eye would let me, was the wood stretching back, creating a tunnel, the branches arched above the walkway. The path we were on curled around behind us and was lost from sight. I turned to resume trudging after Trent and as I did so, before darkness obscured everything again, I thought I saw a pair of hooded eyes, sunk into an ancient face, lined and pitted, staring at me from a few feet away.

The face in front of me was partially covered by her cloak. I had a sense of the complete person, someone so old that the skin had weathered to a thick coffee-coloured leather, but all I focussed on were the eyes. Where there should have been whites there was only black. The irises were a bright luminescent green with tiny black pupils in the centre. Full of misery and hate, they pierced my very core with their malevolence. My memory catapulted me back to the forest on Nabb's Hill. I remembered the feeling of complete horror I had experienced then. This was the woman I had seen on Nabb's Hill. I was certain.

I screamed and bolted backwards, scrambling against the trees to get away from the rustling in the bushes, sensing her moving towards me. I shrieked and skidded away from an imaginary outstretched hand, visualising the curl of her clawed fingers as they reached for my ankle.

Farther up the hill, Trent called my name. I had to get to him. I ran up the hill as fast as I could in my stupid shoes. For a moment I was frantic with terror, certain that Trent would have disappeared and this would be a nightmare that I could never extricate myself from.

"Trent! Trent! Trent!" I shouted as I ran, lost in panic, my heart thumping, my mind recoiling from the image of the eyes I had seen. I was choking back sobs now and when I ran into someone I screamed. Trent grabbed me by the shoulders.

"Heather? Heather! It's ok! It's me! Where were you?" I couldn't talk, I was almost blubbering with fear. "It's ok," Trent soothed again. "We're all right. Shhh." He clutched my shaking shoulders, his forehead close to mine, resting against me until my distress abated slightly.

"We've got to get out of here. I thought I saw something. Someone. No, not a person. The woman I saw the other day." Just thinking about those eyes nearly set me off again. My words were tumbling over themselves, my heart hammering in my chest. "She's stalking me. It was horrible," I stuttered. "We need to get out. We need to get out now!"

Trent turned his head. We both listened hard. "There's

no-one here except for us." The forest had fallen eerily silent, but he didn't appear to find that odd. I'd probably terrified every living creature within five miles. Trent took my hand, and we started to walk again, my chest hitching, as I tried to control my rising anxiety.

We climbed the hill quietly. The trees crowded us, drawing closer and closer, hemming us in. My shoulders brushed the outlying branches, twigs snagged in my hair, and the smell of pine and spruce and damp wood was strong; stronger than the underlying smell of rotting meat. The ground underneath my feet had changed again, became soft and mulchy. It was too narrow for us to walk side by side now, so I clutched at Trent's sopping shirt tail and followed blindly where he led.

The noise of the rain pitter-pattering on leaves above us became quieter as at last the treeline started to thin out. We had crested a hill and come out onto a plateau. Trent shone the light of his mobile down the hill. There was forest as far as the eye could see. We must have wandered off the road and into a wooded area that I didn't recognise in the dark. The rain had not eased up at all. Now that we had vacated the shelter of the trees, we were rapidly drenched.

Trent's mobile switched itself off, and it was then, I was able to spot a faint yellow light in the far distance. I pointed it out to Trent and raised my voice above the wind. "Let's head that way. Maybe it's a house or a farm."

Trent led the way once again, heading for the light. The wind was picking up, becoming fiercer. We had to battle to make any headway. I was buffeted this way and that, and it caught my breath, making it difficult to breathe. I turned my head, cursing the hair that plastered my face.

For a time, we scrambled downhill towards the light, slipping on the wet grass, but soon realised we had to climb again as the land ululated. Every hill we crested was lower than the one before, but each varied in steepness. By now the soggy ground was sticky and slick and difficult to manage in our sandals. I slipped a few times, plastering myself in mud, and

Trent had to help me up. Each time we made it to the top of another of the hills in our path, we paused to get our bearings. There were no other lights in view.

I was so thankful for the warmth of that light, a beacon of hope in the distance. More than anything else I wanted to be at home, sitting in my warm bed with a cup of something calming. I was filthy, soaked through to my underwear, I'd lost my phone, and my dress was ruined. I was exhausted, but I didn't care. I intended to use every last ounce of my strength to get to that light.

The next hill was steeper than the others. As we climbed, I made out a number of large boulders at the top. The shapes were vaguely familiar. I paused for a second to consider them, clutching Trent's hand.

A clap of thunder crashed directly above us, so loud that I was deafened and disoriented. A few seconds later the sky split down the middle, and a brilliant flash of lightning earthed on the hill ahead of us. I ducked, and cried out, slipping backwards. The lightning pulsed again, illuminating our surroundings, and in my peripheral vision I thought I saw movement. Instinct kicked in. Unnerved, I half turned, my heart in my mouth, anxiously awaiting more lightning, and sure enough, I spotted a number of figures following us. The light disappeared. I stared in horror in the direction of the advancing silhouettes. There was something appallingly unnatural about them. My bowels turned to ice.

"Trent!" I screamed. He turned back to me, his face pale and streaked with mud. "There are people following us!" I yelled above the racket of the wind. I pulled him to stand with me, pointing at where I had seen them.

Another flash and this time Trent saw them too. They were gaining ground quickly. They appeared to be wearing heavy cloaks, protection against the driving rain, and yet negotiated the steep terrain, and the wet and slippery ground, with far less trouble than we had. It dawned on me, they weren't so much walking as floating, perhaps six inches above the ground.

"Come on!" Trent yelled in my ear. "We need to get to that house!" He caught my arm and pulled me along. I didn't need much persuasion. Terrified, I turned with him. We moved up and among the boulders as quickly as possible, cresting the hill and not looking back.

Another clap of thunder. The peal reverberated in my head like a gong, my skull vibrating. I cast a fretful glance at the sky above, and at that moment time slowed down. A streak of lightning forked down towards us, striking me solidly in the chest, flinging me backwards as though I had no substance at all. Colliding with a large boulder, I collapsed like a rag doll on the ground.

I lay stunned. At first there was no pain although the edges of my vision were grey and the world slow and quiet. As the lightning tore across the sky once more I saw Trent turning back, his scared, pale face mouthing words I was unable to hear. He battled against the wind, towards me, moving in tortured slow motion. I closed my eyes.

Is this it? asked a small voice in my head. No-one could survive a lightning strike of that magnitude. I was dying. I had to be. "No," I whispered, and opened my eyes again, watching silvery cords of rain fall out of that infinite black sky. I coughed and a breath exploded out of me in a painful gush as the sensation in my body returned. I became aware of the excruciating agony of my back, and my chest burned and tingled where the lightning had hit me.

I put a hand to my chest to feel the damage and instead found Trent's necklace. I clutched at it, a woman drowning, vaguely aware of the heat the charms were radiating. One of them was burning into the palm of my hand.

Trent stumbled to his knees next to me, alarm on his face. He was talking to me but I heard nothing. He reached for me as faces appeared out of the rain above him, shadows of evil. I tried to shout a warning but couldn't form any words. Instead, the voice in my head spoke for me, a thought reaching out beyond this circle of terror, carrying itself across time and space, to a place of light, where a fire burned brightly in a grate, and a woman in a rocking chair dozed. "Danger. Send assistance." The woman jerked awake and stared into the fire, then jumped in alarm. The vision faded.

The spirits' translucent faces flew at us, features blurred, batting against us like sheets in a gale. They had no physicality and yet the energy they generated buffeted and beat at us. They moved too quickly for us to see them clearly; the folds of the hoods of their cloaks cleverly shadowing any defining characteristics, but they were all old women. Extremely old. White wisps of hair stuck out here and there, along with gnarled noses and greedy eyes. Their movements were aggressive, fast, spiky. I sensed their great neediness and anger, their desire to hurt us. They shot through the air around us, veined hands reaching out, skinny and claw-like, concentrating their energy on Trent. He jumped up and slapped their arms away, struck out at one who was particularly insistent, but she shrieked with laughter and soared away. The other women cackled in response, enjoying the fight. The scene was a surreal nightmare.

Trent placed himself between the dashing spirits and me, offering protection while I fought to stay conscious. The hooded women threw themselves at him, he was buffeted this way and that. I willed myself to move, to sit up, stand up, help him—but I had no strength and the pain in my back was crippling. The rain poured down onto my upturned face, ran into my eyes and mouth. With every ounce of remaining strength, I pulled myself into a sitting position and dragged myself backwards to rest against the boulder.

One of the furies was not like the others. She seemed more solid, had more physical definition and was able to touch Trent. She reached out to grasp him, with sinewy arms that were as brown as knotted wood, and she took a tight hold of his shirt, pulling him towards her, her cavernous mouth open—hot and red. I recognised her as the woman I'd seen earlier among the trees, and the woman from Nabb's Hill. Trent gave her a good right hook, and with an angry shriek she relinquished her grip. He stumbled back towards me and threw himself down, throwing an arm against my shoulders. We huddled together as the wind whipped around us, and I held onto him as the shapes turned towards us once more.

The charms on my necklace were pulsing and burning my chest. I used my left hand to reach for them to pull them away from my skin. The charms vibrated as my fingers closed around them. Without thinking about what I was doing, I hoisted the charms by the chain and held them up in front of my face as the spectres approached us. The pentagram glinted as the lightning pulsed around us, sucking strength from the electricity in the air. The chain was cool and yet the pentagram, swinging freely, was burning hot, expanding and shining as I watched. Larger and larger and brighter and brighter it grew— until it was bigger than the palm of my hand and I could no longer look straight at it.

The air was alive with the gleeful shrieking of the shapes around us. Sparks exploded from the pentagram as though it was packed full of fireworks. The wind was frenzied, the needle like rain stung my face and arms, forcing me to narrow my eyes. I was showered in cold white sparks, but beyond me, the spirits were falling back, skittering away in all directions, elbows and knees pumping spider-like, eerily melting into the tree line, waning behind rocks, disappearing as suddenly as they had appeared.

From deep within the wood behind us I heard a howl, a chilling shriek of intense ferocity and anger. I shuddered in fear. Beside me I could feel Trent trembling too, and I squeezed his hand.

Trent tensed again. I followed his gaze. More figures were climbing the hill towards us, coming for us. Would this never end? My pain was intense, and I was exhausted. Trent was as spent as I, his face white. The pentagram in my hand was quiet now, cool and dark. I wouldn't be able to use it again. We were on our own, and we had run out of options.

Except, as the figures closed in on us, I realised that I recognised one of them.

"Claire!" I said. And then everything went hazy.

FIFTEEN

WOOZY RECOLLECTIONS

The oldest of the three women knelt by my side and placed her cool hand on my hot head. I think she murmured some sort of incantation—I assume that's what it was, as the words were rhythmic and meaningful but I couldn't understand what she said. For all I knew it may have been a recipe for chocolate cake. She gave me something to drink from a small bottle extracted from her pocket, and after that I was floating and there was no more pain.

I must have walked back down the hill, but I have no recollection of that at all. The light we had spotted emanated from White Cottage, where a single lantern burned stoically on the back porch. I came to my senses in the kitchen, bundled in blankets as the older woman forced me to drink from her bottle once again. Other figures moved around the room and spoke urgently in low voices. The drink tasted foul, and I gagged. She was firm though, and I gave in, drinking deeply. My head swam. I fought the wooziness. "What happened?" I asked. "Who were those women on the hill?" But everyone was busy, and no-one answered me.

I heard Claire suggesting to Trent that they should retrieve his car. I didn't want him to leave me, but he gripped my shoulder reassuringly, and then, still pale but looking steadfast, he left. I dozed for a while, and the next time I opened my eyes, he was there, looking more shaken than before. If that was possible.

Claire and Trent helped me to the car, and Claire leaned over me to fasten my seat belt securely. "Come and see us when you feel better," she urged, "and this time, we will talk."

Completely numb, incapable of independent thought, I lay my head against the cool glass to the side of me and watched the dark road unroll in front of us. Trent squeezed my hand from time to time. When we arrived back at my house, he took my keys from me to unlock the door, then followed me as I trudged wearily up the stairs.

For once Pip was calm. He watched us with his wise brown eyes. I assume Trent made his way back downstairs and let him out in the garden, but after sitting on my bed, I remembered nothing at all.

SIXTEEN

A DREAM

I awoke the next morning to a terrible shrieking. For one awful moment I was lying on my back in a field, while a group of haggard women with eyes as black as pitch reached for me with talon like nails. I yelped in fear and bolted upright. My mobile phone vibrated on my bedside table, shrilling insistently. Tentatively, I reached over and picked it up, stared at the screen. Unknown number. I rejected the call and lay back in bed. There was a tap on the door.

"Hello?" I croaked.

"Hey." Trent said from outside. He was here? "How are you doing?"

I considered this for a moment, my brain addled by sleep. Everything started to come back to me. I gawped down at my hands, caked in mud. "What time is it?"

"It's nearly one in the afternoon. I was worried about you. Are you all right?"

"I think so," I said. I ached. My back, my chest and legs. "What about you?"

"I'm fine. All things considered. I wanted to stay here last night. I hope you don't mind."

I sat up properly. I was wearing my pants and bra; my beautiful dress, now ruined, was balled up in a heap by the bedroom door. I was filthy. Dried muck stained the bedclothes.

"Wow," I said. "I need a shower."

Trent laughed from behind the door. "Mercy gave you something to kill the pain and help you sleep. You were pretty out of it. I didn't want to force you into the bath in the state you were in."

I lay back down. "All that really happened?"

"Now you're awake I'm going to nip out and get some breakfast, ok? There's nothing edible in this house."

"Oh sure. Yes. I'll get up. Just leave the door off the latch so you can come back in … in case I'm in the bath."

"No!" Trent surprised me with the sharpness of his reply. "I'll wait outside till you let me in if I need to, but whatever you do, keep the house secure, ok?"

"Ok."

"Pip's out here," he said, and I heard him walk down the stairs.

Throwing back the covers, I stared at my body. This hadn't been the ending I was half hankering for after a great evening out.

I padded through to the ensuite and stared at myself in the full length mirror. There was a large red mark, a burn or a scald, in the centre of my chest just above my cleavage. I scrutinized my reflection. The redness was the same shape as the pentagram charm but larger. There were marks, like lettering within the outline. I returned to the bedroom. The necklace was on my bedside table. The acorn and the oak leaf nestled innocently together, looking just as they always had. The pentagram however was twice its original size and where the band around the pentagram had been plain silver when Trent had given me the charms yesterday evening, now the band was etched with letters or symbols, all the way around it.

I was nonplussed, but I knew the pentagram had saved our lives last night and for that I was grateful. I looped the necklace around my neck and returned to the bathroom to run a bath.

*

Trent was as good as his word. He returned with a bag of goodies including fresh orange juice, milk, bagels, jam, soft cheese, smoked salmon and ham, and beautiful fresh tomatoes. After he had made a good, long fuss of the ecstatic Pip, we set about creating a picnic on the table in the back garden. Last night's storm was long gone; the afternoon was sunny and bright. I moved slowly, achy and thick headed, but all things considered I could have been feeling much worse.

We discussed the events of the previous night, it was all either of us could think about, but for both of us there was a large element of doubt and disbelief. I was hazy about what had happened once Claire and her friends had turned up on the hill so Trent began by recounting the location of his lost car. It had been less than half a mile down the road.

"The road was there. It hadn't disappeared. Claire and I walked from the cottage straight to the car. The car was parked in a pulling in space and the hazard lights were on," Trent shook his head. "As soon I turned the key, the car just roared into life. No problem. It was the oddest thing."

"Could Claire explain that?"

"She didn't say a great deal to be honest. I asked her how we had managed to get so far off the road, and she kind of looked at me blankly. If she knew anything, she wasn't letting on." Trent shrugged. "What happened to us? Was any of that real?"

"What do you think?"

He lent forward, elbows on the table, and put his head in his hands. "I thought they wanted to tear us apart … and that one woman. I can still feel her pawing at me. I was there, and yet it's like a bad dream." He took my hand. "And that lightning strike should have killed you, but it didn't."

He was right. The whole experience was something straight out of a nightmare. One that we had both been part of. A shared psychosis perhaps.

"And the necklace …"

"The pentagram?" I clutched it protectively.

"It kind of exploded. It drove them away."

I thought about the mark on my chest. "I know we're not crazy. I've got this to show for it." I undid a couple of buttons on my shirt and moved the necklace aside so that I could show Trent the burn. He leaned in towards me, peered at it closely, and took the necklace in his hand. He examined the pentagram. "It's grown. And these marks … these weren't on there before."

"No," I agreed.

"They appeared last night? After you were hit by the lightning?"

"Or as I was hit by the lightning? I don't know. I remember the necklace was burning me, but when I touched it, only the pentagram was hot. Not all of the charms. It was pulsating."

"How did you know that the pentagram would protect us against those ... things ... spirits ... banshees ... whatever they were?" asked Trent.

"I didn't know it would. It was instinctive." I held the charms lightly in my left hand. They were important to me now.

Trent moved his chair so that he could gently touch the burn mark on my chest. I studied it too. Was it my imagination or was it starting to fade already? I remembered what Claire had been able to do to the deep cut on my hand.

Trent's dark eyes held mine. My stomach did a backflip. His fingers on my skin sent a thrill through my whole body, and I suddenly, badly, wanted to kiss him. I hesitated though, unsure of myself, of him. We had shared something out of the ordinary, it was meaningful, but I shouldn't mistake that for mutual attraction.

Trent noticed my hesitation. Searched my face. What he saw there made him frown. He lifted his hand and gently held the back of my head, drawing me towards him until his lips met mine. He kissed me firmly, lingering for a moment, then drew away and stood up, pulling me up with him, cupping my face between his hands and kissing me again.

"I know what you're thinking," he said softly, his mouth inches from mine.

"What am I thinking?"

"You don't know if this is a good idea."

"It probably isn't."

He pulled me to him, wrapped me in his arms, and rocked with me. "I see how much pain you're in, and I want to take it away."

"No-one can do that," I said, my voice muffled by his

143

shoulder, not wanting to think about Max.

"No. I so wish I could though." I closed my eyes and let his strength flow through me. He couldn't eliminate my unrelenting sorrow, but he could help me get through today, and maybe that was enough for now.

*

That night I had the first of the dreams.

It was a vague dream, without proper form or substance as dreams are wont to be. I was walking, ambling forwards at a relaxed pace, for the longest time. The world as I knew it had ceased to exist, and I could make out nothing of substance, nothing with any colour other than a green-grey mist that wrapped itself around me and clouded my vision. The air felt thick, yet I could breathe and move almost normally. Something wasn't quite right though, my heart beat a little fast and butterflies pulsed in my stomach.

Shapes flickered ahead of me. Shadows or glimpses of shadows. I couldn't tell whether they were human or animal or something else. I wasn't particularly frightened but my senses were heightened. I kept walking, with purpose, very slightly exerting myself, heading towards nothing, nothing that could be seen, but something that I sensed existed.

The air grew thicker and denser and now I found it a struggle to move and breathe, but when I considered abandoning my journey, a figure emerged out of the mist ahead of me. I instinctively knew it was a woman although it was impossible to tell from sight alone because she wasn't clearly in my vision. I kept walking but could never get any closer. In the dream I started to fret about where I was going and whether I would actually be able to get there. My heart thumped nervously in my chest, my breathing became more agitated. Panic was setting in when I awoke with a start.

Lying in bed, slightly out of breath, I noticed that dawn had arrived. Outside the birds were chirruping crazily. Trent was snoring softly next to me. I watched him for a while, grateful to have his company. When I knew I wouldn't get back to sleep, I swung myself out of bed and made for the bathroom.

My feet ached as though I had walked a very long way.

SEVENTEEN

WITCHCRAFT

A matter of weeks ago I would have dismissed the notion that witches had ever existed at all, certainly not in the twenty-first century. Part of me remained unconvinced, and yet as Trent and I walked up the front path to the door of White Cottage I found pondering on the previous night's events and the role the inhabitants of White Cottage had played in them.

We paused at the front door. The garden wasn't merely decorative; it was chock full of herbs. The smells around us were seductive and fresh, they soothed my senses.

It reminded me of my childhood—and my great grandmother's garden. I was very young and she had been incredibly ancient. But kind. Yes, I remembered her as kind, with crinkly eyes watching me as I played. I have a sense that she had enjoyed my company. I liked to romp among her lavender bushes, later relishing the smell of the woody scent in my hair when I went to bed in my grandmother's house. I preferred my great grandmother's garden to her bungalow, because it seemed to me, that even at the height of summer, the inside was always icy cold, and I hated the pervasive smell of cold tar soap and urine. Now I recognise this as the peril of living to a ripe old age in a house without heating or much in the way of plumbing.

I turned at the door and peered back the way we had come, observing the bees, busy among the herbs in their baskets and tubs. The garden provided a beautiful frame to the oak tree in the near distance. It was suddenly blindingly obvious that White Cottage was set at an odd angle to the road. It faced Max's tree and had a direct view of it, so that the gate into the garden framed the whole of the tree. Here I was then, among people guarding the tree.

A number of large black birds were evidently in residence around the oak. One flew from the tree towards us, coming to rest on the thatched porch above our heads. Its beady black eyes appraised us.

"It's a raven," Trent said, sounding surprised.

"Claire can talk to them," I replied, remembering her shooing one away on my first visit.

Trent regarded the bird mistrustfully for a moment and then scowled at the tree. "I don't think I've ever seen so many together at once. Look at them all." He was right. I could see a dozen or so, some crows too, perched on branches, a few strutting around among the flowers at the base of the tree.

"They're creepy. They remind me of death."

"You know, people think they're harbingers of doom but that isn't always the case. Depending on the belief system they can be something else entirely. In Native American folklore they are the stealers of souls but in Welsh mythology there's a warrior goddess—the Morrighan—who can appear in the form of a raven. In witchcraft—"

"In witchcraft they are just birds," said Claire from behind us. She clapped her hands at the raven. It cocked its head and squawked at her. "Go! Go!" she ordered. The bird jumped into the air and flapped its enormous wings, once, twice, and then soared off across the garden and towards the forest behind the cottage.

We watched it as it circled back towards us and then flew towards Max's tree where it disappeared among the foliage.

Claire smiled and stepped politely back so that we could enter the cottage ahead of her. This morning the cottage was smelling particularly fragrant. A strong scent of baking; sugar and cinnamon mixed with something tangy, perhaps lemon. The heavy iron kettle was simmering away on the hob, as it always seemed to be, and small colourful mugs were laid out on the wooden table. Beside them was a large mixing bowl and a number of small glass jars. Claire saw me looking at them and ushered me around towards the bowl. She gave it a quick stir and then handed it to me.

The bowl was full of a thick cream that smelt sharp and fresh, heavenly. "What is it?"

"Extremely Magickal Face Cream," replied Claire with a straight face.

"Really?"

Claire laughed. It was possibly the first time I had heard her laugh, and it was a sweet tinkling sound.

"Not especially. It's basically shea butter, distilled water, and pressed oils." She handed me a vial containing oil. "Bergamot in this case."

I sniffed. This was the lemony smell. "It's gorgeous."

"I'm making some face creams for a woman in town. She sells them in her shop for me. It's one way we keep the wolf from the door." She stirred the mixture once more, then abruptly turned her head and stared out of the window. I followed her gaze. I had a feeling she wasn't just admiring the plants in the garden. I followed her gaze. The hairs on the back of my neck started to prickle.

We were quiet. I followed Claire's gaze and tried to look beyond the garden too. The dream I had experienced the previous night came back to me in a rush. There I was, walking down the long green corridor again. Substance but no substance. My heart was beating solidly in my chest. On I walked. The figure in my dream was nowhere to be seen but there was something, a sense of something, a foreboding. A shadow flitted in my peripheral vision. I turned to look for whatever it was. Nothing. But from deep within me I experienced the sensation I'd had before—something somewhere was uncoiling. Something huge. I had an image of thickness, of scales, and fat greasy coils rubbing against each other. I hitched my breath in and the vision was gone.

Wide-eyed, I spun around. Claire regarded me with evident satisfaction. Concerned, Trent gripped my elbow.

"What happened?" he asked.

Claire nodded. "You saw her, didn't you?"

"Claire!" One of the women we had met the previous night was standing in the door.

"You remember my mother, don't you?" Claire asked.

"Dorothea," said the woman. I could see the resemblance

to Claire now. Dorothea's face was attractive in a homely way, but it was lined, with a sterner set to her mouth. Her hair was long and white. Claire nodded at her mother and turned her attention to the boiling kettle, rearranging the teapot and mugs on the table.

Despite her ordinary appearance and her pleasant face, Dorothea was a formidable looking woman. Her features, even at rest, were naturally wary. She appeared to be on alert, and slightly suspicious of us. When Trent and I spoke, she scrutinised our words carefully, possibly looking for half lies, incomplete truths, or hidden meanings. I decided that Dorothea didn't entirely trust us, but I wasn't at all sure why she needed to. There was something familiar about her. I couldn't be sure, because I couldn't fully remember, but I had a feeling it had been Dorothea in the library that day. If that was the case, she might not trust me, but she wanted to enlist my help for some reason.

Claire had set everything on the tea tray, and Dorothea led the way into the front room. I was eager to see the rest of the cottage, but a much older woman occupied a well-worn rocking chair by the fire, so I stifled an urge to peer around nosily at everything, in order to smile politely at her instead.

"Mother, you remember Trent and Heather?" Dorothea asked, and the woman nodded in affirmation. Dorothea then turned to us. "This is my mother, Rose," she said.

Trent shook her hand and smiled down at her, and then I moved into his place and gave my hand in greeting. Rose clasped it firmly without shaking it. She stared up at me with dark twinkling eyes, appraising me for a moment or two. Her face was soft and pleasant, well wrinkled and framed by silver hair that had been elegantly twisted into a loose chignon. She examined every inch of my face, much as I studied hers. Then her mouth set in a straight line, and she turned to Dorothea. "Yes," she said and her voice was firm. Dorothea nodded.

Rose turned back to me and her look was gentle now. "You have been in the wars, my dear. Some bad luck. The loss of your beloved son."

I nodded. Of course Claire would have told her all of this.

Rose gripped my hand tighter. "There are more trials to come. We have need of you." She patted my hand once, twice and then let go of it.

I was nonplussed and stared down at Rose, not sure what to do or say. She sank back against the pillows arranged behind her on the rocking chair, before looking at her daughter. "Tell them to come," she instructed.

Dorothea went out into the hall and opened the front door. I heard her call. Within seconds several ravens and a few of the large crows flew in front of the parlour window and settled on the fence, containers, and plant pots just beyond. Dorothea spoke in a quiet voice and the birds lifted from their perches, one by one, building up momentum with their great dark wings before soaring high and out of sight. Trent and I stood in the centre of the parlour, mouths open, wondering what on earth was going on.

Trent took my arm and pulled me to a long low bench at the side of the room that had been artfully covered with cushions. We took a seat. I was glad of the comforting pressure of his thigh against mine. I caught Claire's knowing glance at us.

"What do you mean when you say you have need of me?" I accepted the mug of tea that Claire handed to me with slightly shaking hands, and asked, "For what?"

"Patience," she murmured.

*

Claire and Dorothea took a seat on the bench directly to our left. Claire cradled her tea with both hands and smiled at me. It was a warm smile. "I wasn't sure but now I am," she said. I looked at Trent, and he shrugged.

"I would prefer if everyone was here when I explained the matter to you, but I fear that many of our friends must travel a fair distance and it will not be possible to wait for them all. Ah, who is this?"

A woman of about Dorothea's age bustled into the room

150

and greeted everyone. She was a tall woman, thin and angular. Spiky. Her nose was as sharp and pointed as her chin and her elbows jutted out at impossible angles. She was accompanied by an older gentleman who looked a little like Father Christmas. "This is Solange Pendennis," Claire introduced us to her. "She is our nearest neighbour." Solange nodded to us and busied herself pouring a cup of tea. "And Albert Carmichael who lives in the Blackdown Hills."

"I came at once," acknowledged Solange, her voice a soft local bur. "I have word that several will join us. Mercy and Penelope should reach us shortly." As she spoke, another woman arrived, equally without ceremony. This was not my first encounter with Mercy, another woman of advancing years, with hair long and white, flowing down her shoulders. She had attended to me on the night we had trekked across the fields in the storm. She solemnly clasped my hand, before sitting to the side of me. "I'm glad to see you are looking none the worse for your adventure, my dear." Her knees and ankles cracked as she lowered herself onto the bench. I wondered how old she was.

"Excellent," Rose smiled. "Take a seat Solange. We must begin our tale of woe."

*

Trent and I were two pupils, new to school. Attentive, unassuming and well-behaved. Rose had a lilting voice that became quieter in the telling of her tale. The afternoon was warm and yet a fire was burning brightly in the grate. At first, with the window open, the heat was tolerable, but as time went by I found myself lulled, listening to Rose's words. The heat was an embrace, it cocooned me, and my body relaxed, yearning for sleep.

As Rose spoke, her words came alive. They wound around me, weaving their way between my arms and legs, worming their way into my ears and mouth. They were within me. Words strung together like fastenings, clinging to each other to form sentences, weaving ivy around my limbs, tying me to the bench, weighing me down, preventing movement

151

and escape. My limbs were heavy but my mind was clear and focused. I was awake but somnambulant. Other people came into the room and addressed Dorothea and Claire in hushed tones, but Trent and I were largely oblivious.

Rose nodded at Claire, who came forward and threw an herb of some kind into the fire. The flames spat angrily. An intense musky scent filled the room, and I blinked as tears formed in my smarting eyes. I closed them but found I could still see images. I blinked again, my eyes stinging. Tears streamed down my hot face. I squeezed my eyes closed and the images became clearer, matching the tale Rose was spinning. Was it possible? I was looking out at the world through Rose's eyes, listening only to her as she patiently wove the story of Abbotts Cromleigh and an ancient evil that had decimated the settlement many centuries ago.

And then I wasn't simply listening to Rose; I wasn't just seeing the world through her eyes. I found myself there.

EIGHTEEN

DRAWING THE VEIL

A spectacular forest stretched out before me. I noticed two things straight away: the trees were huge, bigger than any I'd seen in any forest; and the air smelt fresh and clean. It was crisp in a way that was appetizing. The sun was high and bright above the leafy canopy, the sky a beautiful azure blue, but the forest floor was cool below my feet. Peering down at my feet, I found them bare and filthy.

The sound of women and their tinkling laughter drew my attention. A beautiful young woman rushed forward and grabbed my hand. "Come. Come!" she said and pulled me with her to join dozens of other women strolling merrily through the forest along converging paths, their feet bare too, and their skirts long, hair loose and swinging down their backs. These were women who had evidently travelled from a number of outlying villages and were gathering together to celebrate their very existence, their femininity, their divinity, and to offer their thanks within this beautiful setting to the goddesses and spirits they worshipped. They radiated joy and gratitude for all that was natural and bountiful.

So I joined them, these women and girls of all ages. Women with shining hair and eyes, women who were quick on their feet and cheery, some with babes at the breast or girls scampering about, who walked alongside the toothless women who shuffled, backs bowed, looking down at the forest floor, those who could make their destination only with the assistance of others.

We came upon a clearing where a bonfire was already burning brightly. Many women were sitting in a circle around it. Some had drums, some clapped, others sang. It was a ululating tribal song, and as we walked into the circle we joined in. We sang the song that all women know, the one that is lodged in our hearts and deep within the womb. A song of joy and heartbreak, of love and loss, of growing, of aging, of desperation and dying. But most of all it was the song of life. Caught up in the moment, feeling a strong connection and a sense of belonging, I clasped hands with the women next to me and I stamped and sang as lustily as they, swinging my hips and circling the fire. We celebrated each other.

We lauded two women especially, heavy with pregnancy. We created makeshift thrones and invited them to take a seat. They were tended to by young girls, garlands of flowers and fresh green leaves were threaded around their necks and wrists and braided into their hair. We honoured the older women too with special status. Many of them joined in the singing and rousing, only one or two sat out, too old now to participate in the dance, but their toes and fingers twitched, and their fading eyes swam with the tears of years of memories.

I swung from woman to woman, clasping hands and jigging. I had never known such love, such high energy, from so many women at one time. It was exhilarating.

But something changed. Somewhere, someone was over-feeding the fire. Sparks flew in all directions, and the smoke billowed out around me. Thick smoke, black and cloying. The atmosphere became increasingly oppressive. I dropped my neighbour's hands and pulled away. Coughing and choking I moved to the outside of the ring to find some cleaner air as the music faded behind me. Saddened by the change in mood, I looked for my jubilant friends but most had disappeared.

The fire was hot, the flames outrageously high, licking hungrily at the branches of the trees that spread their canopy over the clearing. I faded back to the tree line and watched a dozen or so women move as one to circle the fire. They progressed slowly but with purpose, following the lead of one particularly tall woman.

If I was not mistaken, these were not the same women as before. They were naked apart from girdles, draped loosely around waists. Some of the women showed signs of having been shackled. Festering wounds were raised on their wrists and ankles, and in one case around the neck. Other women

154

bore the scars of whippings or beatings. One particular woman stared from two hooded black eyes, blood pooling in the whites, her nose misshapen and her lips split.

Even from my distance—some forty feet away—I could sense the anger of the women in front of me. Despair and desperation, resentment and fear. It emanated from them but particularly their leader. She was stunningly beautiful. Her hair fell in dark red, shining waves to her waist. She was lithe and supple, with perfectly concentric buttocks, and milk heavy breasts. Her stomach was rounded, as though she had recently given birth. In the dimming light I marvelled at her unmarked olive skin and perfect complexion. Her eyes glowed green, her face set, focused on the task in hand.

She gestured to the other women and they took their cue from her, standing in their allotted places in the circle, arms outstretched on either side, pressing their palms to each other before nodding into the fire. They were all beautiful in their own way; short and tall, fat and thin. Big breasts, small breasts, odd shaped breasts, heavy-thighed or athletic. They moved with a graceful fluidity. Partners in the dance.

The woman leading them had a long silver knife that glinted in the light from the fire. She ceremoniously raised the blade high above her head, chanting words I couldn't understand, but the other women offered responses at appropriate intervals. She drew the knife down in front of her face and kissed the blade, then slowly and deliberately slid the tip into her breast and carved a mark there. I gasped. This was no superficial cut. Blood spilled from the wound, and she caught droplets of the oozing crimson flow on the blade of her knife, held it above the fire, and allowed the blood to drip into the flames. The bonfire hissed and spat at her in return. She shook the final drops of blood away and offered the knife to the next woman in the circle before bowing low.

The next woman in the circle went through exactly the same process. She chanted words of an incantation with the knife held high above her head, lowered it to her face. Kissed the blooded blade so that the red stained her lips, before slicing into her own breast. Blood flowed onto the knife and the drops were again fed to the fire. Every woman in the circle repeated the process, one after the other, unwavering, proud. I observed from my vantage point, fear gnawing at my insides.

When the circle was complete, the women joined hands and walked solemnly around the bonfire several times. The fire itself, now contained, was glowing a deep, dangerous red, far hotter than any fire I had seen before. The flames had died down, but it was all the more disquieting for that.

The lead woman broke away from the circle and headed to the undergrowth behind her. She extracted a bundle from the ground. Throwing aside a filthy bloodstained shawl, she uncovered a mewling baby. A boy. A newborn, his umbilical cord still attached, in the light of the fire his face was a balled up, angry red and his cry was high pitched and distressed. His tiny arms flailed, seeking the solace of the warm arms of his mother and an accommodating nipple.

My breath stuck in my throat as I watched aghast. The woman, his mother, lifted the baby above the fire in her left hand and turned around three times. The other women egged her on, chanting and jeering, their eyes burning with hatred and fury. The woman accepted the knife in her right hand from her accomplice, brandished the baby once more, and in one swift action allowed his head to fall back so that she could slice his throat wide open.

I choked on my shock, my body rigid with horror, my arms and fingers outstretched. Blood gushed from the baby's neck, more blood than I had ever seen, in spite of his tiny form. The life drained from him, and his mother threw the tiny, wasted body into the fire. I cried out in grief. I couldn't save him. He was gone. So young. So precious.

The woman turned in my direction. From my vantage point, hidden behind the trees, I didn't think she could see me. She frowned, her head swivelling this way and that, her eyes glowing as they searched. I held my breath. Willed her to look away. She lifted her arms my way and showed me the blood that stained her hands.

"Aefre?" I heard someone ask her, and with a smirk in my direction she turned away.

"My sisters," she said, "our time has come."

The fire between the women erupted, a huge ball of flames spurted towards the sky. I watched silently, still shaking from the loss of the baby. They capered around, embracing each other and shouting. Then they turned as one to look into the fire and waited. With a hissing sound, the fire began to breathe, moving in and out like a diaphragm, before exploding in a shower of sparks and chunks of red hot coal. A great figure rose from the very heart of the flames, scattering burning branches around itself, and holding its arms out to the women. They had no fear. They danced in and out of the flames, to touch it, to touch him, oblivious to the heat or the fire that flicked out at them. Entranced I watched as they offered themselves one by one to the enormous demonic spirit they had conjured through their hideous sacrifice.

I thought I saw the body of the burning baby roll from the ashes. Smoke swirled my way and I inhaled the stench of burning flesh. I backed off. Aefre turned her head my way once more. Coughing and retching, I doubled over in the thick undergrowth and hid myself from her view.

*

A cold compress lay across the nape of my neck, and I could feel Trent rubbing the bottom of my back. I choked and sobbed and someone handed me a piece of cloth to wipe my face. I did so. It came away sooty and blooded. I sat up in alarm.

I was back at White Cottage, surrounded by people. I hadn't met them all before. Besides Rose, Dorothea, Claire, Solange, and Mercy, Trent and I had been joined by another five women. I felt overwhelmed. And why was I the only one overcome by the smoke?

Claire offered me a beaker of water, and I drank deeply. "Better?" asked Rose. I nodded.

Trent frowned, nonplussed. "Are you ok?" he asked.

"They wouldn't let me wake you."

"Did you see what I saw?" I asked him. He shook his head, perplexed.

"He did not," said Dorothea before he had time to respond, and Rose smiled at me, her eyes warm and compassionate.

"Why are you showing me these things? I don't understand."

"You need to see them all, and then everything will be much clearer." Rose was firm.

"But why Heather?" asked Trent.

"We must hurry and draw the veil again," said Rose, ignoring the question. Claire was quick to throw more herbs onto the fire. Rose's voice came again, low and soothing, and in spite of my reservations I was quickly lulled. I followed the sound of her voice, tracked her words, closed my eyes. I wanted to resist, I did. I'd had enough of the horror. But I couldn't stand up or leave the room. There were too many people in my way, sitting on chairs and stools and even cross legged on the floor. They were all watching me, and as the fire smoked, and my eyes smarted, I was lost in the fug of the past once more.

*

Back in the forest I watched the women cavorting with the horned demon that had sprung majestically from the flames. His skin burned a bright red, his forehead jutted above a strong nose and mouth, his full lips were moist and fat, his phallus huge and intimidating. He reached for each woman with hands the size of paddles. Appalled but oddly entranced, I witnessed every woman take her turn with him, each impatient and screaming with some unearthly pleasure, and in every case, they lustily pledged a profane allegiance.

When I could stand no more, I pulled farther back into the undergrowth, rustling among the foliage. The noise was slight, could not possibly have been heard above the women's screams or the crackle of the fire, and yet Aefre's head spun once more, her lips curled in a sneer, her eyes amused, as though she was aware of all I was thinking and feeling.

I threw my head back, contemplated the sky, wishing I could wash my vision of all I had seen. And with that wish, I was a bird, taking flight, high above the scene. Aefre watched me go. I flew above the canopy of the lush forest, higher and higher until the women were dots below me, the fire a red blur. Ahead I could see only rolling countryside and a smattering of small settlements nestled in the valleys. Higher still until I could see the coastline, and the red cliffs of Elbury, and yet I was extant in a time before Elbury actually existed. Beyond, the sea raged, foaming tips on gigantic rolling grey breakers.

From my vantage point, I watched Aefre and her sisters go forth, a band of demonic warriors fuelled by hatred and their murderous lust. Alone, and together, they visited homesteads, farms, and villages, taking what they wanted and slaughtering anyone who dared to get in their way. They killed for the sheer pleasure of it, men, women, children, and animals. Everyone and everything was fair game. And what they couldn't have, they wilfully destroyed. They were wanton in their insanity—burning down buildings and stables, shelters, and shacks. They set fire to fields and hay ricks and danced while the landscape burned. Dozens of families were forced to flee. I watched these unfortunates pack their belongings in bed rolls and walk along the dirt roads to larger settlements in the distance. Places where these innocents imagined they would be safe. Places where Aefre and her sisters were as yet unknown.

Meanwhile, other communities, or those people who were left behind or had chosen to stay after a visit from Aefre, slammed their shutters closed and bolted their doors. They drew into themselves, increasingly insular and suspicious of strangers. They huddled around cooking fires, conversing in hushed whispers, harried and fearful.

But they refused to accept their lot passively. They came together, these persecuted people, and then they sent out satellites, seeking aid from those capable of offering assistance. Out into the verdant countryside, and the tangled forests, went the messengers. Children ran to nearby houses. Women marched along well-trodden riverside paths in order to seek out and speak to other women from neighbouring villages. Men rode ponies and donkeys to market and conversed in the taverns and ale houses. Pigeons and crows flitted here and there, tiny messages sent across the isles. The word went out. The tiny Cromleigh settlement was in dire need of seers, conjurers, wise men and women, witches and wizards, or indeed anyone that could help them to banish the evil forces that were ranged against them.

And they came. They arrived alone, in twos and threes, and in groups. One group of three bedraggled women travelled from the Highlands of Scotland, sharing a mule for part of the journey, walking the rest of the way. A huge man with the blackest of eyes and a shock of matching hair, sailed to England from Iceland. A tiny woman, standing less than three feet tall in her clogs, rowed down the coastline from Wiht-land and had to have her hands bandaged by a medicine man from the North to prevent the suppuration of her blisters. They came in all their infinite shapes and sizes, speaking their own languages, and practicing their own sacred observances and rituals.

Dozens of them answered the call for help and gathered together on the flat ground between the forest and the river to form an alliance of sorts. Passionate discussion ensued among the small groups of travellers, and more than a little in-fighting, until someone had the wit to call a general summit meeting in a wide open space belonging to a local Cromleigh farmer. The travellers set up camp here—makeshift shelters dotted the area, and there were fires every few yards where folk companionably shared whatever supplies they had while arguing loudly about what to do.

I flew down, roosted in a tree, and watched all these good folks, until Rose appeared before me, a much younger Rose that I knew in my own time. I hopped down from my place in the tree and walked on two legs once more.

On the whole the gathering was peaceful and respectful.

160

The villagers appeared in front of their guests and asked for assistance, for something to be done about Aefre and her sisters. Rose and I moved among those on the campground, listening to their discussions, eavesdropping as opinions were put forward, sometimes hesitantly, sometimes assertively. I watched as two women came to blows about something they couldn't agree on, one pulling her opponent's hair so viciously I thought the poor victim would be scalped. A young man pushed past, nearly knocking me into the fire. "Your pardon, lady," he said and rushed to separate them.

Picking myself up from the straw strewn ground, I dusted myself down. When I looked for the squabbling women I saw them, arm in arm, laughing at some common joke. Elsewhere, calmer, quieter circles of wise folk considered their options. Discussions lasted days but at last, the debating was finished. A solution had been agreed.

One aged man stood in front of the gathering and in a willowy voice that we all strained to hear, he announced what must be done. Aefre's power was centred in the clearing, deep in the forest behind us, the one where I had witnessed her dance with her sisters and copulate with the demon. The wise folk issued instructions to the villagers. They must march into the forest, extinguish the supernatural fire still burning there, and generally desecrate the area. They were to remove every speck of dust and ash from the fire, transport all the detritus to the sea, and let the vast oceans dispose of it naturally. They should then take up hoes and ploughs and churn up the ground.

Following this, it was decreed that a tree should be planted in the centre of the clearing, and that the tree should be tended and nurtured, cherished for all time, for as the tree grew tall and strong, it would fill up the clearing. The tree would act as a Sentinel and prevent Aefre from drawing her energy at this spot, the place she had declared sacred for herself and her sisters.

The villagers were bound together in a common purpose to rid themselves of Aefre and her sisters, and so they heeded the word of the wise folk and were quick to undertake all that was suggested. Meanwhile, communities of soldiers and groups of warriors were conscripted to the cause and were drafted in to hunt Aefre and her sisters down.

I took to the skies again, on effortless wing, and watched as Aefre and her sisters fled, splitting up, scattering in all directions, driven away by violence and the threat of total destruction. I witnessed Aefre go to ground in a tiny stone cottage on Nabb's Hill, deep in the forest, hidden away from those that she loathed so totally and who wished harm on her. I saw some of her sisters flee in boats. The seeds of evil scattered across this land and beyond.

The villagers were pleased with all that had been done but concerned that Aefre might return. The wise folk gathered once more and elected fifty Guardians for Abbotts Cromleigh. Fifty of the best among them, whose task it would be to watch over the village, and particularly over the oak tree, now growing peacefully in the clearing.

So now I understood. I could see what Rose had wanted me to see. Aefre had been a curse upon Abbotts Cromleigh and the surrounding environs. What had happened in the area hundreds and hundreds of years ago was still staining the local communities. Aefre and her sisters were out there, somewhere, and they wanted to gather together and dance once more in their clearing and spread their own variety of limitless evil.

I lay in front of the oak tree and looked up, watching it as it grew tall and wide—seeing the branches stretch and the leaves bud, coil and unfold, then fade and shrivel and fall. Again and again and again. The fifty Guardians tended it carefully and they came and went. Each brought a charm or an enchantment or a prayer, and the tree continued to gain strength and height, increasingly broad and beautiful. It had a spectacular reach and within a few years dwarfed its companions in its immediate vicinity.

Abbotts Cromleigh expanded too, growing from a small village to a larger one, before being granted a charter and evolving into a town. Elbury sprang up too, a small fishing colony that became a village that grew and grew. The trail through the forest to the clearing attracted increased footfall and widened with use. In the eighteenth century a dirt track replaced the trail, linking Elbury to Abbotts Cromleigh.

White Cottage had been built where the Guardians could keep an eye on the tree. The road was widened, although it was still no more than a wide lane with passing places. The enclosure act saw the clearing of some of the forest and fields were enclosed beyond the tree. Sheep and cows grazed. The clearing was no more. By the beginning of the twenty-first century both Abbotts Cromleigh and Elbury had two housing estates apiece and were dormitory towns for Exeter.

Aefre did not die. Whatever pact she had made on that first night with the demon had granted her immortality. I took root at the site of the oak tree as the past scrolled by me and turned the pages of a dusty picture book, its mottled colours and blurred, indistinct outlines shooting past me as I watched. Aefre awoke from time to time and ventured out. Each time she was more haggard and wretched than before.

Disoriented and weak, little more than a leathery covering over sallow bones, she had limited power in the early stage but would hunt, find herself an easy victim, an itinerant, an elderly shepherd. Each fresh victim enabled her to feed so she could grow in strength. She was never sated, she kept feeding, destroying life for the sake of it. And the more havoc she created around herself, the more beautiful she became. Her hair shone, glorious and long. Her skin glowed, lustrous in the twilight. Her breasts became high and firm and her hips curved softly, and her lips swelled, a plump red, enticing all who saw her, luring men, and plenty of women, to an unhappy fate.

The Guardians watched her, but they were not warriors. They could not kill her. All they could do was continue to watch the tree and ensure that Aefre never approached it. Occasionally a Guardian would happen upon Aefre and spook her and Aefre would run for home again. As I watched, as the centuries unfolded in front of me, I witnessed how Aefre was rising at shorter intervals and feeding ever more frantically.

With a deep sense of foreboding I instinctively understood that this cycle could not last forever. Something would have to give.

I paused at the gate of White Cottage as traffic passed by. The Guardians gathered beside me and together we watched the tree grow. Rose and Mercy and others I recognised, but as the years flew by, faces faded, becoming ephemeral, temporal, to be replaced by new younger, stronger versions.

The Guardians lived long lives, but they were never immortal. They came and they went. Some smiling at me fondly, others almost oblivious of my presence. One woman in particular stood out from the crowd. She looked like a younger version of my mother and remained with me for a long time. Her eyes crinkled when she smiled, and she smelled of lavender. My great grandmother. She embraced me lovingly, and then she too disappeared.

And now I was standing with Rose, a young Rose, and Dorothea … and now Claire.

Day turned to night, and night to day, over and over, as we observed people travelling along the road in front of the oak. They came on foot, driving oxen, riding carts, horse and carriages. The first motor cars and omnibuses sped past us, impossibly loud and fast, and bicycles, Jeeps carrying American army personnel, bubble cars, scooters, Fords, motorcycles, and … a Peugeot.

My heart lurched into my throat. It was dark, patches of mist ebbed and flowed, obscuring my view for a moment but then I recognised the orange Peugeot as it crested a hill and headed towards me from Pitcher's Field. It was James's car, of course, and he was driving. I started forwards. If I could reach them I could avert catastrophe. I could save Max. My son would live.

I ran out into the road, screaming at the car to stop.

*

"I'm not having this." Trent's voice. Angry. "Whatever you're doing, it has to stop."

I was slumped on the bench once more, sobbing,

hysterical. My chest hitching, my eyes streaming. I'd been within seconds of reaching my son, and now he was gone again. My fingers clutched at Claire who was bending over me. I was vaguely aware that I was the focus of all the attention in the room. Someone was muttering to a neighbour, but all eyes were on me. I tried to pull myself together, accepted the tea that Claire offered, brushed the tears from my face, and caught my breath, holding it just long enough to stop the hiccupping.

"I'm all right. It's all right," I said, trying to appease myself as much as Trent.

"This isn't a circus," he snapped. "What are you trying to do?" This last directed at Rose. I reached out and took his hand.

"I'm fine. I think I know." I wasn't sure what I knew, or whether I knew it all, but I was getting there. I turned back to Rose, who was sitting back in her chair, tired now. "My great grandmother?"

"Yes, your foremothers have been Guardians since the beginning."

"But not my mother?"

"The calling was not so strong in her." Dorothea sounded quietly disapproving, perhaps disappointed. I thought of my mother and her cold relationship with my father and I wondered what she had denied herself in order to please him.

"Am I a Guardian too?"

Rose nodded. "Yes," she said simply.

"But your destiny is not to watch as we do," Mercy spoke out. "The problem is this. When the Guardians were first allotted the task of watching over and protecting the great oak, there were over two hundred within our wider community we could draw on, and fifty Guardians. They were spread throughout the British Isles and even farther afield. There are now just twenty-four including yourself, and we span the globe. Eleven of us are in this room, one is close by."

"We can't do it anymore," said Rose sadly. "Our resources are finite and the Guardians are a dying breed."

"The great oak is not the only portal that Aefre and her

sisters can use. Aefre and her kind can access a number of portals and move around at will, unless we close them down or lock them up. Where possible we enchant the trees and this is enough to prevent Aefre accessing the portal, and joining forces with her sisters. Each portal is a tree, a Sentinel. At any one time we might be called on to increase the enchantment and charms used on trees in Mexico or Nigeria or Myanmar for example. It is vital work, and it is imperative that Aefre and her sisters do not come together. Combined, they are a terrible force for destruction."

"But what does that have to do with me?" I asked. "I'm practically middle-aged. My only son is dead. I can't save the Guardians. I can barely look after myself. I'm not a ... a witch."

Rose and Mercy exchanged a glance, and Mercy smiled at me. "It has been foreseen that you are indeed the saviour of the Guardians."

"How can that be? What do I have to do?"

"You have to destroy Aefre."

NINETEEN

AN IMPOSSIBLE TASK

"Destroy Aefre?" I echoed in disbelief. How was that possible? I turned to Trent, confused. He was following the conversation, and I assumed that although he hadn't been with me on Rose's journey he had heard the tale as she spun it in the room at large. "It can't be done."

Trent frowned and took my hand. "We should go."

"No," Mercy's voice was firm, and when Trent flashed an angry look her way, she glowered right back at him. "Of course you can go, professor. We won't stop you, but it won't change the outcome. Aefre must be destroyed, and Heather can do it."

"How?" challenged Trent. "By breaking the law? By committing murder? How can Heather kill someone? This is ludicrous."

I agreed with him. "You already showed me, in the vision, that the Guardians can't kill Aefre," I shot at Rose.

"The Guardians can't. That's true. But while you are one of us, you are also of this time and this place, much more so than we. And that is why we believe that you can fight back."

"But how? How am I going to do this? I've never seen Aefre. I don't know where to find her, certainly not while she's awake. There was a stone cottage, a forest hideaway, but I only saw it from the air, and I doubt I'd be able to track her down."

There was silence. I gazed around the room at everyone gathered there. No-one avoided my gaze. They all regarded me steadfastly, kindly, expectantly. But no-one offered any answers.

"That we don't know," admitted Mercy.

Trent was incredulous. "You don't know?"

Mercy raised her hand to Trent to quell the anger rising in him. "There is someone who may be able to help you." I looked at the people gathered around me, one by one. Their faces were resolute.

There was a long silence. Finally, Rose said, "It has to be you. But you should know, whenever you have need of us, all you have to do is ask. We'll do all we can to help you."

Mercy nodded at Dorothea who dutifully stood and walked to the mantelpiece to pick up a card resting against the wall there. She plucked it down and handed it to me.

I recognised the name and location instantly. I didn't need the card or Mercy's explanation. "Mr Kephisto is the Keeper of the Tale, the Guardians' tale. He's expecting you."

TWENTY

ADAM

Aefre skirted the cottage from a distance. She could sense the Guardians gathered together in there, spinning their tales and half-truths. They reckoned they had all the answers, but what did they actually know? She had observed them all as they arrived and entered the property. Every time she woke from her rest, they were fewer and fewer. Their time drew short, and she could outlast them—she would go on forever.

Aefre circled the oak tree, hoping the Guardians were too busy having their *tête a tête* to bother with her today. The sun was beginning to set, and they had been hard at it all day. They must be tired.

She could slip closer to the tree while they were preoccupied. She could even, if she was daring enough, lay her hands upon it, but the energy that she needed to receive from her sisters was completely blocked. The tree was an almighty beast above ground and it gave no quarter, even in the fiercest storm. Below ground its network of roots stretched out, deep into the forest behind it, underneath the road and beneath Pitcher's Field. For all she knew, they threaded themselves through the foundations of White Cottage.

She had tried various methods in the past to gain access to the tree, but to no avail. No axe could carve a doorway for her, no automobile could force an entrance. The Guardians were always quick to intervene, and any fire she had lit was quickly extinguished. Seeing their lack of numbers now was heartening. One day she would have as much access to the tree as she needed and she would destroy every charm that bound it, and when she had done so she would conjure the demon afresh. Then she and her sisters would be reunited, free to dance, free to wreak murder and mayhem once more.

Wood smoke scented the air. It was weak. Someone had lit a small open fire in the forest. Aefre lifted her head and breathed in the one smell that most reminded her of village life as a child, many, many centuries ago. She turned and followed the sweet aroma. Absently she assumed the form that many of the male humans preferred. She crossed the road and entered Pitcher's Field. Out in the open. It was risky to cross the field in broad daylight, but worth a gamble today while the Guardians were otherwise engaged.

Pitcher's Field sloped steeply, but she climbed the hill with ease. She was strong. She had been feeding well lately. In her mind's eye she could see the ghosts of the trees that had once graced Pitcher's Field, now torn from the earth and replaced with grazing land. She had paid the farmer who had torn up the trees a less than friendly visit. She existed at one with the forest and would not countenance its destruction.

The scent of smoke grew stronger when she reached the top of the field, but now Aefre could also smell processed meat. The scent was enough to make her gag. How could the inhabitants of this modern world consume such ghastly fare? She spotted the flames of the open fire before her, and for a while she remained still, mesmerised by the flames. A sudden movement drew her attention to a young man crouching close to the fire, watching her.

When she looked his way, he rose awkwardly. He was holding a frying pan, and eight sausages were sizzling merrily away in their own juices.

"Hi love," he said. "Are you hungry? Want to join me?"

He was an itinerant. His shoulder length hair had the start of dreadlocks. Either that or he hadn't washed it in weeks. He sported a ragged beard, making him look older than he was. She guessed he was in his mid-twenties. Had he not been living on the streets he could have been a good looking young man, but alcohol and mental illness were already taking an obvious toll. He was wearing a number of layers, even in the late July heat. The top layer was a thick checked shirt.

A long wool coat lay spread on the ground next to the fire. He indicated she could sit on it. "I'm Adam," he said. "You're welcome to eat with me."

Aefre scanned the horizon. No-one else was in sight. "Are

you alone?" she asked him, her voice seductive.

"I'm not doing anybody any harm," said Adam softly, not fooled by niceties. "I just like to sleep out on nights like tonight. The hostels can get a bit crowded and noisy. I can't hear myself think. Sometimes it's nice just to have me and the stars." He laughed nervously.

She could tell he was appraising her, not sure what he was seeing. Perhaps she appeared out of place in her long black velvet dress, one that emphasised her curves. A mistake. She might have been better placed had she chosen the hiking gear. It made no difference to Aefre, but the young man was obviously suspicious.

She stepped closer to him. Adam placed the pan back on the fire, the sausages spitting in protest, and watched her advance. His eyes were wary.

"Are you the owner of the land? Because I don't mean to trespass. I'll eat my sausages and go." Aefre said nothing. Maybe Adam saw the intent in her eyes because his face crumpled and he shook his head. "Aw," he said, and the desperate futility of his life long fight to survive the criminal abuses and injustices of his life were summarised in that tiny unassuming sound.

Aefre swung at him and knocked him off his feet. Had she been closer she could have taken his head off with one swipe of her claw-like nails. Instead Adam fell to the ground and quickly rolled to his knees. He was faster than she had given him credit for. Crying now he tried to simultaneously crawl and stand up, but he was unbalanced and Aefre kicked his backside hard, sending him sprawling into the grass. The smell of burning sausages was polluting the air that Aefre breathed. Furiously she kicked out at the frying pan, sending it flying through the air, the sausages scattering across the field.

Adam rolled onto his back and raised his arms. Aefre sprang forward and landed on top of him, straddling him, pressing her pelvis down into his stomach. Adam reached out to her to fend her off. She punched the hand that came into contact with her first, breaking his right wrist. He screamed in terror and agony, clutching his arm to his chest. Aware of how close the Guardians were, Aefre took steps to shut him up. She leant forwards, clasped his broken wrist with her left hand and wrapped the other around his neck. She dug her claws into his flesh to break the skin. Rich red blood oozed around her fingers, she stared down in satisfaction.

Adam took a deep breath and opened his mouth to scream again, so Aefre quickly hunched over him and put her lips to his. As Adam breathed out Aefre breathed in. And breathed in, and breathed in. Adam squirmed underneath her, his eyes full of burning fear. Even when there was no oxygen left in his lungs, she wouldn't allow him to draw breath. She kept on sucking the life out of him.

Adam lay helpless beneath her, as Aefre changed form, her face just inches from his. She changed effortlessly, with the merest flicker of a thought in her mind, from a beautiful woman with long shining hair, to her true form: an aging hag, a crone, her skin dry and pitted, her hair matted and straw like. Her eyes glittered down at the dying man, her eyes bright and green, the sclera were as black as pitch.

Aefre didn't care that he was dying, before he had ever had the opportunity to live. He tore desperately at her dress with his good hand, his death throes giving him a strength of purpose he had never experienced in his lifetime, but she batted away his ineffectual struggles easily. Eventually, tired of the game she tightened her grip around his throat, listening to the satisfying clicks of small bones breaking in her grasp.

Adam's head flopped to one side. His eyes sparkling with tears he would never shed. Aefre reached into her dress, pulled out her knife, and sliced his head off with one clean movement. She stared down the hill to White Cottage and the smoke that curled out of the chimney.

Now this was a marvellous way to break up their meeting.

*

Claire was busily making snacks. I had offered to help and had been co-opted into carving homemade bread into edible sized slices at the huge kitchen table. It was not easy. I always opted for sliced bread at home—it was fast and convenient even if it had all the taste of stale cotton wool. The texture on this loaf was pleasantly dense, and with a little practice I managed to avoid turning the sandwiches into doorstoppers. Next to me Dorothea was buttering the slices as quickly as I offered them to her, spreading them with a sweet smelling homemade chutney, before layering slices of pink ham on top and garnishing them with lettuce and tomatoes. In no time at all there was a serving plate filled with the ham sandwiches, and some cheese ones, along with a huge white chocolate and raspberry cake.

I wasn't sure how hungry I was. The afternoon's adventures had left me nauseous and achy. Thinking of the image of the Peugeot driving my way made my heart beat faster. I'd been so close. I was now profoundly weary. Given the opportunity, I could have slept for a week. I began to wipe up breadcrumbs, just as the kitchen window exploded inwards, showering both me and the fully laden table in front of me in shards of glass.

It all happened so quickly. I ducked and screamed in my initial shock, aware that something had landed on the table and was rolling towards me. From my vantage point, the bread knife raised in my hand, I watched it as it came. A ball maybe? No, it had fur. An animal? Time was suspended as I gazed down at it, trying to process the information my eyes were taking in. It took a moment before I realised that what I was seeing was a bearded human head.

It came to rest directly in front of the bread board, its mouth and eyes open, staring up at me.

I didn't react, but I couldn't look away. I heard a commotion from the next room as those Guardians not present in the kitchen, tried to get into the room. Above the noise I heard Trent calling for me. He was stuck behind everyone else and couldn't see me.

Dorothea, sounding more than a little shaken herself, took control. "It's Aefre!" she snapped. "Solange—go and look for her."

I heard the sound of the front door being unlatched and a group of Guardians crowded out into the garden. Voices drifted into the house from the gate and then beyond.

Mercy came into the kitchen, Trent hot on her heels. He stopped uncertainly when he saw what was on the table, then took in the smashed window. "Aefre threw this inside?"

"Yes." Dorothea was perturbed.

Mercy was grim. "She's growing ever more defiant. She would never have come this close to the cottage before."

"This is fresh," said Claire, indicating the head. "She's only just done this."

I stared down at the head, in parts curious, in parts terrified. I observed the yellow teeth, specked with blood, the swollen lips, the tattered beard and the matted hair. This was a man who had lived a hard life, but Aefre had shown no mercy or compassion for him. But then, why would she? She was playing the long game. "What is this ... discolouration around the mouth?" I asked, waving my finger at the lips.

"Bruising. It's the way she likes to feed," Mercy replied. "She sucks life from her victims. The violent sucking elongates the lips and skin around the face, causing stretch marks and bruising as the vessels break."

I conjured up an image in my mind as she described it. "Does she straddle them? Bends down over them as though she's kissing them?"

"Yes."

Trent understood my thought process. "Mrs Adams?" he asked. I nodded.

"Yes," Mercy nodded. "We did become aware of Mrs Adams. But it was too late."

"The homely boarding house owner." Trent sighed. "So Bill saw exactly what he claimed he did." I was glad for Bill, glad we had vindicated him after all these years, but appalled for us. What were we up against here?

Solange returned, paused at the kitchen door, peered through, and spotted the head on the table. "Ah," she grimaced, "there it is. You'd better come."

Dorothea, Trent, Mercy, and I, followed Solange out of the cottage and up the path to the gate. In the fading light of the day I could see the Guardians gathered around the tree. All of them were there, with the exception of Rose and Claire, who had remained in the cottage with her grandmother. I glanced back warily, worried about them, wondering where Aefre was now.

As soon as the thought entered my head I felt the strange slithering sensation I had experienced earlier. In my mind something huge and thick, something repulsive and reptilian, coiled and uncoiled, shedding scales, black and greasy. I stopped dead in the middle of the road. Aefre was here. She was watching us. She watched me as I searched for her. I directed my gaze directly across the road, away from the oak, stared up the hill, past Pitcher's Field to the forest beyond, saw the faint flash of flames from a fire. She was up there.

Mercy had turned and come back for me. She saw the direction I was looking in and nodded. She nodded grimly. "Yes." She took my arm and pulled me gently towards the others. Reluctantly I followed Mercy, but Trent moved towards us and attempted to prevent me progressing any further. I shook my head. I wanted to see what everyone else was looking at.

A headless body had been tied to the oak tree. The arms and legs had been spread out and bound so that the body was displayed in the shape of a star. The stomach had been eviscerated and now gaped open exposing frayed, pale pink flesh. The intestines had been yanked out and dangled to the ground, pooled together on a frying pan in front of the body.

We observed the scene quietly, horrified.

Trent was the one to break the silence. "We need to phone the police," he said, his voice shaky. It was a natural reaction. It was what normal people would do, in ordinary circumstances. Unfortunately, this was so far from ordinary and normal that I instinctively understood that the police would not be able to help.

175

And now I realised exactly why, in spite of the catalogue of accidents and fatalities that had occurred at, or in front of, or near this giant oak tree, it could not be harmed. The tree had to stay, because to chop it down, pull it up, or otherwise harm or remove it, would grant Aefre the access she yearned for. Once she was able to gain the ground that was so hallowed to her, she would gather her sisters together and dance with her demon once more. And who knows, between them they might just be powerful enough to raze Abbotts Cromleigh, other local towns and villages, and even the entire region to the ground. Where would it end?

So I took his arm. "No," I said. "Let's stay out of this." Mercy met my glance and nodded her approval.

Rose and Claire came out of the cottage, backlit by the light of the fire in the living room. "Aefre is still in the vicinity," I told the others. "She's watching us from the top of Pitcher's Field."

"Yes, she likes it up there, doesn't she? Hiding in the foliage. She thinks she's far enough away to be safe." Mercy looked up the hill. Whatever fire had been burning there before had dampened down now, but I could feel Aefre's eyes upon us. It made me shiver. Mercy stood stock still and cocked her head. I imagined for a moment she was reaching out to Aefre. I felt a push, similar to the push I had experienced in the forest with Pip. A howl of pain emanated from the top end of the field. Mercy smiled.

"What did you do?" I asked.

"Just a short, sharp message. I sent her off with her tail between her legs. For now. She'll be back and we need to take care. Carmichael," she addressed an elderly man with a long white beard. "Cut the poor boy down and take him back up to the woods. Nobody must know what has happened here." She turned to one of the women, "Grace, would you be a darling and collect the head from Claire and follow Carmichael up the hill? Strength in numbers?" Solange indicated she would help.

Mercy turned to me. "You should go, dear. Take your young man home. Lock the doors and the windows. And go to see Mr Kephisto as soon as you can. If you have any problems, get word to Claire."

I said I would and linked my arm though Trent's. So tired I could barely walk straight, I leaned against him as we headed towards the car. At the bend we turned to look back. White Cottage was lit up like a Christmas tree, but there was no sign of anyone by the oak, and you would have to search very hard in the gathering gloom to see the tiny figures that struggled to carry their sorry burden up Pitcher's Field.

*

Trent didn't make a fuss about staying over with me. We lay in bed, side by side, staring up at the ceiling lost in our own thoughts. I hadn't felt comfortable turning all the lights in the house off and had opted to leave the light in the hall on. Its glimmer drifted upstairs onto the landing and vaguely lit the bedroom, softening the dark corners and lengthening the shadows. In spite of my general exhaustion, I had gone past the stage where I could actually sleep.

Trent sighed and I rolled over to my side so that I could see him. I put my hand on his chest. "Are you ok?" I could see the outline of his handsome profile and found its increasing familiarity reassuring.

"What a day," he answered.

"Yes. It must be harder for you than for me. You didn't see it all, just heard the words," I said. "For me, it was so vivid. Real!"

"I saw enough of it in my head." Trent's chuckle sounded forced.

"Do you believe it all?" I worried that Trent remained unconvinced. Where once I would staunchly have rejected all we had seen and heard, I now felt that this was no longer possible.

"I guess I do," answered Tent. "But I'm worried about how deeply we're getting into this. How deeply you're getting into it." He turned his head so that he could look at me.

"I'm not afraid," I said softly. I thought again of the

orange Peugeot and my heart ached.

Trent laughed and this time it sounded genuine. He rolled towards me and lifted his hand to stroke my face. "You're a fucking awful liar."

TWENTY-ONE

THE KEEPER OF THE TALE

Number six High Street had a smart façade. I cast my mind back, remembering how Bill Tuckman had spoken of the boarding house. It was hard to imagine that this gloriously restored Georgian terrace, painted in a fresh pale blue, with its wrought iron gates and expertly restored windows, had ever been the shabby house Bill had described.

I studied the roof. I could see an attic window peeping across the town. Bill had waited out the long night there until he could escape from Mrs Adams. The window below, the front bedroom on the first floor, was a much larger bay. Graham Caldecott had died in there and subsequently disappeared. I wondered what Mrs Adams had done with the body.

There was no denying how strong Aefre was. Carmichael had reported back to Mercy that he believed the man had been killed at the edge of the woods on Pitchers' Field, meaning Aefre had carried the body down to the oak tree. I would have struggled to drag it let alone carry it.

I didn't understand why anyone imagined that I was capable of destroying her.

A young woman came to the living room window and glared out at me. I decided I had better make myself scarce before she called the police, so I dropped my eyes and turned about. If I walked far enough down the high street I would come to The Storykeeper where Mr Kephisto resided.

I rambled past a number of closed shops. One had been a printing shop, another had sold cameras and films. I remembered using that one many years ago. One or two of the shops here were completely boarded up, and I had forgotten what they once contained. Then there was a kebab shop, already open for business at two in the afternoon. I was surprised, but perhaps some Cromleigians enjoyed kebabs for lunch. In any case nobody was queuing up to be served, or even examining the menu board trying to decide which delights to opt for.

I passed charity shops and a café, a sandwich shop and a solicitor's, the offices for a local mortgage adviser, and a baby goods shop—where a woman sat alone behind the counter sipping her tea and reading a magazine. This was Abbotts Cromleigh's retail paradise.

At last I saw some signs of life as I moved towards the older part of town. A couple of chemists, the local department store, Boots, Costa, and a well-known clothing brand that Max would have loved. I walked past Taylor's hardware shop and saw The Storykeeper up ahead. I slowed my pace to look at it—the glorious Elizabethan façade with its distinctive bulging front, criss-crossed windows and black and white decoration, and on the top floor, the small window where someone had watched me depart on my last visit. If that had been Mr Kephisto, and if Mr Kephisto had indeed known that I would return, I really hoped that he had the kettle on.

My throat was dry, and I was nervous. I wished Trent could have been with me, but he had gone back to Exeter to attend to business at the University. Although he had no teaching over the summer, he was working his way through last minute applications for the various courses that his department ran, and he had several open days to organise for would-be students who planned to apply to the University for the following year's intake.

I had sensed his reluctance to leave me this morning, but perhaps some relief as well. Completely unintentionally, I had managed to turn his life upside down in the space of a few weeks. He must surely rue the day I had harangued him when I attended his lecture and drew him into this peculiar mess.

And when he left, I was surprised at how much I missed him. There was something about Trent that helped to fill part of the void that Max's death had created. It was a sense that I was no longer so completely and totally alone, that somebody cared about me, and wanted to know what I was thinking and how I was feeling. Yes, I had other friends, but they had their own lives. They were in touch periodically, but I was not the person they thought about when they awoke, or when they went to bed, or when they were hungry, or when they just needed to share something. We all need that intimacy and sometimes we struggle to find it. Trent and I had shared so much, in such a short space of time, and I think that was helping to bind us together.

Of course I had my doubts. Not about my feelings for him—there was nothing complicated about what I felt or how I felt it. Being with him helped to calm my frantic mind. This calmness was something that had evaded me for years now. Deep down, however, I was insecure. Worried that he would decide I was completely barking and run wildly in the opposite direction. I worried about our age gap too, however slight, there were those five years between us. Why wouldn't he want a woman with a longer use by date?

I held my place on the pavement as cars and vans and delivery lorries trundled by in front of me, gazing at the historic building; thinking my thoughts, worrying my worries, until I gradually came to and became aware of the lantern hanging above the door. It was glowing gently, calling my attention. I checked both ways, the road was clear, but looked again, the instinctive reaction of someone whose mother had drummed that behaviour into them at an early age. I made my way across.

I climbed the few uneven steps, paused at the door, took a few deep breaths, and pushed it open. The bell tinkled above my head, announcing my arrival to anyone who might have been interested. Nobody was. There didn't appear to be anyone else in the shop, and Mr Kephisto wasn't immediately apparent. I carefully closed the door behind me and moved out of the doorway. Above me, Caius cawed.

I wandered among the stacks of books, breathing in their enticing new book smell, finding myself in the rear of the shop. Whereas the shop front appeared spacious, the walls closed in on themselves here, and the ceiling was lower. It was a little like walking down a tunnel. The floors were uneven in places and it struck me that the bookshelves must have been purpose built because they were all perfectly straight, there was nothing higgledy-piggledy about them at all, in spite of the irregular nature of the building they inhabited. Here at the back of the shop was the children's section. The walls were lined with books facing out, bright and breezy, attractive to young minds. I smiled to remember Max here, his greedy hands grabbing everything they could reach. I never went out of The Storykeeper without spending more than I had bargained for, thanks to my bookworm of a son.

There was a door at the back here that I assumed belonged to a stock room or Mr Kephisto's personal quarters. I tapped gently on the door but there was no response. Floorboards creaked above my head so I headed for the centre of the shop and started climbing the wobbly stairs I hated so much, keeping a tight hand on the balustrade to protect my balance. Once on the mezzanine, I paused. The crow was perched on the edge of the balcony, its black eyes regarding me with hard intelligence.

"Where's Mr Kephisto?" I asked it and it fluttered its wings, a few feathers and a quantity of dust exploded into the air around it.

"Kephisto? Kephisto?" squawked the bird.

The door at the back of the mezzanine opened and Mr Kephisto peered around it, looking at me questioningly over the top of his spectacles before smiling in recognition.

"Ah, Heather! Good! I wondered when you'd get here. Please," he stepped aside and gestured that I should walk through the door.

"Hello, Mr Kephisto," I said. "But, I, the door downstairs—it's unlocked."

"Oh don't worry about that, my dear." From downstairs came the sound of a distinct click. Someone else was in the shop? "It isn't now. Come this way."

I walked through the open door, onto another landing. There were boxes of books piled high on the bare floor. My feet clumped as I walked after Mr Kephisto. He led me farther in and then turned to his left. Another flight of twisting stairs greeted me, these were even spongier than the ones I had climbed to the mezzanine. I gritted my teeth and followed as fast as I was able.

These stairs opened out onto Mr Kephisto's' living quarters. It was somewhere I could genuinely have imagined him living. The original timbers of the building were on display here, threaded seam-like along the walls and the ceiling beams, and the wooden floor was varnished and shiny clean, covered with old Persian rugs. There were a couple of two-seater sofas, and two armchairs, both covered in green velvet. Mr Kephisto indicated I should sit, so I chose one of the sofas and gazed around me in awe.

There was a wood burning stove on the back wall, glowing brightly even on this muggy afternoon, but even so the room felt cool. In between the timber wall joists were books and every one of them appeared to be leather bound. Some were obviously incredibly old, others more recent. I couldn't see what the subjects were, but they appeared important and weighty: most fitting for someone of Mr Kephisto's dignified appearance.

Mr Kephisto watched me.

"Sorry," I said. "You must be very well-read."

Mr Kephisto nodded. "I've been around for a very long time. I think it's safe to say that reading has provided me with immeasurable joy."

I cut to the chase. "Mercy insisted I come to see you."

"She sent word about what happened yesterday. The poor young man. I had seen him out and about here in Abbotts Cromleigh often. The police have yet to discover him, but they will."

I thought of the headless corpse the police would find. "What will they 'imagine' happened to him?"

"Perhaps a rival, theft, something unfortunate. The shadow of suspicion will be cast over his comrades from the hostels here and in Elbury. Nothing will come of it. His death will be written off. And there will be not so much as a smudge of guilt attached to Aefre, or to the Guardians for that matter."

I got it but felt sorry for the homeless man and for those that would find themselves under suspicion. This would be temporary and the case would be closed unsolved, but that didn't make me feel better. Aefre could screw up many lives, and not just those lives she chose to dispense with.

"Last time I was here you said you expected to see me again," I recalled. "How did you know?"

"It is foreseen that you will destroy Aefre," Mr Kephisto replied.

"But where does it say this? How is it known? How has it been foreseen?"

Mr Kephisto smiled. He took up a box of matches and a handful of what appeared to be cotton wool or fluff of some kind. "Sit back," he instructed, "close your eyes." I sighed. Slightly mistrustfully, I did as he asked, laying my head against the back of the sofa, and resting my eyelids.

I heard a match strike; once, twice, and then a third time. There was a *poof* sound as something—presumably the lint Mr Kephisto had been holding—was set alight. I heard soft footsteps as Mr Kephisto walked closer towards me and then he paused. "Breathe," Mr Kephisto instructed gently. Inhaling, I smelt wood fires, and donkeys, and broth …

*

I walked around the gathering of wise people who had been drawn from all over the British Isles and beyond. I saw again the large Icelandic man, recognised him now as Galdur, and the women from the Highlands. A commotion behind me drew my attention and I watched once more as one angry woman battled with another, grabbing her long plait and dragging her across the ground. I feared for her scalp. A man pushed past me, a young man, knocking me sideways towards the fire. I rolled at the last moment and fell into the straw. The man spun towards me: "My pardon, lady," he said and rushed on to separate the squabbling women. When he had pulled them apart and they were friends again, he turned to look at me. I was brushing straw from my clothes when I realised who the man was.

"Mr Kephisto?" I exclaimed above the general hubbub around us. The man was young, with fair hair and clear, smiling eyes, but it was him, no doubt about it. I recognised him from the way he moved as he came towards me, and up close, the set of his brow line and the colour of his eyes.

"Just Kephisto in this time, my lady," he bowed to me and offered me his arm. I took it, and he led me away from the melee, up the hill a little way and into the tree line. The noise faded enough so we could hear each other speak.

"You were here? In this time?" I gestured at the busy gathering in front of us.

"I am here now, as are you."

I studied my surroundings, watched the people, saw them react to my gaze with stares of their own, smiles, or dismissive head gestures, and it dawned on me exactly what it was he was saying to me. I was no ghost or apparition. I was as real in this time as I was in my own, meaning I was as much one of the original Guardians as any of these people. It was as though I had been cryogenically frozen for many centuries and had now been woken.

"How can this be?" I asked, confused. "I don't live here in this time and then continue to exist all the way through to the twenty-first century, do I?"

"No. You by necessity must come and go. You were not born in this time as we were. You have been summoned here by the Guardians from your own time."

"But how?"

"We are harnessing the power of the Sentinel. Jointly. As a group of Guardians. The tree is enchanted; it is a portal through which the chosen ones may travel. You are one of those chosen ones, as is Aefre, and unfortunately, all of her sisters."

"Because I was there the night they summoned the demon?"

"Perhaps."

"But I didn't make a pact, didn't dance with the devil, didn't …"

"No. So perhaps your access is limited. We don't know for sure. Certainly without us, to you the Sentinel is simply another tree. The Guardians currently control the Sentinel, and this means we can harness its powers. We can bring you here."

"And you know all about the future?"

"We have a combined consciousness. As it happens in your time, we become aware of it here. We can't see any further than that though. Rose and I are here because we have continued to exist. The authority of the Guardians is necessarily limited and finite, we are not, and can never be, omnipowerful, but with the convergence of our various skills we can maintain some continuity. I won't live forever, nor perhaps for very much longer in fact, but there are others to take on the mantle of our combined magick and wisdom and pass it on again."

"Claire?"

"Claire certainly. And yourself."

I frowned. "But I know so little. I don't know where to start. And I certainly don't know how to kill Aefre."

"Then this is a good place to start." Kephisto was firm. He took my arm again and guided me down into the rough little haphazard village of blankets and branches that had sprung up. I moved with the people, became part of them, joined in discussions as they sought the ways and means to prevent Aefre and her sisters from wreaking any more havoc across Cromleigh and beyond.

I attached myself to Kephisto at the summit meeting. Close to two hundred people gathered together in a circle to listen to ideas and formulate plans. The sessions were passionate but disciplined. One elder was chosen to lead each session, and a stick was handed around to those who wished to speak. Kephisto was an active, energetic participant, and was at once encouraging of the more introverted while being conciliatory with those whose zealousness threatened to upset the calm proceedings. At the end of each session, a break was announced, and participants would wander away to eat, drink, chat, or to relieve themselves in the bushes or among the trees.

"There's Rose," I noted, watching as a younger Rose threaded her graceful way through the crowd speaking to those who sought her out and offering counsel where required. Of course she had to have been here, because she had accompanied me when I first came. "But I haven't seen any of the other Guardians that I recognise. Dorothea, Claire, Carmichael, Solange," I trailed off. "Where is Mercy?"

"Those are the Guardians of your time. We still need to choose the Guardians of this time."

I thought with some trepidation of the road that lay ahead for these volunteers.

"Kephisto, you must know, given that you're here and there, that there is so much for the Guardians to fear in the future. These people," I gestured around me, "they'll be hunted down, strung up like animals, because of what they believe in and because of the gods they choose to worship. People will walk on the moon one day, Kephisto," I gestured up at the sky, "and they won't believe in the old ways. They'll eschew what they define as a more 'rational' way of thinking, and witchcraft and paganism—all of the old ways—will be vilified and punished."

"The Guardians will not live forever. We must pass down our skills, our beliefs, our intellect and our resources. Sometimes from mother to daughter, sometimes from father to son. The Guardians that you know in your time, they may not necessarily be here now. They will be second or third generation, maybe later."

"But—" I thought of the sacrifices to come.

"We have a job to do. And we'll do it."

And so it came about that after a number of productive meetings, it was agreed that the clearing would be destroyed and the site cleared. Kephisto was quick to organise a division of labour, and one of the first to volunteer to become a Guardian.

187

"That's as it should be," I said. "I need you in the future, and I need Rose there too." Rose knew that I would arrive at her cottage and join the fight against Aefre because she would be there in the future too. "But how will you manage to survive for centuries?" I asked, thinking of Aefre and the long periods she had spent underground, asleep and out of reach of those who sought to harm her.

"We will use the combined powers we have at our disposal. The Guardians will make it happen. It will be easier for the first millennia or so, but as we lose Guardians, our powers will start to wane. We need you in the twenty-first century to ensure that the final showdown with Aefre does not fail. Rose and I will be waiting. You and I must talk with the Guardians again. They will make it happen."

*

"They elected you as the Keeper of the Tale, and Rose as the Teller of the Tale," I said. I felt woozy coming out of my memories, but Mr Kephisto offered me tea from a tray that had appeared in the room while I was zoned out, and the sugar he heaped into my cup was starting to bring me round.

"Yes, thanks to you."

"But we don't yet know how we are going to destroy Aefre."

Kephisto shook his head. "Admittedly, at this stage it is still a mystery. But things are gathering apace Heather, and I am aware that my time grows short."

"But you've lived for so long, you'll see this through with me, right?" I was alarmed by his fatalism.

"I don't believe I will live to see that great day." Kephisto was calm; I was horrified.

"There are so few Guardians left. We can't afford to lose any more and not replace them."

"If you do what you must do, there will be no need for Guardians in the future."

I rubbed my aching temples. How was it possible to destroy Aefre? The question wound around my head on a constant loop of despair.

"We need to look out for signs. There will be clues to what we should do," Mr Kephisto said. "Professor Redburn will be a huge help to you." He smiled confidently, and I was thankful that he had reminded me that I would not be alone in this quest.

*

Feeling as though the weight of the world was upon me, I headed out of the shop into the daylight and pondered what to do next. I had the beginnings of a stress headache and hadn't eaten all day. It would help to pick up some shopping, go home, and just chill with Pip for a few hours.

Pausing on the pavement in front of The Storykeeper, I considered whether to turn left and call into the small co-op store, or return to my car and visit the larger supermarket, slightly out of town. Remembering I needed dog food, I opted to go back to the car.

It was an overcast day and muggy with it. Perspiration prickled on my forehead and gathered in my cleavage. I waited for a pick-up truck to amble past me. There was never much of a hurry for most of the locals in Abbotts Cromleigh. It was a rural community with plenty of farmers and farm workers whose lives were dictated by the seasons and the weather. Their world wasn't moving anywhere fast, and they had nowhere they really needed to be. When the coast was clear, I stepped off the pavement and walked briskly across the road.

I had almost reached the pavement opposite when the car materialised out of nowhere and steamed up the road, heading straight for me. At the last moment I spotted it from the corner of my eye and tried to break into a run. I almost made it. The car's wing mirror clipped my hip and sent me flying. I landed ten feet away, crumpled.

I didn't breathe, didn't feel any pain. I watched the car drive away; a white Vauxhall, the driver oblivious to what they had done. My mind slipped and the vision of the oily reptilian coils replayed in my mind. The way the scaly tentacles rubbed

189

together, so fat and thick, so ominous, quite turned my stomach.

People were gathering around me now. "It's all right love, we'll get an ambulance," someone was saying. My breath finally came out of me in an audible whoosh.

"No," I said. "I'm fine." I mentally checked myself over. My hip was smarting, and my elbow was hurting, where I must have fallen on it, but other than that, I seemed to be able to move things without much difficulty. I held my arms up, and several people helped to pull me to my feet.

"Are you sure you're ok?" a man asked me. "You took quite a clout there, maid."

He wasn't wrong. My head was swimming. "Honestly, I think I'm fine. Just a bit shaken." I tried to smile at him, slightly embarrassed. My knees were wobbly. "Thank you all," I addressed the growing crowd and that satisfied the majority of them. They started to melt away, leaving just the man with the broad Devon accent and a tiny old lady who must have been about two thirds my size, slightly hunched through osteoarthritis. She was holding tightly to my bag which had been knocked from my arm and regarding me solemnly.

"You ought to have a cup of tea," she said. "With plenty of sugar. That's the best cure for shock." The gentleman nodded his agreement.

"That's a good idea," I said.

"It's what we used to do in the war, you know. Make a nice strong cup of tea, with a couple of sugars if we had it."

"Ok. Yes. I do fancy that."

The gentleman tipped his head to me and strolled off down the road. The woman stayed where she was for a moment. "Sit down somewhere and have a nice cup of tea, dear."

I smiled at her insistence, took my bag from her, and patted her arm. "I will do. Thank you so much. Goodbye."

She turned from me and shuffled five or six feet extremely slowly. I started to walk, tenderly, back towards my car in the opposite direction. "And make sure you wear your charms, dear!" she called after me.

I put my hand on my chest, felt down my cleavage. I didn't have my necklace on. I had taken it off when I washed my hair that morning and left it hanging by the shower. I turned around to take another look at the woman, maybe to find out how she had known. She was nowhere in sight. Sluggishly, my hip bright with pain, I moved to look in the window of the shop closest to me. It was a mobile phone shop. She wasn't in there. The shop beyond was the local coffee house and was doing good business. She didn't appear to be in there either. I hobbled to the ladies' clothes shop farther on, but that was not a place for a woman of her age, and in any case she appeared to have vanished into thin air.

TWENTY-TWO

INTERRUPTIONS

I arrived home, still feeling shocked by the accident and phoned Trent without really thinking about it. He had someone in the office and couldn't talk, so I waited for him to call me back. And waited. And waited.

Why didn't he call? Didn't he know I needed him? All my insecurities started to raise their ugly heads and I worked myself up into a state, deciding that he didn't want to be with me anymore. That he had decided enough was enough with this crazy situation.

I felt hurt, imagining I had been used. All of these thoughts raced through my mind before I had even properly spoken to him. The end result of course, was that when he did finally call, I was short with him on the phone and didn't tell him about my car accident or the strange old woman I had met. I figured I was being strong and independent by not offering this information. He didn't care about me; therefore, he did not need to know.

Trent was perplexed by my shortness, and we had a strained conversation. Frustrated and upset I told him I needed to go, and hung up. I sat on my stairs and wept. I hadn't made it to the supermarket after all. I was in pain, hungry and alone, and I was living in a nightmare that was not of my making. For some reason I seemed intent on sabotaging the one thing in my life that gave me any happiness, the one thing that was stopping me tumbling from the cliff edge.

I was frightened.

*

That night I dreamed again. A similar dream to the one I'd had before. I entered a world shrouded in the densest green fog. The atmosphere was stifling, and this time I struggled to breathe. I needed to find someone. I started to follow the path unfolding in front of me. I walked and walked. My hip throbbed with pain.

I was getting nowhere, and just as I thought I would have to give up, to turn around and go back, a figure materialised out of the mist. I walked on. I could rest as soon as I had spoken to them. My first thought was that the figure in the gloom was Max. He had his back to me and hadn't noticed I was coming. I caught glimpses of his face, even though in reality I was too far away to see him clearly. I was making no ground so I tried to run towards him but my hip wouldn't allow it. I cried and reached out to him, but he was moving farther and farther away. I kept trying, and at last I was getting closer. But it wasn't Max, it was Trent. My heart surged with happiness. I would make it up to him, apologise for being a complete idiot, maybe he would forgive me.

Trent started to turn, and I waved and called out to him, but as he turned in slow motion his shape changed, became a woman, an old woman, a hag. Hunched back like the woman I had seen in the town, a hooked nose and eyes set deeply into her skull. She was lifting a hand, withered and claw-like to draw back her hood, and I realised that I didn't want to see her full face with her cloak down. I was in danger, I needed to run far, far away. The crone kept turning, and I stumbled backwards, my hip impeding me as I fled. She was coming for me and no-one could help me. I screamed.

And sat up, gasping and desperate in the darkness. How had I forgotten to leave the hall light on? I couldn't see a hand in front of my face. Had I heard something? My breathing was loud in the pitch black of the room. I held my breath and listened. Nothing, except the super-fast pulsing of my own heartbeat. I breathed out in a rush and tried to get my breathing under control. Slowly and deeply, in and out. In and out. Until my heartbeat had returned to something approaching normal and I was slightly more relaxed.

My throat was dry and my hip was killing me. My elbow throbbed too. A glass of water and some pain killers would be the sensible course of action. I tentatively swung my feet out of bed.

Walking was agony. Perhaps I should have visited accident and emergency the previous day, after all. I struggled to the door and onto the landing. I'd made this trip so many times, navigating my way around my house in the dark was not a problem. Holding tightly to the balustrade I tried to keep most of my weight going through my left hand side. Gingerly I hopped down the stairs, pausing at the bottom to flick on a light.

Something rattled in the kitchen, and my hand halted in mid-air by the light switch. I listened. Nothing.

"Pip?" I called softly. I heard a rustling opposite me and nearly jumped out of my skin as two bright lights floated towards me at knee height. Pip's eyes shone in the darkness. He had been sleeping in his favourite spot on the sofa, no doubt.

Pip wasn't in the kitchen, so who was? I stood naked at the foot of the stairs, wondering whether to put the light on or not. If someone was in the house the light might scare them away, but conversely I didn't want to be caught naked by a complete stranger.

I became aware of an odd sulphurous smell. Pip sneezed and whined. I moved forwards, inching towards the kitchen, Pip stayed behind, crying softly. The kitchen door stood open as it always did, to allow Pip free access to his water bowl. I put my head around it. Faint light shone, emanating from another house visible through the glass of the back door, illuminating the green mist that roiled and bubbled across the kitchen floor. It was about ankle deep but getting thicker and trying to climb the walls. It stank. I coughed. The source of the manifestation appeared to be the small kitchen window which was open at the top. It shouldn't have been. I knew that. All the windows in the kitchen were locked using a window key. I never opened them. If I needed air in the kitchen, I opened the back door.

I struggled through the mist to shut the kitchen window. It was like walking through water. I slammed the window down and latched it. The keys were in a drawer somewhere; I would need to fish them out. I unlocked the back door and opened it to air the kitchen out, and the mist dissipated rapidly. Pip skipped out into the garden, now wholly unconcerned and perfectly happy. The sensor light clicked on as he moved into its path. Something scuttled rapidly away at the back of the garden. I glared that way, felt something slither against my skin, and shuddered.

My hand reached for my necklace but it still wasn't in place. I reminded myself to put it on as I poured myself a glass of water and fished the ibuprofen from the window sill, quickly swallowing two. Pip returned, so I shut the door and turned the key, double checking that it was actually locked, and then checking that all of the windows were closed and locked.

The sensor light clicked off in the garden and the ground floor of the house was plunged into darkness once more. I made a mental note to switch the hall light on as I went past. Collecting my glass of water, I turned for the hall, whistling at Pip so he would follow me. I jumped a mile as the room was suddenly bathed in light again. The garden sensor had automatically gone on. Something *was* out there.

I peered out, searching the familiarity of my back garden for something that shouldn't be there. I couldn't see anything, there was no movement, nothing to suggest anyone or anything was activating the sensor. "It could be a cat," I spoke out loud, quietly reassuring myself. Or even some other small animal. It wasn't unknown for moles or birds to trip the light from time to time. But I was uneasy. What if someone was there?

I waited for a time, my eyes flicking here, there, and everywhere, but there was no evidence of anything untoward. It crossed my mind that I could call the police, but how seriously would they take me? Pip wasn't reacting to anything specifically. The light shut off again with an audible click.

I breathed a sigh of relief and turned once more for the hall, but drew myself up short. That click of the light going off had been crisp and distinct, as though I were outside, or a window was open. I turned and checked again. The small window was unlatched and open once more.

"Shit."

There was an explosion of light and screeching; I spun around in panic. My mobile phone on the kitchen table was going off. With trembling hands, I reached for the phone as it rang off. I lifted it and stared at the display. One missed call from Sarah. It was 2.52 am.

Why was she calling me at this time of night? I hit the button to return the call. No answer. Perplexed, I placed the phone back on the table then returned to the window to close and latch it once more, triple checking that it was secure.

I tried Sarah's number again. This time it went straight to voicemail. Whatever she had been ringing for, hopefully it could wait till morning. I was exhausted. I hobbled into the hall, switching the hall light on as I passed. Pip headed for the living room again, but I called him to me. I needed his company in the bedroom for the rest of the night.

I struggled upstairs and closed the door, but before getting into bed, I slipped into my bathroom and grabbed the necklace from the hook beside the shower. The pentagram was warm. I snuggled back into bed, gripping the charms in my left fist. I placed my right hand on the pillow next to me and felt the place where Trent's head would have been resting. I missed him. Pip jumped up on the bed and curled up in the crook of my legs and with that I fell into a deep, dreamless sleep.

*

I overslept, feeling sluggish and out of sorts. The windows and doors were all firmly latched. I rummaged in the drawer next to the sink for the window keys and made sure that all the windows downstairs were locked properly. That job done, it was time for tea. Unfortunately, I was out of milk so I was forced to make do with herbal tea which didn't quite hit the spot that builder's tea might have. Breakfast was another couple of ibuprofen. I was famished. I had to go shopping today otherwise Pip would starve too and that was unthinkable.

I grabbed my purse and bag and my mobile phone. Remembering Sarah's late call from the night before I had a quick look to see whether she had been in touch again. There was a text, sent at 3.02. It read. *She turned around.*

She turned around? A chill ran up my spine and goose pimples prickled on my skin. Who turned around? What did she mean? The woman in her dream?

I called her phone. It went to voicemail again. Flicking through my contacts I searched for her home phone number and called that instead. It was picked up almost instantly by a voice I didn't recognise.

"Hello," I started, "it's Heather Keynes here. Is it possible to speak to Sarah please?"

There was a pause on the other end. I listened to the crackles on the line, imagined them travelling along the airwaves. My stomach rolled when the pause stretched out. Something was dreadfully wrong. I heard the person on the end of the phone swallow. "Sorry," he said. "Heather? Yes, you were a friend of my mum's."

He had said were. As in, I was no longer her friend. Not anymore. I waited, my chest tight. Hardly daring to breathe.

"I'm sorry to tell you that my mum passed away last night."

Aefre. I clenched my free hand tightly, feeling the nails bite into the skin of my palm. "How?" I asked. It sounded aggressive, snappy.

"We think it was an overdose. She was found this morning."

We spoke a little more, and I offered my heartfelt condolences before I hung up. I replaced my mobile on the table and slumped heavily on the kitchen chair. Sarah was dead. Sarah had killed herself. I thought of Lewis and Siobhan. Why would Sarah have taken her own life when she still had her other two children? It made no sense.

And yet, the last time I had seen her she had been struggling, and she had spoken about the dreams she had been

197

having and how they were robbing her of sleep. Dreams just as I was experiencing. I picked my mobile up, flicked through the screens to my texts. Sarah had still been alive at 2.52 when she rang me. Had she taken the pills by then? Could I have saved her if I had managed to talk to her? If she had picked up the phone when I rang back? Would she still be alive if I hadn't been distracted by the window in the kitchen and the strange mist in my kitchen?

And then she had sent me a text at 3.02 am. *She turned around.* I had left my phone down here when I went back to bed. Why had I done that?

The woman in the dream that Sarah had been walking towards, was she the same one in my dreams? The same terror from my dreams overtook me. I didn't want the woman to turn around. I had woken up in mortal dread of what I was about to see.

So Sarah had seen her face, and it was so unbearable that she had decided to take her own life.

I slumped in defeat. Sarah had a loving, supportive family and plenty of friends. I hoped I had been of some help to her, but lately, perhaps I hadn't been. If Sarah was unable to continue with life even with all the love that surrounded her after the death of Mikey, then it didn't bode well for me, plodding on through life alone, without Max, without Trent, without anybody to help me.

How could I do what the Guardians wanted me to do? How could I destroy Aefre? I didn't see how I would ever be strong enough. I wasn't the one they needed.

*

I traced the outline of the flowers on my mug for about the millionth time. I had remained sitting at the kitchen table for far too long. Outside it was a warm day, but sitting here, I was cold and shivery. I was running on empty.

There was a smart rat-a-tat-tat on the door and Pip rose from the floor next to me where he had been keeping me company. He rushed to the front door and barked. It was an excited bark, happy, so it seemed unlikely my visitor was the post man.

Stiffly I rose from my seat and limped to the door, staring through the stained glass to see if I could recognise the shape of the person beyond. I thought I did. I drew back the bolts, as Pip wagged his whole behind, and pulled the door open.

Trent stood there, clutching two plastic shopping bags and a large bunch of flowers. He studied my face, frowning with concern. "What's happened?" he asked, moving into the hall, placing the bags on the floor, and scooping me into his free arm.

I opened my mouth to speak but nothing came out. I was so pleased to see him, so thankful that he had arrived even though I had decided he would never want to see me again. I didn't know which emotion to give in to first—happiness or sorrow. I was completely overwhelmed. Trent placed the flowers on the telephone table behind me and wrapped me in a huge hug.

"I'm sorry," he said, and I burst into tears. He didn't need to be sorry. It was me, all me. My own stupidity and uncertainty. My inability to trust anyone, my frozen heart. He rocked me gently for a while, while I sobbed on his shoulder and then he gently extricated himself. "Let's put the kettle on," he said. "I brought some provisions along." He knew me too well.

He handed me the flowers, colourful summer blooms, and picked up the bags of shopping. He noticed the way I was hobbling and frowned again. "Heather, you had better start telling me what's been going on. I only left yesterday morning and since then you look like you've lost half a stone, you can't walk, you're as pale as a ghost, and we've had our first lover's tiff."

Our first lover's tiff, he had said. It inferred there would be more. I held on to that thought, the positivity of it. I began to feel warmer inside.

"I don't know where to start." My voice was husky. Trent bustled around me; put a bowl of food down for Pip and fresh water; boiled the kettle and filled the teapot. In no time at all I had a hot mug of tea and some biscuits in front of me and could feel some warmth coming back to my extremities.

I told him firstly about the meeting with Mr Kephisto and the accident afterwards. I mentioned my feeling that Aefre had had something to do with it, and the odd woman who had told me to wear my charm necklace. Trent reached forward to check I was wearing it, sliding the chain out from under my t-shirt. The pentagram glowed in the sunlight, he clasped it tightly for a moment, met my eyes. An unspoken understanding about the charms passed between us—they were an intrinsic part of this odd journey we were on. He smiled and kissed me. "Go on."

I cradled my flowery mug in my hands and recounted, incredulously, how I had found the sulphurous mist in the kitchen, pouring down from the window that wouldn't stay latched and locked. "Which window?" he asked, so I pointed it out. He checked it and then all of the others, just as I had this morning. Once he was satisfied he returned to the table and poured me more tea.

"But there's more, isn't there?"

I nodded. "My friend Sarah, Mikey's mum. She was found dead this morning. A possible overdose. That's what her family are saying."

"That's terrible news. You don't think it was that straightforward?" Trent pushed the biscuits my way.

"Yes and no." I took a biscuit, dunked it in my tea. "I don't know for sure. But she was having these dreams. The same dreams that I've been having lately." Trent regarded me quizzically. "She dreamt she was walking towards something but never quite getting there and then she would see a woman, and the woman scared her, she didn't want that woman to turn around."

"You've been having these dreams too?"

I nodded. Then I showed him the text.

"She turned around," he read out loud. He stared at the text for a while and then reached for my hand. "It doesn't have to mean anything, you know? Sarah was recently bereaved. Her mind was a little unbalanced emotionally. You're strong Heather. You won't buckle underneath all of this. You've been strong for years. It's one of the things I most admire about you."

"You don't hate me then?" I asked.

"Don't be daft."

"I'm sorry, for being a fool. It's just …" I hesitated.

"Yes?"

"Why would someone like you, want to be with someone like me?"

"Someone like me? Someone who's nerdy and clumsy and can't cook and hates football and can't service his own car or keep a girlfriend for longer than six weeks, you mean? And someone like you who's smart and sexy and beautiful and strong and independent and funny?"

"And old. You forgot old."

"You're a fool, that's what you are." Trent stood and reached down to pull me to standing. "Come on. I want you to show me your bruises and then you can show me how full of life you really are. Convince me you want to live."

I nodded wearily. "I do. I promise. More now than I have for a few years. But this Aefre thing, it's just too much for me. I'm not strong enough. I can't do what they want me to do."

Trent hugged me again. "This isn't your battle; you don't have to be a part of any of it. Just let it go."

"Can I do that? The Guardians …"

"Of course you can. It's your life, not Mercy's, not Rose's or anyone else's. They have no right to insist you help them with anything. You can do what you want."

I nodded. I wanted to believe that. I wanted to feel safe again.

I wanted nothing more to do with the whole sorry debacle.

TWENTY-THREE

OF BOO HAGS AND THINGS

Autumn

The sun was lower over the horizon, and the light through the trees had a glorious golden element to it. I kicked the leaves along the path as I walked, Pip busy sniffing for squirrels. I took a deep breath, savouring the smells and thinking of how I had always loved this time of year. The days were growing shorter now and there was a slight chill in the air in the evenings, but this afternoon it was positively balmy. I was pleased that summer was disappearing though, it had been a crazy time.

Sarah's funeral during the second week of August had been a sad occasion. She had been laid to rest with Mikey and that was fitting of course, mother and son reunited. I'd thought about Max then. I still had his ashes locked away in the bottom drawer of my desk. I had decided when the time came that I would have his ashes scattered with mine. We would be together again, eventually.

Fraser had been at the funeral too. We had exchanged greetings, but I didn't seek him out afterwards. I had nothing of any note to tell him. The police were no closer to uncovering Mikey's killer, and the search had been scaled down. His death was logged as just another mysterious incident.

Trent had accompanied me to the funeral and had been my anchor in the weeks that had passed since then. He spent most evenings at my place, only occasionally staying over in his own flat in Exeter. We had opted for a quiet life, keeping our distance from White Cottage, The Storykeeper, and the Guardians generally, and I had resisted any temptation to visit the oak tree. In return we had heard of no more unexplained deaths or disappearances, and I was now hopeful that everything would remain quiet and that we could move on with our lives and forget everything that had happened. All the magick and mayhem seemed like a distant memory, and yet …

I always wore the charms around my neck. The pentagram nestled with the smaller oak leaf and acorn between my breasts.

I knew I was practicing avoidance behaviour, walking through the local park instead of the forest, hoping to evade the Guardians. Trent and I sometimes drove up to Nabb's Hill and walked together, but usually when I was alone I came here instead and stayed well out of the reach of Mercy and her friends. It was with some dismay therefore, that I realised that the woman striding purposefully along the path towards me was Claire.

She was carrying a small basket. Once I was close enough I could see it contained berries and mushrooms. She had obviously been foraging, but I didn't for the life of me think this meeting was accidental.

"Hi Claire, long time no see."

"Good afternoon, Heather. We had thought to see you before now."

"I've been a little busy," I lied. I hadn't. But Trent had been taking good care of me, and I was eating and sleeping better than I had for years. He had insisted I didn't put myself under any further stress.

"That's good."

I wanted to walk away, not think about Aefre or all the deaths she had caused. I especially didn't want to think about a small group of people who were hoping that I was somehow their salvation. I didn't honestly see how I could be, and as time had passed I had convinced myself that everything I had been through was as a result of drug induced hypnosis. Rose and Kephisto. They were clever. Surely I had been duped.

But in my heart of hearts, I knew this wasn't the case.

"We would like to see you," Claire said earnestly.

"Why? What's happened?" I asked.

"Bill Tuckman passed away."

I was stunned. His story had genuinely touched me. I

swallowed. "Naturally?"

"It's being put down to a natural death, but Kephisto believes ..."

"That Aefre caught up with him at last?"

Claire pursed her lips. I took this as an affirmation. I felt sad for Bill. I had written to him over the summer and sent him some paintbrushes and decent paper to use for his watercolours. I didn't want him to think that I'd forgotten him, or that we had disbelieved his story. We hadn't, far from it.

"Claire, I don't know what I can do. I don't know where Aefre is, and I'm fairly sure that if it came down to it, she would be more than a match for me. How can you think that there is anything special about me?" I shrugged.

"We know there is," she replied. "We will assist you in any way we can."

"But none of us know where to start." I was frustrated that nobody had a plan.

"Come to see us soon," said Claire and began to walk on, "we'll be waiting until then." I turned and watched her until I was sure she wasn't coming back, then I called Pip to heel, sighing. The shine had been taken off the day somewhat.

*

I tenderly placed the urn that held Max's ashes on his bedside table and ran my duster over it once more. How was it possible that Max had been reduced to this? He had been so vital and alive, taller than me already at seventeen and threatening to be broad like his father, but here were his remains in a small urn. I straightened the bed clothes where I had been sitting for a little while, making everything nice, as though it actually still mattered to anyone except me.

Initially, after Max had died, I had left the room exactly as it was on the day he ran out of the house to jump into James's car. His clothes and magazines had been scattered everywhere, and the scent of his aftershave, still so thoroughly unnecessary given he only had to shave once a week, had been strong. After three months without him, I had decided that it wasn't healthy to keep the room as a shrine to that final day of his life, and I had picked up his clothes and washed them, straightened the magazines, and dusted the shelves. Eventually I had laundered the bedding too, and now this room was a memorial to a young man who would never have kept it this neat and tidy.

The front door slammed. Trent had arrived.

"Just a minute," I shouted down to him. I could hear Trent greeting Pip and smiled.

I opened the top drawer of the chest by the window. All of Max's socks and pants were neatly arranged. There was a box of condoms in here too, years out of date now. I'd picked the carton up numerous times. It was open and there were two missing. I had no idea whether Max had actually had sex in his short life, and if he had, as this box of condoms might suggest, I wondered who the girl had been. I would have liked to know. Perhaps that was intrusive, but I hoped he had experienced some of what life had meant to offer him as a man, as much as I had loved the boy he had been.

Perhaps the girl had been Maddie Ledden? I wasn't sure she was Max's type, didn't know what his type had been. But I wouldn't have minded. Whoever it had been, I hoped she had treated him right, and I hoped he had been a gentleman.

I'd put one of his baby toys in here too. It was a blue and lilac teddy that my mother had given him when he was small. He had adored it and chewed on its ears. I had repaired it many, many times over the years. When he was ten, he had decided that he was far too old to have soft toys and I had thrown some out, or passed others on to charity. But not Bear. Initially it had lived in plain sight, but as Max became embarrassed about such things, and his friends were coming over more often, poor Bear had been consigned to dark corners or the space under the bed. Several days after Max died I had found Bear in his underwear drawer, still present though hidden.

Now Bear was looking frail. I picked him up and kissed his threadbare head and held him to my face, missing my son in the simplest and most profound of ways.

I heard movement behind me and turned around in a hurry, feeling oddly guilty.

Trent smiled tiredly. The freshers had arrived, timetables had been fixed, and he had plenty going on. He came forward, hugged and kissed me, then rubbed my shoulders.

"Are you ok?" he asked, looking around the room.

"Yes. I brought Max in here. I don't know why." I indicated the urn I had always kept in my desk. I didn't like it on display. I couldn't work when it was.

"Maybe you think he belongs in here."

"Maybe." I was silent for a while. Trent studied the posters on the wall. There were pictures of scantily clad models, football teams, and Green Day. Max hadn't really been a Green Day fan, but certainly James was, so perhaps Max had put the poster on the wall for appearances sake. There was also a postcard with a picture of George Orwell by his desk, and a black and white printed photo of Rudyard Kipling, whom Max had admired greatly.

"But he doesn't really, does he? He should be out in the great wide world. He would have been twenty-two by now. He would have finished his degree at Sheffield, maybe gone on to do a masters or a teaching certificate. What career would he have chosen? I always thought he would be an English teacher."

"Perhaps he would have enjoyed being an academic," Trent smiled. "Like me."

"Or like his dad," I said, thinking of the hapless postgraduate student who had missed out in being a father to my wonderful son.

"I never really told Max about his father, I guess I didn't have much to tell him. We had already split up when I realised I was pregnant. I found out that he was banging another girl in my seminar group."

"It was his loss," said Trent soothingly, examining the books on the shelves. "Max was a bright young man."

I nodded, appeased, and hugged Bear to me once more. "I'm thinking of emptying this room now."

Trent was puzzled. "Why?"

"You spend so much time in the house, and you need a study, I mean, if we're going to continue being a couple ... and you're going to be here, marking and prepping and writing papers and whatever else it is you do…" I trailed off, panicked by what I was saying.

Trent shook his head, his face loving. "Shhh. You don't have to erase Max. I don't need this room. I can work on your dining table. And no, I'm not going anywhere." He smiled at my uncertainty, always so patient with my insecurity.

"I just wonder whether it's time, you know. To let him go. Am I hanging onto him for too long?"

"He's your son. You'll hang onto him forever, surely." Trent stroked my shoulders.

I showed him Bear. "I sometimes think, if I let him go, if I let all of these worldly possessions go, will the pain diminish? Will I start to feel like a normal person again?" Trent nodded his understanding. "It never leaves me, this knot of hell inside my womb. If I could only understand what happened and why it happened, if it all made sense, would I feel better?" I thought about Aefre. Doubt playing at the edges of my mind. How much was she to blame? Part of me still wanted to confront her.

"But it wouldn't change the fact that Max was gone, just knowing how and why, would it? I'm not sure you would feel better about it. I think you would probably always grieve and always be angry." I listened to what Trent was saying and nodded, replacing Bear into Max's spick and span underwear drawer. Childhood innocence nestling next to the box of condoms. What complicated people we all turn into. For Max that process had just been beginning. For me, it was far advanced.

*

Trent and I were snuggled on the sofa watching something on the TV. Or rather I was watching TV with my head on a pillow on Trent's lap, and he had his nose in a book.

It was something I was getting used to.

"There's something in here you might be interested in," he said, when the adverts came on.

"Oh yes?" I replied lazily, stretching and sitting up reluctantly.

"There's a group of people called Gullahs who live on the east coast of the United States who are descended from African slaves, brought over in the sixteenth century. There must have been loads of them at one time, because they all became pretty tight-knit and formed their own culture, with its own belief system."

"Ok," I prompted him. My programme was just about to come back on and I wanted him to get to the point.

"They believe that everyone has a soul and a spirit, and that when we die, good souls go to heaven and good spirits stay on earth to watch over their family and offer protection if need be. A bad spirit is called a 'boo hag' and it uses witchcraft to steal energy while people sleep. That's the gist of it." I perked up. "But listen to this. Boo hags have been described as having similarities with vampires. They are undead beings that feed off the living. They are skinless and bright red in colour, with bulging blue veins. To survive in the world, they steal a person's skin and assume the identity and thereafter are able to move among the living without suspicion."

I moved so that I could read over Trent's shoulder.

"At night they can shed their skin and hunt for other victims to ride. A common greeting among the Gullahs is 'don't let de boo hag ride ya!'" read Trent.

"Boo hags are said to be able to enter a property through tiny openings, such as a small window or the crack in a door. Once inside they locate their victim and sit on the chest. They will then steal the victim's breath and more specifically, their energy. A boo hag will ride its victim all night long, then sneak away before dawn to return to its discarded skin. If it can't get to its skin before the dawn comes up it will be destroyed. The warning signs that a boo hag is close include that the air will become hot and damp and there may be a strong smell of rotting meat. If you've woken up exhausted after a full night's rest, you may have been visited by a boo hag."

I pursed my lips, my programme forgotten. "You think this could be Aefre?"

"I think that most myths and legends are grounded in reality somewhere along the line. This is in the US. Maybe that's where one or more of her sisters have ended up." That did seem to make sense to me.

"Does it say how to kill them?" I asked, but Trent shook his head.

"It suggests that they are repelled by the colour indigo blue, but this seems to be a cultural thing for the Gullahs, all of the evil spirits associated with them are repelled by indigo blue. The author of this research says that many Gullahs who believe they are being pestered by boo hags paint their houses, particularly doors and window ledges, in this blue colour."

I wasn't convinced that a pot of blue paint would deter Aefre when she set her mind to killing. "Anything else?"

"Salt. 'A salted hag can't get back into its skin,' it says."

I sighed, entirely unpersuaded. "We'd better buy a truck load I suppose. Have you ever come across anything else like this?" I asked.

Trent shrugged. "There's a few. The hag is a popular symbol in European folklore and has almost always been used as a term of derision for older women, so there's stories of them for example, that are quite similar to the boo hag—and in some of those stories they are said to have sat on a sleeper's chest too, causing temporary paralysis. And there are other stories of hags from traditional English folklore, like Peg Powler, who lived in the River Tees and frightened children away."

"Oh I heard a story like that when I was a kid."

"It's a common one throughout England and Wales. She tends to have different names wherever she's based. I think parents used these tales to keep their kids away from the edge of the river by telling them they would be pulled into the river and eaten or something."

"So there's plenty of anecdotal evidence then, I mean that could be taken as evidence of the existence of Aefre and her sisters. But even here in Abbotts Cromleigh, where strange things happen periodically and people go missing or die in horrible ways, it's ignored or swept under the carpet."

"Yes, I suppose so. But how much of that is down to the Guardians?" Trent had not been happy about the way that the homeless man's body had been removed from the oak tree and hidden in the woods. I sympathized, but I understood what the Guardians were trying to do too.

"We should try and find out some more about the boo hags," I answered, trying to change the subject.

"I have a friend at a University in Florida specializing in African-American slave culture. I'll get in touch with him."

"Good," I said and kissed him. I had lost the thread of my TV programme altogether. I switched the TV off. "I'm going upstairs. Are you coming?"

"I'll let Pip out and follow you up."

I nodded. "Don't let the boo hag ride ya!" I said as I left the room, and he chuckled.

TWENTY-FOUR

EUAN

Saturday morning saw me pushing a trolley around the supermarket. It was a tiresome chore, although I had found that now that Trent and I were spending so much time together, between us we were creating some interesting menus and I was experimenting more with food than I had since before Max had died. Once upon a time I had been an inventive cook. Trent was game to have a go too, although he frequently lost track of time when he was working, so we either ate at a stupid time in the evening or he dished up burnt offerings. I'd put on a little weight. Trent liked it.

I hadn't written a list so I went from shelf to shelf and just picked up whatever I fancied that wasn't too expensive. Fruit and vegetables were our staples and I added pasta, rice, bread, cheese, meat, milk, and dog food. I paused in the biscuit aisle for quite some time. Trent liked his biscuits so I spent some time choosing a few complementary varieties.

There among the digestives I had a sudden notion that someone was looking at me. I peered back over my shoulder. The supermarket was busy at this time on a Saturday of course, full of anonymous people going about their business. I couldn't shake the feeling that someone was watching me. I turned around and around, examining the faces of everyone nearby. No-one was paying me any attention. Farther up the aisle other people were pulling bags of crisps down from the top shelf. There was nobody obviously looking my way.

I leaned on my trolley, perplexed. Without thinking, I closed my eyes. I wanted to see if I could sense Aefre anywhere close by. Everything was dark, but as my thoughts reached out to her, I was able to pick up a strong smell of soil for a moment. Had Aefre gone to ground? Maybe she was hiding in her dwelling, somewhere deep in the forest.

There was nothing else. Aefre wasn't stalking me in the

supermarket. I put my hand inside my jacket and checked to make sure the charms were in place. They were warm because I was warm; the pentagram was no hotter than the other two.

I didn't shake off the feeling of being observed all the way around the supermarket. Two or three more times I turned around sharply, including one final time at the check-out, but was never able to catch anyone staring at me. Slightly unnerved, I almost forgot to take my change from the bored young man who served me.

I was relieved to be back outside and rushed for the relative safety of my car, nearly knocking a small child over as I clumsily manhandled my trolley over the inconveniently designed cobbled paving.

I was hastily unloading my bags into the boot when I heard my name called. "Heather?" Fraser and a young woman I assumed was his girlfriend, Sally, were walking towards me. "It is you. Hi Heather, how are you?"

"I'm well," I said. "How are you both?"

"Good, good," nodded Fraser. "This is Sally, my girlfriend." The young woman smiled. She was pretty in a slightly pale, gothic way. I didn't remember her from Max's school days, so possibly she was a little younger than Max and Fraser, or had moved to the area later.

"Have you just finished shopping?" I indicated the supermarket, wondering whether it was them I had sensed looking my way, but Fraser shook his head.

"We're just about to go in actually. There's a party tonight and we need to buy some supplies."

"Oh," I said. "I thought someone was watching me in there. I'm getting paranoid." I laughed, falsely, and instantly hated myself for sounding nervy.

"Watching you?" Fraser and Sally exchanged looks.

"Yes. I think I must have been imagining it. Don't worry."

Sally opened her mouth, glanced at Fraser, and closed it again.

"Enjoy your party," I said. "See you again."

I watched them as they entered the supermarket, shook my head, wondering what Sally had wanted to say, then finished unloading the trolley.

*

"Your bloody mobile was ringing constantly last night," Trent complained as he brought a tray of tea up the following morning. "I had to get up in the end and go downstairs and turn it off." He indicated the phone on the tray.

"Didn't you answer it?" I yawned and snuggled back under the covers.

"It had gone three. No-one sober calls at stupid o'clock with good news." He had a point. I sat up and reached for it and switched it on. It took a while to get going. Trent poured the tea grumpily. I sipped it, too hot, until the phone binged and bonged indicating it was awake and the texts or voicemails were flooding in.

I flicked through the missed calls. It had been Fraser.

I had a voicemail too. I listened carefully before replacing the phone on my bedside table. "It was Fraser. Remember him? And you're right. He was very drunk."

"What did he want?"

"I bumped into him yesterday, I forgot to tell you. We didn't talk for long. He was just ringing me to say that he wanted me to meet someone."

"Who?"

"He didn't say."

"Sounds dubious." Trent didn't say anything but his face queried whether I might be getting involved in the Aefre business again.

"Oh Fraser's harmless. He seems like quite a nice guy to me."

Trent picked up a book from the floor by the side of the bed and opened it up at the bookmark. "So you'll meet him then?" he asked. I nodded. "When?"

"I don't know yet. I'll need to ring him back."

"Do you want me to come with you?"

"I'm a big girl. I can meet him by myself. You worry too much."

"Ok. Well I'll come if you like."

*

I arranged to meet Fraser in The Plough and Harrow later that afternoon. Trent had a mountain of marking to sort out so I insisted he stay at home and finish it off. I suggested he bung a joint in the oven and take charge of the evening meal, but I wasn't entirely sure he would remember to do that and I had high hopes of being home quite quickly anyway.

I was slightly later to the meeting than promised. The Plough and Harrow was busy. They served a Sunday Roast between twelve and three and it was a popular place. I finally spotted Fraser in the back corner in a booth behind the pool tables. He had company.

Fraser stood as I approached and headed me off before I got to the table. "Let's get a drink," he said. He was pale and a little unshaven, the after effects of the previous night.

"Hair of the dog?" I asked and smiled. He nodded but didn't return the smile.

"Yeah. Feeling pretty rough, I have to admit."

"Well you're only young once." I ordered a pint of cider for myself and an Otter Ale for Fraser and stole another look at the man in the booth. Even from this distance I could tell he had terrible skin. "What about your friend?" He would have the same. "This is the person you wanted me to meet?" I asked curiously.

"Yes, listen Heather—" Fraser started to say, just as the landlord placed his pint on the bar. I paid and faced Fraser. "I hope this is all right with you. He wanted to meet you. Has been asking me about it for a while, since Mikey's funeral actually, so yesterday when you said you thought you were being watched in the supermarket I realised who it must be, and so I went in and found him."

I studied the man again. He knew me then. Did I know him? "He was the one watching me in the supermarket?"

"Yes."

I picked up my pint, followed Fraser to the booth, and slid in opposite the man. It was difficult to tell—given that he was sitting—but he appeared to be small to average height, with dark hair. He was painfully thin, but the thing that really stood out was how yellow his pock-marked skin was. A drug addict I surmised. Chronic abuse. Propped against the wall was a standard NHS crutch. I presumed the crutch was his as well. I felt sorry for him.

He offered a self-conscious smile when Fraser put the pint I had bought in front of him. He was missing three front teeth at the top. The rest were rotting.

"Hi," I said.

"Heather," said Fraser nervously, "this is Euan Gatesby."

I rocked back in my seat in shock and stared at the man in front of me. It had been nearly four years, but only four years. I regarded him with fresh eyes, saw the scarring on his face, saw the crutch against the wall. He had been a boy. Fresh faced. Just beginning to enjoy life. He had lived on the council estate on the outskirts of Abbotts Cromleigh. He had been doing relatively well at school and was taking A levels alongside Max and James.

My hand moved to my mouth in shock. I'd visited him in hospital after the accident several times. They had placed him in an induced coma for ten days or so, because his injuries had been severe, but they expected him to make a recovery. Then one day when I went in, he had been moved to a specialist spinal unit in Bristol and after that I had never seen him again. His parents, or perhaps his mum, I couldn't recall the family unit Euan had originated from, had not attended the funerals of either James or Max, and I had never pursued contact with them. I knew he had younger siblings at home.

"How are you Euan?" I asked, and my voice shook. Maybe what I really wanted to ask was, "What happened to you? Why do you look so wasted when you were given the opportunity to live?" but I didn't. I glanced at Fraser, hoping he could help.

"I'm sorry," Euan spoke. He had a surprisingly deep voice. "This must be a shock for you. You haven't seen me in all of these years."

"I've thought about you," I said truthfully. "I think about all of you a great deal." I indicated the crutch. "Did you … recover?"

"No," Euan said. "Well … in part. I had a fracture dislocation in my lower spine and a dislocation in my neck, along with three broken ribs and a collapsed lung. These have mended to a certain extent, but I'm never without pain, particularly in my lower back."

"I'm so sorry," I said. I thought about Max, his postmortem and the accident report. He had a broken femur, two broken ribs, and a broken nose. His airbag had deployed. His injuries had been survivable—possibly not even life changing—but he hadn't made it. James had taken the brunt of the collision. He had been a mess. Euan in the back had had no airbag and had not been wearing a seatbelt. He had been sprawled across the back seat. His injuries had been caused by hitting the back of the front seats with force and then colliding with the side window.

"I survived. I'm glad of that."

"Are you though?" Fraser retorted, scowling at Euan. I was taken aback. "You're screwed up, mate."

"How do you mean?" I asked, holding a hand up to still Fraser's fury.

"Euan's a drug addict. He's in and out of hostels, he's even been done for supply, and he's been inside."

"That's true," said Euan, "but the drugs are a way of managing the pain, you know?"

"What about the nightmares?" asked Fraser.

"I do have nightmares as it happens. I get flashbacks." Euan nodded at me.

"But it's not just nightmares about the accident, neither."

"What sort of nightmares do you have?" I asked as my world shifted slightly on its axis.

"Oh you know." He paused, thinking. "I've been having

them for so long that it seems almost normal to me. But they do disturb me. I'm always walking somewhere. Walking, walking, for ages. I don't walk great anyway. I wake up and my legs ache, really bad."

A pulse started to beat in my temple. Trent had a right to be afraid. I was being sucked into this mess with Aefre and the Guardians again. "Do you ever get anywhere? When you're walking in your dream?"

"Nah, not really, but I always know that the end is in sight. And I think she is waiting for me."

"Who is 'she'?" asked Fraser.

"I don't know. I don't want to know. Sometimes I've glimpsed her and she seems to be luring me to her, and I half want to follow her, and then I don't. I try to run away, to get away from her, but she starts to turn around."

It was the same dream. The same as Sarah's. The same as mine. The one I had, particularly on the nights Trent wasn't with me. I groaned. What did all of this mean? Fraser and Euan regarded me strangely for a moment.

I hurriedly drank some of my cider and decided to change the subject. "You've been watching me in the supermarket?" I asked.

"Yes, sorry." Euan grimaced, a little shame faced. "I have kind of been stalking you when I see you coming in, it's true. I work there, accepting deliveries and checking off orders several times a week. I can't really do much in the way of lifting and carrying, but the government insists I do something for my benefits and so that's what they give me to do. Sometimes they get me to do longer shifts or stay during the day, so I've seen you every now and again." That would explain the other occasions.

"Why didn't you just say hello?" I asked.

Euan indicated his scarred face. "I'm ashamed." He hung his head, and I felt incredibly sad for him.

"Don't ever be ashamed," I said, my eyes filling with tears. "You've been through a hell of a lot and lost so much."

"You're kind, Heather, to try to understand. Most don't,"

Euan said quietly. He sat in silence for a while, and I pulled myself together. "Max asked for you," he said eventually.

My heart skipped a beat. "What?"

Euan gazed at me, his eyes shining. "He asked for you, before he died. That's why I wanted to see you. I wanted to tell you that."

"Max was still alive? After the crash?" My voice was barely audible.

"Yes. But not for long." His face crumpled in pain and suddenly he leaned forwards and grabbed my hand. "Can I tell you it all, Heather? Can I tell you what happened? I tried to tell the police when they came to question me in Bristol. I tried to, I did, but they thought I was hallucinating from the painkillers."

My stomach turned over but Euan was finally offering me the opportunity to know everything. I needed to hear the truth. I held onto his hand, clutching him fiercely. "Yes. Tell me. Tell me," I demanded.

*

"We'd such a good evening. We'd all enjoyed the film and James had treated us to popcorn. He was loaded James was. But he was good with it, you know. Whatever he had, he was more than happy to share with us. He was really great like that. So we all paid for tickets using our student cards, and Max bought a couple of cokes for me and him, and James bought all the popcorn. Big ones. I remember that because I was starving. I don't think I'd eaten before I came out. And Max was always hungry. Getting tall, wasn't he?

"We came out afterwards, in high spirits. James had that car off his aunt and it was quite small really. Not a huge amount of leg room in the back so Max sat in the front, and I had all of the back seat to myself. We were playing these mix tapes that James's aunt had left in the car. The new car she got played CDs I think, so James inherited the tapes as well as the car. We used to laugh about it, but we liked it too. All these tunes from the old days. I think James wanted to have a new music system fitted in it but he thought it wasn't worth it because he was hoping to get a new car when he finished his A levels. If he did well, I suppose.

"So we all piled into the car, and we were driving home. Elbury Road. Black as tar down that road, isn't it? No lights out that way. All winding and blind bends and stuff. James was singing and laughing, but he wasn't going stupid fast, and we hadn't drunk anything or taken anything.

"We got up the road, past Awlcombe. Never saw another thing coming all that time. It was quiet that night. Quite chilly I think. The road wound round and James was manoeuvring well. He was maybe a bit over the speed limit, I don't know. He was in control. Yeah, because you can see if there are cars coming when it's dark, but he knew the road, he wasn't daft, and he wasn't flooring it, 'cause well, you never know, animals and what not on the road.

"We went around that last bend and a woman walked out into the road. In fact, maybe she didn't walk out. I don't know. Maybe she was there already. She just appeared in front of us. One minute she wasn't there and the next minute she was. We all saw her at that last second. Max shouted, and James wrenched the steering wheel and screamed, and then we hit the tree hard. Really hard.

"I felt like I was floating among glass and metal for ages. As though I was in a–a cheese grater or something. I walloped this and I walloped that and I was aware of things changing … of my body changing. I was weightless and then parts of me were warm and floppy and other parts were sharp. And I just thought, *I'm a dead man. I'm a dead man.*

"And then it all stopped. And there was just a dead silence. I was lying in among all this glass, and my face was smarting. The music had gone off. I could hear bits of glass falling somewhere and something dripping. I don't know what that was.

"And Max was calling for you. He kept saying 'Mum' and 'I want my mum.' And he was crying a bit. Snuffley. I could just about make him out from where I was laying in the back.

"And I said to him, 'It's ok Max. Your mum is coming. Help will be here soon. Your mum's coming for you, buddy.'

"I heard a noise outside and I said, 'See Max. Help's coming now. They'll get us out of here.'

"I heard the door by my feet pulled open and I looked over and I swear to god, there was the most beautiful woman there I've ever seen. She was just perfect. All gorgeous dark hair and the most amazing eyes, like jewels they were. And red lips. And I started to say, 'We need help' or something and she put her hand on my thigh to lean over and look in the front.

"Well I screamed. I mean I was in agony, something was broken there. And when I screamed, Max started to cry more.

"She scanned the front and she kind of got up close to James and like, sniffed him. He wasn't moving. I couldn't see him. The coroner said he died instantly, right? Then she looked at Max, and he was crying, and she kind of smiled. My god she was beautiful.

"And then she pulled open his door and pushed him back in the seat, and she lifted his face. I could see the blood from his nose trickling down his chin you know, and she leaned over him and she kissed him. I swear. I thought she was giving him the kiss of life or something but it wasn't anything like that. She held him under the chin and lifted his face, and her lips wrapped around his mouth, and she just kind of sucked on him.

"It was grim.

"I couldn't move. I couldn't do a thing. I was hurting so much. I had little movement in my arms, and I was scared to death, and I just screamed. And then she let go of Max's chin and she turned to look at me and her face was all elongated at the mouth and her mouth was just a black cavernous hole. And I knew she was going to give me one of those kisses and …

"And then car lights were coming. She saw them, kind of squealed and backed away and then someone was there.

"Max never spoke any more. I kept calling to him, but his head was on one side, really I knew he was dead. And I know she killed him. I've never forgotten it.

"I'm sorry Heather. I'm really sorry. Are you all right?"

*

"Are you all right?" How many times had I been asked that in the past three or so years?

I was in the booth with Fraser and Euan but I was not in the booth. I'd escaped to a bubble in my head. The one that kept me sane when the world became an insane place. I had always wanted to know exactly how and why Max had died, and now I did.

Aefre had killed him. Because she could. Opportunity. The car had been driving within her hunting grounds and she had caused it to swerve off the road. She had then opened the car doors, established that James was beyond her uses, and attacked Max. No doubt Euan, immobilised in the back, could wait until last, but she had been disturbed by another arrival before she could get to him.

Euan had a lucky escape. But my darling son had not.

I put my head down on my chest and lived in the pain for a moment. Years of counselling and NLP had shown me what to do. I had to ride it out, ride that wave. Feel it. Live it.

That fucking bitch, Aefre.

I jumped up shakily, knocking the table so that my cider sploshed out of its glass. Alarmed, Fraser stood too. "Heather," he started, but I waved him away. I had to get out.

"Heather, don't leave like this. Let me call someone at least," said Fraser.

I headed for the front door, pushing by some men at the pool table, heard Fraser say to Euan, "Are you fucking crazy?" and that stopped me in my tracks. No. Euan was not crazy. The rest of us were. I turned and walked back, the pool players glowering at me.

Reaching down into the booth, I grabbed the front of Euan's jacket. It was oiled and greasy and looked as though it had never been washed. He was a mess, but he was just as much a victim of Aefre as Max and James and Bill and Mikey. He deserved my sympathy and compassion, not my anger. I

221

choked back my emotion.

"Euan. If you ever need something, you come and find me. Do you hear?" He nodded mutely, his eyes full of tears. "And Euan … those dreams …. Don't walk towards her. Don't ever let her turn around," I said.

*

And here I was in front of Max's tree once more, the bark rough beneath my fingertips, the ground soft and muddy beneath my feet. And this time I knew the truth. Knew it all. My devastation was complete. There would be no more tears for my beloved boy. I had cried them all.

Behind me, Claire, Dorothea, and even Rose were standing at the gate of White Cottage. They had been waiting for me. They had watched me as I had made this final pilgrimage to the tree, to swear on my son's life that he would be avenged.

I was a Guardian. Nothing would prevent me from hunting Aefre down. I wouldn't rest until she had been obliterated from the earth. Trent would not want me to be involved, but he would understand, and he would not try to stop me.

Somehow, someway, I would have my revenge.

TWENTY-FIVE

WINTER

The ground was soft underfoot, although it would harden overnight thanks to a sharp frost. Many of the trees were skeletal now, but still Aefre was able to blend easily into the background. She hid at the edge of the forest at twilight and watched with interest as the proceedings unfolded. Her fetid breath hung in the air, and moisture from the oak pattered on the hood of her cloak. Aefre hardly blinked.

There had been much toing and froing over recent weeks, and she understood the signs. The Guardians were plotting against her. Over the years, over the centuries, the power of the Guardians had been steadily diminished. Back in the dim past there had been dozens of them and they could be called on at any one time to guard the tree or lock it up with their charms and enchantments, potions and magick. In the early days she would never have been able to approach within one hundred yards of it, before someone would send a hex and banish her, sending her slithering into the deep forest away from their prying eyes and pathetic curses. But now as Guardian numbers steadily decreased, Aefre could spend time with the tree if she wished, touch it, rub herself against it, until a watchful Guardian sent her scurrying away.

They were a fading dynamic, and the waning of their influence would only be accelerated by the passing of time. On the other hand, as long as she was able to feed, Aefre knew that her power would continue to grow. And it wouldn't be long, perhaps a century or two, before Aefre would outlive them all. Then the enchantments and charms would disintegrate so that her access to the tree and to the sacred ground lying beneath would be unencumbered.

The Heather woman gave Aefre pause though. She had once haunted the tree like a miserable spirit and taken no interest in Aefre at all, completely unaware of her existence and incapable of searching for her. But now she was a frequent visitor to White Cottage, sometimes alone, sometimes with a man, and periodically, Aefre could sense Heather reaching out for her, searching for her. She could feel the depth of the woman's hatred. It was a hatred matched only by her own for every living being.

Aefre had always been highly intelligent, and over the centuries she had spent a huge amount of time watching people. She had learned from the fox—sly and wily. She observed the comings and goings of the Guardians, had occasionally joined them on their travels, from a distance. She'd had plenty of time to find out where they came from and what they did. On occasion when they had been sloppy about securing their property, she had entered their dwellings and stole around, rattling pots and pans and scaring their cats and dogs.

This had been an amusement for her, a way of killing time when she was prevented from killing anything else, but now as she leant against the great oak tree and considered her options, she realised that if she wanted to, she could take these golden opportunities and weaken the influence of the Guardians even more. The fewer Guardians that were left, the sooner she could assert her own authority on proceedings. Why wait a century or longer, when they were ripe for plucking now?

This Heather though? She was an unknown quantity. Aefre wondered whether it would be possible to break Heather's nerve and spirit. It shouldn't be that difficult. The woman was green and had no true powers of her own. Aefre was convinced that if anyone could break Heather, she could.

*

Solange paused at the back door of her tiny house. The views were breath-taking, overlooking the Norfolk coast, and she stared absently towards the horizon as she stretched her back and shoulders. She had lived here for over three hundred years, and she was beginning to feel her longevity. She didn't know how Kephisto, Rose, or Mercy managed to keep going.

On days like today it was her hands that ached the most. Her knuckles were hot and swollen this evening. Had Solange been a mortal human she might have recognised the signs of arthritis, but she was a witch and a long living one at that, and she didn't have time for human ailments.

Any twenty-first century outsider might have described Solange as a crazy cat lady of late middle age. She didn't mind, and in fact quite enjoyed the stereotype. It meant people kept their distance and didn't pay attention to what she did overly much, and of course, there was no denying that she did love cats—and not just black ones.

She had stepped outside to use the old garden water pump which passed as plumbing for her property. She intended to wet some clay and mix it with herbs to create a poultice to ease the pain in her hands. It was a bracing evening. The icy wind whipped around her tiny stone cottage, and through her clothes, chilling her old bones. She could hear the sea roaring angrily, beyond the cliff just twenty metres or so from where she stood. Many of the neighbouring properties had fallen into the sea over the years, thanks to accelerated coastal erosion, and locals often remarked it was a miracle hers had stayed in place. Solange sniffed. Not a miracle, but magick, and a pure and simple understanding of the power of the world around her and how to embrace the elements.

The pump was stiff, but Solange was strong and she only needed a small amount of water in the earthenware jug she held. She pumped out the vacuum until clear, icy water gushed forth. Behind her, the back door slammed, startling Solange. She tutted, glad that the cats were inside and safe. That could make for a nasty accident for one of them.

Tugging her shawl tighter around herself, Solange walked the few metres to the back door. She turned the handle, but the door was stuck. Solange placed the jug on the step and put her shoulder to the door to give it a hard, sharp shove. For a moment she thought the blasted thing was never going to give, but it sprang open and Solange tripped forwards into her scullery.

Turning back, she hefted the jug once more and closed the door, sliding the bolt easily into place. Her senses tingled slightly. Something wasn't right. The lights at the back of the house had been extinguished. Solange placed the jug on the worktop by the window and fished around for matches. She located three candles where she normally left them and lit them, before creeping through to the living area. The light from the fire was bright, and the air was strangely hot and sticky. Solange unclipped her shawl and threw it on to the back of a chair, before setting about lighting an oil lamp and another few candles. The kettle above the fire was steaming so she knocked it off the flame.

"There we are, kitties. We have light again," she sang, looking around for Bumbles and Fliss. They were her most adoring house cats, rarely venturing far beyond the back door, and her constant companions. They were nowhere to be seen. She hoped they hadn't slipped out into the stormy night. Perhaps they had been scared away by the slamming door.

Solange frowned, unhappy. She turned about, intending to check for them outside. She couldn't bear the thought of her precious cats crying at the door, neglected and half drowned, completely bedraggled by the weather. She pulled up short when the candles in the room blew out, one by one. Solange realised she was in danger, but it was too late. She had missed the warning signs: the heat of the room, the vague scent of rotting flesh and sulphur, her missing familiars—and this was her undoing.

Spotting a movement in her peripheral vision, Solange started to turn. Aefre's hand shot out as Solange rounded on her, catching her by the throat, squeezing hard enough to cut the flow of air to her brain. Solange mentally called out to Mercy and Rose, but her thoughts were disconnected before she had time to formulate a rational message for the elderly Guardians. "No," crooned Aefre. "That's not necessary."

Solange wriggled momentarily but rapidly grew limp in Aefre's iron clad grasp, the light in her eyes fading. With very little life left in Solange, she stared up as Aefre's dark dry mouth bent to hers. There were her two beloved cats, Blossom and Fliss, hanging from the ceiling rafters, their heads unnaturally bent. At the pitiful sight of her beloved familiars, death could not come fast enough for Solange.

Aefre breathed in, sucking the remnants of life from Solange's body, savouring the last drops of her pure goodness. If the Guardians all fell as quickly as this, annihilating them was going to be easier than she had expected.

*

We had gathered together at White Cottage in sombre mood. News of Solange's death in Norfolk had taken some time to reach us. There was a profound sense of shock, particularly among some of the older Guardians, that she had been taken from us with hardly a struggle and no warning that anyone could discern.

For the most part we were astounded that Aefre had wandered so far from her normal hunting grounds, but the murder had the markings of Aefre all over it. When I closed my eyes and reached for her, she was out there. The vision that came unbidden whenever I sought her presence, the coiling and uncoiling of the giant tentacles in my head, was becoming clearer day by day. The feeling of those enormous oily tentacles rubbing against each other made me shudder. The movement, once laborious, was speeding up—Aefre was excited, plotting something.

We were no closer to understanding how to destroy her. I had spent a great deal of time with Mr Kephisto, listening while he read to me from books on folklore and witchcraft. He had countless volumes of old histories, diaries, and letters from the old Guardians, but so far nothing he had uncovered among his attic archive had presented us with a logical possibility.

Trent too had been conversing tentatively with several scholars from Universities around the world. He engaged them with a hypothetical scenario, drawing them into long winded discussions about the symbolism behind any myths they recognised displaying a cultural significance that reflected

227

particularly strongly on older women in far flung communities. Trent found it interesting, as did his colleagues in Florida, Queensland, Johannesburg, and Reykjavik, but so far he had failed to come up with a way to rid the world of Aefre and her sisters, indigo paint and boo hags aside.

As a joke one evening, and a little exasperated by my pacing and bad temper, Trent had suggested that a platoon of soldiers armed with machine guns might do the job. It crossed my mind that he was right, but how did we approach the right people in the military and convince them that we weren't crackpots? I had vague recollections of the Brigadier in Doctor Who from when I was a kid. Oh to have such friends in high places.

Dawn was breaking over the horizon, pale fingers of pink and watery blue bleeding into the dark landscape, as I went to take my leave of Claire. She appeared sad, sitting alone in the kitchen, the smell of nutmeg and cinnamon fragrancing the room, her apron covered in specks of flour, her hands busy folding and unfolding a napkin in her lap. She appeared troubled and so much less sure of herself than usual. The Claire I knew was always brimming with confidence and self-assurance. "What is it?"

She sighed. "There are so few of us left." The skin around her eyes was drawn and tight. "I really fear that we are in trouble. You have to do something Heather; you have to find a way."

"I'm trying," I replied. "I really am."

But Claire was right. So far it wasn't enough.

TWENTY-SIX

AN INSTINCT

There was a thick frost outside. I shivered—partly from cold and partly from fatigue—as I tried to scrape the ice from my car windscreen. It took some time, and the sun had started to poke its forehead above the horizon, the light glowing palely pink, as I finally dropped behind the wheel and turned the heating up full blast. I drove carefully through the icy lanes, aware of how dangerous they could be, given that the gritting lorries were rarely used on these smaller B roads.

Trent's car was parked in its habitual space across the road from the house. It was odd that he hadn't left for work. I checked the time, 7.52 am. If he had any teaching at 9 he was going to struggle to get to the University on time.

I let myself into my house. Everything was quiet. "Trent?" I called but there was no reply. Pip padded softly from the living room and wagged ecstatically. I bent down to him, and he leapt away, running for the back door, in obvious need of a pee. I let him out. The grass was frozen. He didn't stay out long.

I reached for the kettle. It was cold. I frowned. Trent hadn't been down to let Pip out or make himself a cup of tea.

Unhappily I called his name again. There was nothing. No movement, no response from upstairs. A pile of his papers were piled neatly on the kitchen table along with his phone. He hadn't left the house.

My heart beat harder. There was nothing for it but to head upstairs. With deep misgivings I quickly yanked my boots off and trotted up the carpeted stairs. The landing was dark, and my bedroom door closed. Hardly daring to breathe, I pushed the door open and walked in. The room was hot and airless. I could see Trent in the bed, a large hump under the covers. Scared of what I was about to find, I climbed on to my side of bed and put my hand on his shoulder. He was warm. I breathed a sigh of relief and shook him. He jumped awake and groaned.

"Where've you been?" he mumbled.

"Do you know what time it is?"

"No," he moaned and huddled farther under the covers.

Perturbed, I hopped off the bed and pulled the curtains. Weak daylight lit the room and Trent covered his eyes. "God." For good measure I opened the window and let in some fresh air. "Are you crazy?" he demanded.

"It's late, Trent! Up and at 'em, lover boy!"

Trent pushed himself up on one elbow and scrabbled for the watch on the bedside table. "Fuck, fuck, fuck. Why did I sleep in? Where have you been? Where's my phone? I'd better phone the department."

He swung his legs out of bed but rather than leap into action, he remained sitting where he was with his head in his hands, unnaturally pale, almost grey. His eyes were ringed by dark circles and stood out stark against his skin.

"Are you sick?" I asked, handing him my phone. "You don't look great."

"I don't feel great. I feel really sluggish. I need a coffee. Please?"

"Of course." I left him to make his phone call.

*

Trent was out of sorts and generally feeling fatigued so when he opted to spend a few nights at his flat in Exeter, I didn't think it was a bad idea. I phoned him in the evenings to speak to him, but he sounded lethargic and low in energy so we didn't chat for long. I figured it was a virus that one of his undergraduates had passed on; he would rally soon enough. I missed him though and was relieved when Friday evening came and he drove down to see me. I quickly sensed however, he would rather have stayed at home. I cooked a fabulous beef bourguignon, one of his favourites, but he merely picked at it. Secretly a little put out, I gave his portion to a delighted Pip.

Sitting in front of a movie, I found myself drinking wine

by myself. Pip tried to elicit some interest from Trent for cuddles and fuss, but Trent, normally so loving, left Pip in the cold.

We went up to bed and instead of chatting and snuggling, maybe playing around for a while, tonight Trent was distinctly uninterested. When I rolled towards him, he rolled away. I lay in the dark, listening to his heavy breathing, feeling alone, and more than a little rejected.

He slept well though and appeared to have recovered the next day. We spent a few hours Christmas shopping in Abbotts Cromleigh and popped into The Lamb and Flag for a seasonal rum and coke. The only time I ever drank dark rum was at Christmas, when it always seemed spectacularly appropriate.

"Shall we get another one?" It was my round.

Trent checked his watch. "Oh, no, thanks. I'll have to get going in a bit."

"Going? Going where?" It was such an unexpected response that the bottom dropped out of my stomach. My insecurity about Trent's recent lack of interest began to seem well-founded.

"I told you. I have a work do tonight. Professor Thomas is retiring and we're all going out to give him a good send-off."

"You didn't tell me." I was hurt. I truly couldn't remember any mention of a work outing or retirement party. "Aren't partners invited?"

"Don't think so." He was being evasive and refused to look at me. I stared at him in puzzlement.

"You didn't tell me," I repeated and gathered my things together. We walked home in silence. I couldn't think of anything I wanted to say. I was being over-sensitive and more than a little needy, and I didn't want to annoy him, but I didn't know what to say to make it better. Us better.

I saw him to the door as he left. "Have a good time." I didn't really mean it and that made me feel even shittier.

"I'll speak to you soon," he said, and left me there alone, wondering how soon was soon and what he meant by such a vague non-committal phrase anyway.

*

I still had the previous night's wine to finish, but I had a feeling that half a bottle would not be enough. I popped back into town and bought myself more wine and a limp looking pizza from the supermarket.

Sitting on my sofa, watching Saturday night TV without really seeing it, I felt anxious and unhappy and worried about Trent. Unconsciously I cradled the charms from my necklace in my hand. I scrutinized our relationship. Was it stalling? And if so, why? Or was I overreacting?

Probably.

I sighed and fed Pip another crust of pizza. He wagged his tail but even he seemed half-hearted about our meagre supper. Perhaps he wanted pepperoni on his tit bits, or maybe he missed Trent as much as I did.

My phone rang as I was preparing for bed, locking everything up, tidying, and letting Pip out for his final wee. I quickly retrieved my mobile from the sofa arm and had time to glimpse Trent's name, when the ringtone stopped.

I was pleased. Trent was thinking about me. I waited a few minutes. He would call back. But twenty minutes later he still hadn't tried to, so I hit the redial button. It rang forever at his end before going to voicemail. I didn't leave a message. I sat in front of the TV with my phone in my hand wondering what to do. I was wary of bothering him if he was engaged with his colleagues. To keep trying would seem unnecessarily needy.

But something about the situation wasn't sitting right with me. I cast my mind back to summer when Sarah had tried to get in touch with me and I had failed to get back to her. I was never going to let that happen again. If I could have saved Sarah simply by talking to her when she tried to reach out to me, I would have done so. I redialled Trent's number. Again it went to voicemail and this time I didn't wait, I tried again straight away, my heart ticking nervously in time to the ringing in my ear.

The third time I rang he picked it up.

"Yes?" he said. My relief was quashed by the measure of annoyance in his voice.

"It's me," I said, although of course he already knew that.

"Yes, hello." Wherever he was it was busy and noisy. Loud music was playing behind him somewhere—a live band with an enthusiastic drummer—and I could hear laughter. Christmas laughter. Lots of inebriated people. It didn't sound much like a retirement party to me.

"You phoned me?"

"I didn't."

"I had a missed call from you."

"I haven't phoned you, but I can see that you have phoned me. Four times." I was stung. He sounded cold and distant.

"I thought you were trying to get hold of me. I was calling you back."

"Well I wasn't."

Stumped, I was quiet for a moment and decided to laugh it off. I was just about to apologise and make a joke about his mobile calling me all by itself, when I heard a high pitched cheerful giggle and a merry sounding woman flirtingly called out, "Trent! Come on!"

I stared at my phone for a moment as though it could give me the answers I suddenly needed. "Who was that?"

"Who was what?"

"Who is that with you?" The giggle came again.

"I'm with people from work."

"Baby, come on," a woman whispered huskily. I could hear her so clearly, her mouth must have been just inches from the receiver, from Trent's mouth.

"Right." I said flatly. My voice was hollow. No. Not right. Everything was wrong, wrong, wrong. That was not 'people from work' by a long stretch of the imagination.

There was a split second of silence as we both listened to each other think. Insanely furious I pressed the End Call button.

"How dare he? How fucking dare he?" I smashed my mobile on to the coffee table, sending Pip skittering from the living room in fright.

The hot flash of fury passed by in an instant and I felt contrite. I called after Pip to make it up to him. He took a bit of coaxing, but he returned to me, and I sat on the floor in the kitchen cuddling him. I was startled to find warm tears running down my cheeks. I brushed them away. I'd experienced so much pain and loss over the past few years, what was a little more? There were worse experiences in life than a relationship breakdown. Nothing lasts forever, does it? Nonetheless I clung to my scruffy dog and wept.

What will be, will be. I hadn't had many relationships in my forty odd years, but I had realised that you couldn't tether someone to you against their wishes. I didn't own Trent; he didn't own me. We had never said we were in a mutually exclusive relationship.

But letting him go? It didn't feel like it was going to be easy. Trent had grown to mean so much to me, and this betrayal seemed totally out of character for him. Nonetheless, the fact remained that he had been out with someone else and by the sound of it she was on decidedly intimate terms with him. Her husky voice replayed in my memory. I imagined her mouth close to the phone, her lips close to his.

I tidied up the living room and washed my glass and plate. The bottle of wine I hadn't got around to opening was standing on the worktop, as lonely as me. I would take myself up to bed. Tomorrow was another day. I decided I should worry about Trent and his extracurricular activities in the morning.

I was asleep as soon as my head hit the pillow.

*

I watched as they engaged in their lovers' dance. He reached out to her and cupped her head in his hand, pulling her close, his free arm wrapping around her waist. His lips found hers. Gentle kisses that became gradually more assertive and probing. I could recall the taste of those kisses, how his lips had felt against mine, moist and plump. The intimacy of his tongue in my mouth.

They explored each other with those kisses, as he and I had often done, and their movements became more fluid—loose and flowing. His hands slid down, curved around her backside, and he pulled her in towards his pelvis, encouraging her to feel the extent of his desire. She arched back slightly and popped the buttons on his shirt, pulled it open, ran her perfectly manicured fingers down the front of his chest. He had good definition, he worked out, but he wasn't buff. I loved that chest though. Loved to tickle his nipples and watch him squirm.

He lifted the skirt of her dress, slipped his fingers into the waistband of her lacy pants, tugged at them, and with one sharp movement ripped them from her. He dipped his fingers between her cheeks, probed gently downwards. She pulled away slightly. With one practiced hand she tugged at his belt, loosened it so that she could access his fly, flipped the top button, and slid down the zip. He pulled off his trousers and underpants in one swift motion.

She pushed him backwards with a wild laugh, and he fell on to the bed. Starting to rise, he reached for her and grabbed her hand. She climbed onto the bed, straddled his knees, caressed his erection with nails that were dangerously sharp. Her green eyes glinted in the dim light of his bedroom. Then she wriggled farther up the bed, guided him to her, sank down on top of him. His face was alive with lust and desire, and I watched him with an aching heart. He looked at me like that, why did he need to be with someone else? I saw her rock against him, heard his moaning, his voice thick with need.

He reached for her breasts, caressed them through the fabric of the dress she was still wearing. She brushed his hands aside and caught them in one hand, folded his arms back, casually leant so that her weight was pinning him down. He was enjoying it, thought it was all part of making love to her.

But then she hunched over, leaned in to his face, made as

235

if to kiss him. I watched her cheeks draw in and hollow out. She made sucking movements, I saw the rhythm of her throat working. His face altered. One moment he was lost in paradise and the next he realised he was in danger. His eyes opened wide in alarm. She bucked against him, and he tried to throw her off, but she was too strong.

He scanned her face, his eyes wild, squirming beneath her, trying to shake her off, but she had his mouth clamped firmly in hers, his arms secure against the sheet, and her hips pinned firmly against his pelvis. He was unable to release himself. He couldn't breathe, and she was sucking his life dry.

Terrified, I screamed for Trent and saw him try to look my way, desperate for my help, and I lunged forwards to push her off.

*

I sat up in bed with a jolt, my fingers clawing at something I couldn't see in front of me, and my throat constricted with terror. Trent's name echoed in the room around me. Chest hitching, I leaned to my right to check the time on the digital display of my radio alarm clock. It was only 12.40 am and I had already been having a nightmare. It was going to be a long night.

I took a deep breath and held it in until I felt the panic begin to subside.

"It's ok," I said out loud and lay down once more. My heart sank as I remembered the conversation I had shared with Trent earlier in the evening. That's why I had been dreaming about him with another woman.

Aefre.

Aefre?

I pushed myself up again. What if it wasn't a dream? What if the woman Trent was with was indeed Aefre? She and I had a strange connection, not one I particularly sought out, but it was there nonetheless. Did she want to get at me through Trent? My head thumped for a moment as I tried to think.

Fraser had said how beautiful the woman who had chosen

Mikey had been. Bill had mentioned the desirable Mrs Adams. Aefre was ancient, haggard, and leathery. I had seen her with her skin as dry and powdery as a long dead corpse, but it was well within her power to assume the visage of the most tantalising of women. She liked to draw men to her, moths to the flame, lambs to the slaughter.

I remembered too, the spirits on the hill, the night that the pentagram had saved my life, and the way the woman had grabbed at Trent in a frenzy.

I threw back the covers, uncertain what to do. The charms on my necklace were glowing brightly in the dim light. Did that mean something? I could call Trent. He would think I was insane phoning him at this time of night, especially after our conversation just a few hours before. That had not ended well. Perhaps he would accuse me of being too needy and jealous. But if he was really in danger, I should try and help him. I threw on a t-shirt and some jogging bottoms and grabbed a pair of socks from the drawer before dashing downstairs.

In the kitchen I switched the lights on, blinking in the sudden glare, before locating my phone on the table. I picked it up and turned it round, meaning to thumb through to the call screen and access my saved numbers, but the screen was smashed and when I tried to get it to work it made a strange zzzz noise. I threw it back onto the table and dashed back into the hall to use the house phone. Pip came to the living room door and stared at me in surprise.

I lifted the receiver and quickly dialled Trent's mobile number from memory. It rang and rang before going to voicemail. I hung up, waited a second, and tried again. Same result. I didn't know Trent's home phone number from memory and had to locate it from among various scribblings on a notepad. I rang his flat. No answer. I tried again.

"Come on, come on, come on." Nothing.

"What time is it?" I asked myself moving back into the kitchen. 12.53 am. He could be at a club with his work colleagues. He could be having a good time. I was working myself up into a tizzy for nothing.

But he could be with Aefre. It was perfectly feasible that he had arrived home by now. In fact, it might already be too late.

I grabbed my socks and hopped around the kitchen while I put them on. I located my trainers near the back door.

"Back soon." I scratched Pip's head and picked up my car keys and jacket, unbolted the front door, and stepped outside.

It was bitter cold. Locking up the house, my fingers already clumsy and my breath steaming in the night air, I wondered again what Trent would say when he found out I had gone to these lengths because of a dream. I was driving to Exeter on the off chance. If he had decided he wanted nothing more to do with me, I was risking looking a complete fool. And we would be finished forever; I knew that.

The windows of the car had already frosted over in the frigid air. I started the engine, mindful of my neighbours, and let it idle while I frantically scraped the ice away. My breath was coming in quick gasps. I had to calm down. It was a fair way to Exeter, and I needed to drive carefully.

I tried to take it easy on the roads out of Abbotts Cromleigh. The thirty speed limit applied of course, and although I was unlikely to be picked up for speeding this far out in the sticks at this time of night, I didn't want to run the risk of skidding on the roads on black ice or around some of the tight bends. The roads corkscrewed out of Abbotts Cromleigh for three miles before I was finally on the main drag that would take me directly to the city.

Once I had joined the dual carriageway, I floored the accelerator in relief. The image of Aefre hunched over Trent was replaying on a loop in my mind. The road was pitch black most of the way into Exeter, no street lights until I neared the airport and motorway, but I had company. There were plenty of boy racers out and about. I kept my wits about me and drove as quickly and as safely as I could. My heart hammering in my chest the whole time.

Finally, I approached Exeter and joined the ring road. It

was simplest to skirt the city for a way and then head into the centre. Trent lived less than a mile from his department at the University, in a ground floor flat, a handsome converted Victorian house with an enormous bay window in the front. The road outside his house was quiet, and I stole a glance at his windows as I passed. There were lights on. At this time of night parking was difficult, and in the end I parked illegally on double yellow lines.

I remained sitting in the car for a moment, breathless. Was this the right thing to be doing? The pentagram tingled against my skin under my t-shirt. Aefre. I ran to Trent's flat, panting with exertion and fear, and up the path to the thick, white door. I tried to peer through his window to the side of me. The curtains were drawn but there was a slight chink. There was nothing to see.

I tapped on the window gingerly. I was shaking. Partly with cold, partly with the fear that he would be angry with me, but mostly with a rising sense of foreboding that he was in trouble. Of course there was no response, no stirring of the curtains. I tapped harder, but again there was nothing. I had no options left, I would have to ring the bell to his flat and hope I wouldn't disturb anyone else.

I was just about to lean on the bell when I heard a noise behind me. Startled I turned around, ready to lash out at any oncoming threat but it was just the couple who lived on the top floor. She was looking more than a little wasted, wearing a faux fur jacket and a very short skirt. She was clutching an open bottle of champagne. "Hey!" she said brightly. I couldn't remember her name.

"Hi," I said with some relief. "I was just visiting Trent …"

"Has he locked you out?" asked the woman's partner while she giggled. "Silly sod."

"He may be asleep, I guess."

"Likely. Hang on." He dug his keys out and opened the door. The hallway light came on automatically, on a timer that gave them enough time to climb to the second floor. We walked in, and I closed the door behind us, hoping they would go upstairs quickly so that they didn't witness my humiliation when Trent opened the door and confronted my presence with anger.

I flashed them a sheepish smile. "I certainly hope he's in."

"If he isn't, use his spare key." The woman nodded at Trent's door. "He keeps it on top of the door frame. We see it every time we come downstairs."

"Of course!" I said, although I hadn't known this. What sort of an idiot keeps their spare key where everyone can find it? I waved my fingers at the pair as they started to climb the stairs, with him supporting her as she wobbled unevenly, and then turned back to Trent's door. I put my ear against it. There was nothing to hear, but it was in any case a thick door. I knocked. Harder than I had tapped at the window. From upstairs I could hear giggling and a clunk as a bottle knocked into a wall on the next landing. They were still negotiating the stairs. I waited a few seconds, but there was no response to my knocking. The pentagram was hot under my t-shirt. I had to do this now.

I reached above the door frame, praying that the key was there among the dust and dead flies. It was. I hooked it down, rubbed it against my sleeve, and inserted it into the lock. It turned easily. I pushed the door away from myself and stepped inside.

The lounge door was open and a side light was on in there. I could see Trent's deep grey sofa, his books scattered on the floor and piled high on bookcases around the room. I poked my head in the room but there was no-one there. I started to walk down the hall to his closed bedroom door, fearful that I was going to find him in bed with another woman—the young and attractive research student I had always dreaded he would meet—when I noticed the smell.

It was a sulphurous smell, with the faint tang of rotten meat. Either Trent had let his freezer defrost or Aefre was in the building. I recognised that scent from the night in my house when the kitchen window had kept popping open. Oh yes she was here.

I stopped dead in my tracks. A green mist curled in tiny puffs from the gap at the bottom of the bedroom door. She was in there with him. My stomach rolled with a sudden combination of fear and fury.

There was no time to think. I rushed at Trent's door. It was locked. With a howl of rage, I did what I had seen all the heroes on television do an infinite number of times. I put my shoulder to the door and ran at it. Once, twice, and with a burst of strength that surprised me I forced the door open and fell through, onto my knees on the carpet of Trent's bedroom, jarring my wrists as I put my hands out to save myself.

The bedside lights were on in here, perhaps Trent had wanted to set the mood, but the light was a bizarre eerie green and that awful smell was stronger than ever. Rotting meat. And there they were—just as I'd seen them in my dream. Aefre with her back to me. Her long dark hair flowing down her back. Her skirt hiked up around her shapely thighs, straddling Trent who was lying on the bed, eyes only for her. Aefre had his hands above his head, pinned to the bed. Trent lifted his head to kiss her, oblivious of my abrupt entrance.

"Trent!" I screamed, scrambling to my feet, but he paid me no heed. "Don't kiss that bitch!"

Aefre glanced my way and for a second I was stunned into stillness, mesmerised by her flawless beauty. Her skin was creamy, and her plump lips a luscious wet red; her emerald eyes were glowing with life and vitality. She smiled an inviting half-smile at me that warmed me to my core—then turned back to Trent, bending her head to meet his lips.

This was her power. She was disarmingly good-looking, and she could lull you into a warm sense of security. I shook myself. There was no time to lose. I had to separate her from Trent. The closest weapon to hand was a heavy pile of academic books. I picked them up and flung them at Aefre one by one. She lifted her head again, snarling at me. Her lips pulled back from perfectly white teeth, but her mouth was a black hollow now and her eyes flamed a brighter green. She didn't climb off Trent.

I hefted a solid tome from the floor and ran at her, hitting her as hard as I could. She lifted the one arm that wasn't holding Trent down against the bed, to ward off my attack, and then lashed out at me. She was incredibly strong. The force of her hand colliding with my arm knocked me backwards. I ran at her again, trying to grab hold of her and pull her from Trent, but it was like running into a brick wall. She waved me effortlessly away, and I bounced backwards, hitting the sturdy Victorian wall behind me with an almighty wallop.

Trent started coming around from whatever enchantment Aefre had him under. He was looking warily up at her and started fighting to free his hands. Aefre turned her attention back to him. I struggled to my feet and hurriedly searched for something else to attack Aefre with. The bedside light. An Ikea special. I yanked it from the wall and hefted it high before swinging it as hard as I could.

"You fucking bitch!" I screamed as I made firm contact. I swung it again. "Get off him!"

This time I hit my mark well. Aefre snapped at me but tumbled off the bed and landed with a thump on the other side. She lay dazed for a moment, then turned gracefully around onto her front. She wriggled a little and with a grotesque slithering sound she elongated in shape in front of me. In disgust, I moved around to her side of the bed, the standard lamp in my hands, ready to hit her again. To pummel her brains out if I could.

Aefre shrank in front of me. Green dust exploded from her as she moved. Repulsed, I backed away. In horrified fascination I watched as she slid along the floor, more snake than woman before she shot past me, showering me in dead skin and dried moss, into the hall beyond and out of the flat's front door. There was a final clang from the letter box and a puff of green smoke in the hallway, and she was gone.

I jogged down the hall out into the communal entrance way. The front door was locked from this side. Everything was calm and still and the smoke and smell were dissipating.

I closed Trent's door firmly, dead bolting it and snapping the chain into place, before walking back into his bedroom. I suddenly felt exhausted. I dropped his lamp to the floor and moved to where he was lying. He lay naked and pale against the sheets. His passion had ebbed away, but the slick signs of their union remained smeared against his thighs. He appeared disoriented and confused. His face grey with exhaustion.

"How long has she been visiting you?" I asked, and he shook his head, unsure or unable to speak. I wasn't sure which.

He pulled himself up into a sitting position and cradled his head. I reached for him, but suddenly he jumped up.

"I think I'm going to throw up," he announced.

I helped him to the bathroom and turned the light on. Leaving him to it with the door ajar, I moved into the kitchen and set about making some tea. A few minutes later I heard the shower running. I checked on him. Trent was ok. I could see him in the shower stall, beyond the dappled glass bowed beneath the stream of hot water, his head tipped back and his mouth open as though he was trying to fill himself up and sanitise his insides with the pure, clean water.

Steam filled the room. I regarded the small bathroom window. There was no chance in hell I was opening that up.

*

Trent remained in the shower for a long time. Eventually he came to find me in the living room, wrapped in his thick dressing gown, his hair damp and his skin scrubbed pink, thick black circles under his eyes. I handed him a mug of tea, and we sat together on the sofa, side by side. Silent with unspoken misery.

"I'm really sick," he said, and I smiled. It reminded me of something Max might have said when he was trying to elicit some sympathy for a plight he had found himself in. I said nothing at first.

Eventually I squeezed his knee. "The boo hag got ya," I said, my voice so soft and sad I wasn't sure he had heard me, but beside me, Trent nodded. He set his mug down and took

243

my hand. "I'm sorry."

"Don't be."

"I wasn't really aware of what was happening."

"No?" On the one hand this sounded entirely plausible, and yet I wondered how he could have been so gullible. The part of me that was fighting Aefre knew she was devious, but the part of me that was Trent's lover felt horribly betrayed. There was silence between us again until he sighed. I relented.

"What happened?"

Trent shook his head. His fingers felt cold in mine and the skin was drawn and white. I squeezed his hand, trying to bring the colour back. Trent's skin reminded me of how white Max had been in the morgue. But I had lost Max, and I didn't intend to lose Trent too.

"I've been having these dreams. Having nightmares. In the morning I can't quite remember what they're about. And all week I've been thinking that I've got the flu. But then tonight … I … it was … I knew I had a date. That I was going to meet someone. And I turned up to the party, and she was there. I don't think I spent any time with my colleagues. I don't remember doing so."

"You were drinking?" I'd seen Trent's car on the road outside.

"Yes. I was. We were. Maybe I was drunk."

"What do you remember about her?"

"She came out of nowhere, materialised beside me at the bar. Asked me a question. I turned and … with just one glance … I don't remember anything else. She was mesmerising. Beautiful. Her eyes, her hair … her body. And she only had eyes for me. I was enraptured. When she touched me," he laughed without humour, "it was like fireworks going off inside me."

I ran a finger down the hand I was holding. I didn't do that for him? Fireworks didn't go off when I touched him?

"And then nothing … until I felt like I was awakening into a nightmare. My first thought was the flat was on fire, and you were calling my name, and she—that thing—was on top of me. My limbs were so heavy. I couldn't move."

I smoothed the skin carefully around his wrist. I could see bruising, faint finger marks where she had held him down.

"I couldn't get her off me and there you were. My Heather to the rescue. You were so fierce, so brave." He looked at me in wonder.

"I was angry," I said. "But I was scared."

"But you came and you fought her off."

Yes, I had. My dream tonight had been a premonition. I was glad I had listened to my instinct. Trent could have been dead by now, and tomorrow a stranger would have notified me of his death, in mysterious and inexplicable circumstances.

"How did you know?" he asked.

"I didn't. Not for sure. I had a dream tonight. I thought I was being crazy. That maybe you didn't want to be with me. When I spoke to you on the phone, you seemed so distant."

"When?"

"You don't remember that? Around eleven-ish?"

Trent shook his head, confused.

"I had a missed call and rang you back, and I heard you with a woman. You were behaving very oddly. And then I had the dream—you were with Aefre. When I woke up, the pentagram was glowing." I felt for the charms. Cradled them there safely. "I had to come and find you. Just in case."

Trent put his hand on top of mine for a moment and then leant forward and lifted my chin so that I was looking at him. His eyes bore into mine.

"Thank you," he said. "You're the bravest woman I know, Heather. And I love you."

"You do?"

"With all my heart and soul."

"I don't set off fireworks in you the way that Aefre did though."

"You set off cannonballs. You complete me. I want to spend my life with you." He brushed my lips with his. He smelled of toothpaste and shampoo.

"I'm not sure we can ever be safe with Aefre around."

245

"Then let's find her and put a stop to this. Once and for all. And then let's get on with the rest of our lives."

*

Aefre shifted shape, a woman once more, but in her crone form, clad in a long black cloak with a face lined and pitted with extreme age. Hatred etched her face, her luminescent eyes, sunk into the hollows of her skull, glowed dimly and sickly green in the full darkness of the early hours. She watched from the other side of the window, feet away from Heather and Trent entwined on the sofa, whispering their sweet nothings to each other. Vows of loyalty and love. Pointless, trivial murmurings from insignificant weaklings. Loathsome.

Aefre observed them through the tiny chink in the curtain. Watched him as he said the words that would placate her, make her bow to him, do his bidding. Foolish, weak-minded wench that she was.

And yet, they had seen her off tonight.

Heather. Always interfering. It stung that Aefre could not be rid of her as easily as she wished. She would need to force the issue. Take out a few more Guardians. Once their numbers had been decimated, Heather would not pose such a threat.

She waited at the window, glaring in at them, steaming the outside of the glass with her fetid breath. She watched them until they fell asleep on the sofa, wrapped up in a quilt from the bedroom, their easy intimacy an irritation and an insult. The pentagram around the woman's neck glowed softly in the darkness, but Heather didn't notice it.

Such a fool.

As the dawn crept across the horizon, Aefre stole away, intent on destruction elsewhere, and oblivious to the startled stares of early morning delivery drivers.

The Guardians. She would make sure she hurt them all.

TWENTY-SEVEN

THE BEGINNING OF THE END

Mercy lived a simple life. She had inhabited the same tiny cottage in Somerset for centuries, moving in after it had been left deserted during a time of plague. Nobody noticed her then, and even now, her dwelling was remote enough that she had few neighbours, and none of those ever stayed long enough to realise she would outlive them all. In these days of increased mobility and fractured community, who can be certain who their neighbours are anyway? Mercy felt safe in her anonymity.

Nestled in the warmth of her living room, Mercy swayed gently in her hand-carved rocking chair and reflected on her life. It had been both a blessing and a curse to live this long. Before Aefre and her sisters had threatened the existence of Cromleigh, the young Mercey had lived a good and quiet life with her man, Alfwald and their son, whom she had adored. She had been a healing woman, much respected by her neighbours. Her mother and sister were also known as wise women in her community. It was a tradition handed down from mother to daughter, much as property passed between father and son.

The pain of the passing of her loved ones had been something she had lived with for a long, long time. She had grown older, yes, but at a much slower rate than her contemporaries. She had known hundreds of people over the years, dozens of Guardians, but had grown close to few. For a while she had taken lovers, but they too rapidly grew old while she did not, and it became unbearable to watch them wither and fail. Many good people had joined her for part of her journey as a Guardian, but in time she had seen them all fall by the wayside. Each of them had been a blessing, in a life that at times seemed cursed.

The Guardians became her only source of friendship over the years, but since Claire's birth there had been no-one new to join their ranks. The Guardians were a dying breed. There were just the three original Guardians now, Kephisto, Rose, and herself, and while their twilight was growing dim, Mercy understood that her own hours were numbered. Aefre was coming for her. All Mercy could do was wait for her to show.

She had considered summoning the Guardians and enlisting their help. Together they were still powerful enough to fight Aefre off, and she knew her friends would be in parts angry and in parts hurt that she had not called for them, but as she had meditated on what would be and what the future would hold for the Guardians, and in time, a world without them, she had seen clearly that there was no point fighting this particular battle anymore.

She had given her all, and then some. There would be a change now. Her death would be a catalyst for that change.

She remembered standing among the healers, the wise women, the witches, and the wizards in Cromleigh all that time ago. She saw once again the fires, blazing merrily under dark skies; smelt the wood smoke, and the damp moss, and the scent of animals that milled around them. She remembered how she had wanted to put herself forward to protect her village and neighbouring settlements from harm. She had discussed this at length with Alfwald. He had been against it, in spite of his own status as a wise man. Perhaps she had been naïve, she had certainly not realised what a huge task she would be taking on, not understood that it would be hundreds of years before she would be free of the burden. Alfwald had foreseen this and even now the memory of the pain in his eyes when she made her vow to the Guardians was one that could move her to tears.

And so her loved ones had grown old and died, as had their children, and their children after them until Mercy had been all but forgotten by her descendants. But it had not all been a burden. She had welcomed every spring when it arrived in March or April, stood agog as the countryside had burst into life around her and had never tired of the abundance of beauty and life that blossomed annually without fail in her small piece of the West Country.

For many centuries the Guardians had protected Cromleigh and enabled it to grow into a vibrant and healthy community and town. Yes, from time to time Aefre had appeared, but they had been quick to put her down and send her scurrying back to her pit in the forest. Now the time was perfect to make a final stand, but Mercy knew she would not be a part of it.

A log in the grate sputtered. The fire was dying down. Mercy had no intention of adding more fuel to the flames. It would be a waste. Her time was up. She shifted her attention to the front door. Waited. There was a slight noise outside, a scratching. Aefre had arrived.

"The door is open," Mercy said pleasantly. Calmly.

The latch lifted and Aefre walked in, her black cloak swirling around her, the hood covering her face. An icy blast of air filled the room and Mercy shivered but remained seated. The outside was framed through the open doorway—skeletal trees and white sky, a promise of snow—and Mercy gazed wistfully at that picture for a moment, yearning for Spring and rebirth. Perhaps she would have preferred to die outside, where the ancients could look down on her. But this was no time for regrets.

"We meet again, Aefre."

Aefre shrugged back the hood of her cloak, her weary eyes taking in Mercy and her surroundings. In turn, Mercy regarded Aefre with distaste; the leathery skin, the dry flaking lips and rotting teeth, the hair like straw. She stank too. Mercy thought longingly of the fresh air beyond the door. By walking into her cottage, Aefre had corrupted her space.

Aefre cocked her head to one side. "You wait for me?" she drawled, her voice dry and contemptuous.

"I knew you were coming. I won't fight you." Mercy lifted her hands from her lap, showed Aefre her empty palms.

Aefre studied Mercy with interest. "You haven't called the others here?"

"No. There was no need." Mercy folded her hands in her

lap.

Aefre sneered. Her lips drawing back against her teeth, green with infection and black with decay. "Is this some sort of elaborate final sacrifice? Because if it is, it won't make a difference to the outcome. I intend to destroy the Guardians and reunite with my sisters, sooner rather than later."

"And what then?"

"We'll take what we want," Aefre's voice was thick and throaty with greed.

"You have slept for too long these past millennia. The world is altered. You have no idea of the scale of the changes. Cromleigh is a different place; England is a different place. There are millions and millions of people who will seek to destroy you."

"We will take pleasure in unleashing our own horror upon them."

"There are armies of a size you cannot imagine."

"These legions are nothing. We will fight against them as we did before."

"You were brutal, Aefre. You and your sisters. But these armies, they have weapons that can incinerate you where you stand."

"They will have to find us first!" Aefre stepped forward, her face contorted with fury. "These are idle threats. There is nothing that can prevent us from taking what we want. We will destroy all of you—all of your self-proclaimed Guardians—and then anyone that gets in our way. But our success is not something that need concern you."

Mercy rose. "Are you not tired of all this? Tired of being half dead and half alive. Tired of fighting? Don't you yearn for those happy days when you would dance in the forest? When life was a celebration? Why did you suddenly decide to change it all?"

"Hush," Aefre hissed through clenched teeth.

"But remember …"

Aefre shrieked in fury, her eyes growing more animated, her face glowing with hatred. "I don't want to remember!"

"If—"

"Quiet!" thundered Aefre and struck out with one hand. Mercy saw the fist coming for her, but barely had time to blink. Aefre hit Mercy squarely on the jaw, and her head flew backwards, colliding with the mantelpiece. There was a sharp crack in the sudden silence and Mercy crumpled to the floor.

*

Aefre stared down at the untidy body in front of her, felt the rage building inside, under pressure, ready to rip free in a head of steam. She had fully intended Mercy should have a slow and painful death, to go part way towards avenging herself for the trouble the Guardians had caused Aefre and her sisters over the years. Fate, such a fickle beast, had intervened.

Aefre screamed in anger and frustration and kicked at the body. Mercy didn't move. Cursing, Aefre bent down and grabbed Mercy's ankle, then dragged her outside.

A few flakes of snow fell, settling on Mercy's lashes, her sunken eyes gazing sightlessly at the milky sky above. Aefre took her knife from her cloak, carelessly opened what remained of Mercy's jaw and hooked the tongue, slicing it off.

"No more lies," she hissed.

One ancient adversary, gone for good. It was satisfying. She sniffed the air, turned to face the south west. She could sense someone, somewhere reaching out for her again, wanting to know where she was, what she was doing.

Heather.

Aefre scowled, her dry lips shedding skin as she pulled them back in distaste. She needed to finish the Guardians off. All of them, and once and for all. She had made a good start. She should continue her good work.

TWENTY-EIGHT

IN LIMBO

I was sitting in Rose's overwarm parlour, staring out at the snow that danced past the window. Each flake, light and weightless, floated in the air for a fraction of time, before being boosted by the wind, and caught up, was moved elsewhere. This snow wouldn't settle here. Not today. Elsewhere, the country was knee deep in drifts, and public transport had ground to a halt, but proximity to the coast kept the worst of the weather away from Elbury and Abbotts Cromleigh.

The Guardians were mourning the passing of one of their own, for the second time in as many weeks. Heather had not imagined there would be tears; there had been few for Solange, but Mercy had been much loved and as the elder of the Guardians, she had been the source of their combined wisdom and power. Hers was a grave loss for the Guardians.

But Rose was having none of it. "There's no time for wailing and weeping," she scolded. "Don't you think Mercy would have known that Aefre was coming for her."

"Of course she would have," answered Dorothea, her mother's daughter, practical and stoic.

Claire's eyes were rimmed with red. "Well why not call on us then?" she demanded. "Solange may not have been gifted the power of foresight, but Mercy certainly had it. She would have known. She should have called to us."

"What could we have done?" Dorothea replied. "We could not have gone charging off to Somerset and left the oak unguarded."

"More than that," intoned Rose in a low voice, "you have to assume that Mercy knew. Given that she knew but did not send word, why did she choose not to do so?"

There was a general mumbling around the room. Looking out at the snow, I could clearly see Mercy in her rocking chair in her small remote cottage, could see her sitting with her hands in her lap, patiently waiting for Aefre to arrive. The fire was burning low, but Mercy saw no need to bank it. She would have no need of warmth where she was going.

"She knew Aefre was coming. She was completely calm. Welcomed the end because …" I stopped, aware of my own strange voice and the words I was speaking. The images of Mercy were clear and immediate in my mind, as though I was seeing the room with an observer's eyes.

"Because?" Rose prompted gently.

"It was an end, but it is a beginning too." I shook my head, unsure of what I meant, of what Mercy had meant. "She thought that she had done all she could. She thought her death would be a catalyst to the change that must come."

"What change?" asked Claire, but Rose held a hand up.

"The Guardians have done all they can and—" I started in surprise. "Heather. Me? She was thinking of me. She knew I would finish it." I glanced at Rose, woeful, images of Mercy slipping away, panic settling in their place. "But I don't know how. I still don't know how to stop Aefre. I feel no closer to knowing what to do than ever."

Rose nodded knowingly, as though she had been aware of all I had said before I spoke the words. "When the time is right, you will know it, and if Mercy said you will destroy Aefre, you will do that too. Yes, the Guardianship will come to an end, this was always our destiny, but we will have handed over to you."

I returned my gaze to the window and the swirling snowflakes outside. I thought again of Mercy. I felt her loss deeply. She had been a remarkable woman. She had trusted me to carry on her work and I couldn't let her down, but how was I going to rid the world of Aefre? It was a battle that seemed beyond me.

*

Clear skies made for a bitterly cold afternoon but the Christmas lights decorating the town gave me a lift. The red and green of the lights transported me back to Christmases a long time ago when I had helped my mother dress our tree and we had covered the house in tinsel. Even my father had relaxed a little on the few days he was able to take as leave from work.

And then there had been the best Christmases of all when Max was young and my mum was still alive. Max made a rather butch looking angel for the tree in kindergarten when he was four and from then on we had organised our own ceremony every year to dust off the decorations and hang them around the house. My mum and I would drink a little sherry, and we all sang along to cheesy Christmas songs. Max would top the tree with the angel while we all basked in seasonal warmth and well-being.

Christmas had been tough since then, but this year I would be able to celebrate quietly with Trent and Pip, and for that I was profoundly grateful. He had recovered from his ordeal with Aefre and had moved more of his belongings over to my house. He refused to use Max's bedroom as a study, so he was squatting in the lounge, but we were determined that neither of us should be alone overnight again. Aefre was too dangerous, too sly and unpredictable, and I was convinced she wanted to sink her claws into Trent, to kill him as a means of getting at me.

As if it wasn't enough that she had already stolen my son from me.

The coldness I felt inside whenever I thought about Aefre as my son's murderess, wasn't down to the seasonal weather. There had to be a way to rid the world of her. I needed to find it.

I mooched along the high street, looking in windows but not really seeing much, until I found myself outside a gift shop at the bottom of town. I needed a few small presents for clients and fancied something more original than wine this year. I peered through the window at the displays beyond. The shop appeared warm and inviting, glowing with seasonal cheer. A couple of older women were standing at the counter chatting with the assistant. It was worth a look.

As I entered, the women at the counter turned, fear lit

their faces momentarily before the shop assistant smiled and said, "Good afternoon." The looks dissipated rapidly enough but I was slightly taken aback. They had all been talking so earnestly.

I wandered around the shop tentatively, half an ear on the conversation, but whatever they had been discussing had been dropped. Instead they thanked the woman at the counter for her help and left. I watched them go and then turned to the shop assistant, hoping that she would let me in on the secret, but she just smiled and said, "Bless," leaving me none the wiser.

My next stop was a chemist where I bought some odds and ends for Trent's stocking, most notably a rubber duck in a Santa costume that I figured would amuse him. As I queued to pay, I noticed a man leaning heavily on his walking stick, waiting to collect his prescription, staring out of the window and frowning. I followed his gaze. Nothing to see. Whatever was causing him consternation was locked away in his head.

I paid for my goods and stepped back outside into the chill. Looking up and down the street, I spotted a number of older people looking unnerved or unhappy. Even in the coffee shop, there were several older couples, and two small groups of pensioners who caught my attention. Anxiety was etched across their faces, as they whispered together. Something felt off in Abbotts Cromleigh.

I abandoned the idea of doing any more Christmas shopping. I picked up a take away cappuccino and headed for the bookshop. Perhaps Mr Kephisto could offer some illumination on the feeling of unease that pervaded the town this bleak winter's afternoon.

*

"It really seems to only be affecting the elderly," I explained to Mr Kephisto who was shelving some books in the horror fiction section of the shop.

Mr Kephisto peered over the top of his spectacles at me and pursed his lips. "They're not elderly," he muttered.

255

"They're practically kids."

Upstairs I heard the crow squawk as if in sudden hilarity.

"Seriously," I started but the old man shook his head and indicated upstairs. I heard the lock thunk closed on the front door of the shop. "You don't have to close if you don't want to," I said. "If you'd rather be trading? Especially with Christmas coming."

"My dear, I don't run this shop for the money." He led the way to the stairs, and I followed him. He was agile up the rickety staircase, me less so.

"Have you always lived here above this bookshop?"

"I've lived on this site for a very long time. I was always the repository for any knowledge the Guardians accrued, that much is true at least. That was the role allotted to me, way back at the beginning. But remember, I was here in Abbotts Cromleigh for many years before the printing press was introduced. Initially I simply held all the parchment and relics, and the sacred and profane objects that the Guardians wished to keep safe. In the seventeenth century I opened a book shop to the public downstairs. It was a useful front for the Guardians' activities after all. In those days we used to meet here, but so many women coming in and out of a bookshop has at times been suspect, certainly, and eventually we moved the meetings to White Cottage."

We reached the top floor where Mr Kephisto had his parlour these days. The wood burner glowed brightly, always aflame. I was panting slightly, but Mr Kephisto hardly noticed the haul up the stairs.

He gestured grandly at all the books displayed in this room. "This is the centre of all the knowledge we Guardians possess. There are a few pamphlets here written by Mercy several hundred years ago, and there are documents dating back a thousand years or more, written by the wise men among the Guardians, those who could write anyway. We also have a strong tradition of truth telling and story keeping. This too has been handed down from Guardian to Guardian and I have recorded it all, in writing, in case one day it can be of assistance."

When I had visited previously, perhaps I hadn't considered the urgency and the weightiness of the task ahead of me. I hadn't been committed. Now I examined the room with new eyes. This was the legacy that the Guardians were handing on to me. There were hundreds and hundreds, if not multiple thousands of books in the room, all neatly shelved and well dusted. Their spines showed signs of age and yet the gold lettering shone out at me, glinting in the firelight. Hidden here somewhere, I knew there was something I could use to hit back at Aefre.

One slim volume caught my eye. The lettering luminesced with an intense energy, seeming to draw me to it. I examined it closely. The green leather was thick and hard and the gold letters on the spine bore the legend *Carmichael Vol: XXIV*.

"Carmichael?" I asked thinking of the curmudgeonly Guardian I had often seen at White Cottage.

"Ha. Not the one you're thinking of but his grandfather. He enjoyed a great longevity—maybe three hundred or so years from 1389. He lived in a hide in the Blackdown Hills as a virtual recluse most of the time. Had a fondness for botany. He would come and visit me every so often and tell me things he had found out or considered. He liked to run experiments with plants, or just sit in a clearing in the forest and observe life around him."

I pulled the volume down from the shelf and opened it. It was written in a close neat scrawl that I barely found legible. There were diagrams inserted here and there. Plants cut through the middle. Sections of tree. They were beautifully observed pen and ink drawings—the colour as vital as it had been the day they were created.

"The pictures were Carmichael's. He gave them to me to keep safe for him and instructed me to store them with my notes. There's no doubt he was a talented man, and a man out of time." Mr Kephisto smiled fondly at the memory and took the book off me and guided me to his sofa. "So you've come to ask me about the older people in the community."

"Is it just my imagination then?" I felt a little silly.

But Mr Kephisto shook his head. "No. Not really. I don't think anyone in town can articulate their unconscious fears, but there's no doubt that things are amiss. Abbotts Cromleigh is altered. Aefre has grown strong. She walks, and when she walks, chaos reigns. The older people can sense her presence. I believe there may be a deep-rooted social memory among many people here. The fear is handed down from generation to generation."

"But it only seems to be affecting the older people," I replied.

"Perhaps they're the only ones who are making conscious what is unconscious."

I thought about this. It seemed fair. Young people have busy lives, more to fit in to their day—their jobs, families, etc. Perhaps we all live with a certain amount of social anxiety, these days.

"I suppose they have experienced the most exposure to Aefre too." I thought of Bill Tuckman. There were still people in the community who would have known Mrs Adams.

"Indeed. That may be part of it."

I slumped down on the sofa and exhaled in despair.

"There has to be a way. Some way to destroy Aefre. Why haven't we found it yet? There's all this information," I waved my hands at the books and boxes that were lining the room. "All of this—that you have held on to all of these years— precisely so that we can find an answer. And yet we've drawn a blank. Why can't we just mow her down with a tank or something?"

"Because what's to say that she'll stay dead?" I regarded Mr Kephisto uneasily. "Maybe she'll drag herself back to the hell hole she lives in and recuperate for a hundred years or so. She's done that before. And then she'll bide her time until the Guardians are so weak that she can easily pick them off and reign supreme."

"She's been killed before?" I perked up.

"Yes. In 1652 Aefre was hung as a witch. The wife of a

man she was trying to seduce in her own inimitable style, I'm sure you know what I mean my dear, caught her at it. The wife screamed blue murder and her sons managed to catch Aefre before she could do much damage to any of them. She was tried at Exeter Assizes, found guilty of course, and hung along with another two women accused of witchcraft. They cut the bodies down and buried them in unconsecrated ground, but the very next day they discovered that Aefre had been dug up. We Guardians knew that she had never really died, of course. After all, she hasn't been properly alive for over 1500 years. That's why she has very little to fear from lesser mortals."

I slumped again and scratched my head.

"The Guardians were less fortunate. We lost a great number of our fellowship during those years of superstition and suspicion. That was the start of our great decline, and it's the main reason there are so few of us left today."

"And now Aefre is finishing off what was started then," I said. "Poor Mercy. And Solange." I shook my head, troubled. "You must be careful, Mr Kephisto."

"Oh she's bound to come after both me and Rose. Sooner rather than later. We are the final original Guardians." He sounded proud, and while I despaired that he was being so cavalier about the situation we found ourselves in, I was amused by his bravado, dressed in his leaf green suit and surrounded by leather clad volumes—his lifetime's work. And what a lifetime it had been.

I studied the wall of books and parchments again. "There must be something in amongst all this that can offer us some sort of insight into what we can do next, surely?"

"I'm still reading though it all, my dear. You know I am."

I did know he was, but I wanted him to do it faster. It was an enormous job, and he alone could do it. There were no apparent shortcuts. "There's nothing you can remember?"

"From everything everyone has said to me for the past 1500 years? No I'm afraid if anyone has told me how to destroy our least favourite crone, it appears to have slipped my mind."

I sighed and stood. The light was beginning to fail outside, and I had promised Trent that I would not stay out beyond twilight. I worried for him; he worried for me. In some ways we were becoming prisoners, our lives dictated by Aefre. It was frustrating, but there were few alternatives for now. "Let me know if there is anything I can do at all to help you, Mr Kephisto. You know I will." I thought of the densely packed writing, the illegible scrawl. "Or even Trent. I'm sure he could help you, better than me, with all his archival experience."

"Help decipher my writing, you mean? I'm sure he could. Perhaps I should take you up on that offer."

"Trent would enjoy it. Far too much." I laughed and started for the stairs. "Take care, Mr Kephisto. I'll see you soon."

TWENTY-NINE

THE MESSAGE AND THE MESSENGER

Pip eyed me dolefully from his place on the bed as I sat cross-legged wrapping Christmas presents. He flew down the stairs however, barking frantically when Trent arrived home from work. I hurriedly returned presents to their bags and threw them in the wardrobe, before heading downstairs.

"Hi," he said and kissed me. His nose was freezing.

"Cold out?" I grinned.

"I had to park up the road a bit."

"You should be wearing a scarf."

"I didn't think I'd be walking half a mile to get here tonight."

"Oh how you exaggerate. I'll put the kettle on if you like?"

"Do we have any wine?" Of course we had wine. We always had wine. Trent jabbed his thumb behind him. "By the way, you seem to have inherited a crow."

"Eh?"

"There's a crow outside. He's taken up residence on your fence."

I moved past Trent to the window at the side of the door and peered out. It was dark, but the street lamp gave off enough light to reveal the shape of a large bird sitting on top of my metal railings.

I don't know whether it sensed my movement but it turned its head my way—its black eyes glittering—and regarded me solemnly. Perturbed, I opened the door. It squawked at me. I reluctantly went outside, to shoo it away. It stood its ground, fluttering its wings if I got too close. "Go on. Go. Go away!" I urged, but it merely danced on the railings before settling again.

Eventually I tutted and turned back towards the house.

As I went to close the door on it, it squawked urgently at me. Frowning, I closed the door on the noise.

Trent smiled in amusement as I shivered, glad to be back inside. "What did he want?" he asked. I punched his arm.

*

I conjured up a Brussel sprout curry for tea, something that a Polish friend had once taught me. Trent was dubious about the idea, but it was delicious, so he was soon accepting second helpings.

"Do you want to watch a film?" I asked as I started clearing up. Trent shook his head.

"I need to do some marking. I've had stacks handed in over the past few days. Is that ok?"

"Of course," I said, thinking I'd be able to finish my wrapping in peace and quiet upstairs.

"Cool. Ah, shit. I've left the bag in the car." Trent headed out to the hall and a few moments later I heard the front door close as he went out. I started on the washing up and was scrubbing the curry pan when Trent returned, his face red from the cold.

"That damn crow is crazy," he rubbed his arm. "He pecked me."

"He pecked you?" I said, disbelievingly. "Let me see." Trent rolled up his jumper. There was an angry red mark but the skin wasn't broken. "Isn't it a bit unusual for birds to attack people?"

"Unless it's a Hitchcock film, you mean?"

"Well precisely." I headed for the front door and glared out at the crow again. It was in exactly the same spot on the railings where I had seen it before. "Maybe it's rabid."

"Do birds get rabies?"

I shrugged. The crow noticed me and became agitated. It was obviously calling again, although I couldn't hear it with the front door closed. "What if it's a messenger?" I asked, half joking. I felt Trent become still behind me.

"From the Guardians?"

Realisation dawned on us.

"Claire and Dorothea use them to send messages to the other Guardians, don't they?"

Trent nodded.

"But why would they send one to me? I don't speak crow. I don't have any notion what the message could be."

"Maybe it's to tell you they're in danger." Even as the words left Trent's mouth I knew he was right. I placed my hand over the charms on my necklace. The pentagram *was* tingling. Someone was in danger.

"I have to get over there. Aefre is going after all of the Guardians one by one. Maybe she's at White Cottage now."

"But together Rose, Dorothea, and Claire will be fine. There's strength in numbers, surely?"

I studied the crow through the window. Now that I was truly looking at it, I realised how agitated it was. I began to feel panicky myself. "I'd better check," I said. "I won't be long."

"Are you crazy? I'm not letting you go alone. It's not safe."

"I'll be fine. You stay here and do your marking."

"No." Trent was firm and was already pulling his boots back on. I shook my head at him but didn't argue. It cut both ways. I would worry about him being left alone in this house too. We were better facing whatever was coming our way together.

We stepped out into the freezing evening air, the crow squawked loudly once and then rose into the air. He flapped noisily in place as we passed him and trotted down the road to Trent's car as quickly as we could. As we reached the battered Audi, the crow settled on the bonnet. "It's ok," I said to it. "We're coming." Trent started the engine, and I shivered in the front seat. As we began to move the crow took off. It circled above us as we made a U-turn, and then as we headed towards town it flew in front of us, about fifteen feet from the ground.

I sat forward and peered up at it. "If that's not the strangest thing …"

We approached the edge of the town where we needed to

turn right and head towards Elbury. White Cottage was along the way. However, as Trent turned I noticed that the crow was no longer ahead of us. I bobbed my head down and around trying to see where it had gone.

"The bird's gone," I said.

"He's probably gone on ahead," answered Trent, but just at the moment a black shape shot towards us, causing both Trent and I to lurch back in our seats, startled, and Trent to slam on the brakes. Fortunately, there was nothing behind us. We sat there in silence for a moment, until Trent asked incredulously, "Was that the crow?"

"I think so," I answered, scanning the dark skies above. We remained stationary, wondering what to do.

"Here he comes," said Trent and once more the bird was flying at us. At the last second he pulled up, fluttered down and landed on the bonnet. He scrabbled on the paintwork, trying to gain purchase on the slippery surface, and hopped towards the windscreen pecking the glass in front of me. It cocked its head and squawked at me. I wound the window down.

"Kephisto," it called. "Kephisto."

"Oh god. Mr Kephisto. Aefre has gone after Mr Kephisto. This must be his crow, Caius." I tapped my fingers urgently on the dashboard. "Damn it! I was only there this afternoon. Drive Trent."

Trent put his foot down, and we covered the next mile quickly. As soon as the crow realised we were going the right way he shot off ahead of us, flying faster than we could manage thanks to the bends.

On the outskirts of Abbotts Cromleigh I debated suggesting a route that would cut out traffic lights, but in the end decided it would be easier to head directly. We were lucky, the lights were with us all the way. Trent drove down the high street, and I was opening the car door as we reached The Storykeeper.

"Park up and come and find me," I said as I leapt out of the car.

"Heather!" Trent shouted after me, but I paid no heed. I

moved rapidly, stumbling up the steps to the front door. I pushed. Some of the lights were on inside the bookshop, but the door was locked. I jiggled the door, but it was solid, so I rapped hard on the glass and peered inside.

"Mr Kephisto! Mr Kephisto?"

I could feel the warmth of the pentagram underneath my coat. I needed to get into the shop. The door was sturdy. I wasn't going to be able to open this one as easily as I had Trent's bedroom door. I searched for something I could use to break the glass in the door, but I couldn't spot anything obvious, and besides, I was guessing that the manufacturer would have used safety glass.

And Mr Kephisto would surely not be stupid enough to leave a key outside. I reached up and felt along the door ledge, but there was nothing there except a few years' worth of congealed road residue.

But Mr Kephisto didn't use a key anyway, did he? He managed to open and lock the door using something much more powerful. His mind. Could I? Dare I?

I tried for a moment. Envisaged the noise of clicking as the door unlocked itself. Nothing happened. No of course I couldn't. It was a ridiculous notion. I hammered on the door again and shouted his name. This time when I peered through I thought I could see smoke drifting down the stairs. Not green smoke, but the rolling smoke of a fire. The building was alight.

I didn't have my mobile, and Trent hadn't come back from parking the car. I put my hands on the door and in desperation I again thought of the door unlocking in front of me. "Help me do this, Mercy," I begged. I called Mercy to the front of my mind, and then of all the Guardians who had journeyed with her to this juncture. I summoned them all and imagined them gathered behind me, urging me forwards. I remembered the feeling of vibrancy of all the women dancing in the forest so long ago, and I called on their love and energy and the life within them all. The pentagram burned against my chest now and I pushed lightly against the door. There was a distinct click, and the door opened and swung gracefully inwards.

I walked into the bookshop warily, reaching out with my senses to see if I could find Aefre. Deep in the recesses of my mind's eye I saw the coils rubbing together, quickly, thickly. She was close by but she was no longer in the shop. She may have been here, but she wasn't any longer.

I could smell the smoke. We needed to call the fire service. Where was Trent? What was taking him so long? Tentatively I poked my head around the back of the counter. I couldn't see a phone.

"Mr Kephisto?" I called through to the very back of the shop. There was a door here. I didn't think the fire was behind it, but I was cautious. I felt the wood panelling. It was cool. I opened the door and peered through to a stock room, although there wasn't much in it. A few boxes of books marked *Returns* and some piles of paper bags with The Storykeeper logo on them. At the end of the room was a heavier door with a leaded glass window that had to lead to the outside area. It was locked and bolted and didn't look like it had been open for a while.

The pentagram was vibrating against my skin.

I moved back out into the main shop. Mr Kephisto wasn't on the ground floor, I would need to go up to the mezzanine. I glanced hopefully towards the front door for Trent, but there was still no sign of him. I clasped the balustrade and started to pull my way up. The smell of smoke was stronger here, and as I rounded the landing at the top, I could see the smoke hanging in the air, twizzling and turning. The mezzanine area was clear and the crow was not on its perch. Smoke was squeezing its way under the door that led up to the next floor, Mr Kephisto's private quarters.

"No." I regarded the wisps momentarily. I didn't consider myself a hero, but I couldn't leave Mr Kephisto up there.

"Come on Trent!" I shouted, peering over the balustrade at the shop below. He wasn't there and I had no choice, I had to go upstairs. Perhaps someone outside would see the smoke and call the fire service out.

I moved to the side of the door and slowly opened it. Smoke tumbled out to the floor, falling like a huge pile of old grey sheets and then rising like swirling dust into the air. Fortunately, it wasn't as dense as I had feared, and I still couldn't see or hear any flames. I crouched low and started climbing the stairs, the smoke catching in my throat and making me splutter. I tried to hold my breath, but that wasn't helpful. I breathed as shallowly as possible. As I drew level with the door to Mr Kephisto's living quarters I heard the sound I had been dreading. The flames were up here.

The door was open and the lamps were on. I dropped to my knees and crawled in to the room. I could see fire licking at the beams in the corner to the right of me. The bookshelves. My insides quaked with fear but I decided not to think about it.

Coughing and retching, my knees and hands complaining all the while, I struggled on, spotting a body sprawled on the rug ahead of me. Mr Kephisto. I scurried towards him, my own discomfort forgotten. He lay with his head turned towards the bookshelves, his eyes closed, his skin grey. There was a contusion on his temple, and blood oozed from the wound.

"Mr Kephisto!" I cried and reached for him. When he didn't respond, I knelt next to him and lay my ear next to his mouth. I could make out faint breaths, he was alive at least. I straightened his head and smoothed his hair away from the wound.

"Mr Kephisto? It's me Heather. You're going to be all right. We'll get you out." I looked around bleakly at the fire. It was spreading rapidly, and we were trapped here on the top floor. I couldn't carry the old man out by myself. What if nobody came in time? How much danger were we in? The room was warm and growing hotter. All of these books were just fodder for the fire.

I considered making a run for it alone. It was foolhardy to stay here and perish. I could charge back down the stairs and out to the street and wave someone else down. The flames were burning the roof, and it was dark outside, surely someone else had noticed by now. And where was Trent?

But I dismissed the thought of leaving Mr Kephisto here while he was still alive. I wouldn't be able to live with myself. I stood upright, then bent down, clasping him under his shoulders. I pulled him. He was lighter than I had imagined, but nonetheless I wasn't going to be able to carry him. Practically weeping now with exertion, I gripped him hard and dragged him towards the stairs. He moaned as I did so, and I stopped.

"I'm sorry. This is so undignified, I know." I coughed, wiped the sweat away from my face. I leaned over again and put more effort into pulling Mr Kephisto to safety. As I did so, some shelving at the back of the room collapsed and books with pages alight tumbled to the floor, one of them bouncing dangerously close to Mr Kephisto's feet. If I had left him where I had found him he would be burning as well.

I kicked the book away. The rug was on fire now and sparks from the roof were falling onto my head. Like a fool I glanced up, saw the ceiling burning, and wished I hadn't bothered. I stamped on the flames near Mr Kephisto's feet, then moved back to his shoulders. This was impossible. How was I going to get him down the stairs? I couldn't drag him down. I'd hurt him.

"Trent!" I screamed. And then suddenly, miraculously, there he was at last, clambering up the stairs towards me, his forearm across his face, his eyes wide. He pushed me.

"Take his feet," he ordered and hefted Mr Kephisto by his armpits as I had been doing. "Hurry!"

I grabbed Mr Kephisto's feet, and Trent lurched backwards, carrying the brunt of the old man's weight back down the narrow staircase. My lungs were really beginning to hurt now, and again I tried to hold my breath in spite of the exertion. It was useless, I started to cough and choke.

Trent moved quickly and in just seconds we were on the mezzanine. I dropped Mr Kephisto's feet, doubled over and retched. I couldn't seem to get my breath.

"You're going to have to help me down these stairs," Trent shouted. "Can you do that? If you can do that, we can get him out." His eyes were huge in his pale face, but he was determined. I nodded at him, tears running down my face from my smarting eyes. I couldn't waste the breath to answer, instead I took firm hold of Mr Kephisto's feet once more and we moved around to the rickety stairs.

The going here was tougher. The stairs were narrow and uneven and I wavered. I followed Trent down as he moved backwards, once almost stumbling forwards. Finally, we were on the ground floor. From above us came the sound of heavy objects falling.

"Hurry," Trent said. I bent to lift Mr Kephisto's feet again, but Trent waved me away and lifted the man himself. I rushed for the front door, slipped on the steps, and stumbled into the street. Suddenly people were all around me. Blue lights flashed at the periphery of my vision. Someone was asking if I was ok. I coughed and coughed until I was sick, unable to get my breath.

A man in a dark uniform had hold of my arm and pulled me gently but firmly to my feet. "Over here," he said, leading me to an ambulance. The fireman had a kind face, but I tried to pull away, to go and check on Trent and Mr Kephisto, but his hand was firm and he didn't let go.

"That building is so old, it will burn to the ground." A group of bystanders were chatting next to the ambulance. I turned back in fear and the fireman followed my gaze. "Beautiful building," he said and handed me over to a waiting paramedic. She had a bottle of oxygen and a face mask at the ready. She bade me sit on the edge of the ambulance. I manoeuvred myself so that I could see the bookshop.

In between coughing and sucking fresh air, I tried to ask about Trent and Mr Kephisto. I could see the entrance now, but there was a lot of activity around it. The police were moving people back and firefighters were clearly assessing the situation. I caught a glimpse of someone lying on the ground, before more fire personnel obscured my view. The sounds of flames grew louder. The whole building was ablaze.

I felt faint. The paramedic was monitoring my pulse. The

world greyed out for a moment. I closed my eyes. The sound of flames grew louder.

"Die."

The voice was calm and cold. Aefre was here, close by.

My eyes snapped open, and I removed the oxygen mask from my face. I dropped the canister onto the ground. Not a road, but a dirt clearing. The ambulance, the street, the shops, and the people had all disappeared. I was standing in a forest, a great fire raging beyond me, catching at trees and jumping between bushes and clumps of dry bracken. The sky was lit up by an orange halo. I lifted my hands to my already scorched cheeks and turned my face away from the heat. A sudden movement caught my attention.

There she was. Moving off to the side, heading around the flames. She was dressed in a long dark gown, and her hair tumbled down her back in thick, healthy auburn curls.

"I'm coming for you, Aefre," I called after her.

She stopped and turned slowly. She was achingly beautiful; I'd never seen her more so. Her face glowed in the light of the flames, her lips red and full, her eyes huge and dark. "Follow me and you will die." Her words drifted to me, clear above the crackle and roar of the flames, even though her voice was not raised.

"I'm not afraid of you."

"You should be." She lifted her hand and the air shifted. I was knocked backwards, as though a door had shut hard in my face. I fell onto the soft forest floor, put my hands up to protect my face from the heat. Someone was touching me, and I fought them off.

It was the paramedic. Confused, I pushed against her and she backed off, her hands lifted in mock surrender.

"You're all right," she said. "You passed out for a moment. Please just lie still." She turned to seek assistance. "Rob?" she called. Probably her partner. He was out of earshot. She stepped out of the ambulance and walked around the corner to call him. I was out of her sight temporarily.

I took the opportunity to extricate myself from the

oxygen mask and wires, climb from the bed, and jump out of the ambulance. When the paramedic saw what I was doing, she rushed back. I dodged her and rushed towards the bookshop. I felt groggy, and my breathing was harsh and laboured, but I had to see Trent and Mr Kephisto for myself.

There was confusion everywhere. People were moving about and the fire service were pulling out hoses. Police were barking at bystanders and the lights of police cars, ambulances, and fire engines were flashing. The scent of burning filled the air, and ash and debris fell from the bookshop as I walked in front of it.

And there they were. Trent was kneeling beside Mr Kephisto, holding the hand of the old man lying on the pavement. Two paramedics were working on him while a police officer attempted to pull Trent away. I saw Trent shake the officer off and lean in closely to Mr Kephisto as though listening to what he was saying.

With relief I saw that Mr Kephisto was moving. He tucked his hand inside his jacket for a moment and then shakily removed a book. I was close now, standing behind Trent. I leaned over and Mr Kephisto smiled weakly at me. His lips moved. I knelt next to Trent. Mr Kephisto said something, but I missed it. I pressed my hot hand against his freezing cold one.

"You'll be ok," I wheezed. He closed his eyes.

Then someone was hauling me to my feet and pulling me away. I called out to Mr Kephisto.

"We have to get him to the hospital, love. You need to move away now." I doubled over, coughing again.

Trent joined me, looking worried. "How are you?" he asked, his face next to mine as I coughed and retched into the gutter. I nodded and tried to say fine, but it was obvious I wasn't. "Mr Kephisto is being taken to the hospital. I think you should go too."

We walked shakily back to the female paramedic. She eyed me, her face stern, and I shrugged ruefully before launching into another coughing fit. She placed the oxygen mask over my face once more, and I climbed into the ambulance reluctantly. As the doors closed, I spotted Mr Kephisto being lifted onto a stretcher farther down the road. I hoped and prayed he would make it.

The paramedic hooked me up to a machine that beeped as I settled back on the bed. Trent sat next to me, trying to keep out of the way. I watched him thumb through the small notebook Mr Kephisto had given him. From what I could see, all of the pages were blank.

*

I passed the rest of the evening in A and E and the remainder of the night in hospital, but there was no lasting damage. At lunchtime the next day Trent arrived to take me home. That was his intention at least, but I had other ideas.

"We need to go to White Cottage," I said.

"What you need to do is rest."

"How is Mr Kephisto?"

Trent shook his head tiredly. He'd spent most of the previous night with me. At least I'd had a bed and some sleep; Trent had settled for a plastic chair. "They've placed him into an induced coma. They don't think he'll make it."

I collapsed back against the car seat feeling nauseous.

"Home," Trent said firmly. "Doctor's orders." I opened my mouth to protest. "We'll go to White Cottage just as soon as I think you won't flake out the minute you stand up, ok?"

I nodded and closed my eyes.

*

For two days I remained at home, lying on the sofa, watched over by Pip and frustrated by my own inactivity but aware that I needed to build my strength up. My fury at Aefre burned hot. I was full of hate in the dark depths of my heart, but my mind was clear and focused. Where she had stolen so much from me, I fully intended to take everything from her.

When I was well enough I picked up my car keys and signalled my intent to head to White Cottage. Trent, observing the set of my face, let me lead the way. Within twenty minutes we were sitting in Rose's warm living room and filling our friends in on what we knew.

"No change," Trent was telling them. Mr Kephisto was clinging to life. "He has a fractured skull, and there may be some brain damage. Given his advanced age … they're not really sure yet."

"Was it Aefre?" Rose asked.

I nodded. "There's no reason to think otherwise and I certainly had a sense she had been there."

"You didn't see her there?" Rose's eyes were wise.

"Not there, no." I stared vacantly at Rose for a moment. "I did see her though. Just for a moment."

Trent pricked his ears up. "You didn't say anything."

"It was fleeting. I had a vision. We were in the forest. Surrounded by flames. The trees were burning. She was walking away, and I wanted to walk after her. She warned me off. It was a very short encounter."

"She's defensive," Rose mused.

"Yes. I thought so. But given that she has stepped up her battle against you—us—it stands to reason that she's on the ropes. She's desperate. She wants to get rid of us all. We must make a move soon."

"Do we know how to yet? Trent said that Kephisto gave him a book," Claire said.

Trent took the book out of his pocket. It was a small notebook with a thick green embossed leather cover. We had flicked through it numerous times. Every page was blank. He handed it to Claire, and she held it gently in her right hand.

"There's nothing in it," Trent said. "We've been through it," he trailed off as he watched Claire.

She opened her right hand so that the book was lying in her palm, then she held her left hand about ten inches above the book. "Reveal," she ordered. The cover flipped open and then one by one, faster and faster, the pages started to turn until they were flipping over in a blur. Forwards and then backwards. Forwards and then backwards. Abruptly the book twisted, and launched itself into the air before tumbling towards the floor. It smacked the ground with a crack, breaking the spine. The cover fell apart and pages scattered.

I hardly dared to breathe. A tiny slither of parchment had worked its way free of the leather binding.

We all stared at it mutely, until Trent bent down and reverently scooped it up.

"Mr Kephisto told me that Heather could do it," he said. "He said she can destroy Aefre. She just has to believe." He grimaced. "But I'm afraid for you. I'm afraid to let you try."

We held each other's look for a moment. The love I felt for him burned pure, right through the heart of me. The room was silent; the atmosphere strained. "But you have to try, and I have to let you do that," he continued. I tried to smile reassuringly for him, but my jaw had locked tight.

"What does it say on the card?" Claire asked.

Trent reluctantly stared down at the card in his hand. He read what was written there in a neat and tiny script:

"'Dreams are the seeds of change. Nothing grows without a seed, and nothing changes without a dream.' Plant the seed of destruction, Kephisto."

I reached out to take the card from Trent. "What does it mean?" he asked.

Rose patted his arm but didn't answer.

"I don't know," Claire said. "Trust Kephisto to be so obtuse."

My hands were shaking. Finally, I understood where all the visions were leading me.

"I know what it means." I scrutinised the little piece of paper once more. "We need to get busy. We need to summon all the remaining Guardians here. All of them."

"That may take time," Claire interjected.

"We don't have time. Get them here now. It's vitally important. I need to get inside the Sentinel and I can only do it with everyone's help."

THIRTY

NOTHING CHANGES WITHOUT A DREAM

Mr Kephisto appeared tiny, dwarfed by his pristine white bed in the intensive care unit, in a side ward containing one other gentleman. I lied to staff, claiming to be Mr Kephisto's granddaughter, and they allowed me to stay with him for a short time.

I slipped into the seat next to Mr Kephisto and took his pale hand. His skin was translucent, the veins bright blue beneath the surface. His head was bandaged and wires were attached to him in numerous places. He appeared frail. I wondered whether he would pull through, and did he even want to? How old was he? Like Mercy and Rose, he had lived an inordinately long time. The years had passed and left him largely alone—ever watchful for Aefre—with only the support of the Guardians.

Was he safe here by himself in this huge hospital? Would Aefre come for him here? Who would protect him? I studied the man in the bed opposite, his breathing controlled by a machine. He was in an even worse situation than Mr Kephisto, who was breathing by himself at least.

I leaned forward to speak quietly into Mr Kephisto's ear. "I know what I have to do. I'm going in tomorrow." There was no movement, no acknowledgement. I hadn't expected there would be.

"I need your help though. I need help from all of the Guardians. We have to remove the charms. I have to use the portal. If you can ... reach out somehow ... please help me tomorrow." The only response came from the machine monitoring his heart rate, it beeped steadily. I sighed.

Mr Kephisto's eyelids appeared to flutter. I dropped his hand and rose. My pulse raced in sudden excitement. He was coming to. He would be well again. I watched carefully for any other signs of life, wondering whether to call the nurse back, but his face remained still and there was no further movement.

I sank back into the chair beside his bed and put my head in my hands. The road ahead seemed impossible to traverse. To any rational human, the oak tree was just that. A huge solid entity of bark and wood. How the hell was I supposed to find my way into it?

Unbidden I heard Mr Kephisto speaking clearly to me in his soft voice, slightly baffled, almost amused. He repeated the words he had said to Trent. "You can do it. You can destroy Aefre. You just have to believe." I sat up expectantly, my eyes shining with tears. Mr Kephisto lay still and silent on the bed, just one breath away from his long walk in the Summerlands.

*

The remaining Guardians gathered together at White Cottage at last. There were twenty-three of us altogether, a rag tag band of witches, wizards, seers, wise folk, and Druids. We were remarkably ordinary. No long cloaks, no pointed hats, no beards or tumbling locks. Just men and women in ordinary clothes and shoes, with unexceptional haircuts and high street clothing.

But on the whole, the Guardians were elderly. Claire was the youngest by far. She moved in and out of the crowded rooms at the cottage offering food and drinks. There was a never-ending supply of tea and cake. She had obviously been baking all day. She smiled and chatted amiably, but I could see behind the facade, her eyes had lost their sparkle.

Trent too appeared downfallen, lost, sitting alone on the window seat in the main living room, gazing about himself from time to time, listening in on conversations, smiling politely when spoken to, but mostly watching me as I roamed around the garden at the front of the house, watching the oak tree and looking out for newcomers.

The cottage was too warm, and I was nervous. My palms were sticky. I didn't know what to expect, I only knew that I had to try. The garden was bare and stark at this time of year.

Only the hardiest plants survived in their tubs, in marked contrast to the glory of summer. I missed the cottage at its abundant best, when flowers and herbs sprang from pots and cauldrons, and the air was scented and enticing. Now a cold hard frost gripped the earth and the only scent was that of wood smoke.

We had sent word to the Guardians using a variety of means, including telephone and email, as well as birds. One or two of the more elderly Guardians lived in isolation on islands both to the north and south of us, and so Rose had pressed her crows and ravens into action by verbally instructing them to bring the Guardians to us, and so they had.

Dusk was falling, and it was time for us to figure out what we were doing. I had asked Rose to build the fire in the living room as she had before. The cottage had now become uncomfortably hot and crowded, so Claire urged most of the Guardians to move outside. They huddled together, wrapped in great coats, hats, and scarves, their breath steaming in the air as they talked among themselves, gaily swapping stories, but always with a slightly urgent air. We were all aware how important this evening was.

"You look pale," Trent said. He reached out and pushed some unruly strands of hair from my face.

"I'm fine," I smiled, hoping it would calm his fears.

"I don't think you're properly well. The effects of smoke inhalation from the other night …"

I caught his hand in mine. Squeezed it tight. "I have to do this."

"I wish I could do it for you."

"I wish you could too." We laughed together, and I brought his hand to my mouth, kissed his knuckles, then leant my cheek against his palm.

A lone car heading for Elbury drove down the road, passing the cottage. The travellers inside gawped at the group of Guardians gathered in the garden. To all intents and purposes, we must have appeared to be throwing a garden party for the winter solstice.

Some party.

I walked to the gate and stared at the oak tree as if seeing it for the first time. It was a fabulous specimen. Tall and strong, its thick branches spreading into the field beyond on one side and across the road on this side. Dried flowers littered the base of the tree and I realised that if I succeeded in doing what I planned, this would no longer be a place of solace for the bereaved.

I opened the little latch gate and walked across the road towards the tree, then knelt and began carefully gathering up the bunches of flowers. When I had an armful, I moved them to safety farther up the road, next to the stile, the gateway into the field beyond, where sheep were still grazing, enjoying the last of the weak daylight filtering through the trees. When I turned to go back for a second batch, Claire was there, stooping to gather a pile together herself.

"Thanks," I said, taking them from her.

"No problem." We worked quietly and when all of the flowers and small items that had been left at the tree were cleared, we paused at the stile. Claire lifted her head, scenting the air. I was reminded of the first day I had seen her. It seemed so long ago.

"She's close," I said. It wasn't a question. I knew she was.

"Yes."

Aefre was in the trees beyond the field. Hiding from a vantage point that allowed her to see the tree, see us. Out of sight but not out of mind. I could sense her out there. She was agitated, as nervous as I.

"Showtime," I said to her quietly and sensed Aefre's eyes raking my face. She might not comprehend the word but she would understand the meaning.

"Call the Guardians out here and have them begin," I said to Claire, amazed that my voice was so even and self-assured. "I'm going to sit with Rose."

"Wait. I prepared this for you." She handed me a small bundle I'd asked for. "Are you wearing your pendant?"

I nodded, the charms were on their chain, tucked next to

my skin. I checked the contents of the little pouch she had given me and stuck it in the pocket of my jeans. I pressed her hand and walked away quickly, anxious not to discuss the imprudence of what I was about to do. Feeling troubled, and lacking in confidence, I moved quickly between the Guardians in the garden, felt them observing me as I entered the cottage. Rose was waiting patiently for me next to the fire, her wizened face soft and loving.

She indicated I take the chair next to her and then looked pointedly at Trent who was hovering in the background once more. We exchanged glances. There was so much I wanted to say to him. Anxiety twisted my insides. Was I going to come through this? Would I see him again? Instead, determined to appear insouciant, I nodded at him. His head fell to his chest, and I saw his lips sit in a tight line of resignation. He walked out of the room without looking back at me. It felt like a goodbye.

I had a sudden urge to weep. I wasn't naturally brave and here I was, facing the unknown. And now I was alone. Trent's exit had made me feel lonelier than I had at any time since the day Max died.

Rose's cool hand caught mine. She smiled and indicated the chair again. Dorothea slipped in from the kitchen with a goblet full of a thick, hot liquid. I took it from her, held it to my lips, inhaled the steam. It smelt metallic, like blood. I knew what to do. I downed the hot drink in one. It was time to face Aefre.

THIRTY-ONE

THE SONG

The smoke stung my eyes. I blinked back tears and lurched forward in my chair. For a moment I was back in The Storykeeper, the beams in the ceiling burning bright above my head. Mr Kephisto was sitting in his armchair watching me. "This is the wrong place," I said. "I shouldn't be here." There were books smouldering on the shelves. "And why are you still here? You mustn't be!" I cried. "The shop is burning down."

"I'm with you. Be calm. Wherever you are, I'll be there. Remember what I said. Go now." I made my way to the door, stood poised at the top of the rickety steps, hesitated, and turned back. Mr Kephisto was gone, Aefre was sitting in his place, glaring at me with eyes as black as tar.

I backed away, lost my balance, and slipped on the staircase, landing at the bottom with a bang.

"Easy, easy," Rose crooned in my ear and Dorothea helped me back to the chair. I was still in the living room, my stomach churning and head swimming.

I groaned, nauseous and giddy.

"It's the potion," Rose explained. "Give it time. The worst of it will wear off soon enough."

I sweated as Dorothea banked up the fire. It was as hot as Hades. My skin dripped, hair stuck to my face, and I vomited. Dorothea cleaned me up, helping me to remove the jumper I was wearing and applied a cool damp cloth to my face. The t-shirt I wore underneath was damp with perspiration.

"Sit back," she suggested, "rest your eyes."

I closed my eyes and tried to ride the waves of nausea. My pulse throbbed hard in my ears. After a few minutes it began to slow. I listened to the beat of my own heart, breathing evenly, slowing it down.

The chanting began. It was low and deep and quiet. The Guardians had started the process that would remove the enchantments from the Sentinel. At first there was no discernible rhythm to their song, but the more I listened, the clearer and more melodic the chanting became. There were repetitive bass notes, layered with a higher melody and weaving through it all was an alto refrain that tumbled in and around itself, seeming to tie itself in knots. And yet what the chanting actually aimed to do was unravel the magick knots that bound the Sentinel tightly shut.

I pictured the Guardians out there, in the road beyond the cottage, gathered around the tree, but there were too few of them. I needed a larger choir. When the oak tree had been a seed there were dozens and dozens of Guardians to keep it safe. Now the decades and centuries had taken their toll and only twenty of them surrounded it. Rose and Dorothea were here with me. There weren't enough of us. We wouldn't be able to break the enchantment.

As soon as I created that thought in my mind, Mr Kephisto moved into my vision. He walked purposefully away from me, heading for the tree, and as he did that I remembered the words on his note: nothing changes without a dream. I was the tributary to bring about change and that had to start with my dream.

Could I control a dream?

I cast my mind back to the vision I had experienced before when Mercy had been there to guide me. I recalled all of the people gathered together at the summit meeting. They had come together, answered a call for help, determined to solve the problem of Aefre. I remembered their passion, their commitment. I needed to get back there. Could that be done without Mercy as my guide? I willed myself into that past, placed myself back there.

What is imagination? What is memory? The two things blurred and merged in my mind. It was dark. I smelt suckling pig roasting on spits above camp fires, fires that were capable of throwing limited light around the gloom of the camp. I could smell the stink of live cattle and the stench of unwashed men and women. I could hear the clucking of hens and the cries of babies. I felt the roughness of the forest path beneath my feet. I was there, right there with them. This was as real as any dream could be.

Many of those gathered were beginning to pack their belongings, ready to start for home in the morning. There were some—a lucky few—who had carts piled high with bedding and supplies, while others had little more than the clothes they wore. I walked among them, these generous, thoughtful folk, who had gathered here in Cromleigh to do a good deed. A hundred or so pairs of eyes examined me. I must have appeared strange to them in my modern clothes, somehow other, but they did not show unease, did not castigate me, did not question why I was there.

I recognised a young Mercy, sitting in front of a makeshift tent. Her eyes shone happily when she met my gaze. And close by there was Mr Kephisto. A young man, strong and virile. A shock of blonde hair and a healthy complexion. They were gathered with the original group of Guardians, the chosen ones. They had already spent several days working together to bind the Sentinel, while the larger group had looked on and encouraged them.

And here I was to demand that they undo that work. For them, mere hours had passed since they had completed their task. For me it was centuries upon centuries.

And yet they knew.

I recognised the expectation in the Guardians' faces. They were waiting for me as surely as the flower awaits the bee. Mercy rose and walked towards me and held out her hands. I reached for her.

"Do you know me?" I asked.

She shook her head. "I know of you."

"I'm in your future. You're not afraid?"

She shook her head again. "Should I be?"

"No." I tugged her hands. "You must come, and you must bring everybody to help you. I need to have the enchantments broken. The time has come to release the Sentinel. I must gain access."

She nodded, calmly turned, and raised her arms. The camp came to a standstill. No word was spoken. There was a moment's absolute silence and then as one, every man and woman and child walked towards the forest, heading into it, moving towards the Sentinel. The light from the camp fire dimmed as they purposefully headed away. I walked after them a little way, then paused and listened to their footsteps as they shuffled along the soft floor, a carpet of leaves and branches and mulch underfoot, an army on the move. They entered the forest to approach the clearing where the oak was located. Every last one of them headed for the Sentinel, and I watched them mingle with the trees and disappear from my view among the branches. Then I was back in front of the fire with Rose and Dorothea, in real time, and the past had dissipated.

But I could hear the sound of a crowd. Many, many people were massing outside, joining the ranks of the Guardians already present. I rose. Dorothea mopped my face once again. The pull of outside was strong. I had the urge to walk barefoot with the Guardians of old. I needed to bond with the Earth and feel the ground, the mud between my toes. It was suddenly important to me to connect with the old ways and the old world. I was as much a part of this as any of the Guardians. Somehow.

I slipped off my shoes and walked to the front door to look out at the gathering throng. Here were the Guardians of old; they had journeyed from the past to help me. They stood together in unity, those that had survived the passing of time and those that had simply passed away. The chanting was louder now. I could pick out different tones and harmonies. More and more voices were lifted in a complex song, and the magick was hanging thickly in the air.

Dorothea and Rose followed me out of the cottage to the front gate. It was completely dark and yet the air was filled with a certain luminescence. I gazed around me in wonder. Hundreds of spirits had joined us and now they completely encircled the oak tree. Some were standing on the road, many were in the field behind the hedge. Flashes of white could be seen on the hill beyond. The Guardians were here, every single one of them, and they glowed as they sang.

There was Mr Kephisto, pale and translucent, close to the tree, standing with some other men I had never seen before. Their bass tones rumbled through the air, commanding and oddly reassuring. And not far from them was Mercy, a beatific smile on her face as she gazed my way, singing with a soft soprano, clear and true. Pure and good.

The song had changed now to a call and response. I walked towards the oak tree. It swayed in a slight breeze, frost on the twigs shimmering in the strange light. It moved one way with one part of the song, and then shifted the other way when the response came.

I stopped perhaps five feet away from the tree. It emanated a sharp energy, some kind of vibrating force field. I had never sensed this before. Warily, I put my hands up in front of me, my fingers tingled slightly. The enchantment was still in place. I could feel the resistance.

I heard Dorothea and Rose, who had walked with me to the tree, join in with the chanting. Their song altered the harmonies, and the tune shifted again. I closed my eyes and lifted my arms up as though to conduct the sounds around me.

And it was fantastic.

I breathed with the music. I was hearing the sound of a thousand spells being unwoven. Each spell was a key, and each key had locked a chain in place around the portal. The chains falling away, and when I listened, I heard those chains dropping to the floor—even though they didn't exist in the physical world.

The energy from the tree ebbed and flowed with the song. I leant into it, lulled by the power and the beauty. I felt the energy enter me. My body pulsed with heat. I studied my fingers, spread them wide. Light shone from beneath my skin, from within me, turning my skin red, and I felt strong and clear headed, as chain after chain hit the floor and vanished with a flash, until just one chain remained.

It was rusty and strong, as wide as my thigh, and it was

wrapped several times around the trunk of the tree and secured with the most ancient of padlocks. The song strained at the chain, heaved and pulled and wheedled and fondled. The chain shifted against the tree, rubbed the bark away, aggressively abrading the wood beneath, but all to no avail. The song became more desperate, and the chafing of the tree increased, but still the lock held fast and the chain bound the tree.

The pendant around my neck buzzed and vibrated, alive with light. Blood pounded in my ears and suddenly I wanted to sing too. Nothing changes without a dream. I was the last of the Guardians, I had to add my voice to theirs. I didn't know the words to their song, didn't understand the spells they were breaking, so I could only sing my own song and break my own spell. I held my hands forward, directed the light from beneath my skin at the lock. I could feel the energy of the tree, it purred within my soul. "Hear me," I spoke quietly. "You took the best of my life the day my son was drawn to this place. You were the weapon of she who demanded the ultimate sacrifice from me, and the blood of my son was spilt among your roots. You owe me, and so I demand this in return. Open to me. Let me in!"

There was a blinding flash and cold sparks of bright blue light flew from the last of the locks. It fell away with an enormous clang. The great chain reluctantly slithered down the truck to the ground and disappeared in an explosion of smoke and ash. I turned to the Guardians in triumph just as a red shape flew by me with a loud shriek and fingernails as hard as granite whipped at my face.

Aefre.

I flung myself sideways, caught a glimpse of her triumphant smile as she backed away from me, and watched in horror as she ran at the tree and jumped. In a micro second she had disappeared.

I hesitated, but only for a second. I pushed myself to my feet, took a few steps back, and then ran at the tree myself. I leapt with nothing more than a desire to follow Aefre and the intention of never letting her escape my sight again. I heard

Trent yelling my name, but the sound was abruptly cut off.

I remained in the air, in blackness and silence, for an interminable moment, but I could feel my forward trajectory, until I collided with something hard. I fell backwards to the ground. I was somewhere entirely new.

Stunned, I lay on the ground catching my breath, before tentatively sitting and rubbing my elbow and trying to get my bearings. I blinked into the darkness. Pitch black? No. My eyes to became accustomed to my new surroundings. Against my shoulders I felt the pressure of something solid: a round wall, the curve of the oak tree surely? A small hole above my head, a knot in the wood, allowed a tiny chink of light into the space. I put my hand out and caressed the rough interior of the tree. There was no door here. I had jumped through something solid.

The floor beneath me was soft, almost sponge like. As I pushed myself to my knees, earth crumbled around my fingers. I brushed my hands together, then wiped them on my jeans, slightly unnerved by being unable to see much. I sensed movement on my periphery. Aefre? She had jumped in ahead of me. Where was she now?

I stood, bending my neck, frightened I would bash my head against a ceiling or the solid trunk of the tree, but there was plenty of space above me. I held my hands out and moved forwards, ready to collide with the other side of the tree, but there was nothing there. I edged forwards, the narrow space opened out a little, and then a little more. I saw more light in the distance and headed for it, each one of my senses was alert, and mentally I continued to scan for signs of Aefre.

And there was the exit. I bent my head and stepped through the wall of the great oak tree and into a forest clearing. This was Aefre's clearing. The place where she and her sisters had danced and conjured the demon, but instead of her bonfire, the great oak tree dominated the space. There was no road here, no White Cottage, no sign of the Guardians. I was here at a time that was indeterminate. All around me, the trees were tall and twisted, stark against a clear winter sky, my breath hung in the air as I turned about.

I heard a rustling behind me, and I turned in alarm. No-one there. From somewhere in the distance I heard Aefre calling a name. One of her sisters? There was no response. Not this time, but there would be if I didn't hurry.

I had allowed Aefre entry to the Sentinel. What damage was done?

I considered going after her. But what then? She was far more likely to be able finish me off than I was her. And if she located any of her sisters in the meantime …

I had a job to do. Mr Kephisto had told me I had to plant the seed of destruction, and here then was my simple plan. I had to prevent Aefre from ever using the Sentinel to call her sisters and move between realms. With Aefre on this side, as unfortunate as that was, perhaps it made my job easier. I could find a way to trap her here. If I could create a fire within the heart of the oak tree and burn it to the ground, she wouldn't be able to reach Abbotts Cromleigh again. Other Sentinels in other places … that was a different story.

The problem was, I had yet to work out how to get back to my own time.

THIRTY-TWO

AEFRE

Twitching with nerves, I gathered twigs and small branches as quickly as I could, breaking the larger ones over my knee and layering them with dry bracken and gorse to create a pyramid in the middle of the space available inside the huge oak tree. Once I had amassed a large pile, I dug Claire's small pouch out of my jeans pocket. It contained lighter fluid and a box of matches, a sachet of salt and a tiny plastic pot of indigo coloured paint. It was only symbolic, based on what Trent and I had drawn from our research, but I trusted that this was all I needed. Mr Kephisto had seen to that.

Hands shaking, I ripped open the sachet and sprinkled salt over the pile, squirted the lighter fluid around, relieved when I didn't get any on myself. I opened the paint and dipped my finger in, then rubbed paint around the entrance to the tree, before dropping the empty pot into the centre of the pile. It was a representational gesture, but it was all I had. Finally, I struck a match. My hands were unsteady and it took three attempts, but at last a tiny flame spurted into life. I dropped the match onto the wood and watched as the bracken caught quickly, flicking yellow around the smaller branches. I nursed the fire a little until I was sure it had a hold, then I left the relative safety of the oak to step back outside and collect some larger sticks to feed the flames.

I shuffled through the leaves warily, looking about me. Everything was quiet. But then, bending over to retrieve some dried branches from under a nearby beech, something hit me solidly on the side of the head. I stumbled but didn't fall. Groaning, I twisted to see Aefre glowering at me, sporting her true form: a grotesque ancient hag, her jaw hanging by sinews, her flesh green with decomposition, any remaining skin hanging from her, dusty and covered in lichen. In her arms she held the large branch she'd hit me with, raising it above her head to have another go. Adrenaline pumped through my veins. I kicked out and connected with her knee, sending her tumbling backwards. She shrieked and jumped to her feet, as light as a cat, her reactions much faster than mine.

I took off, running back towards the oak, but I didn't get far. She was on me in a second, forcing me down onto the floor, fighting me like a wild cat. I tried to hold her at arm's length, but she was straddling my chest, her fingers digging painfully into my shoulders, trying to wrap themselves around my neck. I screamed and scrunched my shoulders up to my chin, gritting my teeth with the effort of fighting her off. She was insanely strong. I wasn't going to let the battle end this way though, not after everything I'd been through. I wouldn't let her suck the very life out of me, not when I hadn't finished what I had set out to do.

So I reached for her, wrapped my own hands around her hideous bony neck, and dug my thumbs into her slimy macerated throat. She whipped her head backwards, and I almost lost my grip. She shrieked at me as my fingers raked at her skin, and she threw herself forwards once more, her green and black teeth snapping ferociously, her black lips peeled back from cracked and bleeding gums, her breath hot and stinking. Her face was even more grotesque this close. Skin as dry as parchment, flecked with dusty mould, her eyes as black and viscous as oil, rolling in deep yellow sockets. Her once lustrous hair a greasy mess, plastered close to her scalp and hanging in rats' tails around her shoulders.

In the struggle, the chain around my neck slipped from under my jumper and slid into view. Aefre paused and stared at it, her mouth curling in disgust. Then with a screech, she ripped at the chain and threw it away. I yelled, fearful of losing the charms, my only protection, my connection with Trent and the rest of the Guardians. Perhaps my only way home. With renewed fury I cracked Aefre hard across the head with my right fist. She hacked more spittle my way, and dug her hands into my neck once more. I closed my eyes and twisted my head away from her. She released one hand from my neck and gouged at my mouth with her reeking fingers. I pressed my lips together and fought furiously for purchase at her neck.

She yanked her head away again, wrenched herself out of my grasp. She was as slippery as an eel. Adrenaline coursed through my veins, hot and hateful. I had no intention of backing down. I grabbed at her, tried to catch her wrist as she fruitlessly tried to force my mouth open. Her hand slipped as I went for her, and our fingers interlocked. That touch sent a jolt of lightning coursing through me. I gasped and my head and shoulders hit the ground hard enough so that I saw stars.

The features of Aefre's face shifted in front of me, and once more she was the beautiful woman she had once been. Her eyes were mesmerising. Deep pools of fluid green. I found myself swimming in them, through them, deeper and deeper, down into her soul. Deeper still, to a time when she was …

Young.

So young.

Lying on straw in a warm hut, cuddling her younger sisters. Her father sharpening a blade by the fire while her mother nurses the baby. There's a sudden commotion outside, chickens squawking and a bull bellowing. One of their neighbours is screaming, an anguished cry that is cut off before it is fully formed. Her father stands and rushes for the makeshift door of the hut. It crashes open and a huge man plunges a long spear into her father's gut. Her father cries out in pain and lashes out with the blade he was sharpening. The stranger, impossibly strong, catches her father's arm and snaps it backwards. The crack is loud in the ensuing silence.

Her mother screams and stands up. The stranger turns and with one swift movement knocks her mother to the floor, the baby flying from her grasp and squalling as it hits the dirt. More men are at the door now. Aefre sits up in bed, pulling her siblings close.

The stranger barks orders. Aefre doesn't understand the language. One of the new arrivals pulls at her mother and drags her out of the hut by her hair. The stranger looks at Aefre and her younger sisters huddled together in fear. He pulls the skins back from the bed to get a proper look at them. He leans forward to grab hold of Aefre. She scoots backwards. He smiles. It is a cold smile. He lets her back away.

The stranger bends down towards her dying father and catches hold of his blade. It's a knife her father used for butchering rabbits. The stranger catches hold of her youngest sister, only eighteen months old, and sticks the blade into her belly. He moves it upwards, carving a deep line in her skin that leaves a neat mark which belatedly blooms crimson. The little girl starts to shake and mew.

The stranger reaches for a three-year old and Aefre tries to shield her. The stranger knocks Aefre aside, she's a minor inconvenience. He picks up her sister and once more using the bloody knife he thrusts it into her eye socket.

Then he smiles at Aefre again and offers his hand. She stares at him for a moment, her insides turning to ice, but then she takes his hand. What choice does she have? She has two more sisters left alive. He leads her outside. She sees her mother, wants to run to her but is restrained. Her mother is bent double over a pile of logs and the man who dragged her out of the hut has her hair wrapped in his fist as he lunges against her. She grunts and cries with each thrust. When she sees Aefre, she cries out for her biggest little girl. The stranger says something to the man who stops what he is doing to her mother and instead draws out his own blade, reaches forwards, and carves a smile around Aefre's mother's throat.

Aefre watches as her mother's blood gushes against the logs. More blood than Aefre has ever seen. More than the chickens and pigs slaughtered for food for high days and holidays. They bleed, but this is something else. Her mother's blood spurts high and hard at first, then the spray weakens. It is thick and rich, coating the wood, spilling onto the dirt around the woodpile. Her mother twitches and convulses while her murderer thrusts once more and then pulls out of her. He lets her drop among the wood shavings. Her once-sparkling eyes are dull, the life fading. Aefre wants to run to her, to hold her as she dies, but she doesn't dare show any emotion in front of these men. She looks only at the man who took her mother's life. He smiles and waves his cock in her direction, making her a promise, before tucking himself back into his tunic and aiming a kick at her mother's convulsing body. Aefre thinks of her own promise. She won't forget.

Aefre's little community is devastated by this outlaw gang of Roman soldiers. These soldiers round up a number of older girls and march northwards for several days, keeping them without food or water, apart *from what the girls can pillage for themselves as they travel. Finally, the party reaches a settlement where the soldiers have previously taken up residence. There are more women and children there, held as slaves. A silently grieving Aefre joins them to sleep in the long hall, but that same night, her mother's killer seeks her out, and Aefre finds out the savage price of her survival. She is eleven years old.*

*

Caught up in the horror of what I saw through Aefre's eyes, I dragged myself backwards. She had relaxed her grip too and emitted a grunt—of pain or loss, perhaps both. We regarded each other, a moment of brief understanding.

But then I realised she had lost her family and still wilfully chosen to take mine from me. There could be no forgiveness. I wanted her dead.

Recognising I hadn't finished fighting her, eyes glittering, Aefre slammed her hand into my solar plexus, and I curled up in pain, all my breath gone. I lay limp, trying to force myself to breathe and move again and unable to. I waited for the death blow, but it never came. Unnerved, I straightened up, prepared for her to reach for my throat again, but she was distracted. I followed her gaze. Shapes were manifesting themselves near the oak tree. They had the same translucence I had seen in the long dead Guardians when I had called them together outside White Cottage less than an hour ago. Smoky outlines flickered between this reality and another. Aefre rushed to greet them, her lined face shining with longing and excitement.

Her sisters.

That momentary lapse into sharing Aefre's memories had shown the only solace available to Aefre at the hands of her kidnappers was the company of the other female captives. Glimpsing those memories had shown me so much of Aefre's history. I had seen how she had grown to full adulthood and had been a sensational beauty—her dark green eyes, auburn hair, and long limbs had made her a firm favourite among the soldiers. She had been passed around from man to man and forced to do their bidding. She had stoically submitted to their every foul whim, while her heart withered to nothing more than a tight black stone of hatred.

I understood now how Aefre had taken comfort from those women alongside her who had similarly found themselves brutally used and enslaved. She learned quickly from them, these new sisters who had replaced the ones who had died, how to keep the men happy, how to survive their rough justice. She became adept at identifying and using herbs for medicinal purposes and to keep babies at bay. She quickly learned that when the men left on hunting forays or to pillage elsewhere, the women stole away from their drugged guards to spend free time alone in the nearby forest. Aefre joined them time after time, to build a fire and dance and sing. She found joy in such limited freedom.

But I also understood how Aefre's hatred was relentless and enduring. She wanted to be rid of the soldiers once and for all, yet feared them because they were warriors and she was an untrained, unarmed woman. She knew that with luck she might take one out with her butchering knife, but the rest would take her down before she managed to make good her escape. She was strong but she was no match for the warriors with their swords and daggers.

Aefre was bright, and she learned quickly. There were a number of cunning women among her friends who knew how to use the old magick, and so she sought their counsel. These women persuaded her that something could be done if she gathered the strongest and most virile women together. She could dance up a storm and conjure a demon, to ask for his assistance.

All she had to do was sacrifice her firstborn son.

And so she had.

I had been there when she had killed the baby. I had watched her as she performed that monstrous requirement without blinking. And the demon had granted her what? Along with her sisters she henceforth had the power to take the lives of the soldiers, and anyone else that dared to cross her path. And for a time she had enjoyed the freedom to do as she wished and to wreak her hatred and revenge on the people in the settlements she stumbled across.

But evil cannot set you free. The price she had paid was to be locked in eternity with her hatred and her anger. The Guardians had separated her from the only companions who had ever shown her love and gentleness after she had lost her family. Her beauty had decayed as her body aged, and in order to maintain any semblance of how she had once looked she now forcibly sucked the life from innocents to win back a temporary ability to shapeshift. She ate and slept. Where was the joy in that?

I could see it all now, and I pitied her. I did. As a young girl she had lost so much.

But she had killed many innocent people. She had preyed on the elderly and the vulnerable and stolen the future of many who had their whole lives in front of them. And she had killed my son. For that alone, I wanted to wipe her from the face of the earth. And what about Mercy, Solange, Mr Kephisto. I had to avenge them all. I would not be defeated.

And yet, here now, at last, were Aefre's sisters. They were coming to join her. Aefre twirled and cried out in happiness, holding her arms out to them in welcome. The transparent figures streamed towards her, weaving in and out of the trees, dead leaves dancing underfoot. I watched this new hypnotic dance as the spirits faded in and out of colour. Graceful figures, women of all shapes and sizes and of all ages.

One passed by me, so close I could have reached out and grabbed her foot, except there was no substance to her. No physicality or at least nothing I could have caught hold of. She floated two or three inches above the ground, her bare feet skimming the air. The bottom of her feet were calloused and filthy as though she had never worn shoes. Her calves were shapely. I admired her abundant hips and her swelling belly and breasts, and she casually glanced down at me. Her long dark hair fell around her shoulders. She had two hooded black eyes, with blood pooling in the whites, her nose was misshapen and her lips split and stained with blood. I'd seen her before, she had conjured the demon with Aefre many centuries ago, another victim of Roman oppressors.

The ghost smiled, and it was enchanting, warming me through, assuaging my fear and anger. I was filled with a longing to be with her, share her life, go where she went. I wanted to dance with her. I wanted to be one with her. I wanted to be as divine as she was. I wanted to wrap myself around her, feel her softness, embrace her wetness. I wanted to ooze sexuality as she did, wear it casually, offer it freely. I wanted to feel the love of her sisters as they wrapped me in their comforting embrace.

The ghost swayed in front of me, her head tipped to one side, curious as to who I was. Maybe I was as opaque to her as she was to me. Beyond her, Aefre was reaching out as the other spirits joined her. They were at once sparkling and bright, then pale and muted once again. They weren't fully formed yet. They weren't entirely here with Aefre and myself.

I sank back to the ground in despair, worried I had already lost the fight, but looking up at the ghost woman once more my eye fell on something hanging from a branch behind her head. It shimmered in the moonlight. My pendant, hanging where Aefre had tossed it while she was trying to kill me.

I shook myself, trying to clear the fug of indecision away. My mind was disoriented. Part of me yearned to join these women, this sisterhood, but the pendant shining on the tree reminded me who I was and where I had come from. I couldn't allow these spirits any more time to manifest, otherwise Aefre and her sisters would be reunited once more in their evil dance, and I couldn't possibly know how many more lives would be laid to waste if I failed in what I had set out to do.

I had to stop them.

If it was possible to trap them on this plane, in this time, wherever it was, away from my own reality, I had to do it.

The second I had that thought, the ghost closest to me became more agitated, as though my thoughts were not my own. Her head swivelled to look directly at me, her stained mouth pulled open—a dark cavern of hell beyond. Her eyes widened, black and soulless, and her skin shrivelled and split. She raised her arms towards me and stepped forwards. Repulsed, free of the spell she had cast, I leapt to my feet and jumped high to capture my pendant above her head. Grasping it firmly in my left hand and tugging it away from the tree, I spun around and darted away. The ghost danced up to me, moving easily, fluttering in my face. I tried to bat her away, but I only swatted thin air.

Our movement caught Aefre's attention. An expression of hatred passed across her face, replacing the love she'd shown her sisters. With no time to lose I scarpered towards the oak tree, ducked in through the opening, and returned to the fire I had built. It was still aflame, the limited space in the hollow of the tree smoky. Just feet away lay the can of lighter fuel I'd dropped. I picked it up and threw it carefully into the flames, hoping it would explode and take the tree with it, then dashed towards the area of the tree where I had first jumped in.

The wall of the tree was solid. I didn't know how to break out. I hammered against it in frustration. "Get me out!" I screamed, hopeful the Guardians beyond could hear me. The fire crackled merrily behind me, and I turned. I was running out of time. I slumped against the tree, thinking, my back raking against the bark. The fire was burning well, but not necessarily enough to destroy the tree.

Aefre had followed me in. She circled the fire cautiously. I saw her in both of her forms. In the light from the fire she was beautiful, young, her hair glorious, her skin as ripe and smooth as a peach. In shadow she was the ancient crone, haggard, bent, hair lank, and skin dusty.

She flitted half in and half out of the shadows. I watched her mouth work, ruby lips versus dead grey ones. Emerald eyes versus eyes as black as melted tar. Her pink tongue, fresh and sweet, juxtaposed with the green fur of decay.

"You will die today," she said, and her voice was at once melodic and sweet, corrupt and dead.

Death was becoming a distinct possibility, but I would not give in easily. How could I? Every fibre of my being wanted to survive. I touched the wood behind me again, soothed by the presence of something so familiar, this tree, Max's tree, and then I became aware of the pentagram throbbing in my left hand. I clasped the charms tightly. Her eyes narrowed. "You cannot kill me," she grumbled.

"No," I replied. Perhaps that much was true. But maybe it wasn't necessary to kill Aefre herself. If I could just trap her here with her sisters and destroy the portal, would that be enough? What had Mr Kephisto said? I needed to plant the seed.

Plant the seed. There was no physical seed. I had to plant the seed with the only weapon I possessed. I'd already used it once—my dreams, my imagination. I had to merge the past and the present, fact and fiction, truth and myth. Somewhere where those worlds met, I would find a way home; Aefre would be destroyed.

Aefre smiled and moved into the shadows. "My sisters are here now and we are too strong for you. We are not afraid. Never afraid. We will offer you as a sacrifice to our gods and goddesses. We will hoist you into the branches of this precious tree, hang you by the neck, then cut you down, torture you and kill you, and then we will build your dismal fire higher and place your pathetic body on it. We'll dance in delight as your skin melts, as your hair turns to ash, as your fingers and toes curl, and your tendons shrink and snap."

I breathed deeply, looked inside myself, and stood tall, holding my left hand out and high. The chain swung, catching the firelight, and the pendants tumbled free of my grasp, swinging underneath my hand: an acorn and a leaf and a pentagram. I caught them in my right hand and pulled the acorn free of the broken chain. The acorn: a seed. If my aim was true …

I drew the acorn to my lips and breathed on it; thought of Mercy and Solange, of the itinerant on the hill, the hitchhiker, Margaret and Bill, and all of Aefre's other victims, and I thought of Max and James. I took all of my sorrow and my hatred and imagined it growing, becoming something black and diseased that settling into the roots. I created an image in my mind of the tree turning putrid, beginning with its heart, decaying from the inside out, becoming a wet stinking mass. I conjured the death of the great oak by harnessing the old magick that resides within us all, not just Aefre and her miserable band of sisters, but in me and all women, in all people. The destruction of the tree would lead to the eradication of Aefre and her sisters. The seed was ready for planting.

"Rot in hell," I said and threw the tainted acorn charm into the fire.

Bullseye. The charm bounced once in the air but fell directly down and hit the can of lighter fluid.

I dropped to the ground and covered my face. The can exploded. I heard a horrendous shrieking and peeked up quickly. Aefre was covered in flames, desperately trying to pat them out with her hands. Her skin was smouldering and flaking off in large papery chunks.

I felt my back scorching through my t-shirt. I rolled to smother the flames. Aefre's unholy screaming provided a musical backdrop along with the roaring of flames around me. The wood was catching, and the tree was going to burn. What didn't burn would be destroyed by disease. I instinctively understood that. It was time for me to find a way out and leave Aefre and her sisters to their fate.

I struggled to a standing position. The smoke was thick, making me cough, my lungs not fully recovered from the fire in Mr Kephisto's shop. The billowing black clouds made it difficult to see. I had to find the exit from inside the tree. Aefre's screaming went on a little longer and then stopped abruptly. I heard the crackle of flames behind me and desperately scraped the wall with my fingers. Still no door.

How to get out? In desperation I hammered against the wall. My left hand clutching the pentagram made contact with the wood of the tree and there was a flash of bright blue light.

The wall crumbled away, and I fell forwards into darkness.

*

I lay for some time, my breathing laboured, sobbing, and hiccupping in fear. I could smell my singed clothes and hair, but I was out of immediate danger. When I felt strong enough, I pushed myself up into a kneeling position and looked about.

The air was fresh and cool, there was little light. I was in some sort of tunnel, ten feet wide or so. I pushed myself to my feet and warily reached out. In the dim light I could feel the walls, and when I touched them I understood they were made of thousands upon thousands of branches, knitted thickly together. They stretched above my head on both sides and joined together in an arch.

Perturbed, I took a few steps. The ground under my feet was no different to that of the hollow oak; soft, loose, and damp, the natural detritus of thousands of years of forest decay. I turned slowly, making a full circle. Behind me was a mirror image of what was in front. A long corridor. No windows, no escapes. I could go forwards or backwards, the end result would be the same, surely?

There was nothing for it. Remaining in one place was not an option. I elected to go forwards, and so I began to walk.

And walk and walk.

At first nothing changed, the walls remained the same tangle of branches, and the light was non-existent but eventually, just as I was about to slow to a stop and reappraise the situation, I noticed that something ahead of me had changed. I had been walking towards nothing but darkness, now I could see the first pin prick of light. I sped up and eventually the pin prick became a small circle and then a larger one. I began to rush forwards, feeling the elation of freedom.

But then an arm reached out from the wall and a small hand grabbed me, spinning me off course. Horrified, I turned, ready to lash out angrily, but the form that slipped out of the branches was slight and pale and no threat to me at all.

"Sarah," I gasped and stepped towards her.

"Turn back, Heather," she urged. "Don't let her turn around."

I glanced back at the light ahead of me, the horrible truth pricking at my insides. "Where is this?" I asked. "Where am I?" But when I looked for Sarah, she had disappeared.

I stumbled backwards still facing the light, seeking what was there. With a shudder, my mind reached out and touched Aefre's. I saw into Aefre's black heart, saw the maggots crawling in the cold dead flesh and the serpent coiling and uncoiling, thick and greasy, shedding scales.

Should I go forwards? Confront her?

Sarah had said not to. Was she here? Trapped here? In this tunnel with Aefre? Such an ending would be unbearable. I cried afresh. A loud rumble caught me in mid-sob, and the ground rocked beneath my feet. Alarmed, I looked ahead, the light had changed, become murkier, and a mist rolled towards me, low to the ground but trying to climb the walls. The stench of sulphur mingled with decay infiltrated my senses, and I gagged.

"Go back," said a voice at my elbow, and I jumped a mile. It was the itinerant from the hill. "Go back," he looked at me sadly.

"I'm sorry," I said. "I'm sorry, for what she did to you."

Another roar, louder than the first and the ground split beneath my feet. Chunks of the roof rained down on me, and I crouched by the side of the wall, clinging onto a sturdy branch for dear life. When the tunnel had stopped shaking I stood. I needed to heed the warnings and retrace my steps.

Turning my back on the light, I trotted away, avoiding the rip in the ground.

The ground shook again. This time I ran hell for leather back the way I had come. I didn't know how far I needed to go, or if I had even reached my starting point. I just kept running until I had no breath left and then I ran some more, until I collapsed to my knees. Casting a worried glance over my shoulder I could see the mist still rolling relentlessly towards me. It carried only death.

"I can't get out. I don't know how to get out!" I screamed, and my voice was full of fear and cowardice and defeat.

"You do, Mum." A voice I had never thought to hear again. I turned to my side, tears streaming down my face. Max. My boy. Standing tall and slim, ethereal in the half-light of the tunnel, his eyes shining with love.

I reached for him, my hands trembling, my mouth wide with disbelief. "Max?" I whispered. He had no substance but he was there, in front of me. "Baby?" I was undone by my love for him, flailing in a lake of emotion, shaking with the elation of beholding him once more. My only child. My lost boy. The most precious of jewels.

"There's no time, Mum. You have to get out of here."

"You'll come too?" I demanded, my voice shrill. "I can't leave you again. You must come too."

"You have to go, Mum!" The floor beneath our feet rocked, a fissure appeared in the wall next to me.

"How?" I said, and Max indicated the fissure in the wall. It was too small. I would never get through.

"Come with me!" I begged my son.

"Go Mum! I'm with you. I'm always with you."

The fusty stench of the mist was suffocating me and I ducked at the sound of another tremendous crack from directly above my head. It was now or never. Max pointed at the widening gap between the branches, and I stooped my head to peer out.

"Now!" cried Max and something pushed me hard. My shoulders collided painfully with the branches and then I slipped sideways and fell hard onto a rough, stone-strewn trail.

THIRTY-THREE

BENDING TIME

I lay sprawled on the ground, momentarily winded. My wrists ached and my palms were grazed and bloody. Groaning inwardly, I hauled myself up once more, inspecting my hands, brushing tiny chips of stone from where they had embedded themselves into the flesh. The pentagram and the oak leaf hung from their broken chain, looped through the fingers of my left hand. The pentagram glowed with warmth.

I looked hopefully for Max but he was nowhere in sight. Perhaps he had been a hallucination. My shoulders slumped, and I cried bitter tears. He was lost to me again, and the pain was as bright and sharp as it had ever been.

"I wanted you to come with me! You said you were always with me." I sobbed, a little girl who wanted her own way, pleading with the universe as I had after my son had first died and wiping the snot from my face with the back of my hand.

What now? I sniffed hard, my tears subsided, and I was able to take stock of my surroundings. The oak tree was behind me. Smoke was emanating from a few of the knots that I could see. It was burning from within. That was the good news.

But here I was on my hands and knees on what should have been a tarmacked road directly opposite White Cottage, with a welcoming party that consisted of my friends: the Guardians and Trent. There was no-one to be seen, no person in sight at all. There was no road and no cottage and very little light.

The moon was out. Layers of clouds were flitting across the sky at a superfast pace. As I stared up morosely, the first drops of rain pattered down on my upturned face. Although I was accorded some shelter by the wide sweep of the oak's thick branches, without the foliage I was going to get wet very quickly. I decided that as the tree was burning, it was safer to move away from it, so I headed down the stone path a little way and sheltered under a cluster of smaller trees.

I examined the landscape. Not much to see in the dark. There were trees everywhere, densely packed on either side of the stone path. The undergrowth was thick and twisted, brambles intertwined with the lower branches of trees. Some of this forest would be impassable for all but the smallest of animals.

The noise of scraping gave me pause. I turned my head, my heart beating hard in my chest. Had it originated from the oak? Holding my breath, I listened. Yes. There it was again. A heavy rasping sound, wood on wood.

Breathing fast, I panicked. It wasn't over. She was coming for me, and I was lost and alone. I didn't know how to get back to my own time. What had I done wrong? Should I have imagined myself back at White Cottage? I turned and ran down, brushing past the trees as I went; they reached for me. The path dropped into the dip a little, then started to climb steeply, following the lie of the land I recognised as that which ran alongside Elbury Road in my own time.

In my reality, there was farmland to the right that had been cleared of trees, and Pitcher's Field was over the road to my left. The forest began farther up. But here I was now, in dense woodland, so thick it brought on claustrophobia. I was breathing loudly, laboured gasps for air, so I couldn't hear the noise of anyone—of Aefre—following me. I just kept going, running blindly, wherever the gap in the trees deigned to lead me.

The stone path disappeared as I stumbled on a small clearing. The trees were spread out a little here. Blue moonlight filtered through a damp mist. I remained still, panting noisily with my mouth open, for a moment, fighting to bring my breathing under control, my eyes darting here and there, searching for danger.

If Aefre was following me she was doing it quietly. I couldn't hear a sound except for the muted pitter-patter of rain hitting the leaves around me. No animals, no wind. My heart seemed to be the loudest noise in the forest.

A small trail showed an exit from the clearing, the only alternative open to me. Reluctantly I followed it. The ground was level and meandered here and there like a misplaced stream. I kept my eyes peeled for any movement, twitching nervously.

I was lost. I couldn't place myself on a map in my mind. Maybe I should keep an eye on where the moon was, or something. Perhaps I should just turn around and return to the oak tree.

I stopped dead in my tracks. I could see something up ahead. An outbuilding or a grain shed? It was small. Somewhere the farmer would store food for his animals. I approached the building. It was a tiny stone cottage, sunken into the landscape, with a door and a window and a chimney. A dim light flickered through the glassless hole that was the window, some sort of hessian covering flapped gently, catching the frigid breeze. The wooden door stood slightly ajar. A dark curl of smoke wound its way from the chimney. Someone was at home.

I half-heartedly wondered whether someone here could help me. Maybe they had a phone. But I already knew that wasn't likely. I raised my hand to tap on the door but pulled myself up short. From inside came a rumbling noise. It came in short rhythmic bursts. With trepidation I moved forwards.

"Hello?" I called. My voice thick with dread.

The rumbling noise stopped.

"Come in dear," came a female voice. A musty, thick voice. Cracked with age.

I knew even before I entered the room whom I would see, but it was my destiny. I was powerless. I had to confront her once again. I peered around the door, and there was Aefre, the crone and not the maiden, slouching in a rocking chair.

She smiled, her wide black and green grin, and slowly rocked the chair forwards and back. Forwards and back. The rumbling noise was the rockers rolling across the rough wooden floor.

My head brushed against something, I turned to look, gagged, and stepped away from the overpowering stench. Dead animals hung from the ceiling—pheasants, foxes, badgers, and even a small fawn. They dangled from their hind legs, or were hung by the neck, in varying states of decay, sunken eyes dull and beyond pain.

Aefre rocked, watching me, her dry lips drawn back in a smirk. Her clothes were smouldering, and the hands that gripped the arms of the rocker were burned. There were holes in the fabric of her cloak across her chest, burned through and exposing the dead flesh beneath—grey mottled flesh.

"You seem disappointed to see me, Heather," she hissed. "You can't kill me. I told you that."

"It would seem not." My voice sounded hollow and defeated. I hated it.

"You have a powerful magick within you. You can shift time. Move around and through it. I admire that."

"I don't know how I do it," I said. It was the truth.

"All the more remarkable then. Very few of the Guardians have the strength and skills that you have." Aefre rocked, and we observed each other for a moment. "Kephisto is a powerful wizard, and Mercy, she was a great witch, yes. But you, you're something else. You should join my sisters and I. We'd be pleased to have you."

I remembered the yearning for companionship I had experienced back in the clearing with Aefre's spirit sister but shook my head in defiance. "No. That's not for me."

Aefre stopped rocking and stooped forward, scooped up a log in one wizened hand, and threw it hard into the fire. Sparks exploded from the grate and smoke billowed into the room. My eyes watered. The aggression belied her tone. She was angry. "Then I'm afraid I will have to kill you."

I rocked on my feet, blinded by the smoke. Aefre was shifting shape in front of me, twisting and winding around herself, folding in half, coiling like a serpent. Huge and grey, her coils rubbing and twisting, knotting and slipping free, thick with age, her demonic form. Her true form. Aefre had sold her soul as a young woman many centuries ago. The beautiful fresh faced girl she had once been, all shining promise, had ceased to exist the moment the soldiers had burst into her family's dwelling.

"You think you'll live forever Aefre, but that can't happen. We're both going to die here." I looked away from her and stared out of the window into the darkness beyond. Felt a heat emanating from somewhere in the forest. Saw the light glowing and growing. Somewhere out there, not so very far away, the oak tree was burning. Regardless of where I was now, and how I could get back to my own time, the tree would burn. The oak was going to die, and Aefre would be trapped somewhere between her sisters' world and mine.

"You aren't afraid to die?" she asked curiously.

Trent's face appeared in my mind, perhaps my last regret. I loved him. And then I thought of Max. "Of course I am. But a huge part of me died the night you took the life of my son."

"Your son?" Aefre scrutinized my face. Her black eyes rolled in their sockets. She pushed herself upright and made a show of examining her putrescent palms. She waved her hands in front of her face, hooked her fingers and waggled the thick discoloured nails, seeing something there that I couldn't. "No. No. Not I."

"But you did!" I said, furious that she would deny it. "A few years ago—"

"You can't know that it was me!" she roared, her sudden anger ferocious in the quiet of the night. "It wasn't me! What if it was you? I think it was you!"

"Don't be absurd," I retorted.

"But you move time! You don't need the portal. You travel where you wish. Perhaps he isn't dead. Perhaps it hasn't happened yet?"

"What?" I stared at her, full of confusion and pain.

Aefre burst out laughing. It was a horrible sound, wheezing and bubbling. She sank back in the rocking chair, her black eyes bright with hatred.

"Perhaps he left the town with his friends a few minutes ago. Maybe he's on the road travelling home in his metal carriage as we speak," she spat.

This was cruel. If it hadn't happened yet, I didn't want to go through it again. "What do you mean? What are you saying?" I asked her. She threw back her head and guffawed. I whimpered, closer to insanity in that moment than I had ever been.

If it hadn't happened yet … if this was the past, or if there was any way I could turn back time and save the life of my son … I didn't have to go through it all again. I could go down there to the road and head him off. I could stop the car.

I darted out of the door of Aefre's tiny cottage and ran the way I had come. This time I wasn't careful or quiet. I pounded along the dirt path, coming to the clearing quickly, then turned down the hill, slipping and scrambling on the loose wet shale beneath my feet. On and on I ran, the blood pounding in my ears, my breath harsh and ragged. The undergrowth cutting in on me, brambles slicing at my face and hands as I pushed on.

My foot caught a larger stone, and I tripped and fell, banging the side of my face as I went down. Pain exploded in bright light, and I cradled my lower jaw for a moment, but I was back on my feet when I heard a rumbling noise, slightly tinny, the sound of an old car heading my way on the road nearby. A road that hadn't been there before. Time was playing tricks on me, or I was bending time to my will as Aefre had said I could. I didn't know which. I didn't care.

The landscape had changed again. The hedge to my left was high but beyond it I could make out a field. White shadows told me there were sheep grazing there. The moon emerged from behind the storm clouds and confirmed it. Ahead of me the stone path ended and tarmac began. I was on a side road, a farmer's lane. Elbury road was ahead of me and there was indeed a car coming. The ground was dry, small pockets of mist hovered in the air like spirits from the past watching to see what I would do.

I started to weep desperately. I'd never wanted anything as much as I wanted this moment. Time was short. I found myself praying as I raced down the remainder of the track. Through the trees to my right I could see the headlights. If this was Max, I had to stop the car. But how could I know whether it was him?

What the hell.

I couldn't take the risk of missing the opportunity. I threw myself out into the road in front of the oncoming vehicle and prayed it was the right one.

Too late I realised with horror what I had done. It was James's car. He wasn't travelling particularly quickly but he was an inexperienced driver. As he swerved to avoid me, I clearly saw the look of shock on his face, and then the car crashed headlong into the oak tree. There was an explosion of metal and glass, followed by the thud of several branches falling from the tree, then complete silence.

All of the strength seeped out of my limbs. I sank to my knees in the middle of the road, clutching my head in my hands. What had I done? What had I done?

Behind me came the sound of hysterical laughter. Aefre. She was enjoying this, relishing the fact that I was reliving what had happened to my son, witnessing it; had in fact caused the accident myself.

She passed me in the road, still chuckling but ignoring me, heading directly for the car. As she passed me she began to shift shape. She wanted to finish what she had started. I remembered only too well what Euan had told me about his encounter with the stunning woman after the crash. Euan had survived because she had been disturbed. Max had suffered, but he should have survived. Aefre had killed him.

I stared after her. This was exactly the scenario Euan had described, the very same. Yet wasn't it different too? Aefre was walking towards the car, her shapely hips swaying and her long luscious hair swinging as she went, but her clothes were full of burn marks and were smouldering as she walked. Her hands were scorched an angry red. Her shape shifting wasn't complete. Aefre was damaged. I had done that to her.

I looked up at the oak tree. Sparks flew around the naked branches like a halo, bright against the dark sky. The tree was burning. It was dying, and Aefre could die too. I had set the wheels in motion, now I had to make sure they didn't fall off.

Aefre reached the car. She opened the back door and leaned in over the figure on the backseat. I heard a scream of pain. Euan. I scrambled to my feet and ran to the foot of the oak. I picked up a sturdy branch, one that had fallen when the car hit the trunk. I had my weapon.

"Aefre!"

Startled she drew her head out of the car and looked my way. I took a few paces forwards, drew on all of the fury I possessed, and hit her full in the face with everything I could muster.

I managed to knock her sideways. I didn't give her a chance, I hit her once more. She fell to the floor. I hit her again. And again. I smashed her skull this time. The sharp cracking sound was a tonic for my furious soul. Thick black goo oozed from her, dripping onto the Earth, then sinking like fingers into the dirt. Elated by the sight, I hit her again and again, with a cold fury that had built in me over the previous few years. When I was absolutely certain she wouldn't ever get up, I threw the branch aside and grabbed her arm. She was skin and bone again; her shiny hair drying out. As I watched, her skin began to stipple and crisp and her eyes sank back into their sockets.

Clenching my teeth in disgust, I dragged her towards the tree and lay her next to it. The tree was warm; I could feel the heat when I placed my hand on it to steady myself. I nudged Aefre with the toe of my shoe. Her body twisted and curled, much as bacon will in hot oil. She withered in front of me, shrank, dried out to a husk, and sank part way into the Earth, grey and mottled and little more than ash, becoming part of the landscape she had dominated for so long. I kicked leaves over the small bump of her hips that remained. No-one would ever know she lay here.

Urgently I moved to the side of the car and put my head around the open door. Euan was wide eyed, crumpled on the back seat, clearly seriously injured. I couldn't move him. "It's going to be ok," I promised, "you'll be fine." I looked past him into the front. James was already gone. No doubt about that. His head was lolling at a terrible angle. I could not save him. I had to get to Max.

Headlights lit up the road in front of me. Another car was coming. I prayed they had a phone on them so we could call for help.

I moved to the passenger door, next to Max, and tried to open it. It was stuck. I pulled hard. It wouldn't open for me.

The car pulled up and a man jumped out. "What happened? Are you all right? Have you phoned for an ambulance?" he yelled.

"No," I shouted back. "I don't have my phone on me."

I turned my attention back to the car and heard the stranger speaking into his phone urgently. I rattled the passenger door hard to no avail.

"Help me!" I cried. "My son is in here."

"Hold on. They're asking where we are exactly?"

"Elbury Road, past The Traveller's Rest, at White Cottage." He relayed the information, repeated the words White Cottage a few times, pocketed his phone and rushed to my side.

"Let me try," he said and together we pulled at the door. "Is it locked?" he asked. He went in through the back door. "Hey son," he said to Euan, "help is on its way."

I heard the lock click. This time when I pulled, the door scraped open reluctantly.

And there was my son, seventeen years old, crumpled against the airbag, pale and bloody, obviously in pain, but alive. Alive! I sank to my knees next to him, grabbing his hand and sobbing, delirious with relief. Four long years of grief flowed through me, and I wept hysterically. The stranger gripped my shoulders for a moment and then turned to comfort Euan in the back.

Above us the tree continued to burn. Sparks rained down on the scene. Through my tears, I watched as the Sentinel became a roman candle, lighting up my darkness.

.

THIRTY-FOUR

THE END OF THE BEGINNING

I stood at a safe distance, observing the emergency services as they sprang into action. By the time they arrived the oak tree was well alight. They were quickly able to extract Max from the car, and more carefully, Euan, but getting James's body out was immensely problematic. In the end, the fire service rigged up a tow truck and pulled the car back from the tree. As they did so, the tree imploded and showered Aefre's remains with hot ash.

"Damn tree is rotten to the core," I heard one of the firefighters exclaim.

Good. I had been successful.

I watched them work, one eye on the treatment Max was receiving and the other on the tree, wrapped in a silver foil blanket a paramedic had lent me. No-one had asked me why I was out in the middle of the night, in just a t-shirt and jeans, barefoot in spite of the weather.

"They say your son will be fine," murmured a gentle familiar voice at my side. I turned and looked. The man who had arrived in the car, my knight in shining armour with a mobile phone. He shouldn't have been there. Was part of a future that was in my past, a future that would never occur now.

"Trent Redburn," he said and offered his hand to shake.

I nodded. "I know. You're a professor at the University of Exeter."

"Not a professor." He was handsome.

"You will be," I said.

His eyes lit up in amusement. "Have we met?"

"We have." I hesitated, and he regarded me curiously. I shook my head. What could I say? He didn't know me from Adam. "Now."

He followed my gaze towards the burning tree. "It's

desperately sad, for that poor boy." We stared at the flames together. James had been the final sacrifice. I would think about that a great deal in the years to come. I nodded.

"Thanks for coming to my rescue."

"I'm just glad you knew where we were. I don't know this area at all. Mind you, the White Cottage reference seemed to help the emergency services."

"It's just here." I indicated behind us, turned and looked with him. The cottage nestled in the hollow, in complete darkness. No plume of smoke wound its way out of the chimney. The garden was overgrown and full of decaying weeds. Pots and containers lay smashed or on their sides. A *For Sale* sign had been strapped to the gate. Where were the Guardians? Who would look after the Sentinel now? The tree was dead, Aefre was dead, but what if?

I looked in sudden panic towards the town. What of Mr Kephisto? Would The Storykeeper still lie in ruins?

One of the paramedics called to me, they were ready to take Max to the hospital.

I nodded at Trent, uncertain of what to say, loathe to leave him but intent on never letting Max out of my sight again. Not until he made it to his sixties at least. Trent caught my arm as I turned away and held something out. "Wait. I found this next to the car. You dropped it when you were struggling with the door." A broken silver chain with a single charm on it. I held out my hand, and he placed it on my palm. It tingled slightly as it lay there.

I gazed down in disbelief at the one charm that remained of the three that Trent had given me once before. Here he was offering it again, but with no memory of ever doing so. An oak leaf. "A symbol of strength and longevity, perhaps?" he said earnestly, referring to the survival of my son, no doubt.

I looked once more at the cottage standing quietly with its unencumbered view over the ruins of the tree. Was it waiting for new Guardians to move in? I glanced back at the man I loved. I dangled the oak leaf on the chain, letting it dance in the space between us, and smiled up at him. In our future I could see us making a life together at White Cottage, and I would grow old, happily so, the teller of the tale and a crone, bouncing her grandbabies on her knee, and chasing them through the lavender bushes. And Trent would be the keeper of the tale in Mr Kephisto's stead.

"Here's to strength and longevity," I said, and my heart soared with love and gratitude for the Guardians who had protected us so recently, all who came before them, and all who were yet to come.

ACKNOWLEDGMENTS

East Devon is one of the most beautiful places on earth and I thank my lucky stars that I live here every day. The landscape is a constant source of inspiration to me; this glorious mix of coastline and countryside, forest and sky. The dappled light and the salty breeze. What is not to love? This is where I first came across Aefre. I was driving home from Sidmouth to Ottery St Mary in 2014, along the winding rural road that was my commute at that time. She was hiding in the hedgerow and I imagined glimpsing her as I ambled along (you amble by necessity down most of our lanes). From that moment on, her story needed to be told, and Crone is the result.

I would firstly - most importantly - like to thank my husband John Wycherley for his patience, support and enthusiasm. It can't be easy being married to someone who dreams up horrible ways to kill people for fun. He puts up with my crazy ideas when few other people would, and doesn't (often) moan about the amount of time I spend in front of my screen. Cheers mi duck.

Also thanks to my Mum and Dad for being the most wonderful parents anyone could ever had. They must have often thought I was bonkers to walk away from my career, but they have never said so. I love you both. Thanks too, to my brother Rich, sister-in-law Victoria and nephew Toby, and to my wonderful Auntie Lindy. Family is everything and my family really are the best.

Big grateful feisty shout outs to the wonderful writers at The Urban Writers Playground. To the brilliant cake goddess that is Charlie Haynes for providing the virtual space where we all hang out, as well as the Devon retreats where we physically toil. And a loud huzzah! to my other playmates – Julie Archer, Janet Baird, Yvonne Parsloe, Shanthi Sam, Sarah Jeffery, Jennifer Syme et al., for their warmth and support. When the going gets tough, these women have my back. Truly amazing!

To my extra-special pom-pom waving beta readers Vanessa Wick and Debbie Jefferson Zhao: you're both awesome.

To Simon Broughton and Richard Sharp – thanks for providing the expertise I desperately needed in some of these pages.

To the inestimably brilliant Amie McCracken for cheerleading as I wrote, and then for editing this monster. I remember shyly emailing Amie to ask her whether she could possibly/maybe/perhaps see her way forward to consider editing the novel, but only if she had time and was a teensy-weensy bit interested. I'm still waiting to get my hand back, but in the meantime she has weaved her magic and I am humbled and grateful beyond measure. She has helped me become a better writer, a journey I take seriously. Thanks Amie.

To Jennie Rawlings at Serifim.com for her generosity, and for going above and beyond. You've helped me turn my rough stone into a diamond. The book cover design is stunning and adds so much to the finished product. Thankyou!

And thank *you*, my readers. It is a dream come true to get this into print and to write something that other people choose to read. I have lived with Crone for a few years now, picking up the MS and setting it aside, but Aefre has proven to be difficult to keep quiet. In fact she remains pretty unquiet in my mind! If you think Aefre's still out there somewhere, you'd better let me know – please get in touch!

Finally, this novel is dedicated to my best furry friend forever. He was my constant companion, lying under my desk by my left hand side throughout the writing of numerous drafts, nursing me through meningitis when I was really poorly, and even sticking with me while I rewrote and edited the unwieldy MS the first time around, but he isn't here today and my world is incomplete without him. Taken too young, leaving me broken-hearted, he lives on in these pages as Pip.

Forever on the breeze, always loved, my precious Herbie Longfellow Alderdice.

Jeannie Wycherley
24th April 2017

ABOUT THE AUTHOR

Jeannie Wycherley is a writer, copywriter and gift shop proprietor who resides somewhere between the forest and the coast in East Devon, UK. Her work is inspired by the landscape, not least because her desk affords her sweeping views over a valley and the glorious hills beyond. Why this translates into horror is anybody's guess.

Follow Jeannie

Twitter @thecushionlady
Facebook: https://www.facebook.com/jeanniewycherley/
Website: jeanniewycherley.co.uk

Made in the USA
Middletown, DE
17 January 2018